Nikita's Story

Part I
Tenzenar

Gayle Hansen

ISBN 978-1-64191-534-2 (paperback)
ISBN 978-1-64191-535-9 (digital)

Copyright © 2020 by Gayle Hansen

All rights reserved. No part of this publication may be reproduced, distributed, or transmitted in any form or by any means, including photocopying, recording, or other electronic or mechanical methods without the prior written permission of the publisher. For permission requests, solicit the publisher via the address below.

Christian Faith Publishing, Inc.
832 Park Avenue
Meadville, PA 16335
www.christianfaithpublishing.com

Printed in the United States of America

Kings of Airies is a continuing saga spanning thousands of years. *Nikita's Story*, the second book of the saga, appears in five book-length parts (volumes) due to its length. Other *Kings of Airies* books include *Valcree's Story* and *Nathaneyellan's Story*.

Special Thanks to:

Dan Ellrick and Jody MacArthur for all the time and encourage-
   ment you gave me.
Without you both I would never have gotten here.
May God bless you greatly.

Contents

Prologue		11
1.	Home?	15
2.	A Starting Over	28
3.	The Expedition	56
4.	Pride's Folly	80
5.	The Answers Are Given	94
6.	What Is Love?	119
7.	The Breaking of a Heart	144
8.	Whateshan Eyette Sontall	160
9.	Jeanitear	176
10.	Disclosures and Discoveries	198
11.	Among the Tenzenar	224
12.	A Clearer Understanding	257
13.	Promises to Keyenoa	275

Author's Note:

The Airian people are a people very similar to human's in appearance with the exception that they glow and are generally quite beautiful to look at. The reason why they glow is because God created them from His energy, power, or essence, rather than the clay of the earth. The amount that they glow is dependent upon the gifts God bestows upon each individual.

The Airian language is a language of emotion and deep feelings. Even nouns, such as zewaller or dree, call up not only the image of the creature, person, or thing but the emotion that goes with them. For instance, zewaller, a large dragon-like creature, conjures up the strong emotions of fear and danger along with the image and smell of the creature all expressed in one word. Whereas the word dree calls up the image of a small frightened creature, bringing with it the feelings of timidity, inadequacy, empathy, and often humor, as well as the woodsy odor they carry.

Because Nikita is writing his own story it is 'translated' from his language to English, with many Arian words not translated. All other languages in Nikita's Story will have their own font or style to differentiate them from Airian. For example, all Tenzenar words will be in *italics*.

Airian rules of writing while comparable to English rules of writing, have a few differences.

Capitalization: Airians capitalize words that are important or are powerful to them, and therefore are not necessarily words that would be capitalized in English. Due to their history for example, Kings and Kingdoms are two examples of the words that have a greater importance or power to the Airian people, and so are capitalized where they would not be in English.

Quotations: Airians use double quotation marks " " for spoken statements, and single quotes ' ' for thoughts or non-spoken statements. Single quotes are also used when quoting another person even when the quote isn't spoken or within double quotes. Airian's believe that making this distinction makes it easier for the reader to understand when something is spoken out loud or simply thought or repeated for emphasis or importance.

Example 1: 'I so wish she would look my way. Should I do something to cause her to notice me?' my thoughts were distracting me from where my attention should have been. 'Okay, so stop looking at her and pay attention to the discussion at hand, you mootan!' I corrected myself.

Example 2: It is times like these that Mothers' words, 'Distraction is Castrin's favorite way of causing us to make teepatins of ourselves,' is important to remember.

These are likely only a few differences that will be found while reading Nikita's Story or subsequent books concerning Airians. If I have forgotten any other differences, I apologize now…

Toenda sorice omprice.

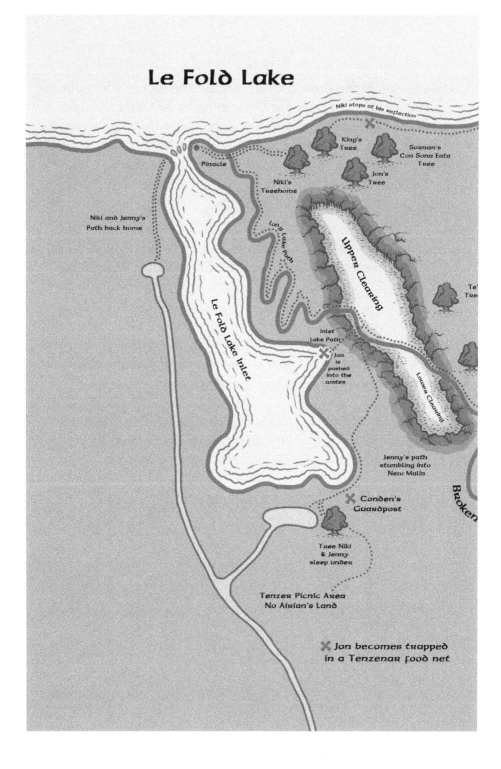

Le Fold Lake

Niki's path when running from father's death

...aiu's
...ehome

Corina's
Treehome

Niki's attack
from a zewaller

New Malin
in Dindieum Forest

Dindieum River

Path to Malinieum City

N
W ✦ **E**
S

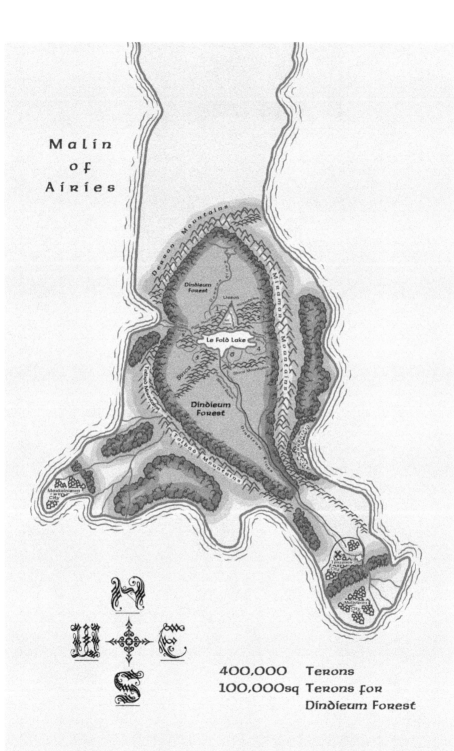

Prologue

A child of fourteen aanas wrote the following essay during the reign of High King Sayleen Cantabo, Seventh King of Airies. The original remains preserved in the Malinieum City Museum. The reprinted text here follows the partial translation performed by the museum's second curator for cultural history. **Some Airian words and all errors remain faithfully preserved with no helpful transcription.**

The People of Airies, Their Powers, and Their Kings

We have not always been nikca of Keyenoa. Back in a time of which we are ashamed, our people were ruled by Sontall, greed, lust, and blood. Keyenoa, at the cry of one man, came to our aid and enriched us all with His essence and power. It was at this time that Airies was established through Keyenoa's gifts of power, thus giving to us the way of life we now hold dear.

Each Airian, man or woman, has the power to become invisible; the time which they can remain invisible depends upon their age. Under nineteen aanas old, invisibility is drastically shortened by youth and lack of power. Usually at the age of nineteen, we receive power from Keyenoa, and our time of invisibility is then increased to match the amount of power given.

NIKITA'S STORY

At this time, every male also receives the power of fight through Con Sona Eata, or Coming of age. Thus, if attacked or provoked, he is able to use his mind to inflict severe pain on another, in the place of using fists or weapons for defense.

The women of Airies do not come of age as men do, though I am told that at this age, they go through a change of some kind and are then considered adults. Once this change takes place, their Keyenoa-given sensitivity increases, and they are able to sense future changes or occurrences, which Keyenoa confirms to them. The accuracy of these predictions depends solely upon the limited amount of power received during their time of change.

It is because of the differences within Airian people and Keyenoa's choosing that not all people have the same power-given abilities and strengths. As with every kind of talent, some have more power, while others have considerably less.

On Airies, hundreds of aanas ago, because of that one man's cry, Keyenoa decided that there would always be seven kings to rule our planet, six to reign over the six continents, and the seventh to rule over all of Airies. Every king on Airies is chosen by Keyenoa alone, and is then usually forced into Con Sona Eata an aana earlier, at the age of eighteen. Having chosen His kings, Keyenoa then gives to each a range of power, which is increased in proportion to the size of the kingdom they are to rule. All kings, with the exception of the High King, take on the name of their kingdom as their sir-name. This is done to honor the first kings arecta by Keyenoa's power. The First High King requested that he not be so honored, and to honor him, our people have obeyed his request through the ages.

Here follows the list of kings, and Keyenoa's given power during Eata Cantabo:

Lord Richon Locar now fully rules as the First King of Airies, with the recent passing of Lord Dokadan Locar through Sontall. He rules the continent of Locar, our ghea minca-eye kingdom. Keyenoa has ghea arece every First King with the power of mind transportation. With this power the king is able, through a simple thought, to take himself wherever he desires, so long as it does not exceed the 15,000 square teron size of his kingdom.

PART I TENZENAR

Lord Kreatar Dorna, the Second King of Airies, was also gifted with the power of mind transportation. Yet his gift of power was strengthened, both allowing him to take another with him, and to encompass the greater size of Dorna, which is 20,000 square terons.

In the giving of the powers for The Third King of Airies, Lord Ceranon Letark, Keyenoa gives to him the added power in which to hear the thoughts of those near him. As with all kings, Lord Ceranon holds also the power of each king before him, strengthened to a greater degree and the size of his island kingdom of 30,000 square terons.

The fourth, fifth, and sixth kings, each are also blessed with the power of the kings preceding them, yet always in an enhanced form. Therefore the powers of the Fourth King of Airies, Lord Alon Tarton, are expanded to include the touching of thoughts chosen from those within the square miles equal to the size of Tarton, and communicating with them through his mind alone. He is also able to block other Kings from reading his thoughts if he judges it necessary. The Fifth King, Lord Palona Cetar, is arecta with the added gift of Keysa~narann. This literally means that he is able to move objects from place to place without the need to go with them. Lastly, the Sixth King, Lord Markain Malin, rules Airies' largest continent, which spans over 400,000 square terons and is the kingdom in which I live. Lord Markain's power of fight is so strong that with one simple thought, he has the ability to instantly take the life of another. Our king has also been given the power to transform the matter and structure of objects, such as changing a rock into a flower, or sand to glass, through the simple use of his mind. The kingdom size of Tarton is 45,000 square terons, and the size of Cetar, the fifth kingdom, is 80,000 square terons.

The Seventh King of Airies, because Keyenoa chose him to rule all of Airies and to keep our people unified, was given neye continent to rule. Nor did Keyenoa place upon him any limits as to what he would be able to do with his power on our planet. It is, therefore, the High King's responsibility to care for Airies' needs. He chooses when the rain should fall, or when the sun must shine.

He keeps this planet moving about the sun, as it turns upon its own axis, making for us night and day, as well as fortauns, tuevtauns, and aanas. Met Lordship is Airies' protector, and Keyenoa guides Met Lordship. Keyenoa does this by not only being that power which He gives to our High king, but also by living and speaking within him, instructing him gently in His ways, as He does with all Airians. Because the High King must have a place to rest his head each night, he lives in a castle known as Oreon at the of top Mt. Oron, almost directly in the center of Malin, but never does he interfere in the ruling of Malin in any aspect. At this time, Airies is ruled by Met Lordship High King Sayleen Cantabo, Seventh King of Airies, though Eata Doege is close on the way.

Chapter I

Home?

"When things are quiet... *that* is the time to grow concerned."
—Thaytoric Book of Wisdom

I was fourteen aanas old—nearing fifteen in a minca over half an aana more—sitting in the learning house, listening to Cessan Rugan drone on about our history and the first High King. I was thinking that I was too old to have to endure such torture and was wondering what keezworky reason had me returning to this nonsense today. 'Haven't I already skipped weeks of this torture? Neye trouble came of that. Therefore, Father must agree with my conclusion—since he always knows everything I'm doing—because trouble certainly would have come to me by now,' I thought.

As my gaze wandered around the room, I suddenly jerked upright in my chair and muttered a quick prayer of leki that I had listened to reason and decided to attend the learning house today. Standing in the doorway, backlit by the bright morning sun, was one of my father's personal guards, Conden. There was neye way to avoid it; I was doomed. It did not take long for Rugan to notice the man's presence, and without even needing to ask the guard his purpose, I was instantly instructed to follow Father's guard from the Cessan's learning house so I could face my father's wrath. I left eagerly. I was at least happy to be free of the learning house master's incessant droning and scowling glances. Following close on Conden's heals, it took only about an ona before I fell behind.

The city of Malinieum, where I lived, always captivated me. Each time I walked along its streets, the city seemed to reveal its many surprises and examples of our joyous way of life. Being in serious trouble made minca difference when it came to Malinieum City's effect on my attention. I could not seem to help my desire to watch and absorb everything that might present itself along the way to Castle Loreann and my father's wrath. The city, as usual, was bustling with people. Mothers were ghea Keyen or chiding their nikca. Nikca were busy at play, and men worked at their jobs while young boys learned their trades at those men's side. Malinieum literally sang with the people and life within it. Color and sound were everywhere… and I lagged behind, eagerly trying to become a part of it all.

Smiling indulgently, Conden retraced his steps, knowing me well and the infatuation I felt for my home. "Your affection for Malinieum City is apparent, Niki. I would guess that it is this affection that is at the root of the trouble you soon shall face. What do you think?" he asked with a chuckle.

I smiled sheepishly. "I can't seem to help myself, Conden. I've grown so bored listening to Rugan's mind-numbing words buzzing in my ears day after day. When just outside the learning house, Malinieum City sings. The city is bursting with life and crowded with so many exciting things to discover." I paused, watching a stone carver add a nikca's name to the lintel of the house. "Conden, do you know what causes the buildings of Malinieum City to sing?"

He grunted in thought. "Ta. When a person with even a minca amount of power passes by, their power creates a current of energy that stirs the air. It is this power-infused air current that filters through the latticework, arches, and carvings on the buildings and makes musical notes. How these notes come out so pure and wonderful, I don't know, Niki, but then I am a guard, not a skilled stonemason." He shrugged, unconcerned over his ignorance.

PART I TENZENAR

"I guess you're right, Conden, how matters minca. Just knowing I like it is enough," I said, looking around with a sweeping gaze, hoping to delay us a minca longer.

He shook his head, a knowing smile touching his face. "Neye, young lord, you cannot divert me any longer, or it will not just be your punishment being met this day but mine as well."

I sighed and followed the guard through Malinieum City, across the square, passed the massive flowing fountain to the front of Loreann—the private home and palace for the administration of the Sixth King of Airies. It was the place where I lived because I was the Sixth King's only nikca and son. We turned down a hallway that led to my father's private chambers, just beyond the main entrance. As we neared his private council room, fully aware of the trouble I was in and not eager to ponder the punishment that was all too soon to come, I contemplated my relationship with my father.

I believed in many ways we were like most normal father and sons, but for us, we had a strange sort of closeness. I was free to share whatever I wanted with him, though my sharing was often unnecessary because of his given power as the Sixth King. Generally, Father knew almost before I did what I was up to—whether I wanted him to know or not. However, neye matter what I did, whether it was right or wrong, Father was there to instruct me on how to pick up the mess and set me back on the smoother course. He was also a fair man, ready to listen to whatever explanation I had. I never had to worry that I would be left on my own or unprotected in anyway. Yet even assured of all that, I nonetheless found it very difficult to talk with him. Father seemed to keep himself purposely distant and emotionally independent where I was concerned. I never doubted his Keyen, but he always seemed to struggle in expressing that Keyen. I had long wondered if he chose to emotionally distance himself because I was a male image of my mother. Sontall had claimed her sometime around my Santall, and this, of course, grieved my father deeply. I imagined that the pain he must experience every time he looked at me, only to see my mother, would cause any man—even my father—to put a wall of protection between him and the cause of that pain.

NIKITA'S STORY

The door of Father's private council room opened, and with knees trembling, I entered. Stopping in the center of the room, I stood before my father, the Sixth King of Airies. Aware of his attention—and suddenly feeling terribly guilty—I looked at the floor between us, hardly daring to move. Even before Conden's confirming statement of my being in trouble, I knew that my truancy from the learning house must have been discovered. So I felt it was wise to ponder my situation in silence and allow Father the opportunity to speak first. Having purposely been absent from the learning house for fortauns, I was humbly leki'anee that I had followed the urging of Keyenoa and attended learning house today, especially since Father had decided to summon me for judgment on this particular day. (It never even crossed my mind that he had used his given power to discover what day I had decided to attend the learning house before sending Conden to get me.)

Father cleared his throat, putting a halt to my thoughts. "Nikita Markain Malin." His voice resounded with commanding power and heavy reproach.

Looking up at him, his gaze bore deep in my soul, as a merciless smile touched his mouth. All my blood quickly pooled at my feet, and I turned as gray as the stones covering the floor. It was clear I had really managed to raise his ire this time. Father planned to squeeze every lastna of discomfort from me and then crush what minca hope might remain by revealing my punishment. What made the situation worse was knowing that the squeezing discomfort, as miserable as it was going to be, was the least of my worries.

"Due to your intentional and numerous truancies from the learning house, I've reached the decision to remove you from the learning house forthwith. Therefore, my son, you are neye longer expected to attend lessons under Cessan Rugan's tutelage. You are, as of this day, finished with learning house teachings."

My mouth fell open, and my heart pounded with delight. Instantly, I began dreaming of what I would do with my newfound freedom. Watching me closely, Father simply smiled. His expression, one filled with tender patience and sympathetic indulgence, easily lulled me into forgetting my own warning concerning my up and coming punishment.

Clearing his throat, Father drew me back from my dreams... "Nikita, it is time you learn—through diligent and focused study—exactly what it means to be the son of a King and a possible heir to the throne of one of the Six Kingdoms... if Keyenoa so wills that your powers prove strong enough."

He waited, watching me from his seat at the far end of the hall. Suddenly, still standing in the center of that room, I felt very much like a nematoe hopelessly trapped in a minsle~ar web. A web so cunningly spun I was unaware I had been caught until I saw the minsle~ar rushing toward me.

"So," Father continued without mercy, "you're to be placed in the capable care of your Thaytor—someone whom you cannot abandon from time to time simply because you enjoy your freedom far more than your studies. Nikita Markain Malin, from this day forward, your Thaytor, Master Jontair Alcone, will be teaching and advising you at your side until your Sontall."

A pain leapt from deep inside. The minsle~ar stung and swiftly spun me tightly in a prison of thread. Greedily, it sucked the hope of my newfound freedom dry. Caught and defeated, I followed the direction of my father's hand as he indicated the man standing a pearon away from his side.

My Thaytor loomed, seeming larger than the hall and more menacing than any punishment that had ever before been loosed upon my misdeeds. Jon actually stands about three learons, eight furons tall. However, at that moment I would have argued up, down, and sideways that he had grown as big as the council room. He wore a billowing black cape that surrounded him, cloaking and protecting him as if it were a living entity all its own. It covered his broad shoulders and draped passed his chest and arms, all of which were clothed in a deep-black, wide-sleeved shirt. The cape then fell past his equally black slacks and a pair of tight, thigh-high ebony boots, before it finally reached the floor.

Slowly, I forced my gaze toward the face of this black apparition of a man who loomed before me. His hair, as black as his clothes, surrounded his face in wild disarray before meeting with his cape at his shoulders. Drawn to the glowing countenance of my new Thaytor's fair face, I was met by a pair of smoldering, ebony eyes that instantly pierced my soul with the thrust of two fiery lackna blades. Terror shivered along my flesh and slammed through my blood as I struggled to break free of his gaze. As my knees buckled, I met the floor in a humbling display of weakness while that inky blackness, which came from and around him, slowly consumed me. I fainted.

As I floated in that place of semi-consciousness, Jon approached me while quietly quoting from the Thaytoric Book of Wisdom. Lifting me in his arms, he carried me from Father's council room, reciting from the Book of Wisdom all the way to my rooms. "Once a prince and his Thaytor are introduced, and Keyenoa chooses to anoint their union, a power escapes from the Thaytor and touches his prince, branding each for all time.... It unites us, Niki, and binds us. It is this bond that lets neye other Thaytor or man—with the exception of myself—hold or have any power over you."

He chuckled. "Nikita, all Kings and prospective Kings must have a Thaytor to guide and teach him. At first, I will be your instructor, guiding you to understand what it takes to make a benna and just ruler. At times, I will be something of a prophet, pulling you out of scrapes almost before you manage to find yourself in them. Now, hear me well on this, Niki, not only am I and always will be these things, I am also your mentor and Fortulaynan as well. I will guide and counsel you, through both my wisdom and my power, always leading you toward manhood and a crown—if Keyenoa so wills that you be a King." He chuckled again. "But as I have said, I am most of all, Nikita Markain Malin, the closest Fortulaynan you'll ever have. Truly, a taun will come when you will realize your life would have been long forfeit it weren't for my hand. When that taun comes, our lives will be bonded not only by power, but also Keyen Fortulaynan."

As the days and tuevtauns passed, I learned these shared facts firsthand. As I came to know and understand Jon better, his Keyen for life combined with the all too Airian mischievousness and curiosity—which we, as a people, all seemed to have in abundance—caused my feelings for him to expand, until I found I could not, and did not want to live without him.

⌘ ⌘ ⌘ ⌘

Nearly an aana after Father had introduced us, Jon and I were leaving Malinieum City to travel to Oreon where I was to meet with Met Lordship High King Sayleen Cantabo. We were walking through Malinieum Forest, a minca band of trees that surrounded the outer edge of Malinieum City. I, as usual, was hardly listening while Jon droned on over some interminable fact or other which he seemed to never cease prattling about. While, ignoring him, I was enjoying the breeze in the trees and the smell of the soil beneath our feet after an earlier rain.

"The castle where Met Lordship resides is known as Oreon. It's actually the top of Mt. Oron, located in the center of the continent of Malin. Surrounding it is the thick forest called Dindieum, which spans over a hundred terons in every direction. Oreon houses thousands of guards and some hundreds of orate, as well as—" He silenced himself and looked at me before raising an eyebrow. "You've barely heard a word I said, have you, Niki?"

I smiled mischievously and shook my head.

He sighed. "Have you at least kept your ears open in these last few tuevtauns while wandering about Loreann, as I've asked?"

Even as I tried to ignore it, I could feel his gaze pierce me while he awaited my reply. "About the Eata Doege?" I asked uncertainly.

He nodded, his expression relaxing. "Now, what that means is Met Lordship High King Sayleen Cantabo expects to pass in Sontall sometime during your generation of Kings, and Keyenoa will choose someone—most likely a prince—to take Met Lordship's place as the Seventh King and ruler of Airies."

I stopped and stared at him in horror. "You mean I could become the next High King?"

Jon had continued along the path, nodding absent-mindedly in agreement, never noticing the terror that filled me over such a possibility.

Ashamed of this unconfessed fear while hoping he wouldn't notice it—as Thaytor's have a bad habit of noticing such things—I continued quickly, "But why now? I mean, Met Lordship doesn't look old enough to pass in Sontall?"

He glanced back and smiled, "In two aanas, Met Lordship will be one hundred aanas old." Aware of my surprise, he chuckled, "I know, our High King looks much younger, but looks are deceiving, especially in High Kings." Sensing my confusion, he stopped and waited for me to catch up. "Sit down." He pointed to a rotting log just off the path.

Knowing that Jon, when he wanted, could make anything he had to share come alive I sat and waited eagerly, hoping this would be one of those times.

"Okay." He began pacing back and forth. "As I said, Met Lordship High King Sayleen Cantabo has aged while being King, ninety-eight aanas... but because he is the High King, he actually ages one aana for every two of ours. Therefore, if we count the natural aanas that have passed in his lifetime, Met Lordship has lived close to two hundred aanas... plus, eighteen more before he Conay Sona Eata." Jon sighed, and turning away, began to do the math in his head.

I listened as Jon mumbled to himself.

"Let's see... he's ninety-eight plus ninety-eight, for his doubled aanas, which is... one hundred ninety-six, plus eighteen more before Con Sona Eata... and that makes him... 214." He turned back to me. "Met Lordship is actually 214 aanas old," he said proudly, unaware he had been talking out loud all along.

"Think about it, Niki, and remember... even though he has all that power, Met Lordship is still just an Airian, and a tired Airian at that," he added, helping me to consider the man rather than the King.

"How can anyone be so certain that he's going to reach his Sontall in my generation?" I asked, looking blindly in the direction I knew Oreon to be and wondered what the castle looked like—having not paid attention to Jon's earlier description. Too far away from the castle to possibly see it, I saw only a faint glimpse of Golden Meadow through the trees around us as their branches swayed in the gentle currents of air.

"Because Met Lordship told the Kings and they in turn told the Thaytors." Jon leaned against a tree beside me and continued to explain, "Keyenoa reveals to the High King when his taun for Sontall is near. With Met Lordship forewarned by Keyenoa, our High King then can use his given power to begin to search for the youth who Keyenoa has likely chosen to become the next High King. Met Lordship's given power is often able to discern the amount of power lying dormant in his predecessor long before the boy nears his time of Con Sona Eata."

"Then, mustn't he know who'll be the next High King by now?" I pressed, hoping his answer would assure me that I was not that youth. Ashamed, I wondered why I felt so uncomfortable with the prospect of becoming the High King. Most boys' dream of what it would be like if they were the High King. I simply didn't want such a gift from Keyenoa. The thought of trying to care for myself was difficult enough, let alone having to care for all of Airies.

Jon had continued down the path, and discovering him gone, I quickly followed after him.

When I caught up, he answered my question, "Neye, not yet that I know of anyway," causing my heart to sink. "But that's why we're going to Oreon. Met Lordship High King Sayleen Cantabo has summoned the princes, one by one, so he may meet them. This helps him to determine—through his given power—if anyone of you are to be the next High King. You, Nikita Markain Malin, are the last prince to meet with Met Lordship. And," he added swiftly, knowing my next question before I could ask, "if he finds that none of the princes are to be High King, he will then release his given power to search all of Airies for the boy whom Keyenoa has chosen to replace him."

"Jon?"

"What?"

"Let's say it is one of the princes who will be the next High King. Will Met Lordship know exactly who it'll be once he has met us all?"

"Well, not exactly—but he'll have a benna idea.…" Jon was obviously distracted. His expression had grown concerned and a frown cut deep grooves between his eyes and along the sides of his mouth. Aware that I had planned to ask another question, he silenced me with the force of his glance, before he explained, "Hush, Met Lord. I need to get my bearings. There is something strange with the silence of Malinieum Forest and Golden Meadow beyond," he whispered, causing tingles of alarm to slide up and down my spine.

The air had suddenly grown still, unmistakably and unnaturally warm and heavy. The burr of scureel in the grass, the ever-present song of birds, and the scurry of minca animals moving along the underbrush… were nonexistent. Jon and I stood alone at the meadow's edge, while every living creature around us waited in hiding as if preparing for something to swoop down and swallow us all. I could smell the anxiety in the air as the tension around us thickened and grew. Jon grabbed my tunic-vest and pulled me beneath the cover of the trees.

"What's wrong, Master?" I squawked. My voice pierced the silence like an arrow.

Jon glared at me and then struggled to regain his frayed temper. "I know not," he whispered, and despite his displeasure, he kept his voice soft and low so it sounded like leaves rustling in the trees. His words did not disturb anything, nor did it alert anything to our presence. "Grab my cape, Niki, and go invisible… and for Alleanne's sake, don't talk until you can control the pitch of your voice," he commanded in that same soft whisper.

Crouched in the underbrush, Jon strove to discern what the danger might be before it found us. Trusting his instincts over my own, I did not look around. Instead, having gone invisible, I let my mind wander, imagining some of the possibilities that might be out there.

"Jon," my voice was now controlled and but a mere whisper, "could it be a zewaller?" I asked, having instantly thought of the hideous half-dassishon, half-lizard–like creature that stood as tall as a tree and had teeth as long and wide as a man's hand. The only way a zewaller could be killed was through the power of fight (of which I was too young to have)… and even then, zewaller didn't meet Sontall easily. "Maybe it's ghea neye but a lumballer." I added, yet still shivered over the thought. Lumballer, while normally afraid of their own shadow, were sometimes worse than a zewaller, especially if their territory was invaded. Lumballer are large, deceptively fuzzy, and somewhat adorable-looking creatures, but they have poisonous spines growing within their fur. The spines can be easily flung from their bodies over a hundred learons with frightening accuracy.

I shuffled a minca closer to Jon. "What can it be?"

"I know not. It is unnatural, Niki. Look, even the breeze is still and heavy with heat. The forest and meadow may look void of life, but the creatures in both environments are more alert than ever before. It's like.…"

The wind suddenly thundered over the trees, causing their tops to bend and sway violently. Everything grew dark. Clouds of smoke and fire shot from the sky above the meadow. I screamed and released Jon's cape, ready to run back for home. My Thaytor's hand lashed out, catching me before I could move a furon. Pulling me nearer to his side, his touch reached through my terror and calmed me. He said something, but the wind and noise took his words away before I could understand them.

The fierce storm slowly descended. The trees began to crack and fall as if they were twigs beneath an invisible foot. The fire sank, first scorching and then incinerating the grass in the center of the vast meadow. Jon threw his cape over my body while I tucked my head against my chest, temporarily shutting out the sight before me. Too frightened to move, we huddled near one another as the unnatural darkness deepened and the fire sank slowly to the ground with each ena that passed.

"Be this our Sontall… are we soon to see Keyenoa?" I asked, shouting so he could hear me above the holocaust.

"I know not, Niki. It isn't natural. Look closer, you'll see it is neye storm," he shouted calmly, drawing my gaze from beneath his cape. "I don't even think the people in Malinieum City can see it. It looks to be centralized right there."

The fire slowly sank into the ground. The wind now buffeted us viciously, flinging dirt and debris in our eyes, while the tops of the trees neye longer seemed to be moving. The heat became intense as burning embers flew with the wind stinging our faces, and singing our hair. We ducked beneath Jon's cape, protecting ourselves against the punishing lash of debris as the fire slowly smothered itself against the meadow floor. As suddenly as the din began, the silence returned. The unexpected and instant cessation of noise felt all the more ominous than the cacophony only enas before. There now was ghea neye—not a sound to shatter the sudden oppressive silence.

"Remain invisible, Niki."

I barely heard him, as we struggled to untangle ourselves from his cape while careful to remain close enough to each other that our invisibility shields overlapped allowing us to be able to see one another.

"Ghea Alleanne! Look at that!" I blurted, my voice carried all too easily in the suddenly heavy silence.

Jon flashed me a dark look of warning.

"What beast can it be, Master?" I pressed, carefully quieting my voice.

A huge cylindrical creature, almost as long as Golden Meadow and nearly as wide, lay like a sleeping mantobar in the burnt grass. It didn't seem to have a front, back, or even eyes. Nonetheless, I feared that if I drew its attention by some ghea teepin action it would decide to eat us.

"It is not a living thing, Niki," Jon replied. "Look closer… there are doors at its side. Do you see them now?" Even as he spoke, the doors had begun to open. "It's a lunata."

"A what?"

PART I TENZENAR

He stared at me with Thaytoric censure. "If you had paid more attention in the learning house, Met Lord, you would remember that a lunata is used to carry beings across space, so that they may travel to other planets to live—after they destroy the creatures and beings that lived there before them."

As he was explaining, **they** climbed out of the lunata... people that looked so much like Airians, yet... bland... with none of Keyenoa's light surrounding them.

"Tenzenar, Niki. Tenzenar," he whispered. His voice, while devoid of emotion still managed to carry a threatening ring of warning and terror.

I remembered the teaching of Tenzenar and lunatas then.

"If thee fear ghea neye more, fear the Tenzenar for they bring the hand of Sontall wherever they go," I whispered, reciting what I had learned in the house. "I don't know how I could've forgotten, when it's been taught to me aana after aana," I murmured, ashamed of myself.

He gave my shoulder a gentle squeeze. "Worry not about it now, Met Lord. Fear has a way of causing even the most learned to forget his own name." He squeezed my shoulder. "It also causes others to snap and say hurtful things... toenda omprice sorice, Niki."

I smiled and nodded, aware that he was apologizing for his comment about my not paying attention at the learning house.

Noises drifted toward us as the Tenzenar continued streaming from the doors of the lunata. While we were too far away to hear what was being said as the Tenzenar spoke to one another, we quickly realized our danger. Rising to our feet, neye longer close enough that we could see one another, Jon squeezed my shoulder then tugged on it, urgently passing along the message to run. Firmly grasping his cape, allowing him to take the lead, we ran back to Malinieum City.

We knew if we were quick in warning our people, Father would send word to Met Lordship, and then all the people of Airies would be safe and protected before the Tenzenar even managed to discover Malinieum City.

Chapter II

A Starting Over

"When one seeks, he usually finds; but often what one seeks be not what one finds. So take care in what thee seek, or chance receiving what Keyenoa decides one needs to be given."
—Valcree Metlan Sontall,
First High Kingof Airies

Met Lordship High King Sayleen Cantabo, fearing delay, transported the people of Airies to Mt. Oron. The power he had received from Keyenoa revealed that with the exception of the continent of Locar, the Tenzenar invasion encompassed every island continent on Airies. Certain none of his people were safe from discovery on their separate continents; he brought all of his people close to Oreon, transporting us to the base of Mt. Oron. While he called his Kings into council within Oreon, Met Lordship asked his people, through his given power, to await the King's decision. He instructed all his people to take rest and shelter however we could along the base of Mt. Oron. While on the mountainside awaiting word from our Kings, everyone began to realize that our homes would neye longer be the same homes we had known throughout our lives. Many Airians lifted their thoughts and fears to Keyenoa —aware that such things were best entrusted there.

PART I TENZENAR

Jon and I sat under the low branches of a gungas tree, well above the vast camps of people, hoping to avoid the numerous questions nagging us all. With our arms wrapped around our legs, and our chins resting on our knees, we too struggled with our private fears and thoughts brought on by the Tenzenar invasion.

"What are you thinking, Niki?" Jon asked quietly.

"Why? I was wondering why," I sighed, keeping my head on my knees.

Jon crawled out from beneath the low branches, pushing though the large, thick leaves at the end of the branches and walked to the edge of a babbling mountain stream several pearons away. Curious, I followed. I was uncertain of his mood, yet hopeful he would give me an answer.

He looked at me. "Why run?"

His voice was without life. His eyes looked suddenly dull and were almost gray in color. They reminded me all too much of the Tenzenar faces I had seen that morning. This unexpected change filled me with despair for my Thaytor and fear for us all. Could the Tenzenar eventually take the light of Keyenoa from us as well?

Jon didn't wait for my confirmation but quietly answered my question, chilling me with the sorrowful lack of life apparent even in his voice. "Because the Tenzenar would have destroyed us all if we stayed in our old homes."

"Neye, Master. I want to know why they've come here. What made our planet a place they wanted to claim and, most of all, why do they feel they have a right to claim it?" I corrected.

He looked at me in stunned surprise but remained silent a long time. Knowing better than to press for an answer, I waited for him to speak, eager for his reply.

"Well," he sighed, smiling gently. "You've finally asked a question for which I have neye answer. Honestly, Niki, I don't even think Met Lordship knows why they chose to come here, let alone why they believe they have the right to do so." Disappointed with his answer, I nonetheless realized that by his confession over his inability to answer it, he was telling me I was growing up. This made me smile.

NIKITA'S STORY

We walked down the mountain's slope together, joining many of those we recognized from the Castle Loreann. Jon went to have a private word with Bonfinar, my father's Thaytor, leaving me alone in the crowd. At loose ends, I decided to take advantage of my… unique… freedom and retraced my steps up the mountainside. So much had happened since rising that morning. I wanted taun alone with my own thoughts and fears, hoping to somehow come to terms with them.

Passing a few acquaintances and guards, I offered a muttered greeting, but chose not to stop to talk with them. Moving past the crowds, I continued to climb. I wanted to know how the Kings were going to keep us safe and where we were going to live; most of all, I wanted to know what they were going to do about the invading Tenzenar.

I was jarred from my thoughts when the ground dropped beneath me, and my boot landed with a splash in icy cold water. Looking down in surprise, I discovered I had stepped knee-deep into the mountain stream near where Jon and I had stood earlier. Looking around, I noticed that the stream cut into the mountainside, falling swiftly in the direction of LeFold Lake. Glancing up, I followed the course of the stream with my gaze. I was pleased to note that the stream could well lead straight to Oreon's golden doors.

"Hmmm, I wonder…" I said aloud as a plan swiftly formed in my mind. Glancing furtively over my shoulder, I made sure I was completely alone, afraid someone might see me and guess my intentions. To my relief, neye seemed to notice or care where I was. Ascertaining I was safe, I smiled victoriously and began my climb. I was going to Oreon and find some way to listen to what the Kings were deciding rather than wait around the base of Mt. Oron in fear and awful wondering.

Night fell and still I climbed, determined to reach the top. I was often forced to walk in the icy mountain stream when the mountainside itself grew steep and impassable. My feet had long grown numb from the ice-cold water, causing me to slip and fall all too frequently. Wet, bruised, and tired, I paused. While wiping my dripping hands on my tunic, I looked back to discover how far I had climbed. I could neye longer see the people below. The only sign of their presence were the dots of flickering light from their camp fires. For a moment, I wondered about Jon. The thought that he might even now be looking for me sent shivers of terror down my spine. Afraid he might have guessed my intentions, I pulled myself out of the stream and scrambled up the steep rocky slope, forcing myself to go on at an even faster pace. If Jon had guessed my intentions, I realized that he could easily be less than an oona behind me.

Reaching a point in the night where it became so dark, I was unable to see my hand before my face, I had decided to give up and return to the base of the mountain. Then, as if I had called them to do so, the clouds departed and released a full moon's light over my surroundings. Pearons ahead, tucked in the craggy, turreted mountaintop, shimmering in the muted light, stood the massive Gates of Gold—the entrance to Oreon—the doors were even beginning to swing open. In my joy and excitement over having discovered that I'd reached my destination, I took it as a sign that the Gates of Gold were beckoning me to enter. Taking neye time to consider the possible wrong of my actions and so forestall my going in, I rushed through the opening doors. Then, thinking that while the doors welcomed me, others inside might not be as cordial, I raised my shield of invisibility and clung to the shadows and walls as I went on my way deeper inside Oreon. Remembering the number of people Jon had mentioned living in the castle, I kept my ears alert while I swiftly began to read the walls, looking for some indication of where the Kings might be found.

Even as I searched the walls for directions, I found myself longing to stop and read more of the stories and tales about the past Kings or brave soldiers that were carved in the walls along the hallways. Just as I was about to give into that desire, I read an obscure mention of a Chamber of Kings beside a long, curving staircase. Taking those steps, still carefully hugging the stairwell's shadows, I climbed to the top. Once there, I discovered that what lay in front of me was a solid balcony that spread out and clearly circled the high ceiling of a room. Hesitating, wondering if I somehow missed a door or turn in the dark stairwell, I considered turning around and trying again. Then, hearing the power touched voices of several men coming from the room below, even recognizing many of those voices from the councils taken at my father's home, I cautiously crept to the rail to peek my nose over its edge.

I had indeed found the Kings!

Immediately, the man at the head of the table drew my attention. His voice caressed my ears with its soft, deep, and mesmerizing melodic power. It quickly hypnotized me into forgetting my caution until I discovered I was leaning far over the rail in an effort to get closer to the man and his voice. The powerful melody of his words slowly began to penetrate my fogged mind until I managed to comprehend what he was saying.

"The Tenzenar won't even think to enter Dindieum Forest. The forest is far too deep and wild for such exploration. We will be safe here, my Kings." Met Lordship paused.

Ready to toast this wisdom, Lord Richon Locar lifted his goblet. It was the quick and concentrated motion from Met Lordship that caused him to pause and remain silent.

"It seems we have an unexpected visitor, tomenan," the High King calmly informed his Six Kings.

Lord Richon lowered his goblet to the table in surprise, as the Kings began to angrily mumble to one another. Alerted to the danger of my situation, I slid from the railing, hastily raising my invisibility shield, while turning toward the stairs. I had intended to flee Oreon.

"Now, now, Met Lords," Met Lordship's spellbinding voice seemed to flow right through my intentions, leaving me frozen in my retreat, "you are frightening our young visitor away with such angry murmurings," he chastised his Kings lightly, silencing them instantly. "Come, young one, come to the rail so we all may see who visits our council," he beckoned with tender amusement.

Unable to deny him, I closed my eyes and began silently praying for protection as my shield dropped against my wishes, "Dear Keyenoa, Father is certain to be ashamed and angry with me. I have done it again—acting before thinking. Tella saa, Keyenoa, have Father not be too angry," I pleaded, overwhelmed with shame and embarrassment, knowing that once again my desires and curiosity had put me in a situation from which I had neye way to escape.

Chuckling, aware of my thoughts and prayers, Met Lordship continued to cajole me with his words and power, "Thy father, young one? Truly, I would worry not. If I were him, I would be… most… proud," he hesitated purposely over the words, "of a son who had managed to get so far into Oreon undetected by guard or orate. Come now, return to the rail, and allow all my Kings to learn who you are and how you managed such a feat."

Gently pulled to the rail by a simple nudge of his power, I discovered each King staring up at me, eager to discover their "spy."

Met Lordship looked toward my father. "Your son, I believe, Mark? He is the only prince I've not had the pleasure of meeting—as yet." The laughter that escaped his lips was enchanting. Suddenly, I longed to be nearer, forgetting the trouble I faced and the wisdom to stay far from the man who sat next to the High King, knowing he would meet out my punishment.

Father, with a stiff nod, confirmed Met Lordship's statement, before he leaned near the High King to speak quietly with him. Met Lordship chuckled and nodded, his laughter still holding me in thrall, while Father turned to look up at me on the balcony.

"Nikita Markain Malin, thee will get thyself down here and explain thy actions to this council immediately," he demanded with a frightening amount of control, while his displeasure clearly revealed itself through his formal speech.

I swallowed, looking around the encircling balcony for a way down. I looked again, and then a third time before giving up and shutting my eyes. "Father?"

I felt his irritation. I knew it for a certainty, though he had not said a word and would not say a word until I explained myself.

Taking a breath, I continued, "There are neye, stairs that lead into the chamber.…" I hesitated, hoping I had said enough, since my dilemma seemed obvious—at least to me.

Father said not a word.

"Met Father, there be neye door that I can see into the room. How am I...?"

The Kings all began to chuckle—except Father. All I wanted to do was find a hole to climb in, rather than face further humiliation. Again, I tried to turn back into the stairwell. Met Lordship's gentle chuckle seemed to suddenly override all the other Kings, holding me in my place and removing my shame as if he had snuffed out a candle.

"This room, young one, is the Chamber of Kings and was so named because only the Seven Kings have the right to use it and the ability to gain access inside. All who enter here must do so through the use of their given power. It was through Keyenoa's command and direction that Met Lordship High King Valcree Metlan Sontall built all of Oreon. Having neye aid of tool or man, this room alone in all of Oreon was built solely through Keyenoa's gift of power to the first High King. It was purposely built with neye doors or portals of any kind. Thus ensuring that only through the given power of the Seven Kings of Airies is anyone ever able to gain entrance." He paused a moment, looking up but not quite meeting my gaze. "Young one, do you know your history? That Oreon was cut, hollowed, and carved by the finest stonemasons, artisans, and the first High King of Airies, Valcree Metlan Sontall, through Keyenoa's direction, thousands of aanas ago? Keyenoa even ordered that Oreon's exterior remain as He created it at the beginning of taun—with only the Gates of Gold added to its exterior, and even the Gates had to be hidden deep in the mountain's shado...." Stopping himself, Met Lordship looked stunned as all heard him mutter, "By Alleanne! Keyenoa knew of this day all that long ago, and so told Met Valcree to build Oreon in such a way for the protection of his people at this time." Lowering his head toward the table, he closed his eyes and focused his power in prayer, ghea leki Keyenoa for His farsighted care.

Suddenly freed from the High King's mesmerizing focus, I again thought to slip away. Only to feel the touch of his given power before I could even take a step, "Any further lessons of Oreon must wait for another time. For now, young one, I would be most proud to bring you into the chamber," Met Lordship added while seeking Father's nod of approval. Then, even before he had finished his sentence, I was standing between the High King and my father at the head of the table.

"Well, Nikita, explain thyself," Father demanded in the tightly controlled voice he used when dealing with my infractions. "And where in Alleanne's name is Jontair!" he shouted before I could even formulate an answer to his first demand.

Everyone was quiet.

I stared at my boots. Father's questions and my reasons had become hopelessly garbled in my head. Even as I struggled to straighten them out, they continued to get tangled up with my fear and my thoughts over my numerous possible punishments. I didn't think I would ever be able to answer him. Especially since I wasn't even able to remember how I had managed to get my boots so wet. Desperate for help and some minca offer of understanding, knowing I would not find it from Father, I looked around the table at the other Kings. While each man met my gaze, expressing both humor and pity, they offered minca comfort and neye help.

Met Lordship put his hand on my shoulder. That light and comforting touch easily plucked my heart from my throat and cleared my mind of confusion. "Now, young one, tell us how you found your way to Oreon and through the Gates of Gold to this chamber, leaving your Thaytor unaware of your actions?"

Grateful, I looked into his eyes and was instantly held by those ice-blue orbs. I was caught by the incredible power within them. Unwilling—and unable—to break free, I admitted my gaffe. I had forgotten one of Jon's most repeated and incessant instructions as we had prepared to travel to Oreon. I must never ever look directly at the High King's face, neye matter how compelling an urge I may have to the contrary. Held by Met Lordship, I gazed at the man before me and was surprised to find tiny wrinkles creasing the corners of those ice-blue eyes and his firm, expressive mouth. His round face was barely marred by age, expressing a youthful, almost innocent awareness. His hair, mostly black and only slightly streaked with gray, surrounded his face magnifiently, stopping when it touched his shoulders close against his neck. He was a man that would be easily liked and trusted even without his gift of power. His whole demeanor actually deceived the onlooker concerning the amount of given power he truly held. The truth of his almost incomprehensible amount of given power was found only within the depth of his ice-blue eyes and glowing in a light surrounding his body.

Met Lordship smiled tenderly. Lowering his gaze, he looked at the floor between us, gently releasing me from his hold. Gasping, I sucked in a deep breath of air. Ghea leki'anee—though unexpectedly—I had neye trouble remembering where I was, or the questions he had asked of me.

"As far as I know, Master Jon is still at the base of Mt. Oron, Met Lordship High King Sayleen Cantabo," I explained without hesitation. "The last time I saw him was when he went to speak with Bonfinar, leaving me on my own. I was so tired of waiting to hear what was going to happen to us. I wanted to be alone, so I began to wander up the steeper slopes of Oron where neye was waiting."

Each King listened intently, interested in what I had to say, as they drank casually from their goblets or snacked from the plates before them around the large rectangular table. I stared at my feet. I felt more comfortable looking at them rather than the Kings, especially my father. Thinking of my climb to reach Oreon, I almost laughed aloud when I suddenly remembered how I had gotten my boots wet.

"Well…" I continued, "While I was thinking these impatient thoughts, I stepped right in the middle of a stream. Looking up the mountainside, this stream appeared to lead straight to Oreon. And since I really wanted to hear what was being decided… well… I followed the stream to the Gates of Gold. Discovering that the Gates were opening, I walked in. I was careful not to be spotted by any guards or orate along the way by raising my invisibility shield," I added proudly and then nearly kicked myself for having volunteered far too much incriminating information.

The Kings began to murmur uneasily about the Gates of Gold opening for me. Afraid I had done something very wrong, I looked quickly toward my father, seeking his reassurance. As our eyes met, he smiled stiffly, assuring me that my infractions were neye greater than I had first assumed while fighting his own reactions over my announcement. Father wasn't certain if he should be proud because I had the courage to find a way into Oreon, or reprimand me for daring to enter without being invited inside and welcomed by my High King.

"Someday, son, your curiosity will put you in a situation so troublesome, you will not be able to charm your way out," he said quietly. He had obviously decided to feel both angry and proud over my accomplishments, at least for the time being.

Unable to help myself, I looked toward Met Lordship. He smiled with understanding, careful not to meet my gaze or that of my father's. "Well, Mark, since Nikita has climbed such a long way and obviously gone to a considerable amount of trouble to get here. Why not let the boy remain and hear what has been decided? It's up to you, forlaynan. He's your son… in many more ways than your common bond of blood," he added with a telling chuckle.

Father began to laugh quietly, twinkles of mischief and memories danced in his sharp green eyes. "Met Lordship, I admit there is minca sense in sending him back to the base of Mt. Oron. I am certain that if we did, he would simply turn and rescale the mountainside. As you've said, he's my son in more ways than blood. And who am I to argue with my High King?"

"Then he stays," Met Lordship commanded, laughing along with Father.

The High King produced a chair and a plate of food though his gift of power, setting both in the space between him and my father. Hesitating a moment, he glanced at father, being careful not to meet Father's gaze. "Mark, do you object to his having the wine served at this table?" he asked.

"I've neye objections for this night," Father answered quietly.

With a wave of his hand, Met Lordship set a goblet of wine at my place—much to my delighted pleasure. Sitting, I began to eat and drink as though I had not done either in several days. Between the wine and Met Lordship High King Sayleen Cantabo's melodious voice, I soon drifted off into a dreamy sleep, neye longer concerned over where I was going to live, or the safety of Airies due to the Tenzenar invasion.

While I slept, it was decided that the Kingdoms of Airies would resettle in the heart of Dindieum around LeFold Lake and Mount Oron. All the Kingdoms were purposely situated close to Oreon and the High King's protection. They were nestled among the rolling hills of the Sinca Range, deeply surrounded by the ancient forest of Dindieum, where neye Tenzenar would think to trespass.

The First Kingdom, Locar, was located the farthest from the Tenzenar landing site, in the valley of the river Derran. Locar had a minca frontage on LeFold Lake over the gentle hills west of Oron. The Second Kingdom, Dorna, was to settle on the western shore of LeFold Lake. Dorna's borders then extended west toward the sea along the valley formed by the river Tolbad. The foothills that rolled from Oron to the northeast became the home of the Third Kingdom of Airies, Letark. These three ghea minca Kingdoms were purposely situated closest to Oreon and the farthest from the Tenzenar presence.

The larger Kingdoms, with their more powerful Kings, were located along the southern shore of LeFold Lake. The Fourth Kingdom, Tarton, was placed east along the Miramar River and the Miramar Mountain Range. The Fifth Kingdom of Cetar was to settle to the west, nestled within the southern stretch of the Sinca Mountains and the Tolbad Range. The Sixth Kingdom of Malin was to be settled between the Kingdoms of Tarton and Cetar, straddling the Broken Dindieum River with the Sinca Mountains as its southern border and LeFold Lake as its northern border.

Immediately following the King's departure from Oreon, they told their people what was decided. Then, Met Lordship transported every person, along with their property and livestock, to their new Kingdoms. Throughout the remainder of that long night, the people of Airies were forced to find shelter for themselves and their livestock however they could within the wilds of Dindieum. The people of Malin chose to settle high in the thickly branched and heavily foliaged gungas trees, sheltered by the leaves. Whatever livestock they had was allowed to roam freely on the ground beneath the branches or beyond.

I entered New Malin in the arms of my Thaytor, sound asleep and oblivious to all. Waking the next morning, slowly reaching consciousness through layers of a confused wine-induced haze, I discovered I was precariously close to falling out of my 'bed.' While grasping tightly to my unreliable and very firm 'mattress'—a wide tree branch—I ever so astutely ascertained that I must have been put there while deep in a drunken stupor. Peering through the branches, gazing a minca over a pearon straight down, I tried to discover just who—or what—had awakened me. I hoped to give who or what a piece of my mind without my sour stomach and headache growing worse from the effort.

Despite my blurred vision, I found Jon standing between the branches with his hands on his hips gazing up at me. He began laughing hysterically while I glowered at him through the branches, struggling to keep my balance and not fall out of the tree.

"Come on, sleepy one, princes and even Kings have to work today. We need to make New Malin into a home as soon as we can," he called up, having managed to contain his laughter.

Still clamoring for stability with my head swimming over each clumsy movement, I began to make my way down. I struggled to untangle my sluggish limbs from around one branch after another while still maintaining my dignity as well as my balance. By the time I reached the ground, my humor was all but gone. Jon's continued chuckling only added insult to my efforts. I honestly couldn't understand why I was feeling so disagreeable, but—even as I pondered the oddity of my mood—I admitted I was perversely enjoying my foul temper. I was most eager to vent my mood upon my Thaytor. When I reached the base of the tree, the first thing I did was scowl ominously at him. I grumbled beneath my breath, careful to say ghea neye that he could understand.

"Okay, so, what has you in such a pleasant state of mind this fine morning, Met Lord?" Jon asked sarcastically.

I simply scowled at him all the more, certain his bright and cheery disposition was far from necessary.

Finally frowning in return, Jon centered his black gaze on my sour countenance. His cheerfulness quickly faded when having to face my expression for even a few mere enas. "I will have neye pity for you if you tell me you have a hangover from all that wine you consumed during last night's escapade."

I ignored his jibe, realizing he had just given me a reason for not only my foul mood but my sour stomach and head as well. "I don't enjoy sleeping in trees, Jon. What mootan would?" I snapped.

The memory of my actions of the night before suddenly burst forth from my pounding head and sluggish memory. Instantly, I realized the absolute teepin of incurring my Thaytor's wrath when he might be my only ally, especially if I had to face my father this morning. Closing my mouth, I urged myself to behave normally, while fighting to ignore my queasy stomach, shaky knees and aching head as we crawled out from beneath the tree and began to walk together through the forest.

"Master?"

I waited for him to look at me.

"I only drank one goblet of leeksha wine from Met Lordship's table. Surely that's not enough to cause drunkenness. If I feel out of sorts, it was caused by whatever mootan stuffed me in a tree last night," I added peevishly.

Jon chuckled with minca mercy, "Niki, one goblet of wine at Met Lordship's table is equivalent to over half a bottle. Plenty to cause drunkenness and a hangover in a grown man if consumed too quickly, let alone a young boy accustomed to only warm saflee" He looked at me with malicious glee. "Oh, and by the way, I'm the mootan who stuffed you in the tree."

Aware that I had just planted my boot firmly in my mouth, I ignored the fact that he had insulted me by calling me a young boy when I was fifteen aanas of age. I thought it best to change the subject. "Tell me, Master, what exactly do we have to do today, anyway?"

He chuckled again, his eyes glittering like black diamonds. He was enjoying my suffering and peevishness far too much to let my mood sway him. "Ask me what we don't have to do, Niki. That question would be easier to answer. Come now, Met Lord," he urged with barely contained humor, "and do yourself a favor. Keep that foul mood and temper you seem determined to share with me from manifesting itself further, or you may find yourself in more trouble than even you can charm yourself out of."

I was shocked into silence. I remembered those same words uttered by my father the night before and couldn't help but wonder if they were a prophetic warning from Keyenoa.

We were walking through the dense forest at a jarring pace, passing many people working on various projects. I took minca notice of what they were doing. Instead, I continued to suffer through the pain in my head and my queasy stomach in silence, until my curiosity finally got the better of my wisdom.

Glancing at Jon, I dared another question, "Where are we going, anyway?" To my shame, I still sounded peevish.

"To your father" was his reply. "He expressed a strong desire to see you as soon as possible this morning," Jon continued, having cast a quick and satisfied glance at my stricken and sick expression.

I said ghea neye more, finally heeding the many warnings I had already received, and concentrated on the people we passed. Very few of them were familiar to me. I thought I recognized some of the people from the cities of Lizingham and Markainieum, yet there were very few people from Malinieum City. Most surprising of all, I began to recognize through their different clothing, that some of the people had to be from the Fourth Kingdom of Airies, known now as New Tarton. As I looked closer, it became clear that the people of New Malin were gravitating toward the men from New Tarton, as if seeking instruction or guidance.

Dismayed, I grasped Jon's shoulder and pulled him to a stop. "Where are the people from Malinieum City?" I demanded. "And... why are the people of New Tarton here giving what looks like instruction to our people? This makes neye sense, Jon!"

"Well, 'tis nice to see you're finally alert—if still not in the best of moods," Jon replied with a sarcastic drawl. Having mercy on me, he decided to answer my demand. "The people from Malinieum City who have chosen to remain in New Malin are building their homes nearer to the lake. Many of the people from Malinieum, and even some from Markainieum and Lizingham, have chosen to live in one of the other Kingdoms. Met Lordship High King Sayleen Cantabo suggested this option for your father's people, because… well… our Kingdom's population needed to be reduced to live comfortably on what land we now have. Most of your father's people were relieved and eager to go, feeling quite uneasy about living in the Kingdom closest to the Tenzenar."

Stunned, I pressed him with another question, "If we had to reduce our population, then why are there people from Tart… I mean New Tarton here?" I corrected myself.

He smiled and started forward, leaving me to follow. "I think many of them are making furniture. As far as I understand it, your father urgently requested of Lord Alon as many of the finest woodcarvers and artisans he could spare. I'm not quite certain everything your father has in mind. Almost all of Tarton's builders and woodcarvers are here, while quite a few of our finest stonemasons are—I believe temporarily—in New Tarton. If, you delay me neye longer, young lord, we will likely learn your father's plans shortly. What do thee think? Can thee hurry along a minca more?" Jon fell into his formal speech with the lifting of an eyebrow and a telling gleam in his eye.

Father stood in a huge clearing talking to a few men from Malinieum City. Bonfinar, Father's Thaytor, was as usual, standing silently at his side. Jon and I stopped about ten paces away and waited for Father to finish his discussion. With Father facing Jon and me, his voice reached us easily. Being more concerned about the possible punishments I faced, I paid minca attention to what was being said. Until Father said, "Ta, build the homes in the trees."

Unhappy with the sound of that, I decided to pay less attention to my worries and more to the conversation. Just the thought of spending another night in a tree had my stomach churning and my head spinning in rebellion.

"The gungas trees are perfectly suited for what we need." Father's expression was alight with enthusiasm and eagerness.

I groaned silently as I remembered my descent from that type of tree not that long ago.

"Neye! Not stone" was his emphatic reply, when one stonemason spoke up.

"Ta, right," he acknowledged another man's comment before continuing, "using the wood from the zumfouler and tezzar trees—both producing a light, yet sturdy wood—will easily support the weight of the occupants. These types of wood will also not cause the weight of the home and its occupants to be too heavy for the branches of the gungas tree to sustain.

"This is why I requested Tarton's woodcarving skills," he continued, his eyes focusing on a man dressed in Tarton clothing. "Borman, here, will explain what he discussed with me earlier this morning. Heed him well, tomenan both his skills and yours are necessary for building our homes. Every dwelling must be built with precision and care so that they are invisible to any unsuspecting eye."

As the New Tarton man, Borman, began his detailed explanation concerning the construction of our homes, Bonfinar leaned over Father's right shoulder and murmured something in his ear. Father's eyes lit up as he glanced toward me and Jon. When one man interrupted Borman to ask Father a question, Father quickly returned his attention to the men before him.

"We must to hide our homes in the event of invasion. If the Tenzenar were to enter New Malin and find our dwellings, they would never leave until they found the occupants and destroyed us all. Using New Tarton's woodworking skills allows us to place our homes in the gungas trees. Utilizing their natural abundant foliage and evenly placed branches, our homes can be built and easily kept hidden. I am assured that neye would ever suspect a home to be the trees… unless they knew exactly where and what to look for."

The men murmured in approval and dawning understanding over what the men from New Tarton had in mind. Father indicated that after they listened to Borman, they should attach themselves to one of those men from New Tarton, who were out searching for the best trees so that building could begin immediately. He also requested that each man learn and then take the time teach others how to build our new gungas tree-homes. When Borman again began his explanations, Father turned his attention in our direction. There was a strange expression on his face, one I had not seen before.

"Well," he said, looking at me, "you had quite an adventure last night, Met Son. How do you feel this morning, after all that"—he cleared his throat—"excitement."

Remembering the many warnings I had received concerning my mood, I forced myself to sound more cheerful than I actually felt. "Fine," I said.

Father said ghea neye; he just smiled and looked at Jon. While he didn't acknowledge or make reference to it, he knew I had just ghea castrin.

"Jon and I had a long discussion earlier this morning over our meal," he began. "It was concerning your actions of yesterday. After all we discussed, he and I have reached an agreement as to how you should be dealt with." His expression brightened as he watched me fidget.

"Dear Keyenoa," I prayed in earnest silence, while waiting for the lackna to fall. "Are not my aching head and queasy stomach more than enough punishment for my behavior of last night?"

Father continued without mercy, "You, Met Son, as all know well, have several aanas to grow before Con Sona Eata and being considered a man. I am aware that your sixteenth day of birth now looms near. However, even at sixteen, you have at least two more aanas before you move into manhood."

Wondering why he was stating the obvious, I waited, prudently keeping silent. I would hear my punishment quickly enough, and I didn't need to add insult to further my injury.

"Therefore, your Thaytor and I have decided, because of your behavior when the lunata landed and your actions last night… to forget your age and treat you as a man."

My mouth fell open.

He continued, a twinkle of humor flashing in his very green eyes. "Jon and I felt the most important thing a young man must have is a home of his own. Niki, it is clear to me that you have earned the right to possess your own home. You are free to choose any area within New Malin you desire."

This stupendous news had been stated so matter-of-factly and with such minca emotion, I wondered if I had heard him right. However, taking a hard look at Father, there was neye denying his earnestness or his Keyen Donolyn. All I could do was stand there and stare at him in flabbergasted disbelief. While I had believed in his Keyen, Father had never been one to express his feelings openly or comfortably. Finding his Keyen, pride, and understanding so openly expressed with such depth of feeling, I was overwhelmed. I so wanted to say something, only to find myself so stunned by it all that I couldn't utter a sound.

Father continued as if he were saying ghea neye out of the ordinary. "I have only one request before you search for a location to build your new home, Niki," he began in a regal and terribly fatherly tone. "I want you and Jon to help build the homes of my people before your own. Give your assistance wherever you can, lending aid to those families who have nikca, first. I don't want any of our nikca sleeping under the stars another night if it can be helped. To accomplish this, we all need to work hard this day."

"Even if I weren't given my own home, I would gladly do as you've asked, Met Father," I answered with lame formality, not knowing how to tell him sorice leki omprice. The dangers for any nikca left to sleep in a tree for too long, having neye floor under them or roof over their head, were too many to count—zewaller not being the least of these.

Jon and I caught up with one of the master builders from New Tarton and went to work. Before night fell, all but a few people had homes ready to occupy. Every family that had nikca had a roof over their head that first night. When Father received word of those few that had to wait for their homes to be built, he urged those that had homes to offer shelter to those still waiting for a home. This suggestion was eagerly accepted and neye spent the night nestled uncomfortably or precariously over a tree-branch mattress, including myself. The construction of Father's home had begun just before nightfall, so we had the first floor and most of the ceiling completed where we could sleep protected.

The building of our new homes was surprisingly easy and they went up quickly. Though constructed of wood and of simple design, the homes were as strong and sturdy as the intricately carved stone buildings in Malinieum City.

The gungas trees, themselves, were one of the major reasons for the ease in building the new dwellings. The trees resembled enormous green eggs, averaging twelve pearons in height and ten pearons in diameter at its widest point. Each of the twenty to forty levels of branches, which on average began at the base of the tree approximately two learons above the ground, contained between ten and sixteen branches, which grew around the trunk in a symmetrical pattern, somewhat like a horizontal wagon wheel. The vertical spacing between the groups of branches grew closer together at the top and bottom of the tree than in its middle. The average vertical space between the spokes of branches at its widest was six learons, and only one learon at its ghea minca. Every branch on a gungas tree is bare of leaves until its end, or newest growth. At the end of each branch, a network of limbs branch out into thousands of long stems. Each stem then holds three very large, dark green leaves, approximately the size of an average male foot—or just over half a learon in length. These leaves shield the inner parts of the tree so completely that even when storms blow, the wind is unable to reveal anything beyond the leaves.

Every home was built in the center of the tree, between the widest groups of the spoke-like branches. The lower branches of the tree made natural steps, allowing the owner or visitors to climb easily to the tree's center. Where the branches grew at wider intervals, steps were added to fill in the gaps to reach the front door. Every floor and roof of the home was laid on and supported by the symmetrical grouping of branches. The outside walls were constructed with many shuttered windows that faced the leaf side of the home. These shuttered windows allowed in as much of the sparse gray-green light as possible. Every home butted against the trunk of the tree. There were even homes that were constructed all the way around the trunk and a few that were even built with two or more stories above the first.

Father was as busy as the rest of New Malin. He spent most of the first day using his given power to change twigs into stone nails and convert the fine sand along the lake's edge into glass panes for the windows. Once all the building materials were made, he spent his time and his muscles with the other men, sanding, refining, and finishing the roughly cut wood needed to build the homes or to make our new furniture. Then, he used his given power to transport the furniture inside the homes.

After a much-needed night's sleep on Father's main-room floor, I went back to work alongside my Thaytor, finishing the work we had begun the day before. A short while past mid-sun, we were notified by one of Malin's guards that all the homes had been completed with the exclusion of my own.

"Well, Niki, where do you think you'd like to live?" Jon asked, his eyes twinkling with wicked delight. "Knowing how you feel about sleeping in trees, once you've decided on the location, I'll have one of the builders dig you a large hole and throw in a blanket. This way you can stay warm and dry—and well out of the trees, just as you vowed."

I shrugged a shoulder, scuffing the toe of my boot into the ground. "You know, Master, trees aren't so bad to live in once you have a floor under you, walls around you, and a roof over your head," I said, laughing with him over my ridiculous declaration. Receiving a benna night's sleep and waking with neye hangover to plague me, had a miraculous effect upon my attitude.

"Ta, you do have a point, Met Lord," he chuckled while he grimaced in mock pain and rubbed his back. "So where would you like your tree-home built? Have you any preferences?"

I sat on a nearby rotting tree trunk. "I've been giving the matter a great deal of thought while I've been working," I said. "I really felt that my choice needed to be prayerfully considered and areceta by Keyenoa's wisdom." I looked up at Jon and blushed. "Do you know if there are any more mature gungas trees down by the lake along the eastern boarder?" I asked quickly.

He took a moment to consider, "Possibly, we'll have to ask one of Tarton's builders. Why?"

I sighed, "I hope to live as near Met Father as possible," I murmured, digging the heels of my boots into the rotting log beneath me. "I still need his watchful eye and example… at least until I Con Sona Eata." I waited for some comment but received only his silence. I pressed on, "Jon." I concentrated on coating the toe of my boot in the heavy detritus and rotting humus I had just loosened from the log, "I saw how hard it was for him to let me go… so I don't want to go too far from him… at least until I must."

Wondering over his continued silence, I looked up to find him staring at me. Jon's expression was filled with amazement and—to my surprise—deep respect. "Sometimes I am certain I know thee, Met Lord, only to find thee doing or saying something so unexpected, it destroys all my confidence that I have ever known thee at all. Perhaps, Met Fortulaynan, I'll never know thee completely. Lately, I find thy actions to be most unexpected," he murmured, flowing with formal speech.

Aware of my puzzlement, he smiled. "Niki, all I am trying to say is that I am finding, as every day passes, you are growing into more of a man than the day before. It is just rather confusing when I know you have aanas to go before reaching your manhood following Con Sona Eata." He paused. His eyes gleamed with sudden insight, causing my heart to race in fear thinking he would announce that I was to be the next High King or something just as undesirable. Then, blinking once, Jon shook his head and dismissed his deep thoughts. "Come let's see if we can build you a home near your father, young master," he said with a smile.

PART I TENZENAR

Father sent four of Tarton's finest builders to help us. Borman, the Master Builder, approached respectfully when Jon and I had finished talking.

"Benna arecean, tomenan," he greeted with a mixture of formality and open ghea forlana. "We've been sent to construct your home, Met Lord. Speak only of your desire concerning its location. All else has been planned as a gift and surprise from Lord Malin... including the furniture that goes inside."

Embarrassed over Father's incredible gift, I began to stammer incoherently. Jon took pity on me and explained to Borman what I wanted. "Actually, he hopes to live near LeFold Lake, as close to Lord Markain as possible."

Smiling, Borman urged us to join his crew as they scouted for a tree in my chosen area. When the tree was found, they presented their choice ceremoniously. I gaped at the green monstrosity the builders had shown me. I was astounded that they felt I needed a tree so large. It stood nearly one hundred fifty learons high and spanned approximately one hundred learons wide.

"Jon, what makes them think I need a tree this big?" I asked with a wave of my arm toward the tree. Turning to my Thaytor, I discovered I was alone.

He and the four builders stood several a pearons away murmuring secretly together. Curious, I slid nearer to the group. Borman quickly stepped in and forestalled any chance of eavesdropping.

"Tella saa, Lord Nikita, understand that Met Lord Malin desires to surprise you with this home. He greatly hopes to keep you from seeing it or knowing anything about it—except its location—until it is completed and ready for your habitation. Met Lord, truly, all plans are made. The building will begin"—he stuttered and cleared his throat—"as soon as you find another location within New Malin to wait. I assure you, that if you are needed for any decisions, we will have neye difficulty finding you." Smiling at my Thaytor, he steered me away from Jon and the other builders.

Finishing his conversation quickly, Jon took me in hand and dragged me into the clearing where we had found Father speaking to the men of New Malin the day before. Jon informed me that I was to wait there until my home was completed. He also promised that he would remain at my side to see that I did what I was expected—for once.

When Father received word that I had chosen to live near him, he came to the clearing to tell me leki omprice. Jon and I were sitting by the fast-running river, which was called the Broken Dindieum. This fast-running river had been once a part of the Dindieum River before Lord Valcree became our first High King. When all the other changes were wrought upon Airies at Lord Valcree's crowning, the Dindieum River was broken within the Sinca Mountains, causing the Broken Dindieum River to flow into LeFold Lake, while the true Dindieum River continued on its original course south to Dreamer's Lake, through Malinieum City and into the ocean. Where Jon and I sat, the Broken Dindieum cut its way through the west side of the Upper Clearing before crossing the large clearing making a clear boundary between the Upper Clearing and Lower Clearing. Finding us sitting there, Father joined us. We all sat together for some moments in silence. My boots lay idly on the bank, while I dangled my feet in the cool, swift-moving water, wiggling my toes delightedly. Uncomfortable with the silence, I struggled to find something to say while Father and Jon watched my feet moving through the water.

Looking toward him, Father met my gaze. What I saw in his deep green eyes held my tongue. Gratitude, pride, and profound Keyen Donolyn were reflected there as he smiled at me. To spare us both any embarrassment Father didn't speak about how he felt. However, despite his silence, for the first time in my young life, Father freely offered me insight into his heart as he shared his pride and Keyen through the power-filled depth of his gaze.

After a long and comfortable silence, he spoke, "I've conferred with Tarton's master builders. Because cooking in our new homes could be—to say the least—very dangerous, our meals are to be shared in this clearing with all the people of New Malin. Though we won't have tables, it will be much like the Ryder's and Leagonenn of old, before Valcree became our First High King."

PART I TENZENAR

I pulled my feet from the water and looked around the clearing. Its vast size naturally cut into the forest, with the Broken Dindieum winding its way along one side. To the south just before the river separated the two clearings, a few stonemasons were busy building a bridge to span the river to the west. Then further south where the river separated the clearings another group of stonemasons worked on a bridge that would give access to both the Upper and Lower clearings. Down at the far end of the Lower Clearing, almost a teron away, the trees grew all the way to the river's edge and reached their grand limbs down to the water, as if wanting to soak their leaves as I did my feet. Slowly taking in all I could of my surroundings, I turned back to my father and Jon, sighing contentedly.

I was certain that New Malin would grow to be an even better home, more ghea keyen than Malinieum City. Living fifteen aanas of my life in one place had, unknowingly and unintentionally, limited my experiences and subsequent knowledge. Looking to the sky, I silently leki'an Keyenoa for all He had shown me in that moment and the past few days. Then, I eagerly asked Keyenoa to lead me into the new adventures I sensed were waiting for me just beyond my understanding.

⌘⌘⌘⌘

Life in New Malin settled down to an aclusceaun and happy existence. Every day, after partaking of one of the first of three large morning meals, some of the men would set out into the forest to hunt food for the main meal every evening. Malin's skilled stonemasons continued building bridges or clearing paths through Dindieum Forest, always taking care to antiquate each stone or marker and make certain that every path looked wild and long abandoned. Despite the fact that everyone believed the Tenzenar would never venture this far into Dindieum, all things were done as a precaution, hoping to deceive any possible invader into believing this land had not been occupied for eatas.

Whenever some new piece of construction had been completed, Father carefully inspected every detail. He also made certain the bridges and other visible dwellings had the look of abandonment and that there was neye place in New Malin where our flight into Dindieum was recorded, carved, or written. Father diligently made certain that neye detail was overlooked that would keep our presence in Dindieum hidden, thus protecting us from the Tenzenar.

As life settled down into a normal routine, the people of New Malin quickly became filled with tranquility and felt a renewed sense of joy. Father gave Jon permission to take me to the new Kingdoms of Cetar, Tarton, and even Dorna. On my travels, I discovered how each Kingdom took care to hide themselves from the possibility of invasion. First, we journeyed with Borman and the other builders to New Tarton, remaining in New Tarton a few days under Lord Alon Tarton's generous hospitality.

We had begun our journey to New Tarton's center by traveling along LeFolds' shore, following the instructions given by the swift-footed shaliyle sent to us by Lord Alon. Leaving New Malin, we soon discovered that the only type of growth that Tarton could boast was thick, tall under brush and groundcover that grew everywhere beneath tall tezzar and zumfouler trees, and seemingly even over solid rock. This underbrush resisted cutting, even with the use of an axe. Therefore, the only way to travel to and through Tarton was to remain close to the LeFold's shore.

Our minca group arrived at the instructed location later than expected and found neye sign of New Tarton's people. There were only birds and scurrying rodents flitting among the tangled underbrush. Confused, yet certain this was where Lord Alon had indicated we would be greeted, we looked around hoping to find some sort of indication of New Tarton's inhabitance. Suddenly, there was a pronounced movement in the brush. Terrified, thinking I'd soon be facing a zewaller, I nearly let out a bloodcurdling shout… only to find myself face-to-face with Lord Alon Tarton, himself.

"You can close your mouth, Met Nikita, I am neye zewaller," he said, laughing.

I blushed and closed my mouth with a snap.

Lord Alon described the imaginative construction of New Tarton's dwellings as he led us through the underbrush. "With the help of Malin's master stonemasons, we've built one-story homes here within the brush. Every home and public building is ingeniously connected to all others through a maze of stone archways, ensuring that every family is able to reach my castle in the center of the complex as well as their neighbors. Malin's stonemasons were clever enough to do this so that neye need travel through another's home in order to reach their desired destination." Lord Tarton looked back at me. "Your father's men, Niki, have created an impression of space and intriguing freedom, despite the fact that our homes are enclosed in the brush," he told me excitedly once we reached the archways and were able to stand upright. With underbrush all around us, and stone archways above us, we followed Lord Tarton along the maze-like passageways to his castle.

Following our stay in Tarton, we returned to New Malin with our stonemasons. Jon and I kept silent about our homes having been constructed in the trees and weren't disappointed by the men's surprise. They, too, were startled into nearly crying out when Conden climbed out from under the branches of Father's home and welcomed them to Kingstree. That night sitting with Father we told him all we saw in Tarton. Everyone had a benna laugh over Airian ingenuity and our fickle imaginations, which seemed to get the best of us at the worst times.

A few fortauns later, we set out for New Cetar, with plans to continue on to New Dorna from there. New Cetar was spread out over minca rolling hills, covered by trees and plant growth very similar to those of New Malin. However, New Cetar chose to dig their homes into the rolling hillsides. They adapted minca rodent holes and other openings that couldn't be seen by the naked eye for ventilation and light. The entrances into the dwellings were wood-backed slabs of sod, overgrown with the vine-like plants that covered the ground and trees all across Cetar. When the doors were shut, they blended completely into the hillside and were undetectable to the eye. Inside the dwellings, the fine networking of roots were left exposed, enabling the owner to hang items from them for easy access and handy storage. The walls were not musty or damp. There were neye odors of mold or dank fungus, because the mud and sand mixture that had been plastered against every surface of the home's interior kept them clean, dry, and free from such growth.

Eager to spend as much time as possible with Prince Kreatar Sornan Dorna, my forlaynan, we left for New Dorna the morning after our arrival. New Dorna was scattered with high, craggy cliffs and rocks covered with spiny, dwarfed tezzar trees. Within the cliffs were thousands of caves of various sizes and depths, where rock outcroppings or trees hid most of the openings. It was within these hidden caves that the people of Dorna chose to live. They had long rope ladders, which when unrolled and lowered, were the only way to reach the homes of New Dorna.

We were sitting around the fire pit in Lord Dorna's luxurious cave home, when Sornan began to explain his father's trials while the people of Dorna worked together to make their caves into homes. Laughter rang in his voice when Sornan leaned near, as if in confidence, but spoke loud enough that we all could hear, "First, Father had to go from cave to cave, securing the rope ladders into each, and dropping them down so the new owners could climb them and inspect their new home. I swear to you that Father and Cadell, his Thaytor, took two long days doing only this. Then Father had to repeat the process, taking all the furniture that the people of New Dorna had been constructing and transport them into the caves. Well, by the end of the first fortaun, poor Father was so confused he had a hard time telling up from down for nearly another fortaun."

While everyone was laughing uproariously, Lord Kreatar Dorna added with a wink, "I suffered all this, Met Niki, because Keyenoa has so decreed that we lowly Kings are not to receive the power your father has been arecta with... so I had to transport myself with each item that need to go into the caves or that item would never have made it to its destination. Needless to say, Sornan is correct, I became one very dizzy and confused King after days of up and down, in and out."

"I was at least spared the furniture moving trial, as my King could not transport me along with the furniture," Cadell added, laying a hand of amity upon his King's shoulder.

"Poor Father," Sornan laughed, his teasing expression and attention never leaving his father who sat across the fire from him. "After so many days using his given power every few onas, Cadell and I still wonder if he can tell up from down."

"Oh, don't exaggerate, Sornan," Lord Dorna laughed. "I know with a certainty we are **standing** with our feet firmly on **ground level**!" Each of us—including Lord Kreatar—burst out in uproarious laughter. Not only were we in a cave, but we were also sitting in very comfortable chairs with our feet up on stools.

"Met Lord Kreatar Dorna," I teased, "I do believe thee need a very long rest!"

This caused us all to laugh again.

I then told them about the other Kingdoms we had visited. Both Lord Dorna and Sornan were fascinated by the creativity of the people in each Kingdom and the ingenuity used in hiding all our homes. During the last onas before retiring that first night, we talked about what we thought the future would bring to our people. Because I chose to keep my deeper fears and concerns of the future to myself, I suffered some rather lively and uncomfortable dreams throughout the night.

Jon and I remained in New Dorna for a very happy and busy fortaun. Then, with great reluctance, we said benna soreleann and returned to New Malin. Again, we reported to Father, telling him all about our stay. He, too, was pleased to hear how Lord Dorna had hidden his people in Dindieum's caves and of New Cetar's creativity as well. Laughing, Father confessed he was glad that all he needed to do was make nails and glass. When it had come time for him to use his given power and transport New Malin's furniture into our tree-homes, he was not burdened with the job of transporting himself into his people's homes as well.

Chapter III

The Expedition

"The harder the path, the smoother I shall make it, if thee will but take My hand and follow Me."

—Book of Keyenoa

Nearly four tuevtauns had passed since our move to Dindieum. In that time, I had come to believe that everyone had forgotten the Tenzenar—except me. Since returning from Dorna, the dreams I first experienced there began to intensify. I would wake several times each night from horrifying nightmares filled with Tenzenar invasion and Airian Sontall. I was often left every morning drenched in sweat with my heart pounding fearfully. And every morning, in light of day with aclusceaun surrounding our new homes, such nightmares seemed ghea teepin and without merit, so I kept the dreams and worries to myself. Yet one morning, after screaming myself awake twice in a matter of onas having fallen back to sleep and picking up where I left off in my dream, I knew I had to speak to someone—if not about my dreams, about what was troubling me.

Climbing wearily out of my massive bed, I pulled at the coverlet and mopped the sweat from my face. "Enough is enough," I muttered. "I must talk to Jon. I just hope he'll agree with me on the cause—and my solution—to these fearful dreams." Stumbling across the chilled floor, I grabbed up my strewn clothing, dressing as I went. "Perhaps it would be wiser to omit mentioning my dreams and just tell him about my solution of how to be rid of them," I continued talking to myself and Keyenoa as I left my tree-home. "Jon can't be ghea teepin enough to deny that someone needs to discover what the Tenzenar are doing, despite the fact that we're safely tucked away in Dindieum. This issue has to be important to someone else and not just me. We need discover why the Tenzenar chose to come to Airies in the first place and discover what they are doing." I fell silent after climbing beneath the low branches of my gungas tree, aware of those around me and not wanting to look like a mootan talking to myself.

Jon was sitting in the clearing, enjoying his morning meal of honey bread, cooked theron eggs, and quintie. After nodding to one of the women that I was ready to eat, I sat beside Jon and waited for him to speak first. While I needed to talk to him, I decided I could wait awhile longer for his response. There was certainly neye reason to interrupt his meal with my worries as they were certainly not going anywhere.

"Benna aray, young master," he said absently, his attention never quite leaving his plate.

I was served the same fare as Jon and quietly told the woman leki omprice for her trouble. 'You wanted to talk to him, Niki—so talk!' I shouted at myself in my thoughts, then delayed further by pondering just how to broach the subject tactfully. Coming up with ghea neye helpful, I tried to eat, but rearranged my food around my plate more than actually putting much of anything in my mouth.

Finished, my Thaytor began to study me between lingering sips of warmed saflee. Unable to sit still under his power-sensitive scrutiny, I gave up all pretense of eating. Flinging the plate to the ground in frustration, chagrined when the food was scattered in the grass, I stood. In one last attempt to forestall the inevitable, I feigned ignorance of his attention and my spilled food, and walked to the stream.

Jon calmly followed, "So what brings you to me this sun's rise in such a mood, Niki?" he asked, placing a comforting hand on my shoulder.

Staring at the bridge several pearons away, remembering how I had watched it being built, I sighed, "Can thee walk with me to the lake's edge, Met Fortulaynan? There, where the water caresses the shore with its gentle melody, I hope to be able to talk with thee uninterrupted. What plague's my mind this morn', be in need of both the water's song and thy wisdom, before I shall find aclusceaun," I replied, not daring to look at him.

His hand slipped from my shoulder as he led the way across the bridge. "With your formal speech ringing its gentle rhapsody upon my ears, I gather that you are quite troubled," he said as I followed him across the bridge.

The path we took was originally made by ledo and lox traveling to the lake's edge for water, and was therefore very rough and narrow. Forced to walk single file, it made any serious conversation impossible. When we reached the end of the path there was about two learons of grassy turf before ending abruptly at the lake's edge. At the sudden cessation of land was an abutment a bit over a learon above the water. The lake lapped at this buttress with soothing, musical repetition. Just to the right of the path, along the meager, grassy expanse was an intricately carved stone bench that faced the lake. Jon and I sat down in silence.

I stared at the water while Jon's cinder gaze, aflame with curiosity, watched me while he struggled to wait patiently for me to speak.

Sighing, aware that what I had to say would not be easily heard, I forged ahead, "Master, it is mootan to remain here in New Malin, ignorant and unconcerned about what the Tenzenar have done, and are doing at least here on Malin. It's important that we try and discover several things, such as their reasons for coming to Airies and how much of Malin's continent they've already come to occupy and what they know or believe concerning our existence." I fell silent, my expression urging him to recognize the burning determination and desperation I felt. It was important that he understand the danger I was convinced our people faced. "Jon, we can't just live here and blithely assume that our vacated cities will remain undiscovered, and that these insatiable explorers will remain content with what land they have so far discovered. We must discover what knowledge they've gathered concerning our people, and what plans they have for Airies."

A flicker of surprise danced swiftly across Jon's face before he turned away to stare across the lake while chuckling hollowly, "You've done it again, Niki," he sighed, his expression rueful. "Why is it that you never seem to worry about the common things most boys of your aanas do? Why can't you come to me with the simple troubles one is to expect at your age, such as having picked a fight you shouldn't have, or losing a bet you should have never made?"

I smiled, chagrined, aware of the frustrated wonderment in his voice. He did not want or expect an answer from me.

"I must say, Niki, when you worry about something, it's important enough that I find myself hard-pressed to give you an answer." He sighed, placing his hands on his knees, finally turning from the lake view to look at me. "So you're right… if it isn't already being done, learning about the Tenzenar and what they're up to is something we, as a people, should be doing. Now," he pinned me with his stare, "I ask, how you would suggest this be accomplished?"

I stood, shivered from the intensity and power in his stare before I turned away and picked up a minca stone from the grass. Pitching it lazily into the lake, I answered, not daring to face him, "Simple," I stooped for another stone and studied it carefully while I continued. "You and I should return to Malinieum City and discover all we need to know." Then, with a determined jut of my chin, I defiantly threw the stone as far as I could out into the lake before turning to face my Thaytor.

Jon's composure had slid away in astonishment. "You, Nikita, are either a mootan, or you have gone totally keezworky," he shouted. "If you're serious about suggesting such a kutated idea as that. What in Keyenoa's name do you know about Tenzenar and their ways? Do you honestly believe that anyone would allow you to go traipsing off—Alleanne only knows where—virtually unprotected, so you could watch what these Sontall worshiping creatures are doing? By Alleanne, I've never heard such utter and ridiculous drivel in my entire life!"

"Then I guess I must be a kutated mootan, as well as keezworky, and… and spouting utter and ridiculous drivel, **because I am very serious about this**!" I shouted back.

"Well, just get that kutated idea out of your head right now! You are ghea neye but a boy, Niki, innocent of so much—just a nicka, immature and unready for the world—especially with Tenzenar in that world. There is neye way on Airies your father—or for that matter, I—will ever let you go. Do you hear me?" he barked, glaring at the defiant glint in my gaze.

"Then I won't tell Father and I'll find some way to go without you stuck to my back like a billon burr!" I retorted, flopping on the bench, so provoked I sounded exactly like the immature nicka Jon had likened me to.

"**Nikita, that is enough**! Now, listen to me carefully… before I wring your stubborn, royal neck!" he shouted, having turned to face me, putting his back to the lake with his feet balanced on the edge of the abutment. He bent over the bench where I was sitting and pushed his face so close to mine that his nose nearly touched my own, while I glared defiantly up at him. "**Your idea won't work**!" he shouted. "By Alleanne, I promise you that I will do everything I can to find answers to your concerns… but you aren't going to Malinieum City, with or without me. **Do you hear me**?!"

"Try and stop me!" I dared. "Just try!" I repeated, jumping to my feet and shoving him backward.

Mouth open and arms flailing, he went in the lake, making a magnificent splash. His waterlogged cape wrapped itself about his legs, frustrating and forestalling his every attempt to rise from the water. I didn't remain to laugh at his comical appearance or his unsuccessful attempts to rise, but quickly made my escape. With my thoughts still fogged by rage, I started down the path fully intent on leaving him there until he drowned.

PART I TENZENAR

I had nearly made it back to the clearing when Father appeared suddenly in front of me on the path. Forgetting all of Keyenoa's teachings concerning respect for one's parent, I turned my rage on him. "Oh, neye! I don't want to hear from you right now either! So if that's what you have in mind, you can just forget it!" I shouted, thinking to shove him out of the way.

Father's whole body seemed to vibrate as he struggled to restrain himself. Then, grasping my shoulders, his expression tight with his own anger, he held me in my place. Instantly my fury was quashed by cold and unflinching reason.

"Hear from me you shall, Nikita Markain Malin. After I help you chalday your Thaytor from LeFold Lake, you shall both hear from me." I was then forcefully turned around and urged back up the path with a firm push. "Now, return to your Thaytor, Met Son, or I promise you that you will find it difficult and painful to sit for at least a fortaun… or more!" he threatened through clenched teeth.

Jon still had not managed to get out of the lake but had managed to get himself straightened out enough that he was neye longer in fear of drowning. Sitting in the water, with his hands braced behind him for greater balance, he gaped at Father and me in shock and bewilderment. His coal black hair dripped water into his eyes and made minca streams of water that trickled down his face and along his neck before disappearing beneath the collar of his black shirt. The lake's gentle waves lapped around his chest and upper arms, while his long black cape, freed from his legs, floated gracefully over the water behind him, undulating with the waves. He looked miserable and waterlogged. Had I not already managed to get myself into enough trouble, I would have broken into uproarious laughter over the sight of him sitting in the lake.

"Met Lord Markain!" Jon exclaimed, desperately trying to stand, only to be repeatedly pulled back into the lake by his cape and the mud sucking at his hands and the ankles of his boots.

Father offered him an arm, providing enough leverage so that Jon managed to free himself from the lake's hold. Stepping onto the shore, Jon disentangled himself from his cape that had

NIKITA'S STORY

once again clung to his body and lifted an appreciative expression toward my father as he bowed in respect. "If I may be so bold, Met Lord, what brings you to this part of LeFold Lake?" he asked.

Father smiled wickedly. "I sensed this sudden storm," he explained, waving a distracted hand toward Jon's wet clothing, graciously drying them with his given power. "However, such storms usually end quickly and life then continues on much as it always has… though, I do hope that those who were caught unaware have grown wiser from the experience." He sat on the stone bench looking sternly in my direction and then Jon's. "Now, it is time we discuss the cause of this minor storm and thus ensure that you both might gain some of that wisdom I mentioned."

Sulking and nurturing the last remnants of my temper, I remained standing as Jon kneeled before Father on the thin strip of land in front of the bench. His position revealed his deep devotion and respect for my father. Jon clearly valued my father's knowledge and wisdom, and wanted to show Father his repentance for his temper toward me. I watched the two men in wonder, aware I usually responded in that same way whenever Jon prepared to teach me something I was eager to learn. I had yet to understand in full just how special my father was. Because of our move to New Malin and my Thaytor's actions in that moment, I finally began to see my father in a new and honest light.

"You are aware of all that has been said and done here, aren't you, Met Lord?" Jon asked, lowering his eyes in shame when Father nodded.

"Niki, sit here, next to Jon," Father ordered, struggling not to smile through his frown of disapproval. As with any parent who knows their nikca well, Father understood that my pride had been hurt by Jon's thoughtless name calling, along with his refusal to hear anything I wanted to tell him. It was this understanding, as well as the humor he saw in my ridiculous expression, combined with his Keyen Donolyn for me that caused the fleeting smile he struggled to hide.

"Sulking gets an Airian ghea neye but misery, Met Son," he said as I sat down beside Jon. "Now, concerning the Tenzenar…

Niki, you've shown intuitive discernment... though, you are not the first to have this concern. Met Lordship High King Sayleen Cantabo and I spoke just last evening over this matter and agreed someone must go to Malinieum City to learn what has transpired since our hurried departure."

"But who, Met Lord?" Jon asked, leaning forward. "Certainly Niki can't be considered—he knows ghea neye of Tenzenar and their dangers."

"Ah!" Father lifted his finger and an eyebrow. "You are right about his ignorance, Jon, but it is exactly that ignorance and his concern which makes me think he should go and learn all he can."

My mouth fell open as my gaze darted from one man to the other.

Jon smiled, his ebony eyes glittering with growing understanding. "Lay alda, Met Lord," he chuckled.

Father nodded.

"Well, I... I don't," I piped in, only to bite my lip, afraid Father would change his mind.

He chuckled, reading my thoughts. "It's rather simple, Niki," Father began as he shifted in his seat to look at me. "As you should know by now, it is believed that you'll become a King upon your eighteenth day of birth. This is one reason why you are being trained by Jon on the matters of governing and leadership.

"Now, with the Tenzenar on Airies, your training needs to expand to include them. It's important that you gain as much knowledge of these beings as you possibly can. In this way, you can protect both yourself and your people from any danger they might cause." He paused, spearing me with his sharp gaze. "Tell me, Niki, what better way to learn than by firsthand experience?" he asked with patient logic.

"Neye better way, at all, Father!" I exclaimed as I began making plans for what I'd do upon reaching Malinieum City. "I knew I was right about my going, I just knew I was," I murmured.

"Nikita Malin." Father waited until he had my full attention. "There are a few matters I insist be understood—and accepted—before I'll sanction you joining this expedition."

My heart sank. He had stipulations.

Reading my thoughts, he just smiled knowingly. "Last evening, Met Lordship and I decided to send three guards to Malinieum City, Conden and Salitarin from Malin, and Scaun from Oreon. If you are to accompany them, Jon must also go. With your Thaytor—and the guards—it should be easier to find some way to curtail that unquenchable urge for freedom you try so hard to obtain at every opportunity and so hopefully keep you from mischief.

"The guards' duties will include keeping you safe, hunting for meals and returning to New Malin with news of the Tenzenar. Your Thaytor's duty will include keeping a close watch on you at all times and scouting the Tenzenar areas. Your duties will entail not only an equal split of camp chores, but you will also—at times—accompany either Jon or the guards when scouting the Tenzenar areas. **This means, Niki, you are never to be out of Jontair's sight, unless he knows where you're going and has permitted you the freedom to go**! If you can accept these rules you and Jon would most likely be doing most of the scouting in the Tenzenar areas." Father paused a moment, eyeing me intently. "Niki, hear me well on this. If you disobey any of these rules even once, the guards will follow Jon's orders to march you right back home. That, my son, is an order—firm and unshakable. **Do you understand me?**"

Leaping up from my place in the grass, I grasped both his shoulders tightly while gazing excitedly into his bright green eyes. "Ta, Met Father, I understand and would do anything to go on this expedition… even wrestle a zewaller if that's what it'd take!" Giving him neye chance to respond, I embraced him enthusiastically, only to feel him stiffen beneath my arms. Pulling back hurriedly, thinking he was rejecting what I offered, I tried to pretend ghea neye had happened. I did not understand that Father had frozen in surprise because he had not received such a display of affection from me in a very long time, rather than in rejection.

Fearing what I'd find reflected in his gaze, Keyenoa, nonetheless, urged me to look at him. While struggling with the urge to

PART I TENZENAR

hide all I felt, I lifted my gaze to my father openly revealing all the affection I felt for him in my expression. Then, knowing it needed to be said, I pushed the words of gratitude beyond my uncertainty, "Sorice leki, Met Father. Leki omprice," I whispered, before turning away in embarrassment.

"Niki, go with Jon. Begin your preparations," his voice, hoarse with emotion, was somewhat difficult to understand. "Your journey… begins tomorrow at sun's rise."

Father stood, with his attention focused across the lake he effectively communicated his desire for solitude. Later, I came to understand that I had so moved his heart he was at a loss as how to express his Keyen in return.

⌘ ⌘ ⌘ ⌘

"Ten long days to Malinieum City, Niki, do you feel up to the walk?"

Smiling at Conden, I ignored his teasing while lifting the heavy pack to my shoulder. With a shrug and a snort of laughter, the guard pulled his pack over his shoulders as Jon helped shift mine into a more comfortable position. Then my Thaytor, Salitarin, and Scaun readied themselves for the journey, talking quietly among themselves about rest-bits, meal stops, and the first night's camp.

"Master Alcone," Scaun, the guard from Oreon, spoke up, "I'll take the rear position."

"Salitarin and I will take lead," Conden volunteered cheerfully.

I frowned as everyone stepped into place, with lacknas, leaknas, and Loreann bows placed ready on their persons.

"Master, why do the guards—and even you—feel it's necessary to protect me this way?" I whispered, waving an arm to indicate their positions. "My birth is a minca matter, and I'd prefer it be forgotten."

Conden looked back and smiled knowingly, "It isn't your royalty we protect, Niki."

Scaun coughed and Salitarin flinched as both men caught the teasing barb, which I did not. I looked to Jon for clarification.

"It is your lack of power we protect, Niki, not your position of birth."

My face heated instantly in a white blush. I could have booted Conden—except that he was right—and I was a teepatin for not thinking of it myself. Clamping my mouth shut, I determined not speak again until I had something intelligent to say. 'And that might be a long while in coming,' I thought to myself.

"We also seek food as we go, Met Lord, and being both in the front and at the rear opens the range in which our weapons can fly without chance of striking a fellow traveler," Scaun interjected easing my embarrassment.

I smiled at the guard, "Then, I will strive to remain silent so as not to frighten away a possible meal. Sorice leki, Met Scaun."

The first six days of our journey were enjoyably uneventful. Conden kept up his teasing banter, sparing neye. It wasn't long before Salitarin and Scaun also relaxed around me and Jon. Everyone easily joined in the conversations and bantering, often giving Conden a taste of his own medicine. I was glad for their joking and Jon's quiet watchful manner. In those six days, we became forlana through the fun, bantering, and work.

The day before we would reach the end of Dindieum Forest and the beginning of Golden Meadow, we became silent and watchful. Tense and ready to go invisible at a moment's notice, we took care to even quiet our footsteps while searching for any sign of Tenzenar, ghea leki'anne, finding none. Late on the seventh day, we reached the edge of Dindieum Forest.

Speaking barely above a whisper, Jon halted the group, "We are at the place where constant invisibility is a necessity, tomenan. The moment we leave the protection of Dindieum, our shields must be raised. Niki, you are to remain here in the trees, at least for now. It isn't necessary to push the limits of your shield just yet."

"In other words, Niki, sit tight and don't wander. It is safe for you to remain visible within the trees," Conden murmured as he and Salitarin moved beside me. Malin's guard knew he needed to be blunt in order to cement the rules in my head so that I would not have any wiggle room to subvert them.

Jon ignored my indignant scowl and addressed Scaun, "Would you be willing to scout ahead from here? While your given power might not be as extensive as mine, your skill in defensive training far exceeds anything I know."

Agreeing to go, Scaun chuckled, enjoying the adrenalin rush as he moved with Jon nearer to the forest edge.

"Go southeast, following the river path neye farther than three terons. If you encounter any sign of Tenzenar existence before those three terons, return to us immediately." Jon's voice deepened with sincerity. "Scaun, whatever you find, te salma do neye exploring where danger is apt to come upon you unexpectedly. Let not an ena of curiosity take seed. I want you only going out to determine how near to Dindieum's edge we should make our camp safely this night."

"Alda soona leone, Master Alcone," Scaun replied. "I plan to be very cautious. Enjoying an adventure is one thing. But my skin crawls over the thought of encountering Tenzenar. I am as weary of travel as the rest of you and desire neye contact with any of those creatures—at least for tonight." He let his gaze scan far into the meadow. "Met Lordship carefully showed me where the lunata landing took place on one of the maps in Oreon. We remain quite a distance from that landing sight, so I doubt I'll find any Tenzenar nearby anyway," he added with a chuckle.

Gazing up at the night-darkened sky, I took note that it was about an oona after night fall. In less than another oona, the moon would rise. I shivered as I thought of Scaun and what he'd been asked to do. While it was clear neither Jon nor Scaun expected Tenzenar to be this close to the forest, both men were aware of the dangers out on that vast, open meadow. After assuring his Loreann bow, arrows, and quiver were ready and easily accessible from his back, Scaun gave a jaunty wave, raised his shield of invisibility and left the shelter of the trees.

NIKITA'S STORY

Our minca group remained silent. All of us seemed affected by the unusual tension that surrounded the vast meadow. Looking around the forest edge, I was aware that it was unusually quiet and was reminded of the horrible silence just before the Tenzenar had landed. As I peered through the darkness into the meadow, I wondered if this tension was caused by Tenzenar being far closer than anyone wanted to believe.

Conden and Salitarin shifted restlessly, unconsciously moving deeper within the trees. Jon remained at the forest's edge, his glowing presence visible in the darkness to guide Scaun back to our group. Comforted by Jon's presence, I moved to stand behind him, also remaining visible. He seemed unaware of my approach as he continued to stare across the undulating grasses of Golden Meadow waiting for Scaun's return. Following his gaze, I saw a glowing dome of light which cut into the Airian night sky. It dimmed the luminosity of the moon's arrival and simply snuffed out the light of many stars. Stiffening, I sucked in a deep breath of air unable to take my eyes from the strange dome of light on the horizon.

Jon glanced back. "Malinieum City would glow a minca like that on a night as dark as this. Though, she never put the moon to shame or doused the light of so many stars with such a vast and bright light as that. It is the light made by a large city, but, I think not Malinieum. Perhaps it will dim when the moon fully lifts her head, but the glow will not be completely overwhelmed by the moonlight. It seems they've built a city, Niki. So one question has been answered. The Tenzenar intend to remain on Airies' soil for a long taun to come, rather than coming for just a short and unwelcome visit," he said quietly, his attention returning to the glow across the meadow.

I watched the moon rise, floating high above the horizon. As Jon had suggested the moonlight did slightly dim the Tenzenar glow. Seven onas later, with my eyes still focused on the familiar moon, Scaun called out to Jon.

"He is back far too soon," my Thaytor muttered under his breath, as the guard lowered his shield of invisibility.

PART I TENZENAR

I was close enough to see Scaun's fear and bewilderment, as he jogged swiftly toward the forest to reach Jon's side. "There be a dwelling but four onas walk away! Master, they're closer to the forest than even Met Lordship knew!"

Having spoken recklessly, Scaun looked around for the rest of the company, hoping his revelation of the High King's limited power had not been overheard. Conden and Salitarin's approach kept the guard from noticing me tucked within the shadow of Jon's cape.

He spoke openly before the other men, assuming I had remained beneath the forest's canopy. "What I've seen this night has caused me more fear than I care to admit," he continued honestly, his gaze growing glassy as he began to chant in fearful recollection, "May Keyenoa have mercy on us all! 'Tis a sight I wished never to have witnessed. Like a living thing, it spreads from the Tenzenar dwelling covering our path as far as my eyes could follow toward our city of Malinieum. Oozing across the ground, snaking as if a serpent, it swallows the grass and smothers the land. This thing that the Tenzenar have vomited over our ground be made of horrid things for which I want neye knowledge or explanation. Black as night, warm as day… it reeks of flesh rotting forever in shenon."

It was unusual for an Oreon Guard to express such emotion, especially while on duty serving the High King. I shifted, leaning nearer to Jon, shaken by the images Scaun brought to my mind with such dread. My movement drew the guard's attention as he became aware of my presence. Turning away, he stared across the meadow while struggling to regain control of his emotions.

Jon glanced at me, giving Scaun the taun he needed, but offered me neye rebuke for being so near. Returning his attention to Jon, Scaun continued his descriptions with greater control of his emotions, "I was drawn from the river's edge by an unnatural light less than a teron from here. Heading toward it, I quickly discovered that the light was coming from a large Tenzenar dwelling. I decided to sit and wait where I was for the moon to rise high enough so I could see the dwelling and make note of the changes the Tenzenar made to the land around the dwelling. That was when I saw this... this"—he cleared his throat, fighting with his emotions once again—"covering I described." He paused, "Jon, as I said, it continues as far as my eyes could see in the direction of Malinieum City. And the smell—I can't describe the smell. It reeks."

Jon seemed to accept this news calmly. The uncertainty I was experiencing was also reflected in Salitarin and Conden expressions. Both men had placed their hands on the hilts of their lacknas, their gazes watchful and wary of every shadow or shift in the breeze. Scaun glanced at me as he waited for Jon's decision concerning what would be done with his news.

"Did you get close enough to see if the Tenzenar were awake in this dwelling?" Jon asked, ignoring the mounting tension around him.

"Neye. I went neye further than the strange covering, which lays several pearons from the dwelling. I saw only a large dwelling and an unnatural light spilling from the front windows. I went neye closer... and was leki'anee for your orders that instructed I was not do so."

Jon continued to gaze across the meadow. I closed my eyes, seeking Keyenoa's advice and was quietly assured that we were perfectly safe. There was ghea neye to fear, except my own imagination. While waiting for my Thaytor's decision, a sense of aclusceaun filled my soul.

Sighing, his expression resolved, Jon nodded. "Scaun, you, Conden and Salitarin go back at least half a teron into Dindieum. There, set up our camp, not far from the path." He glanced at me. "Niki and I are going to take a look at these Tenzenar, the covering, and their dwelling."

I shivered with a mixture of excitement and fear.

Conden stepped forward, his hand still resting on the hilt of his blade. Even knowing that Jon's given power was more than enough to protect us both, the guard was uneasy. "Wait. Allow me to follow you to this dwelling once the site of our camp has been selected. This way, we will all know where the camp will be and none will have trouble finding it."

Jon shook his head, smiling at the guard. He understood that Conden's motive for joining us was to offer added protection. "Niki and I will simply enter Dindieum visible. One of you only needs to wait on the path for our return, and we won't be missed."

Salitarin shifted uneasily, hesitantly stepping forward. "Master?" he forced himself to speak, buffering his impudence by the use of the highly respectful title for Jon's position. "Tella saa, why go to so much trouble when it seems simpler to remain invisible and allow Conden to escort you back?"

"You forget, Salitarin, Niki's ability to remain invisible for any length of time is limited due to his not as yet having passed through Con Sona Eata. I am also well aware that he has minca ability to protect himself and will watch over him most carefully. Need I remind you, tomenan, I've enough power to spare him all I have?" Jon added calmly with a telling smile.

Scaun coughed and chuckled, understanding Jon's gentle rebuke completely. "I must confess, Master, I had not thought of Lord Nikita's shortened invisibility. While we have been aware of his other handicaps and teased him unmercifully about them—to the young lord's irritation—that handicap seems to have slip our minds these last few onas, neye matter how often it has been mentioned."

Salitarin and Conden agreed, and Scaun continued, "I confess, Master, that both Met Lordship and Lord Markain made it clear to all three of us here, Lord Niki's potential for indiscretion when even a hint of independence is offered to him. We have been warned, Master, your young ward is a wily one. And with the warning ringing in our ears we forgot that you know him far better than we. You have managed him very well these aanas he has been in your care. I ask your forgiveness for our doubts."

Laughing outright, Jon looked at each guard, "I had neye idea that both Kings spoke of Niki's predilection for trouble. I confess openly before all of you that I am far from proficient in dealing with his recklessness and so welcome your extra vigilance. Question me often and continue to test my plans in your hearts. If those plans feel wrong to any of you, te salma, voice those concerns. This night is a test of both my ability to watch out for Niki, and his ability to follow my orders. Let us all see where his predilection lies."

Putting an arm around my shoulder, he turned me in the direction of the meadow and the Tenzenar dwelling. Accurately reading my emotions after hearing this discussion concerning my predilections, he chuckled, "Didn't your father say that sulking gets an Airian ghea neye but misery? Give yourself taun, Niki, you'll most likely have more power and wisdom from that given power than anyone else here."

We moved out from beneath the trees.

"Raise your shield and take hold of my cape so I may know where you are.… And do stop feeling sorry for yourself. It is most unbecoming, do you hear me?" he chided as he raised his shield and disappeared.

I laughed, agreeing with him, "Ta, I hear you," I chuckled and took hold of his cape while raising my own shield of invisibility. We moved together quietly along the old path that cut though the meadow.

After climbing a minca rise and dropping out of sight of Dindieum, an odd sickening stench began to tickle my nostrils. Tugging on Jon's cape, I gazed blindly in his direction, "Master," I whispered hoarsely, "can you smell that?" Jon knew it was a question he didn't need to answer. I looked swiftly in all directions, afraid if I let my guard down a Tenzenar would spring up at me out of the grass. I tugged on his cape again. "Jon, what do you know about Tenzenar?"

He continued walking, pulling me along by his cape. Tugging on it for the third time, insisting he answer, I finally heard him mumble under his breath, "About as much as you, Niki."

His answer, while honest, did ghea neye for my sense of well-being. I decided that since his answers were as un-palatable as the air around us, silence was the wiser course. Illuminated by the moon's light, the worn path that led from Malinieum to Oreon had not only been widened, but also carefully leveled by Tenzenar hands. As we continued on through the changed landscape, my head began to reel and ache from the increasing stench, foreign to my nose. It seemed not only to fill the air but coat it with a cloying taste. I felt as though I were drowning in its noxious intensity and suffocating on it as it coated my tongue and throat.

"Master!" I whispered, terrified by the changes around us. "Can this be what Tenzenar smell like? How can they stand themselves without choking?" I fell silent, having exhausted what breath I had while fighting to hold down the meal in my stomach.

"Breathe through your mouth, Niki, it's the only way to tolerate it for long," Jon replied, calming me by the simple sound of his voice. "All we can do is to continue toward the dwelling Scaun mentioned. There we may discover your answers... not to mention some other answers to questions that plague my mind." He paused, his step hesitating, "Unless you'd rather return to Dindieum?" he asked.

"Neye, Jon. I want to go on," I assured him.

Jon pressed forward.

Clouds moved in shrouding the face of the moon, causing all to become cloaked in night's blackness. Without my sight, my other senses intensified, heightening the fetid odor and my fear. Breathing through my mouth, the air continued to wrap around my tongue and cling to my palate as though it were a solid mass, befouling my taste. My stomach lurched and I fought with each step to keep it still.

I was so focused on my own discomfort that I didn't notice when Jon took a step up on to something. Suddenly the toe of my boot became stuck in a strange glutinous mass, throwing me off balance and pitching me forward. My offended nose fell smack into the cause of the noxious odor. Blindly, I thrashed my arms, scraping my palms along the rough surface, seeking escape, while coughing and vomiting in uncontrollable spasms. Awash in panic, I couldn't seem to find a way to free myself. Jon, realizing my difficulty, blindly grasped my vest and hauled me to my feet.

"Niki...." His hands searched my body. "Let me see you. I need to know that you're all right. You hit that stuff pretty hard," his concern rang in his voice.

NIKITA'S STORY

I forced myself to lower my shield. "What are they doing to Airies, Jon?" I asked, focusing on my Thaytor when he also lowered his shield of invisibility.

"Your nose is bleeding, and your palms are scraped," he said, ignoring my question for the moment. "Sit down and drop your head back... we need to get the bleeding stopped."

"Master...?" I pressed, refusing to sit, until he answered my inquiries.

"I don't know, Niki. I really don't know," he sighed, turning away in shame. "I know as much about Tenzenar as you. That's why we're here—late at night, waiting for your nose to stop bleeding—hoping to learn something about these... these..." Jon lifted an arm to indicate the land around us, "Tenzenar." Smiling with humor, he then met my gaze. "Now sit down and.... Don't touch that!" he snapped as I raised my hand to my tender nose.

My whole face ached, not to mention my hands.

Defeated, I let him minister to my wounds. With ghea neye but my pain and my surroundings to focus on, I began to wonder how our people would survive while the Tenzenar remained on Airies. Finding that same anxiety in my Thaytor's expression, I was strangely comforted not to be alone in my thoughts. Ignoring my watchful attention, Jon began searching my body for any additional damage. Once he declared me fit to continue, I raised my shield, took hold of his cape, and followed him.

Stepping onto the odoriferous substance, I noticed a large, two or three story box-shaped building covered with wood slats some pearons to our left. Light spilled from several windows, but did minca to illuminate the detail of the structure, except its size and boxy shape. Moving closer to the structure, Jon paused on a grassy embankment ghea leki'annee putting the noxious surface behind us and down wind. There, we watched the structure and waited for the clouds to release the moon.

When the moon's silvery light shone on the dwelling, the surprising beauty of Tenzenar craftsmanship was revealed. A myriad of latticing, molding, and imaginative carvings adorned nearly every window, corner and straight line of the dwelling. The windows were placed along the structure in a balanced order. Inside each window, a cloth was hung, outlining the glass with a splash of muted color while a sheer panel of material was hung directly over the window. Therefore, the light spilling from the windows was diffused by the material, greatly limiting our ability to see inside. The Tenzenar had colored the outside of the dwelling a strange, unnatural tint and used another darker tint on all the latticing, molding and carvings. However, because the night transformed all color to various hues of gray I couldn't discern what the colors were that they had chosen.

Frustrated by this glimpse of their way of life, which only wet my appetite for more, I looked to where I sensed Jon waited beside me. "I want to see in!" I whispered, urgently tugging on his cape. My Airian curiosity had easily overwhelmed my fear of possible Tenzenar hazards.

Jon's cape shifted in my hand as he looked carefully around for danger. "All right, Niki, go ahead and see if you can look in the windows... be careful and quiet!" his urgency for caution was clear despite his subdued voice.

Afraid he might change his mind, I ran down the embankment toward the dwelling. Reaching a wide stone walk, I followed it to a short set of stairs that led to a raised area that wrapped its way around the front of the dwelling. At the top of the steps, I paused, allowing my eyes to adjust to the light spilling through the cloth-shrouded windows. Desiring the security of something solid beneath my hands, I darted to the wall. Running my hand along the wooden planks covering the structure, I inched my way toward the first illuminated window. Strange music drifted out from the slightly open portal, as I stepped from the wall and cautiously peered inside.

Adjusting quickly to the light, I focused on a large room with walls colored a soft blue, and floors coated in a spread of unnatural looking grass nearly the same color as the walls. Along the walls hung unfamiliar, yet extraordinarily beautiful paintings of a foreign land; each one held my attention a moment before my eyes moved to the next. Sprouting from the ceiling, an ornate object of glass and gold, that was rather pleasing to the eye, hung down into the room producing much of the unnatural light that spilled through the windows. Flanking what looked to be some sort of fire pit at the far end of the room, were two tall bookcases, each overflowing with books, all of various sizes and colors. As I scanned their titles, I was disappointed to find the inscriptions were completely incomprehensible. The oddly fat and disjointed symbols on the bindings were totally foreign and unfamiliar. Across the room from the window, the music seemed to emanate from two large boxes, placed on either side of a large, cloth-covered, overstuffed… chair. Both the chair and the bloated bench that sat directly beneath the window were a comical sight to behold. Somehow they reminded me of a pair of overweight woman who had forced themselves into apparel far too minca for their massive bulk, and certain their minca clothing made them beautiful and slim, they would stand before you with seams strained and flesh bulging in lumpy proportions… looking utterly ridiculous. Struggling to confine my sudden need to laugh, I focused on the Tenzenar within the room.

There were nikca with strange toys scattered around them, playing on the blue fibrous grass in the center of the room. I was surprised to see that they played with these intriguing items with the same typical sibling interaction as Airian nikca—which was as companionable as it was antagonistic. There were two adults who watched them indulgently from the stuffed bench beneath the window. As the nikca's voices rose with their play, I was caught up by their excitement—though I understood ghea neye that was being said. The nikca seemed alive with a vibrancy of life that reminded me of my own people. I was drawn to the minca ones rather than fearful of them. Even the adults seemed less horrifying than my lessons in learning house had taught. I was curious and bewildered by all I witnessed in that room. How could it be that a people we feared, seemed to have Keyenoa's presence within them and their home?

My attention shifted as the adult female glanced at a minca mechanical object on her wrist and unexpectedly rose from her place. Instinctively, I stepped back from the window as she began to speak to the nikca. Her voice did not sing with the same vibrancy as the nikca, yet I still heard something that was nearly lost in her voice which seemed to hold a hint of Keyenoa's presence in it. Did these Tenzenar loose Keyenoa's joy as they grew older—a joy that Airians never loose... unless they chose to walk away from Keyenoa. Then, the woman turned, revealing a glimpse of an undeniable light deep in her eyes. A light I recognized to be Keyenoa's. With my curiosity heightened even further—I was glad to find that this woman, while she didn't glow, had some sign of Keyenoa's presence inside her. Again, I wondered why we needed to fear such people if He lived in them, at least in some way like us.

Tenderly the woman gathered the two nikca together. After they hugged and kissed the man who had remained seated on the puffy bench, the woman and nikca left the room. Each one, mother and nikca alike, hugged, kissed, pinched, and poked the other up the stairs, their mingled laughter filtered out through the minca gap in the window. The male Tenzenar watched them go up the stairs, a book forgotten before him, with an expression of ghea Keyen indulgence. I leaned closer to the window to glance at the book, only to find the strange, fat, and disjointed symbols which I had seen on the bindings of the books in the shelves across the room.

Feeling the strain of holding myself invisible for so long, I reluctantly left the warmth of the scene. Moving to the edge of the platform, ignoring the stairs, I jumped off the raised boards and ran up the embankment.

"Well, Niki, what did you see?" Jon asked with a chuckle, hearing my approach.

I rushed to his side, almost bouncing with all my news. Unable to see him, I turned and stared at the dwelling while I answered. "It was so strange... and rather wonderful, Master. I found them frightening, and happy and sad all at once. Oh, but neye matter what I saw, all of it was unbelievably intriguing." I turned blindly in his direction, expressing my fascination with my hands and face, not considering that I was still invisible. "They must be royalty, Jon, because they have even more given power than Father. It's incredible, all the things they had and could do."

"Sit down and release your invisibility before you strain yourself," he instructed with a mixture of Thaytoric understanding, excitement, and indulgence.

Neye longer concerned over the dangers of Tenzenar proximity, I gratefully lowered my shield and sat down. Jon dropped his as well, and listened to everything I had to say and all I described. I fell silent after sharing every detail of the dwelling that I could remember, awed again by everything I described.

My attention slowly drifted toward the Tenzenar house as I continued with my description, "To have the power to make the room glow without candles—and to make music emerge from magic boxes… their power must at least equal Father's. Jon, do you think it's possible they get their power from Keyenoa, as we do?" I asked, remembering Keyenoa's presence in the woman and her nikca. "Master, the people… well they're so different—yet also so very similar to us." I looked at him not waiting for his answer, "I'm not sure I can describe them so you'd understand, because I honestly don't understand myself. They frighten me, excite me, and baffle me all at the same time. I really must learn more and then even more about them! Oh, Jon, they must be very powerful, not only because of all they are capable of doing, but because I am drawn to them despite how dangerous I've been taught they are," I confessed almost overflowing with excitement. "They have books, too, Jon. But I couldn't read their words. Oh, and I heard them speak. But their language… I couldn't understand them." Horrified, I gasped, "Master, if we can't understand them, how are we going learn more about them?"

He sighed, looking aanas older and weighed down with grief. "Niki, listen to me carefully. These Tenzenar have neye power in the way our people have. They have neye more knowledge of things than your father—if even that much. While I admit to know minca about the Tenzenar, this much I know: Tenzenar have a fascinated obsession with mechanisms and machines. It is these machines and mechanisms that have created the light and make music come out of boxes. Niki, it takes a minca bit of knowledge to build these things, not Keyenoa's given power to make them work. And it takes even less intelligence to simply use the machines." Sighing again, he stared at the house below. "About their language, well, let us go back to camp and send Conden to New Malin on the morrow with the information we have concerning the Tenzenar and our language problem. Your father or Met Lordship will likely have a solution to this language barrier we face. And while we wait for this problem to be solved, we can all do some hunting."

We sat on the embankment a few moments longer, allowing me a minca more time to gather my strength so I could raise my shield of invisibility and hold it long enough to return to Dindieum. Watching the Tenzenar dwelling, we saw a shadow of movement behind one of the windows in the room I had looked into, and I guessed that the woman had returned to the room to join the man. I imagined her sitting next to him on that ridiculous puffy bench and wondered if the nikca had returned with her or if they were in one of the upstairs rooms which now glowed ever so faintly with a soft light.

I looked at Jon. "I don't ache from the strain of holding myself invisible any longer, Master. I'm ready to go back to Dindieum, now," I said, feeling tired and suddenly very eager to crawl into my bedroll.

Jon nodded and rose from his place beside me. As I took his cape, we raised our shields of invisibility and returned to camp where we were met by three impatient guards. They kept me from finding the inside my bedroll, until I had again described everything I had witnessed after peering in the window of the Tenzenar dwelling. Though they had known about the Tenzenar fascination for mechanical devices because Father and Met Lordship had told them about this, all of the guards were as amazed I had been with everything I described.

Chapter IV

Pride's Folly

"Be careful, Met son, in what punishment thee decrees, for it may well be that I have allowed the circumstance to punish thine errant nikca more justly than thine hand could measure."
—Book of Keyenoa

Conden left for New Malin at dawn. During his absence, we agreed to remain close to camp and only leave it to hunt for food in the wilds of Dindieum. We would do neye further exploring of the Tenzenar area until Conden returned with a solution to the language problem. An oona after Conden's departure, however, we were forced to reevaluate part of our plans. Less than an oona after dawn, our camp was bombarded by horrendous noises—the likes of which we had never heard before—thunderous rumbles, unnatural hums, screaming creaks of metal as it grated against metal and shouts of Tenzenar voices that mingled with the horrifying shrieks of Sontall from the trees. My perceptions of Tenzenar as benign creatures had been instantly destroyed while we wondered if all life—as we knew it—was being extinguished along the path leading to Malinieum City while the cacophony moved slowly closer to our camp.

PART I TENZENAR

By midday, the horrific shrieks of ghea Sontall trees being ripped from the ground and flung to the forest floor nearly overwhelmed the horrendous dissonance of the monstrous machines. When dusk approached, harsh and angry Tenzenar voices were clearly discernable despite the continued roar of machinery as they trampled the underbrush not but ten pearons from our camp. Just as we were certain we were about to be overcome by Alleanne only knew what, the sounds of demolition and machinery stopped. Dindieum was awash in a total eerie and uncomfortable silence.

Onas later, the air slowly became permeated with the noxious odor, familiar to me from the night before.

"Keyenoa has certainly been watching over us today," Scaun murmured uneasily in the sudden silence, his hand covering his nose in an effort to hold back the stench.

"Ta, and I've spent these several unnerving moments of silence expressing my gratitude for His watchful protection," Salitarin agreed. "Jon, do you think they're finished killing… at least for this day?"

"Ta, as you said, at least for today" was Jon's answer as he turned toward the Oreon guard. "What say you to joining me on a short walk, Scaun?"

The Oreon guard smiled grimly. "Hmm, a benna stretch of the muscles was just what I was thinking." His expression as he looked at Jon was sharp with challenge.

I stood, preparing to join them, only to face Jon's frown and shake of his head. "Neye, I need you to stay put this time. None of us needs the extra worry of wondering what you might find to get into while we're looking over the Sontall the Tenzenar have brought our way. Salitarin, you have my permission to sit on him if you must. But **keep him in camp**," he added firmly, aware of the glint of rebellion in my gaze.

The guard smiled wickedly and nodded as he turned his focus on me. Much to my frustration, I was humbled to discover that Salitarin followed orders with a literal interpretation. The moment I tried to sneak out of camp—thinking I had lulled him into believing I was off for a moment of needed privacy in the bushes—I found myself flat on my back, with his knee resting firmly on my chest, while he grinned at me in unbridled glee.

Following this altercation, to assure himself that he would be able to keep an eye on me, Salitarin volunteered my services in preparing the evening meal. Dusk had begun to fall within the forest and our meal was warming on the fire when Jon and Scaun returned to camp. Aware of their troubled expressions, Salitarin immediately served the meal, despite the fact it was only late afternoon. The guard gave me a pointed look telling me to keep silent and allow both men time to adjust to all they had seen.

"We can neye longer remain in this camp safely," Jon explained, leaning his back against a tree trunk while resting his plate on his knee. "The Tenzenar have removed the trees, roots and all, five hundred pearons into Dindieum. The putrid substance that chokes the life out of the ground now covers the path up to the forest's edge.

"Being discovered by the Tenzenar is the least of our worries, tomenan. What Scaun and I have seen, tells me that we are in a far greater danger than that. The Tenzenar have massive metal machines that uproot trees, wrenching the massive root systems from the ground, and gobbling the tree whole. And other machines of the same size that level the land with one pass. We will be squashed like nematoes, or eaten alive when these machines are unleashed on this camp. And it is certain they will be unleashed upon this camp very soon."

I shivered uncontrollably as my imagination worked exuberantly to conjure up images of what Jon had described. Scaring myself, I looked at my Thaytor, remembering that Conden wasn't expected to return for many days. "Master, what about Conden? How will the guard find us if we leave this camp?"

Jon lowered his jott to his plate and stared blankly at the fire, as he struggled to find an answer to this new dilemma. I set my meal on the ground, leaving it half eaten and began to share my thoughts and fears with Keyenoa. Scaun and Salitarin ignored their food while also searching their thoughts for a solution.

PART I TENZENAR

"Jon, our minds have been too full of ghea teepin worry to think straight!" Scaun blurted, grinning ear to ear. "Obviously we need to move north, further into Dindieum. Going that far into the forest, Conden who's unaware of the danger, won't have his shield raised. If, we simply make camp close to the path and Salitarin and I stand guard along the side of the path in shifts, we will be able to intercept him when he comes along."

Jon sighed, "So simple an answer, and we all nearly overlooked it in our panic." Lifting his jott, he scraped the remains of his meal into his mouth. "Now, let's get to packing! If we wait till morning, Dindieum's trees will be literally falling on our heads before we're half packed."

Scaun and Salitarin instantly began scraping their half-full plates back in the pot on the fire and began to pack up the camp. I jumped up and made an effort to help, but soon realized my efforts were more of a hindrance than a help. After being barked at for the third time having gotten in the way and causing everyone more work than aid, I went off to sulk. I was instantly forgotten and left to my own devices.

Full of youth and the ghea teepin-eye that goes with it, I decided to take advantage of the freedom unintentionally offered. Creeping from the quickly disassembling camp, I headed in the direction of the Tenzenar dwelling. While I remembered Father's orders and my promise to obey them, I was feeling hurt and useless. I was too immature to care about those rules and the promises I had made to follow them.

I soon wandered into the area where the trees had been wrenched from the ground, and gobbled whole by the machines Jon had described. I quickly skirted the huge machines sitting idly within the cleared land. Afraid they would come alive and eat me if I lingered even an ena, I didn't dare stop to look closely at them. Dusk had yet to fall beyond the shade and shadows of the trees, so I ran past Dindieum's Sontall and on to the malodourous covering which had crept to the forest's edge.

Curious, I knelt on the covering and put my face as close to it as I could, forcing my nose to nearly touch the surface, causing the putrid odor to be all the stronger. My eyes watered and my nose burned, but I kept my face where it was. I was determined to get a closer look at the substance and try to discover why it smelled so of untold things. What I found was tiny stones and sand smothered in a thick, gooey black substance that held the whole mess together and caused it to harden. Sticking my finger into a pool of the black muck that had puddled on the ground at the edge of the surface, I discovered that it not only clung tenaciously to whatever it touched, but was the cause of the stench. Wiping my finger against my tunic britches, then leaf debris, and lastly even the surface itself—all to no avail—I was resigned to the fact that I managed to not only make my finger filthier with my efforts, but I had also created more questions than answers. Being typically Airian concerning such frustrations, I shrugged my shoulders and walked away from the surface and my questions, knowing they would still be there when Keyenoa was ready to reveal the answers I sought.

Reaching the Tenzenar dwelling, I sat on the grassy embankment and watched the two nikca playing out front. They ran and laughed, alternately chasing one another with open and joyful abandon. More often than not, neither nikca was quite sure who was chasing whom, but both obviously didn't care. Their voices were clear and almost as full of melody as Airian nikca. I could clearly hear Keyenoa's presence in their voices and so forgot the dangers around me, and, even for a time, where I actually was. By Keyenoa's grace alone, I never forgot to keep my shield of invisibility raised.

The door of the house swung open, reawakening me to the possible danger in my situation. Fortifying my invisibility shield, aware of the strain it put on my body, I watched the woman step part of the way out the door. Calling to the nikca, they immediately stopped playing and ran eagerly past the woman and inside the dwelling. As the door closed, it shut out the woman's laughter that mingled harmoniously with her nikca's.

Surrounded so suddenly in silence, I felt alone and abandoned sitting on the embankment. Giving myself a mental shake and a quiet talking to about my emotions not being very Airian-like, I looked around to assure myself of my safety. "With neye around… instead of sulking because you feel lonely and abandoned, take the opportunity and drop your shield, Niki," I whispered just to hear someone's voice. Then, taking my own advice, I lowered my shield and became visible.

Having already noticed in the late afternoon light that the ground along the side of the house had been covered with the same black substance that covered the path, my indomitable Airian curiosity stirred and I went to investigate. A minca dwelling set a few pearons toward the back of the house had been built at the end of the covering. There were two large doors which encompassed the whole front of the building, with rough-looking handles hammered on them near the bottom of the doors. I tried pulling and pushing on the handles, but the large square doors refused to budge. Spying a window along the side of the building, I went to peek inside.

There, before my bewildered eyes, was a large metal object. It sat on four fat, black, grooved wheels. The object seemed to have a long nose and round clear globes on its front that looked a bit like eyes. In between these 'eyes' hung a shiny metal grill, mimicking a toothsome grimace. The brightly colored metal sides were buffed to a high gloss and had what might be doors molded into them. There were windows above each door and cushioned seats inside. Shaking my head, I stepped away from the window of the minca building. Confused by the object and its use, wondering why it needed its own building, I decided that Tenzenar were simply keezworky.

By this time, dusk had truly fallen, limiting my vision. A full oona needed to pass until the moon's rise when its light would offer me aid, but I didn't want to wait for the moon, or return to Dindieum just yet. Having only discovered more questions, I wanted to find something that would offer some answers rather than more questions. Wandering to the back of the ghea minca dwelling, I noticed a portion of land had been fenced in directly behind the larger Tenzenar dwelling. Wondering why they would erect a tall metal fence to enclose less than a tenth of an aron of land; I didn't hesitate or stop to think. I simply climbed fence and began walking into the center of the fenced land. By that time I had completely forgotten that I had left my shield of invisibility down and was walking around fully visible.

Suddenly, I heard a low menacing growl rushing toward me. Turning—not bothering to stop to see what might be making such a sound—I bounded back toward the fence as fast as my feet would allow. Just as I gripped the top of the fence and started to swing my legs over, something latched on to my ankle. It penetrated my flesh and sent shooting pains up my leg. The sharp teeth of some creature had punctured my boot and my flesh and held me tenaciously. In a panic, I just worked all the harder to bring both my legs up and over the fence. The force of my vault and my added effort to clear the fence managed to tear the creature free, ripping my flesh and rending my boot. But I managed to make it to the over the fence to relative safety.

Turning to look at my attacker, I only then remembered to raise my invisibility shield and vanish. Gazing at the creature now clawing at the fence, I finally discovered my first answer—the reason for a fence—a strange-looking logone. It growled, barked, and clawed wildly at the metal meshed fence and ground, eager to garner another taste of Airian. Cautiously, I backed up not feeling terribly confident that the fence would hold. As I moved away, the beast became even louder as it tried harder to reach me, creating such a deafening ruckus in its desperation that the back door suddenly opened. From the door, the man called out to the logone in a sharp, commanding tone. Instantly the frantic clawing and barking stopped, but the beast stubbornly remained at the fence, staring hungrily in my direction while continuing to growl in menacing tones. This behavior drew the man out of the dwelling. The man again said something to the despicable creature. But rather than looking at the logone he was intently stairing in the direction of the logone's frenzied stare. I froze, throwing all my energy into fortifying my shield. If the man chose to let the logone out of that fence, I wasn't worth a lestna. Knowing my shield was raised I was positive the Tenzenar couldn't see me, yet for a moment I suffered the eerie sensation that our eyes met. Shaking his head, the Tenzenar looked down at the logone. His voice, ripe with irritation, he said something to the beast a final time, before he turned back to the house, leaving the logone at the fence.

'I mustn't move a muscle. Oh, Alleanne, my ankle hurts!' I thought to myself, never taking my eyes off the logone. "I guess this is one of those times that Father and Jon told me about, when I wouldn't be able to charm my way out of trouble," I whispered aloud, trying not to laugh at myself and my circumstance. Looking up, I began to silently pray, "Keyenoa, what am I to do?" I asked. My thoughts quickly turned to my Thaytor and I again whispered aloud, "Oh Jon, I'll take any punishment you think I deserve, if you just come quickly and get me out of this!"

The logone hadn't stopped growling. It only increased in volume when it heard my voice.

There was more movement at the back door as the woman stepped outside along with the man. She carried an odd-shaped sphere in her hand that emitted a bright focused beam of light, which she waved back and forth along the grass as they walked toward the fence and the logone. Something on the ground near the edge of the fence caught the light and sparkled iridescently. The man quickly retrieved it and turned it over in his hand as the woman shone the light on it. They had found the piece of my boot the logone had torn off.

'You kutated mootan teepatin,' I silently berated myself. 'It's most likely coated with your blood too. Why not simply announce to every Tenzenar on Malin that they are not here alone.'

The man and woman talked quietly about their find. Then reaching an agreement, he nodded and tucked the torn piece of my boot into his pocket. Facing the logone, he spoke sharply—silencing the beast—before he and the woman returned to the house.

I closed my eyes as the pain from my ankle and what I'd inadvertently done washed through my body. By jumping that fence, I had put all of my people in danger. The Tenzenar now had evidence there were other beings living on this planet that had the knowledge of curing and treating skins for clothing. What the blood would reveal to these Tenzenar, I dared not consider.

Unable to hold my invisibility—even if it meant my life—my shield shattered, leaving me further weakened from the physical strain I'd put on myself to hold my invisibility for so long. The logone instantly increased the volume of its growling. I paid the creature minca heed. All I wanted to do was jump the fence and find some way to retrieve what the Tenzenar had found. Even if I could have raised my shield, the teepin of such a desperate act simply continued to growl in front of me. Glancing at the beast uneasily, I pondered entering the house another way, 'If can't get in by the front door, then maybe one of the windows might be opened,' I thought to myself, growing hopeful. 'Could I dare gather my strength and courage, and then give it a tr....'

"Nikita Markain Malin!"

Startled by the angry voice not even a pearon away, I nearly jumped out of my skin. The logone stiffened, its hackles raised and the growling again increased in volume. I was momentarily too startled to recognize my own Thaytor's voice as I turned only to find neye there.

"By Alleanne, I hope you're pleased with yourself, Met Lord," he continued, enabling me to put a name to the voice.

"Jon?" I asked, not really sure what else to say.

"Ta" was his curt reply.

"Oh," I mumbled, struggling with the overwhelming emotions of relief and terror. All I could think was, 'What is he going to say when he learns what I have done?'

"Oh, what?" he barked, his last shreds of patience vanishing. "Oh, it is you, or... oh, that's nice? For Alleanne's sake, Niki! What were you thinking? You could have been hurt by this logone or even killed by the Tenzenar. Have you gone completely keezworky, leaving camp without escort or permission and wandering around out here alone?!"

During this dressing down, the logone began to bark and lunge at the fence in frantic frenzy. Jon, his patience having departed long before, turned and jolted the beast with a minca of his given power. Frightened, though not seriously hurt, the logone ran to the other side of the fence with its tail between his legs to sulk in silence. Turning from the fence, Jon's full anger fell on me.

"Now raise your shield and start moving—quick as a ledo stag—back to camp, before I give you the same as the logone," he barked, sounding very much like the creature sulking on the far side of the fence.

I remained visible. "Master?" I interjected meekly, aware my news would most likely get me exactly what the logone had gotten.

"What?" he snapped through clenched teeth.

"About that possibly of being hurt by the logone…?" I faltered to silence.

"Ta," he said, again through his teeth.

'This is not going well at all,' I thought. "Well… Master… it… umm… kind of… happened," I squeaked.

"What!" he shouted, forgetting where we were. Then sighing, he struggled to restrain his anger. "Are you bleeding?"

"Ta… enough, I think, for it to drip into the grass as we go."

"Well, this isn't the place for assessing the damage. Where exactly are you hurt?"

I mumbled something about my ankle, too ashamed and frightened to mention the missing piece of fur.

He moved nearer. "Come on, climb on my shoulders so we won't leave a trail of blood back to camp," he muttered, while kneeling down and taking my arm to guide me onto his shoulders. "Now, Niki, you have to raise your shield," he suggested while shifting my weight evenly across his back. "Seeing an Airian floating about, well… I think you get my point?"

I chuckled at the thought and raised my shield. I spent the remainder of that time focusing my energy on keeping my shield raised until we reached Dindieum.

By the time we made it to the new camp, my ankle ached miserably, yet I said ghea neye. Not only was Jon still angry, but we were surprised to find Conden sitting comfortably near the fire with Met Lordship High King Sayleen Cantabo warming his hands next to him. Not a soul made mention of our late arrival or why I had arrived seated on Jon's shoulders. Prudently, I felt it was wiser to simply sit down and remain in silent agony, rather than draw any further attention to my misdeeds.

Drawn to Met Lordship, I was struck by how much he had seemed to have aged since we had last met. Looking at him even in the muted firelight I could tell that his time for Sontall was nearing. I couldn't help but wonder—with a sense of foreboding—who it was that Keyenoa had chosen to take his place. Fearful I might receive an answer I didn't want, I pushed those thoughts aside. Conden's chuckle turned my attention in that guard's direction. Suddenly, I wondered how Conden had managed to return with Met Lordship in tow when he had only departed this morning.

"Oh, Niki," Met Lordship laughed, "the thousands of questions that so fills the minds of youth," he said, keeping his attention on the fire, aware of my gaze. "I'll answer your question first, young one, and then perhaps your guards and Thaytor will answer mine," he said with an indulgent smile. Shifting, he glanced at each one of us, but carefully never quite met our gaze. "My dreams were restless through the early oonas of this morning. Enas after waking, I knew there was benna reason for having such troubled slumber. The problem was I couldn't seem to discover just what or where that problem lay. I regret to say, my power simply won't pierce the darkness that now covers this part of Malin. It wasn't till dusk, when Conden emerged from beneath this layer of darkness heading to New Malin, that I realized the trouble emanated from around the five of you. Not wasting even a moment, I used my power and transported myself to Conden's side. I was then close enough to this company that my power could pierce just far enough to reveal the dangers you faced. I regret that my power didn't warn me of your danger earlier. But I'm most grateful that Keyenoa's hand protected each and every one of you.

"I didn't even offer Conden a moment to explain why he was returning but transported us both here to your new camp so I could hear all of your news firsthand." Met Lordship looked in Jon's direction, "So, Master Alcone, what have you learned?"

PART I TENZENAR

Keeping his eyes focused on the ground, Jon told Met Lordship all we had discovered. Conveniently, he left out my most recent adventure among the Tenzenar. Met Lordship listened attentively then stood and carefully held of each our gazes for a very short moment. I felt a sharp stab of pain shoot through my head when it came to be my turn. Held by Met Lordship's given power, I suddenly felt trapped and desperate for release. When his gaze left me, I then felt empty, wanting his gaze to return.

"Well," Met Lordship sighed as he resumed his seat by the fire, "While I am tempted to remain, translating the Tenzenar language by going with you on your forays into their territory, I know I would get ghea neye done that needs doing in Oreon," he said with a chuckle. "Therefore, I have given each of you the power to understand and even speak the Tenzenar language with ease." Met Lordship looked at me.

I dared not look up. I understood another reason why it was wise not to meet his gaze having experienced that minca touch of his given power.

"I did not give any of you the ability to read their written word, and I hope that you may learn what you must without it. What I have given is quite a bit of knowledge to amass in an instant, and that was dangerous enough, especially for Niki. His mind is young and unchanged by Con Sona Eata. It is most difficult for him to deal with the amount of given power I needed to force into his mind to accept what I have done. The four of you know the pain you experienced by what I have given. Be aware that pain was intensified for our young prince. What I've done for you, young one, painful though it was, I had to do, but I will do neye more. It was a painful process for you all," he added, aware of my embarrassment over my handicap of youth.

Jon knelt at Met Lordship's feet, lowering his head to one knee. "Colen en donahae, Met Lordship, Sorice leki'anee, for thy generous gift," he replied properly, speaking for us all, as the guards also fell to one knee and lowered their heads in respect.

I bowed but remained seated because my ankle ached too much to strain it to kneel. Peeking through my lowered lashes at

Met Lordship, I caught sight of the smile that flit about his mouth as he looked at me, aware of my attention.

"Oh, Jontair," he said, as if something just occurred to him. Yet this clearly was not the case, "as you are well aware, it is not uncommon for the one under your care to seek trouble without an ena's consideration." Met Lordship struggled not to smile. "As you are aware of this, I ask only that when such an occurrence takes place, you consider Keyenoa's wise words: 'The trouble they find, often serves justly for the punishment they deserve.' In such cases, I feel extra punishment becomes unnecessary."

Jon carefully lifted Met Lordship's cape to his lips and kissed it, before he stood and bowed with respect over the offered advice. Met Lordship then vanished, taking himself back to Oreon instantly.

Turning, not even blinking at the sudden disappearance of Met Lordship, Jon's gaze burned into mine. "All right, Niki, let's see exactly what punishment you received for your… adventure," he barked angrily.

I shifted gingerly on the log where I sat and lifted my ankle, setting it on my other knee. "The logone got my ankle," I explained to the curious guards then closed my eyes. I didn't want to look at Jon or the throbbing wound. All I could do was pray he wouldn't ask me where the missing part of my boot happened to be.

Jon knelt to get a better look at the damage, while I continued to pray. "Niki, turn around and lay over the log on your stomach. Salitarin, get me some light so I might have a better look at Niki's… reward," he mumbled distractedly.

Finding a dry piece of wood, Salitarin soaked one end in a jar of keyloss and poured a bit of our drinking water over it. Instantly it burst into flame, and he quickly brought the torch to Jon.

"Only through mootan stubbornness, could you have withstood this pain for as long as you have without so much as a whimper of complaint," he said. "That logone tore part of your boot, not to mention a good portion of your ankle wide open. How in Alleanne you managed to hold your invisibility through this pain, I don't know," he muttered to himself.

I winced over his description and opened my eyes turning to solemnly meet his gaze.

"Well, there's neye sense trying to put this delicately," he sighed. "Niki, that boot must come off so it can be repaired and give me access to clean the bite. I will not tolerate a word of protest from you either. You will need that boot to wear for the rest of this journey, and it cannot be repaired with you still in it," he added aware of my intention to argue.

I closed my eyes in defeat. "Why didn't I wear the other boots, which lace up—instead of the ones that have to be pulled on?" I grumbled piteously, knowing my ankle had swollen to twice its normal size.

"Niki, just lay yourself across the log on your stomach and hold onto the log to keep yourself steady." Doing as I was instructed, Jon took hold of my foot, while Scaun made another torch. Salitarin and Conden straddled the log on either side of me and held me by the shoulders. Gently cradling my foot in his hands Jon pulled, while the two guards held me in place, and Scaun held the torches so they could see what was going on. As waves of wrenching pain surged through my leg, I began praying my ankle would simply come off with the boot. Then, I wouldn't have to suffer the pain when the wound was cleansed after the boot's removal. Keyenoa though offered neye such mercy. I was forced to endure the excruciating pain of having the wound soaked in burning nema leaf juice and cleaned by my Thaytor's hand. Jon quietly told me that both agonies would help me heal faster and keep out infection.

Before I fell asleep over a plate of food, I was hastily fed and put to bed. The last thing I remembered was Jon leaning over my pallet and brushing his fingers across my forehead. Touched by his power and the words he uttered, my pain left me and I fell asleep to his murmuring, "Ta, Keyenoa, the circumstance certainly was punishment enough for his misdeed this night. Dachta ulenor, my young master," he added and that was the last thing I remembered as sleep claimed me.

Chapter V

The Answers Are Given

"An Airian's curiosity—if not curtailed—will take him places all common sense would demand he run from.
—Thaytoric Book of Wisdom

Jon had already consumed his morning meal and was ready to travel to the Tenzenar dwelling when I woke the following morning. He had planned to leave me in camp because of my injured ankle while I was determined to go, ankle or not. Eating hastily, careful not to reveal any pain to my watchful Thaytor, I argued stubbornly about my going with him. Confident that my youthful exuberance and persistence would defeat his every objection, I never let up.

We set out shortly after I had finished my meal.

There was neye sign of noise or activity when we neared the section of forest invaded by the Tenzenar. The massive machinery sat dormant and quiet. Jon quickly explored the machinery more closely, wondering if he could discover why there were neye Tenzenar about and the machines were idle. I stayed as far from the machines as I could, certain if I got near them they would somehow start up and eat me alive. Jon didn't linger long, afraid the Tenzenar might arrive at any moment. With our shields raised, we continued on to the Tenzenar house. Reaching the embankment, we gazed at the Tenzenar dwelling in the light of day.

"I remember standing near here only a few tuevtauns ago with my helop at my side, watching the meadow grasses stirring in the wind, and the scurry of dree as they ran for their holes at the slightest sound. It looks so different now," I whispered sadly.

"I'll go around to the back, Niki… you explore the front," Jon murmured, grieving as much as I for what was gone.

I was relieved he'd chosen to explore the back. Having neye power to protect myself, I didn't relish the idea of exploring anything that may involve that logone. Clearly, Jon was much better equipped to deal with that situation.

Then, aware of the power in his gaze as it found mine, despite the fact that we were invisible, I waited for him to speak. "Niki, promise me that you'll think before you act, and then act with caution and forethought. I tell you these people are dangerous. Swear to me that you'll not drop your guard for an ena."

Embarrassed, yet admitting he had good reason for such concern, I looked away, breaking the hold of his power. "I swear, Master, I won't lower my guard for an ena," I promised, forgetting he had asked much more than that of me.

Jon set his hand on my shoulder, "Benna." There was a smile in his voice. "Meet me here on this offensive black stuff when you've quenched your curiosity—or in twenty onas—whichever comes first. You should be able to hold your invisibility for that long, but not much longer."

Leaving me on the embankment, Jon wandered around to the back of the dwelling. I approached the building, stepping onto the raised platform to look in the window next to the door. Suddenly, the door opened. I quickly backed toward the edge of the platform. Landing wrong on my ankle, stars flashed before my eyes as pain shot up my leg in agonizing currents. While biting my lip to keep from making a sound, the young boy—about ten aanas old—stopped not three paces away. Still holding the door wide open, he stuck his head back inside the dwelling.

NIKITA'S STORY

"Sure, Mom, I promise to stay at Jimmy's house. I'll be home in time for lunch," he hollered through the doorway in a tone of tolerant exasperation. I smiled, aware of the numerous times I also had to repeat such parental orders. Promising to follow those orders the instant they were issued, despite the fact that I had promised the same thing so many times before that I thought it unnecessary to promise them again.

His mother called out, keeping the boy where he was. Without hesitation—or any thought at all—I limped past the boy into the house. He shivered uncomfortably as I brushed passed him, his expression softening to bemusement. Having made it into the house, I turned and watched the boy recover from my passing so close to him. Shivering again, he shrugged his shoulders and, forgetting the whole experience, focused his attention down the hallway.

"Hey, Mom, can I bring Jimmy over for lunch?" he hollered.

"Yes, of course" came the laughing reply from the back of the dwelling. *"Now hurry up and shut that door, young man! Who knows what crawly things you're letting in by leaving it opened like that!"*

I smiled. She had a point to her complaint... especially this time. 'Okay, so... I may not be crawling, but I was hobbling, and I was in the house only because the boy had held the door open!' I thought, feeling very proud of myself.

When the door slammed shut behind me, I suddenly realized I had neye certain way to get back out. It was only then that I remembered Jon's warning and the request he had made, that I think carefully before acting.

"So, Keyenoa, when am I going to learn to think before I do something instead of after?" I asked in thought.

The clank of dishes and the odor of freshly cooked food wafted toward me from the hall and drew my attention.

'All right, standing in the hallway worrying isn't going to get me back outside, so why am I wasting time doing just that? Explore and learn... that's what we're here to do... and what better way to learn than being among them?' I thought to myself.

Then, without further delay, took a quick inventory of my new surroundings as I headed to the back of the dwelling.

Behind me was the front door. In front of me just a minca to my left was a long, curved staircase, its rails polished and smoothed to a beautiful sheen. To my right was an archway that opened into the room I had seen two nights before while looking through the window. In front of me along the side of the stairs was a hallway that ended at another window with a door to the right. It was from that direction that the mouth-watering odor and clattering noises came. I was drawn forward. Being a boy of fifteen aanas, I was always hungry. This made the combination of sounds and odors impossible to resist. Once again, without thought and minca caution, I quietly wandered down the hall to investigate.

There was a large wooden table in the center of the room, covered with an enormous amount of food. I found the sight strangely similar, yet also very different from anything I'd seen before. Remembering caution, aware that my curiosity and continual state of hunger would likely entice me to snatch some tasty-looking tidbit from the table, I forced myself to remain in the hall and focus my attention on the Tenzenar.

The man sat with his back to me, somehow reminding me a bit of Met Lordship High King Sayleen Cantabo. I sensed he ruled his family with the same gentle authority as our High King ruled Airies. The woman sat at his right, as aware of him as she was everything else, ready to serve his any need. Across from her sat the minca female nikca. This minca nikca fascinated me with her bright, perky expression and mischievous grin. She, more than the others, seemed to almost glow with Keyenoa's presence. She bubbled with a youthful exuberance—so like my own—and this confused me. From all the lessons drilled into my head at learning house, I never imagined there would be anything I would even remotely have in common with a Tenzenar.

Sighing, the man leaned back in his chair, pushing his plate to the center of the table. *"I'm sure glad it's a weekend!"* he exclaimed, a note of pure contentment in his voice. *"No infernal machines creating a racket and scaring the livestock,"* he continued, speaking to neye in particular.

"Daddy, how far is the road gonna go?" the nikca asked, her attention darting all over the place at once.

"I'm not sure, Lisa. I think they plan to extend it all the way to a lake, deep in the forest. Once it's finished, why don't we all take a trip and see this lake for ourselves?" he replied.

Lisa shrugged her shoulders, her gaze darting into the hall where I stood. Her attention remained there a long moment before moving on. A knowing smile played around her mouth. The gesture revealed to me that she was up to something, but that she wasn't quite ready to reveal what it was at that moment. Neither parent chose to pressure her for an answer as to what she was thinking.

After a long and comfortable silence, the woman took in a deep breath and sighed contentedly while looking out a back window. *"I like it here, Bill. It's like a dream come true… especially on a glorious day like today. I believe the Lord has truly blessed us all by letting us come here to live."* Her voice held the dreamy quality of true happiness, again confusing me; these beings weren't supposed to be happy. Hearing her speak of Keyenoa—while she didn't glow, He did seem to shine in her eyes—further perplexed me, contradicting all I had been taught. Wasn't it the nature of these beings to prefer invading and killing to Keyen?

"Yes, Ruth," Bill agreed with the woman while setting his hand over hers and giving it a tender squeeze. *"I remember our anxiousness, just a few short years ago when we didn't think they'd ever open the permits to this planet and allow us our dream. I remember, too, those many nights that we prayed God would somehow make it possible for us come here and free ourselves from the sterility of progress and the over advancement of technology we found ourselves living in. Oh, how we had both longed to live life simply off the land like they used to do so long ago on Earth, and thought it would never come to be. Our prayers have been answered better than either of us dreamed, haven't they, sweetheart?"*

PART I TENZENAR

Ruth looked at her man's face and smiled with Keyen, "*Yes, Bill, He has... but what about your church? I know you love the farm and the work, but I also know your first love is to serve Him through pastoring a flock. If that never comes to fruition, will you remain as happy?*"

"*It will come when He chooses, Ruth, not when we do. I'm content now with the work of my hands. How many times have you chided me to wait on Him and not plunge ahead out of impatience? Yes, sweetheart, I will be happy.*"

Ruth smiled with embarrassment and squeezed his hand. The room was silent a long time as they gazed into each other's eyes, sharing a deep and tender communication only they could understand.

Lisa watched her parents some moments before she looked around the room again. Strangely those searching eyes darted to the hall and seemed to land on me. Afraid that she could somehow see me, I fortified my shield and started to step back from the doorway thinking to find some place I could hide. Then, her attention moved away and I realized how ghea teepin I was acting. Checking to be sure my shield was up and strong, I assured myself that *Lisa* couldn't see me any more than she could the air around us.

"*Momma,*" she spoke up. "*Shouldn't we think about the people who have been living here before us?*"

Suddenly, I wondered if I were ghea teepin or not. Her parents turned from each other and looked at her in confusion.

"*My teacher says they're called* Airians,*"* she added helpfully.

Ruth smiled patiently, "*Well, honey, no one believes they're alive now. They think they died off thousands of years ago. But, honey, if they were alive... well, things have a way of working themselves out, in the end.*"

Lisa was perfectly happy with that non-answer. She smiled and returned to her meal. It seemed to me that *Ruth* hadn't really given the matter much thought. It was clear the answer was given simply to placate the nikca's mind, rather than as a solution to a very real problem.

Ruth stood and began to gather the plates around the table. *"Now hurry up and wipe your face, young lady, so you can go out and play. My heavens! Half the morning's gone already and you've been here wasting it away sitting with your Mom and Dad,"* she exclaimed in mock horror, causing *Lisa* to giggle.

Wiping her face hurriedly, *Lisa* dashed passed me to the front door without a moment's hesitation. Seeing this as a chance to leave the house, I limped as fast as I could after her. As I hobbled along the hall, I found *Lisa* standing at the front door calmly holding it wide open… as if suddenly in neye hurry to leave. With her attention focused down the hallway in my direction she smiled, and for that moment I had the uncomfortable feeling she was smiling at me.

"Can I play with Sam in the front yard?" she called out.

Feeling terribly uneasy, I started out the door. As I slipped by, *Lisa* giggled joyously… staring right at me.

"I don't know why you didn't go out the back door if you wanted to play with Sam, but yes, Lisa, you can play with him. Just be careful he doesn't run away from the house on some wild goose chase. Sam's been acting rather strange lately and it's gotten worse since last night, so if he doesn't want to leave the fence, play with him in there all right?" her mother called back, not expecting a reply.

With a wild whoop of joy, *Lisa* dove out of the house and slammed the front door, nearly running me over on the minca set of stairs leading off the raised platform. She ran past me and hurried around to the back of the house forcing me to jump aside to avoid being run over. I grimaced in pain as I landed wrong. Again I couldn't help but examine my thoughts about the girl being able to see me. Sighing, I hobbled up the embankment to sit wearily on the edge of the black covering—or *"road"*—and wait for Jon's return. Relieved to be off my ankle, I watched a few rentins singing and playing in the trees and grass nearby. I marveled over how the minca birds seemed to feel at home so close to the strangeness of the Tenzenar and all they'd done in altering this once familiar land.

PART I TENZENAR

"Niki?" my Thaytor's voice reached me from about a pearon to my left.

"Ta. I'm sitting here, on this *ro*... er, black stuff," I answered, realizing the questions I would arouse if I suddenly used its proper name.

Accurately reading the distance between us through the sound of my voice, Jon sat at my side. "Well, tell me, did you learn anything that was helpful?" he asked, our shoulders brushing lightly as he made himself more comfortable.

"What did you learn, Master?" I stalled. While I may have received most of the answers we had come here searching for, I was certain his pleasure would fade when he discovered how I had acquired the information. So I was in neye hurry to share my news.

Jon sighed in frustration. "I found a very large building some pearons from the end of the fence. Inside are many animals penned in minca enclosures. Some of the creatures appear to resemble Airian animals, though only slightly. The Tenzenar creatures, however, are tamer to the point of being quite docile actually. It seems the beasts are quite content in those minca pens." He sighed again. "Actually, Niki, I learned ghea neye… unless you want to count the obvious fact that these animals were brought here with the Tenzenar from wherever they've come and not culled or cultivated here.

"Now.…" His hands hit his knees. "What did you learn? Did you discover anything of importance?"

I began to share my news, hoping he would be so flabbergasted with my revelations that he would forget to ask how I had acquired such knowledge. "Well, Master, it seems these Tenzenar have come from a place called *Earth* and are here to… let's see how did they put it? Oh ta, *'free ourselves from the sterility of progress, and live life simply off the land.'* Oh, and they don't think we're alive any longer, though they do know we call ourselves Airians. And this covering of black stone and gook is called a *road*, and the reasons why they aren't working on it is because it's now a *weekend*… whatever that is exactly, I'm not sure, but

I do know it implies something about designated days of rest," I mumbled to myself, before remembering a very important piece of information. Reaching out, I blindly grasped his shoulder. "Oh, ta, I almost forgot! Jon, they plan to take this *road* thing all the way to LeFold Lake! How can Father keep New Malin safe if they plan to come right through our Kingdom?"

Jon sucked in a deep and uncomfortable breath. In the ensuing silence, I decided not to tell him about the food, the room, or anything else inside the house, knowing that sharing such details would more than likely to get me in a great deal of trouble.

His boots scuffed along the gravel. I knew by the sound that he'd turned to face me. "Niki, how in Alleanne's name did you learn all that? Everything I saw left me with more frustrating questions than I started with."

I was sunk! He'd asked and I had to tell the truth. I owed my Thaytor at least that. So quickly lifting my thoughts upward, I prayed, "Keyenoa, I confess that honoring You is often inconvenient. In speaking the truth—as I know I must—I have to try my Thaytor's patience… and Keyenoa I really hate trying Jon's patience. I know, Father of all fathers, I should have thought of that before I went into the dwelling."

Sighing in defeat, I muttered the truth, "I went inside the Tenzenar dwelling when the male nikca was leaving to play with a forlana."

Jon was silent.

I held my breath waiting for the explosion of temper I was certain would come.

Finally he sighed. "I don't want to hear any more, Niki. I am certain I'd regret it if I did. What's done is done." Then to my further surprise, he began to chuckle quietly over my audacity.

"Master," I spoke hesitantly. Glad of my reprieve, I felt the need to share what truly perplexed me about these beings. "The Tenzenar in that dwelling… Well they're… well…. They're…" I stumbled over the words, trying to explain what I'd witnessed and what they made me feel. "Well, they're not what I expected at all!" I blurted out in frustration, aware I'd explained ghea neye of what

I wanted to say. "The nikca, Jon, they are so… well…" Again, I stumbled, "Almost Airian! I… I think… well, I think Keyenoa lives within them… and even within their parents," I forced the words out, aware of how keezworky it sounded even to me, and I was the one who had seen and heard what I was trying so hard to explain to Jon.

Lisa came running around the side of the dwelling laughing and jumping, while calling for… *"Sam!"* Bounding along behind her was the black and tan colored logone, mouth open, tongue lolling, and large ears alert. With a sudden burst of speed, the logone rushed toward her, purposely knocking her flat on her back.

I surged to my feet, ready to rush to her protection. Jon, sensing my intentions, grasped—the only part of me within reach—my injured ankle. Instantly, I halted all forward motion as excruciating pain shot up my leg. Falling forward with a grunt, I stared in horror as the logone stood over *Lisa*, its mouth open and fangs bared. Then, to my utter amazement, it began sniffing and licking her face, with its stubby tail wagging wildly. *Lisa* wriggled, squirmed, and laughed hysterically in return, encouraging the logone to offer more of the same.

Laying on my stomach, my body pointing down the embankment, with Jon still hanging on to my very tender ankle, I looked blindly back in his direction. "A tame logone… named… *Sam*?" I asked incredulously.

Jon released my ankle and simply began laughing at the oddity of it all. "I guess it must be, Niki, but… *Sam*? Why couldn't they come up with a better name than, *Sam*? 'Tis a very silly name to pronounce. It falls not gently from the tongue, but rather plops off and lands… splat on the ears. And that logone is definitely not a silly looking beast."

I started laughing harder. To my shame, I laughed so loudly that the logone heard me. Suddenly, it became focused solely on protecting its dwelling and its people. With a deep and low woof, it charged at us with teeth bared and hackles raised.

"Sam, come back here!" Lisa yelled. *"Leave them alone, they aren't bothering you!"*

Sam paid her neye heed. Jon, having neye choice, gave *Sam* a second taste of his power. The jolt tore through its charging body, tossing the animal backward and tumbling it down the embankment. Giving a heartfelt yelp, *Sam* turned and ran back to *Lisa*, trying to tuck his stubby tail between his legs. There, sitting protectively in front of her, *Sam* leaned against the nikca needing to receive a bit of comfort from her.

Lisa looked at the logone—who, when he sat was nearly the same height as she—and shook her head from side to side as she stroked his head. *"Tsk, tsk, tsk,"* she reprimanded, sounding very much like a scolding mother or Thaytor, I nearly chuckled again, *"Well, that should teach you, you bad ole dog."* She bent over and spoke directly into his tip-tilted ear, still stroking his head, *"I'm sure they're very nice people… if you don't go around trying to bite them."*

I looked at myself, and then at Jon. I was afraid one of us had accidentally dropped our shield of invisibility. I could neye more see myself or Jon than I could the air around us. Yet it was obvious this Tenzenar nikca was able to see both of us even when we weren't able see each other. I suddenly felt chilled to the bone and sick to my stomach.

"Master," I whispered, checking again to make certain my shield was in place, "how can she know we're here? Why aren't we invisible to her? You can't see me, can you?"

"Neye, Niki, I can't see you," he murmured, his voice troubled. "Whatever the reason… it is clear that we are visible to her, and that makes it ghea teepin to remain here discussing it. Come, let's get back to camp… and quickly. You should be feeling the strain of holding your shield this long, anyway." He grasped blindly for my elbow and helped me to my feet.

I leaned heavily on him, as we hurried back, but said ghea neye about my pain. At camp, we told the guards all we'd seen and learned at the Tenzenar dwelling. Following our mid-meal, Scaun prepared to return to New Malin and share with Father and Met Lordship the news I had acquired. Jon told the guard that he need not try and return to us because we would also soon be on our way home. Once he talked with Father and the High King, Scaun was to return to the Oreon guard for reassignment.

I held out my hand when the Oreon guard was ready to depart, "Benna ghea arecean. Met Scaun. I've been honored by… well, your simply being able to put up with me and treating me as a forlana. Sorice leki omprice, I have learned much from you these past days," I said.

After his departure, Conden and Salitarin went hunting while Jon and I remained in camp. I went to my bed pallet and lay down, shutting my eyes to everything around me. Jon, as troubled as I, busied himself by straightening the already neat camp. The Tenzenar, *Lisa*, had greatly disturbed our thoughts.

"How could she have seen us sitting on that embankment?" I asked Keyenoa in my thoughts as I struggled to recapture the aclusceaun I'd lost. Heaving a deep sigh, I rolled over. "Keyenoa, there is neye denying that she is very much like us because of her joy and openness. Actually, I could not see any of the harsh lifelessness in any of the Tenzenar where *Lisa* lives as I had seen in the people streaming off that lunata. Why didn't I see it? And why did I see You? There is an openness to the nikca's heart, where You are seen so clearly. Your presence is just barely visible in her parents, but it is also there… and these are parents who—if I understood correctly and I am certain I did—spoke of You with honor and respect and affection, as if You lived in them as well.

"Keyenoa, how is it that *Lisa* can see Jon and me? And why is it that she was the only one able to see us? By the way, sorice leki omprice that neye other than *Lisa* saw me… not even the boy. Tella saa, Keyenoa, show me why this minca nikca is so different from those older than her? And why are these Tenzenar—whom I've been taught to fear—not so fearsome… or different from us?"

I squirmed uncomfortably, my thoughts and prayers shifting with me. "Keyenoa, why is it that all I've been taught of these people contrasts with what I saw? Father above all father's, I saw their capacity for Keyen and their true belief in You. Oh, their name for you was different, but I know they spoke of You… and neye other. Tell me, Keyenoa, te salma, how a people who feel Keyen and speak of You with honor are able to kill and destroy so much that is Yours? This Keyenoa, I don't understand neye matter how hard I try. How can two such opposite attitudes coexist in one being, and how can You live in a being of such opposites?"

I rolled again. Staring at the green mist of leaves above me, I confessed my impatience. I didn't want to put aside my questions and wait for Keyenoa to reveal the answers in His taun. My soul burned with a need to know. And this also frightened me because I had never before felt such a straining and tearing impatience and confusion. As I confessed these things to Keyenoa, I wondered if my unnatural impatience was bred by these strange, yet similar people. Keyenoa quietly urged me to simply and honestly give them into His care. I needed to remember to trust… if I could do neye more.

My sense of aclusceaun restored, I rose from my pallet and began to help around the camp, thinking as minca about the Tenzenar as I could. I so wanted to trust that Keyenoa would bring the answers I sought.

It was later in the night when my mind refused to allow me to sleep. With ghea neye but darkness to occupy my mind, I could neye longer turn my thoughts from the Tenzenar as I believed Keyenoa wanted me to do. Then, laying my assumptions out before Keyenoa, I realized He wanted me to understand these people so I could help my own people to live with these beings on Airies. However, He didn't want me frightened of them or the truth I had come to know where these Tenzenar were concerned. Keyenoa urged me to talk to Jon.

I moved in the direction of the neglected fire, hoping there'd be a few embers to keep me warm as I contemplated waking my Thaytor. I carefully stumbled past the two sleeping guards, and sat wearily on the log in front of the fire. There were only a few coals glowing deep in the center of the fire making the darkness of the night seem impenetrable.

"Well, Met Fortulaynan, what keeps thee from slumber on this dark night?"

I jumped, staring hard across the fire pit trying to find my Thaytor. There was only the blackness of the night to greet me. For a moment, I wondered if I were imagining voices where none existed.

"Thee are not hearing things, Niki," Jon chuckled. "'Tis the black clothes I wear. They are an arecean in the darkness. Even the sharpest Airian eye cannot discern them from the night... unless I wish otherwise." Raising his head slowly, he revealed his face.

"How was it you saw me, Master?" I asked curiously.

"The silver fur of the neron lox gives thee away. Thy clothes set thee aglow even in the blackest of nights." His formal speech had grown heavier with every word, telling me that he was deeply troubled.

"Master, what so plights thy mind that thee find sleep as hard to find as I have?" I asked, slipping into his same speech patterns.

"I believe, Niki," he smiled, "I asked thee first."

"I think, Jon, our troubles are the same... a minca Tenzenar named *Lisa*?"

"*Lisa*. Ta. Our speech always gives us away, Niki, when our minds won't rest," he murmured.

He hadn't been aware he was speaking so formally until I had begun to emulate him. I smiled, comfortable with the fact that Jon and I were very much alike.

"Master, how could the nikca have known we were there? How could she have seen us, when we couldn't even see each other? What makes her different from the older Tenzenar, and so like us in spirit? I need to know these things, Master! I know I'll not find sleep this night, until I make some sense of this."

Jon smiled slowly. "I have been sitting here most of this night, struggling desperately for a few answers concerning her ability to see us... and now discover you've had the answer all along!"

I stared at him thinking his mind had snapped.

"Just listen... and stay quiet," he added, aware of my tendency to interrupt him incessantly. "I'm not sure how well I can explain this." Stepping over the fire, he straddled the log beside me and held my gaze as he began his story. "Many, many eatas ago, at the time the Tenzenar first became known to us, we had a High King whose powers were so vast they spanned the universe. He was urged by Keyenoa to search the stars with his thoughts. When he did so, Keyenoa directed his gaze to these people flying among the stars in their lunatas. The High King, sensing that they might someday find their way to Airies, felt compelled to learn more about these beings. So this High King remained in one of the towers of Oreon for many, many aanas, watching these people who lived trillions of terons away. He slept minca and ate erratically, spending every free oona focused on these beings.

"As the aanas passed, the other Kings began to realize that Met Lordship was allowing his care for Airies to slip. So they went to Oreon to urge their High King to come from his tower and tell them what he'd learned. Reluctantly, he came down, staying only long enough to tell them all he'd seen. The things Met Lordship told his Kings have been etched somewhere on the walls inside Oreon and have also been passed down through the telling of his story as I am doing now. It's a tale that should never be overlooked, Niki, for deep in its telling is a warning to all Airians concerning obsession.

"These people, which Met Lordship called Tenzenar, had begun to explore the stars and planets, first they did so by using huge machines that enabled them to see other worlds close up. Then they began sending lunatas out to other worlds in great hopes of finding some sort of life. But neye life was found close to their home. So they continued to build more of these machines, making them larger and grander, enabling them to see even farther into space. They also began creating other machines that transmitted sound waves out among the stars, hoping to hear an answer back. As they waited for a reply, more lunatas, larger and farther reaching were built and sent out. They even began to build dwellings in space around their world, spreading them like stepping stones deeper and farther out into space.

"When Met Lordship discovered this, he then turned his focus from their doings and on to the Tenzenar themselves. He wisely realized that because of their relentless push into space and desire for discovery that they could someday find their way to Airies. He knew his people had to know what kind of beings these Tenzenar were and what to do if this invasion happened.

"The High King had quickly learned how these Tenzenar prided themselves on their knowledge of making powerful machines—so much so that their world was filled with a massive assortment. Tenzenar spent their time on the pursuit of things and machines, caring minca for each other and Keyenoa. The people were divided and their lands also. Niki, the High King learned that they even killed their own kind for the sole purpose of gaining more land and machines. Tenzenar seem to fear everything they don't understand, and what they least understand is their own kind. When our High King watched them, it became apparent that their selfishness and greed drove them to destroy anything and anyone who dared step in the way of what they desired, especially Keyenoa.

"Because of this, Met Lordship recognized that they were actually destroying themselves and their world with their selfish pursuits. He knew that unless the Tenzenar changed, they would continue to search out other worlds that contained and sustained life, conquer that world, move in and begin to destroy all life there. This destruction, while it might not be done intentionally but through the senseless use of their machines and the feeding of their own greed, fear, and selfishness, there would still be ghea neye left to take or fight over."

Jon fell silent, and I struggled with a feeling of great regret for these people he had described. I still couldn't understand what answer I had given him or how my questions had much to do with his story. Jon was so lost in thought I'd become forgotten along with his reasons for telling the story.

"Master," I waited until he met my gaze, "Toenda sorice, I don't understand. What has this to do with *Lisa*, how she saw us, or why she's so different from the older Tenzenar?"

He smiled with chagrin. "Toenda Niki, I will explain. When this High King left the Kings, he returned to his tower high in Oreon and focused his thoughts on the nikca. He had become obsessed with these beings and was deeply concerned over their destiny as well as what would happen when they came into contact with us. He hoped the nikca might, when they grew, change their own destiny. It wasn't long before the High King became thoroughly obsessed with them. He had such hope because the nikca seemed so different from older Tenzenar. They were happy, free of distrust and full of Keyen. Met Lordship began calling them minca Airians because they seemed so very much like us. In their innocence and lack of worries, the nikca seemed to radiate with the joy of Keyenoa in their hearts.

"Just as his hope for these people blossomed, he discovered that as the nikca grew older, they became as cruel, selfish and destructive as their parents—if not more so. Despondent, he mourned for these people and their nikca. He realized, in the taun to come, they would not only destroy themselves but many other beings which they would encounter on their explorations. The High King remained in his tower, weeping and grieving for many days before the orate sent word to the other Kings concerning this development. When the Kings returned to Oreon, they broke into the tower and carried the High King out—he was by then too weak to leave on his own. Met Lordship lay in his bed a few scant days, telling the Kings everything he'd learned, while they fought desperately to keep him alive. Due to his lack of food and sleep combined with the grief he suffered over these people, he had lost the will to live. He passed in Sontall a few onas after completing his story to the Kings about the Tenzenar and their nikca."

Jon's voice was heavy with grief, "He kept telling the Kings: 'They don't listen to their nikca, who, for so minca a time, walk with Keyenoa in their hearts, but with the example of their parents, they follow what they are taught and walk away from the hope they had.'"

The gentle rustle of the leaves and the forest night noises that mingled with the slumbering sounds of the guards were all we heard for several onas. Pondering Jon's story, I wasn't sure I understood what it had to do with *Lisa*'s differences.

I looked at him. "Master, are you saying, she is different because she is young?" I asked.

"Ta, mostly. Maybe it also has a minca to do with a person's gifts, talents, and abilities. Perhaps, Keyenoa gave minca *Lisa* a gift of greater sight."

Cocking my head to one side, suddenly curious, I watched him closely. It wasn't like Jon to be so quiet after finishing a story of such importance. Normally, he would question me thoroughly on the many hidden lessons within it. There was something more to this story that he was reluctant to reveal.

"Master," I said with just the right amount of innocence, "Why haven't I heard this story before?"

"It's a story all Airians would rather not tell. This High King was one of the greatest and most ghea Keyen High Kings in our history. Yet, because of his obsession with the Tenzenar, he forgot his own people and passed in Sontall when he was but nineteen aanas of age."

"Nineteen? Jon, how could he have passed at nineteen when you said he had studied the Tenzenar for many, many aanas?"

"He was nineteen aanas, by his aging, Niki, but he'd been High King for five hundred aanas as you and I count them. You see, because of his vast amount of power, he aged one aana for five hundred aanas of our lives.

"Do you remember how I told you about Met Lordship High King Sayleen Cantabo, and that he is actually two hundred fourteen aanas old by our aanas, but by his, he's only one hundred?" I nodded and he continued, "Well, simply put, it was the same with this High King... but because his power was so very much stronger, he aged more slowly than Met Lordship High King Sayleen Cantabo."

I stared at my feet, while Jon watched me. I had learned more of the story but knew he still hadn't shared all there was to it. Looking up at his silhouette in the darkness, I decided to question him point blank.

"So, Master, what was the name of this High King?"

He smiled, his teeth reflecting the iridescent glow from my tunic in the darkness. "I didn't mention it because I was afraid you might choose to follow in his place," he replied.

NIKITA'S STORY

"Why would I think myself to Sontall? Master, have I ever been the thinking kind of Airian?"

"Neye, but thinking wasn't what killed him, obsession was. And why I am worried is because his name was Nikita Seylong Anliegh. Niki, he was your great-great-grand uncle. You were named after him, along with your mother, father, and your father's father. I've been long afraid if you knew your uncle's story, you'd close your mind to all else and live as he did. You're fully aware that such things have happened before in our history, and in this case, it be not something any of us want for you, as you have a tendency to become obsessed with something to the point of acting upon it without thinking it over first." He leaned forward, placing a hand on my shoulder. "Niki, always remember you were first named after your mother, and that you carry a second name, Markain, a name of strength, life, and loyalty."

I nodded, taking his concern seriously. I was aware how names and their personal history did seem to repeat themselves on Airies. "I understand, Jon. Father honored me with two names, hoping I would care deeply for all peoples, like my uncle, but also be strong in wisdom and choose to live my life to the fullest." I silently wondered why Father had also given me the name of my mother but dared not ask. I had yet to talk about her with anyone.

"Come, master," Jon purposely used the title with teasing affection, as always putting a smile on my face. "I believe we have had enough with questions and talk for now. The sun is rising and we've not as yet slept as all things should. Let us retire to our beds and sleep during this short time before true day. It will be a benna taun to ponder all we've discussed this night."

⌘ ⌘ ⌘ ⌘

I woke slowly, pulled from a deep sleep by the increasing warmth of a new day. When I crawled from under the low gungas branches, I discovered it was near midday. Except for my Thaytor, the camp was empty. He sat close to the fire watching me instead of our mid-meal warming over the flickering flames. Aware of his speculative attention I joined him by the fire.

"Where are Conden and Salitarin?" I asked, watching the fire.

"I sent them to Dreamer's Lake and Malinieum City. Understandably, they were eager to go and I hadn't the heart to turn them down. You and I didn't need any more of the tension we Airians seem to gather when around the Tenzenar, and to be honest, Niki, I was simply too tired to consider another trek." He leaned forward to stir the pot bubbling over the fire before looking back at me. "Do you mind?"

I thought about all we'd been through and weighed it against my desire to see Malinieum City. "Neye, Master, I think I'm relieved that the guards have gone rather than you and I. I don't think my ankle could have tolerated the long walk. And neye matter how badly I would like to see my old home, I've had my fill of Tenzenar. Their strange ways and their machines have an equally strange effect on our emotions. Have you noticed that?" I asked, watching the flames flicker hypnotically before my eyes, not wanting to look at Jon.

He sighed with relief as he gathered up our waiting plates and filled them with food. "Ta, now that you mention it, you are right." He glanced at me sharply before turning back to his chore as he continued talking to me. "I think we'll be going home as soon as our two adventurous guards return. I estimate it should be neye later than ten days from today." He began to laugh rather hollowly, "Though Tenzenar are sometimes hard to understand, they really are rather uncomplicated beings. With the exception of discovering what has been done with Malinieum City, we have acquired the information we set out to learn. I see neye need to remain here any longer." He passed me my meal with a rueful grin, "Therefore… I hope you agree that the wisest thing you and I could do would be to remain in Dindieum until the guards return."

I chuckled at his not so subtle statement. "I can't help thinking that we'll be leaving with more questions than we came to learn, but honestly, Master, I am eager to separate myself from the uneasiness that has settled on me like a fraw-nall since our arrival here," I murmured, before lowering my head and ghea leki Keyenoa for the meal.

Glancing at me from over his plate, his eyes intently watchful for a long moment, he said ghea neye of what he was thinking. Following his example, I put my own questions aside with a shrug of my shoulders and began eating.

⌘⌘⌘⌘

To our surprise, Conden and Salitarin returned late in the evening five short days after their departure. Aware of the guards' shock and exhaustion, we quickly fed them while keeping our questions at bay until they were ready to offer some answers. As they ate, they calmed and began to tell their story. Jon and I listened eagerly to their experiences. Salitarin, the more articulate storyteller, told of their experiences, while Conden interjected periodically.

"When we left camp, we decided to leave the path and enter the forest before nearing the Tenzenar construction area and *road*, but as we neared the construction site we only heard the usual forest sounds. After some discussion we went to investigate...."

"Three Tenzenar males were there. The massive machines were lifeless. It didn't look to us as though anyone planned to use them for some time," Conden interjected, sending a smile of apology to Salitarin.

Ignoring him, Salitarin continued, "We decided to listen in, hoping to discover what was happening. These men—who called themselves *surveyors*—were discussing their plans to travel deeper into Dindieum to look over the land. While we weren't able to discover how far they planned to go, we did learn that the machines would be halted for at least seven days following another day of this *weekend* you told us about, Niki." Salitarin paused, his expression suddenly haunted. "The rest of our story is not as easy to tell, Master Alcone," he spoke directly to Jon, "in our ignorance concerning Tenzenar, we did many ghea-teepin and dangerous things."

Conden interjected quickly, "Niki, toenda omprice sorice. All this time, Salitarin and I condemned your behavior, thinking we would be much wiser in our actions around these beings than you. I cannot tell you how wrong we were."

Salitarin nodded with emphatic agreement and then continued his tale, "After looking over the dwelling near here and its Tenzenar, we traveled slowly south noting the many changes made to Malin. To put it mildly, Master Alcone, all we saw made us very uneasy. Everything you, Niki, and Scaun described concerning your journeys were difficult for us to envision... until we saw it ourselves."

Salitarin looked at me. "We discovered the purpose of the strange-looking machine you described resting in its own private dwelling beside the larger dwelling, Lord Nikita. They're used for holding Tenzenar in them and zooming along their *roads* at unheard of speeds. This gets their occupants from place to place in a great hurry. Conden even learned the Tenzenar called these machines... *thacar*."

"I'd rather leave the tale of that discovery up to Salitarin... but later, forlana, much later," Conden said while he shuddered with dread.

"Okay, I'll explain—but later—like you said, much later!" Salitarin agreed, his eyes glazing with fear. "The first three days we followed as near to the *road* as we dared, and the closer we got to Dreamer's Lake, the more *roads* we found. These *roads* traverse the ground in all directions like slime trails of some large noxious beast. The number of dwellings also increased—like so much mold feeding off decay—the dwellings looked as if they'd sprung up suddenly overnight." Salitarin shivered with revulsion. "Well, enough of that," he muttered concerning his morbid descriptions before continuing his story. "Most of the dwellings are tall, with windows laid out in neat rows, square in shape, and made of wood. There were Tenzenar everywhere, zooming along in their *thacars*, scurrying along the streets or moving about inside their dwellings... there was neye place we could go to escape them.

NIKITA'S STORY

"When dusk fell on the fourth night, Conden and I reached the Tenzenar city. Fearing all we saw, we... well, we ran through much of it in a panic, searching for a place to hide. We chanced on a group of large tang bushes, outside the main part of this city and crawled among them. There we slept fitfully till dawn."

"That's when we really saw the city and decided to turn back and have a look," Conden said as Salitarin gathered his thoughts to continue.

"I don't think even the High King would believe it, Master Alcone... unless he saw it with his own eyes. There were buildings stacked four to twenty levels high, built square, with harsh, sharp angled planes and windows all in rows. Learons separated one building from another, and each building looked exactly like its neighbor. Some were built so tall they blocked out the sun, shadowing the ground with fearsome and grotesque shapes. We felt cold and frightened, and longed only to reach Malinieum City...."

"But by that time, we had lost our bearings and couldn't seem to find our way out of the grey forest of buildings. Each time we were certain we traveled in the right direction, we found later we had still walked the wrong way," Conden interrupted, giving us a clear idea of their fearful dilemma and their growing panic.

Glaring at him, Salitarin continued with his story, "When we were able to find our way to Malinieum City, we learned—like everything else outside Dindieum—the city is neye longer ours. They've built their horrible dwellings right to the edge of Malinieum forest, surrounding and taking over Dreamer's Lake. Behind Malinieum's walls there were at least a hundred Tenzenar digging and scraping, desperately trying to discover all they can of us and our history—most particularly the cause of our sudden disappearance."

"Niki's right. They believe we've all passed in Sontall through some horrible holocaust... but they're confused because they cannot find any *burial sites* that would hold the remains of our bodies," Conden murmured in confusion.

Jon chuckled, "Tenzenar don't turn to dust when they reach Sontall. Instead they take hundreds of aanas to return to the earth

PART I TENZENAR

from which they come," he explained, clarifying the humor he had found in the Tenzenar's dilemma and Conden's confusion.

After a few enas of quiet chuckling, Salitarin continued, "While wandering through Malinieum City we discovered—by pure accident—a strange bit of information, which prompted us to return to camp as soon as we could. When we had made it to Castle Loreann we discovered a Tenzenar man standing there. He was staring hopelessly at the symbols on the fountain. Another man approached him, and disturbing the first man's concentration, he excitedly told the first man that they had managed to complete a *road* all the way to another Airian city. Together these two men began to make plans for an exploration of this new city's interior. We tried to discover which city they had found, but they have neye idea how to read our symbols and so still don't even know the name of Malinieum City."

"Knowing that Lord Markain and Met Lordship needed the information we'd gathered, Salitarin and I chose to return here as quickly as we could," Conden interrupted then seemed to turn slightly green.

Salitarin, though irritated with all the interruptions, took pity on Conden's suddenly green expression and quickly explained why the guard had turned green. "We arrived here in such an unbelievable amount of time because Conden recognized the man who resides in the dwelling near here. We saw him standing near the gates of Malinieum City, talking to a young boy—we think was his son. When the man opened a door to his *thacar*, Conden impulsively grabbed my arm and climbed into the machine after the boy. We were so concerned about the news we received that neither of us thought about what we were doing. By Keyenoa's great and mighty power, it was a horrifying ride! And that's all I'll say about it! I've neye wish to relive that experience ever again, even in my memories!"

While Salitarin shuddered and turned a strange color of green himself, Conden sheepishly provided a minca more information, "I happened to learn the machine's name when the man called to his boy to, *'Get in thacar.'* That's also what made me think to climb in as well." He paused a moment, his teasing spirit quickly recovering, "I just couldn't let Niki have all the adventures and be the only one to make kutated mistakes, could I?" he asked with a twinkle in his eye. Then sobering, he shook his head, "If ever there is a next time, I plan to leave all the kutated mootan actions to Niki alone. I never wish to do anything as impulsively teepin as that again," he added with determination.

"There will be neye more kutated actions by Niki, either!" Jon exclaimed. "We are leaving at dawn." This caused each of us to laugh, fully aware that leaving was the only way to guarantee I'd discover neye further trouble with the Tenzenar.

As the silence of the night fell over the camp, Jon sighed. Setting his hands on his knees, he rose from his place by the fire. "Well… that's it then," as he spoke, his worries seemed to drop from him as though they were dust. "We head home in the morning to tell Lord Malin of our discoveries. He'll know what's to be done in response to all our news… if that is, anything can be done."

Chapter VI

What Is Love?

"Teepin is the man who gives his heart away while his eyes are closed."
—The Book of Keyenoa

Four nights later, long after moon's rise, our company made it back to New Malin. It was too late to speak with Father and not wanting our time together to end so suddenly, we spent the night under the roof of my tree-home. Within the oona of dawn Jon woke us all. Following a hurried meal of dried fruit and nuts found in my defacka, we left for Kingstree, Father's home.

Sitting in his massive chair in his hall of audiences, Father listened attentively to all we had to say, his face grim and unhappy. Needing to know if our travels had done any benna for our people, we asked him—rather boldly—what would be done concerning the Tenzenar's encroachment into Dindieum.

"I must take your news to Met Lordship. The Tenzenar are beyond my control... even when it comes to the land I once ruled. Wait in Nikita's home, I'll come to you there and gladly share Met Lordship's plans."

Oonas following final meal in the clearing, Father arrived at my home as promised. Taking a seat in one of my mainroom chairs, he told us of Met Lordship's decisions.

"Within a day's time, all I'm about to tell you will have begun," Father said with a weary sigh. "The Fifth Kingdom, Lord Palona Cetar's, and the Fourth Kingdom, Lord Alon Tarton's, have been alerted that the one of the old cities of Markainieum or Lizingham have been discovered. Because the cities are also near our new borders, and because the Tenzenar *road* to LeFold Lake will pass between Lord Palona's and my Kingdom, every Airian living within all three Kingdoms—Lord Alon's included because of Lizingham—have been instructed to set up warning systems. By using a sequence of whistles, our people will be warned if a Tenzenar enters our land. Three long, shrill whistles, at least five enas in length, shall be New Malin's warning. If such a sequence of whistles is heard, all are to immediately raise their shields of invisibility and run for the nearest shelter or hiding place. The people of New Malin will hear this directive on the morrow. Tarton and Cetar each have a strikingly different sequence of whistles, so anyone living close to the borders would know from which direction the danger was coming and run in the proper direction for shelter and safety. Also, on the morrow, my guards will be assigned rotating duty, several tuevtauns in length, to guard the borders of New Malin. Worry not this night, your assignments will be given on the morrow," he added, looking directly at Conden and Salitarin.

⌘⌘⌘⌘

Despite such changes to New Malin, being home filled me with serenity. New Malin was an allearan I had missed greatly. I hadn't been aware of how strong a sense of unrest and confusion the Tenzenar presence had placed on those of us who had traveled within their presence until I had returned home. Jon and I returned to our usual routine as the days moved on, and soon the Tenzenar memories faded from my mind.

There was neye time to spend with the three guards who had traveled with us, much to Jon's and my mutual regret. While Scaun had returned to New Malin to help train the guards in the defense of our Kingdom, he returned to Oreon swiftly after his assignment was completed. Conden and Salitarin volunteered to take the southwestern border to stand guard there for a tour of seven tuevtauns and so departed shortly after Scaun.

It was a few fortauns following our return when I found myself faced with another dilemma. I was sitting in the clearing an oona or two after midday, and Jon was retelling the stories and legends of one of our past heroes. He was teaching me the importance of several virtues, instructing me concerning the use of such qualities—if I were to become King. While in the middle of the well-known story of our first High King Valcree Metlan Sontall, I became so noticeably restless and inattentive that even Jon fell silent to look at me sharply.

"Do you want to explain what has you all fidgety this day, Niki?" he asked in exasperation. "You've had difficulty keeping your body still and your mind on business all morning. What be troubling thee so, young master?"

Unwilling to answer, I lowered my gaze looked toward the grass, "I'd like to go walking someplace and just think, Jon… if that would be all right with you?"

"Do you wish to think alone, or to me?"

"Alone," I whispered.

"All right, Niki. I understand your need for taun and will not deny you," he reassured me. "Each of us has such a need to work things out for ourselves first, it's ghea neye to feel ashamed about." He held my shoulder gently, pulling my attention to his deep, black gaze. "But remember, you can come to me with anything and I'll be ready to listen and help. I'll not let you down, I swear this to you." He released my shoulder as he stood. "Come to my home when you've had enough of solitude. Tomorrow is your day of birth and we've the matter of your celebrations to discuss," he added with a smile.

"Leki, Jon," I said, taking my leave of him.

I wanted to discover a new path which would challenge me and so possibly divert my thoughts. There was a trail that remained on the clearing side of the stream and looked as though it would take me north along the Broken Dindieum River in the direction of Oreon and the main part of LeFold Lake. Knowing I had not taken this path before, I decided to follow it.

I quickly turned west, then south away from the inhabited gungas trees and soon found myself traveling along in twisting turns beneath the canopy of uninhabited gungas and tezzar trees. It wasn't long before I gave my surroundings minca acknowledgment. I was, by then, deep in thought.

"Tomorrow I'll be sixteen aanas old," I said quietly to Keyenoa. "Two more aanas before I'm to be a man." Lifting my eyes to Alleanne, I revealed my agony in my expression. "Then why do women interest me now, Daddan? It's not right to feel as I do! Jon has explained—until I think my ears will fall off—when such feelings for women are expected to blossom and change. And that is always after Con Sona Eata. Keyenoa, you have made this a fact of life for all Airian men. I shouldn't be having these feelings now! I've two or three aanas to wait before Con Sona Eata... yet here I am declaring to You, Keyenoa-mine, that I find one particular woman oh so incredibly desirable."

My prayer was disturbed by the lonely cry of a theron. Looking up, I watched the magnificent animal fly overhead before disappearing within the trees. His breast was sun-yellow, his head blood-red and his top notch a royal purple all blazed brilliantly in the intermittent sunlight. His magnificent wings nearly spanned my height, and burst with colors of yellow, red, and purple as the sun kissed them through the gaps in the trees. His long, scissor-like tail caught and held my gaze. In awe, I stood frozen, watching as the length sailed past my seeking eyes. If I had dared to reach out, I could've touched the tail's feather-softness. For a moment, I wondered why we Airians marveled over these creatures when we raised them for eggs and food, and so made them quite a common sight.

"This creature though, has lived many aanas in this forest before his eyes beheld the sight of a single Airian... or an Airian beheld the sight of him," I said to myself and Keyenoa, answering my own question as I moved on.

The river babbled noisily beside me, while the trees seemed to whisper to each other in the breeze about the disturbed prince who walked alone among them. Unwilling to ponder my dilemma, I paid closer attention to the path and its direction. It had turned west, south, east, and north. The further I walked, the more curious I became about the path and my destination. With time, as I continued my walk, the river neye longer babbled along, but roared at my side as if suddenly in a great hurry to complete its journey. The trail continued to follow the river, twisting and turning in all directions, seemingly having neye more end than the rushing water beside it.

Stopping, I put my hands on my hips, aware that despite the twists and turns, I was heading mostly north toward the lake. "But I should've reached the LeFold Lake long before now," I said, not caring if anyone was around to hear me talking to myself.

Shrugging my shoulders I gave the matter neye further thought. The trail would have to end somewhere, and I was now determined to discover where that would be, so I continued to follow it. As I rounded a curve, I found a rock pinnacle, as black as Jon's powerful eyes, several pearons ahead placed in the center of the path. Beyond the pinnacle, I could see the vast expanse of LeFold Lake shimmering in the sun. Spurred on, I picked up my pace. It looked as though all land ended where the spire stood, leaving ghea neye beyond it but air and the water of the lake several pearons below.

As I reached the rock pinnacle I discovered that the stream beside me tumbled wildly over a cliff. Walking cautiously forward, I looked between the spire and the waterfall and discovered a twenty four learon drop to the base of the cliff and the sand at the lake's edge.

Examining the pinnacle, I realized that it had been formed over many aanas when the stream had been wider and the water had been forced to surge around it with great force as it fell over the cliff. The pinnacle was made of a vein of a stronger and denser rock that withstood the water's force while the softer stone around it eroded away. On closer examination, I discovered that it was connected to the cliff's edge and had crudely carved gouges cut into its surface. The gouges spiraled around the outside of the black stone all the way to the beach below. Smiling, realizing they were crudely carved steps, I put a hand against the side of the pinnacle and took the steps down to the lakeshore.

As my worries once again surfaced to the forefront of my mind, I sat on the sun-warmed sand near the lake's edge and continued my prayer to Keyenoa. "It isn't all women that I find attractive, just one. So I keep telling myself that I've neye need to get so un-hinged by my feelings.… Oh, Keyenoa, who am I kidding? It doesn't matter what I tell myself—I am un-hinged! I even asked Sornan what he thought of her when he and his father visited. And all Sornan said was that while Te'air was nice looking, she was not nearly as beautiful as Beblina Aaleyen. Then he even went on to explain that he couldn't understand what made Lady Beblina so great!

"Keyenoa, even I have heard how everyone goes on about Lady Beblina's beauty, claiming she is the most beautiful woman on Airies. I thought Sornan was just, You know, talking big, so I asked him how he could judge Beblina's beauty against anyone else's when he hadn't even seen the lady. Then, he told me he'd met Beblina when he and his father visited New Letark before coming to New Malin for a visit.

"Oh, but it gets worse, Keyenoa. Sornan then went on to tell me he had enough of talking about women, asking me, 'What was great about any of them, anyway?' He changed the subject quickly, pressing me for information about Tenzenar. Well, from all that, even I could tell it was obvious that he wasn't interested in girls… and he's an aana older than me! So what is wrong with me? What is it I'm supposed to do?!" I cried out, putting my hands over my face as her name echoed in my mind, taunting me with my desire. "Oh, Te'air, what makes me think of thee always?" I moaned into my hands.

'All right, Niki, think!' I ordered myself silently. 'You feel this way, and neye matter how hard you try to forget her, you still want her… and neye matter how differently you want it to be, your feelings for her are not going to change… so why worry about it?

'That's it! What's the use in worrying myself fraw about how I feel, when it changes ghea neye? I'll simply accept that I feel what I feel and go on. It's not necessary to speak with Jon about it. Actually, it'd be pointless. I mean there's ghea neye he can do about my feelings... any more than I can. Ta, I'll keep my feelings for Te'air to myself. I don't need Jon teasing me about them the way he teased Conden about his feelings for... whatever-her-name-was. Neye, Keyenoa! I couldn't handle it if Jon teased me about Te'air!' Certain I had made the right decision, I stood intending to follow the lake shore toward home.

Just as I turned... there she was, carrying a bunch of tiny flowers in her hand. Oh, but she was beautiful, so fragile and delicately female. Her hair was the color of sun-bleached sand shimmering with life in the heat of the day. It seemed to caress her cheeks then rested lightly on her shoulders before spilling in gentle curls down her back. She had soft-blue flowers woven among the silken strands of her hair that matched the color of her large, innocent eyes. Her face, so fair and petal-soft, was graced with lips enticingly kissable and as red as a keya fruit just before picking. Her cheeks were blushed with just a touch of pink from the sun and the breeze.

She wore a cropped top handmade from tiny, dried, flower petals of dusty blue. It was drawn up and around her shoulders from across her back to tie in the front. Her waist was bare, causing my hands to tingle with the need to caress her flesh. Her skirt, made from blue and pink flower petals, draped just below her waist on one side and angled down with careless abandon to rest a furon above her thigh on the other. The skirt was full, draping in even waves around her, ending just below her knees in a perfectly even line of cloth. Her tiny feet were unshod and barely depressed the soft sand where she stood only ten pearons away.

I stared at her, mouth gaping. She was never aware of me, but she seemed always to be somewhere nearby. To her, I was neye more than an unseen spirit or an unimportant nematoe buzzing irritatingly close at hand. I remained terrified to even strike up a conversation with her, while my obsession with her had been building since my return to New Malin. Every time I saw her my tongue seemed to grow fat and my mind would go blank, while my body simply seemed to get spastic inside.

I was certain that if I did not escape Te'air's presence immediately I would do something to embarrass myself. Frantically, I looked around for a way out. Immediately, I saw the path that followed the lake shore... but going that way would force me to walk right by her. Afraid I would manage to trip over my own feet and push Te'air into the lake, I knew I had to find another way. Turning, I was confronted by the waterfall. Feeling my hopes dashed, a voice in my head shouted triumphantly, "Climb the pinnacle! Just go back the way you came, you mootan!"

Striving for every lestna of nonchalance I possessed, I scuffed my boot into the sand, while smoothly turning toward the pinnacle. Then offering an audible sigh, I ambled to the stairs and began my climb. All the while, I prayed that my actions seemed normal to the woman below... Te'air.

An oona later I returned to the clearing. Several women were bustling about, working on prepairing the evening meal. Remembering my promise to Jon, I hurried through the clearing aware he must have been growing concerned over my long absence. I found him sitting in the mainroom of his tree-home watching the open door, waiting for me.

"What happened to you, young master? Did you mean to walk so long?" he asked calmly, though concern remained shadowed in his eyes.

"I took a new path and didn't realize how long a walk it was," I answered quietly as I sat comfortably at his feet. "Jon, why do you call me master, when that's what I call you? How is it we both can be masters when we're referring to each other?" I asked, really wanting to know while at the same time hoping to divert him from his next question.

I was successful.

He smiled, his eyes glittering like black starlight. "You are my master because I serve you with my life while teaching and advising you. Yet you are bound to me by the Keyenoa areceta

Thaytoric bond between us, needing all that I can give. I'm your servant as much as you're mine, Niki, because that's the way Keyenoa so wills it to be. Each of us has the right to call the other 'master,' while neither of us has the right to think of ourselves as being a master over the other. We are to be servants to all and masters over none, as it says in Keyenoa's book."

I set my hand on his leg. His words touched my heart, warming me to my soul, doing far more than I hoped when I had questioned him. My deep Keyen and respect for him welled to the surface, and as our eyes met, his Keyen and power touched me with gentle strength, cementing that bond he had mentioned even further.

"Do you wish to tell me of your problem so I may help?" he asked, holding my gaze.

I fidgeted, desperate to tell him, yet still feared his teasing. Suddenly, I was also afraid that by telling him, he'd pull away from me as a forlaynan and Thaytor because I was strange and different.

"It's ghea neye, Jon," I murmured, lowering my eyes to keep him from seeing my castrin.

Jon leaned back in his chair, his attention wandering to the window panel behind me, as he chuckled lightly. "If I didn't know better, I'd believe it was a very pretty girl which has you all flustered," he commented, laughing quietly.

My head shot up and my mouth fell open. I was unable to hide my shock and surprise and so began to blink wide-eyed at him. My stomach lurched painfully, and my heart felt as though it were pounding its way out of my chest. Jon, seeing my reaction, only laughed harder. Gaping at him, I was sure my fears had come true... Jontair Alcone was laughing at my Keyen for a woman. Almost ready to pop up and curse him for his callousness... I realized that my assumption was wrong. Jon's expression was one of innocent humor rather than malice. He had neye idea how true his comment had been. He was laughing at my expression because he believed that I was shocked and offended over the absurdity of his comment rather than its accuracy. Quickly, I looked away afraid he might realize how correct his comment actually was.

While absently picking at the sole of my boot, I struggled for some reason to justify my recent… distraction. "Actually… I was thinking about my sixteenth day of birth. As you said, it is taking place on the morrow," I murmured.

"Well… it's the truth… sort of!" I thought to Keyenoa, having heard His reprimand concerning my… prevarication. "It's not really a castrin at all. Being sixteen is definitely the wrong age for me to be thinking about women. And I was thinking I wouldn't have a problem… if I were only a few aanas older."

Jon, unaware of my thoughts and justifications to Keyenoa, leaned forward, excitement shining in his eyes. "Since you've been spending all this time dreaming up plans for your celebration, I would guess you've some rather extravagant ideas to share. Tell me, and we'll see what's possible," he urged almost boyishly. Every Airian loves a benna celebration.

Trapped, I had to think quickly and hope my ideas would satisfy him. I certainly didn't need a suspicious Thaytor while dealing with a day of birth celebration and my painful longing for Te'air.

"I'd like a big feast, with all the people of Malin… and ta, even a few people from the other Kingdoms, to be there. I want all the princes… and I guess princesses as well… to celebrate with me.

"For the meal… I'd like to have roast creasion with billons and gravy and all the trimmings… like honey bread and spiceon jelly—and of course a moreanne cake! After the feast there should be singing and dancing… for those who like that sort of thing. Oh, and of course a theron hunt for the boys! That way we won't be stuck having to listen to the singing or be forced into dancing with the princesses and such."

Jon chuckled, "I'm certain, Niki, everything you've mentioned can easily be arranged. Now, if you can forget your day of birth wishes long enough to put some food inside of you, let's go eat—I'm famished! All that talk of creasion and spiceon jelly hasn't helped much either," he teased.

We went to the clearing laughing and joking about unimportant things. For a short time, I was able to forget Te'air and my longings. Arriving at the clearing, Father signaled his request that we join him. Throughout the meal he and Jon discussed my day of birth wishes, while I listened half-heartedly and choked down my food. The minca I managed to glean from their discussion was that Father had agreed with all my wishes. At the meal's end, he winked in my direction as he asked Jon to talk with him privately in Kingstree.

Forcing down the last few bites of my food, I escaped from the meal in an agonizing rush. After making certain neye noticed me or my destination, I crossed the bridge and ran to the lake inlet. Sitting on the ornately carved bench, I let the memory of Jon sitting chest deep in the lake bring a smile to my face. The memory and smile lasted less than a moment, however. Troubled by what happened throughout the evening meal, the humoriouis image of Jon in the lake faded quickly. Looking up at the stars, I desperately tried to clear my mind of all confusion.

Te'air had served Father, Jon, and me our evening meal. I'd never been that close to her—let alone had I dared to dream it was possible. Even with her that near, she still she seemed so distant and unattainable. She never looked at me or acknowledged I was there, yet she had pressed herself against me in order to set my plate in front of me or refill my drink. And each time she walked passed or brushed her arm by my ear, the air was filled with the sweet aroma of solleeta flowers and honey. My heart had hammered throughout the meal and my breath caught in my throat, making food nearly impossible to swallow. And now, even sitting here, every time I inhaled I remembered her body pressing against my back, the slight unintentional caress as she served me, and the alluring aroma of soleta flowers filling the air.

"Oh, Keyenoa, what am I to do?" I cried out loud. "Whenever she's around I lose control of my body and mind. She's flooded my thoughts and filled my heart. Why can't I control what I feel… and why do I feel what I shouldn't? What am I to do?" I called up to Alleanne.

The only answer I heard was the lonely cry of a theron and the amfracks singing in the lake. Keyenoa would answer in His way and His taun, and so I didn't pressure Him. I remained at the lake until the chill of the night crept into my bones and the moon lifted her face above the trees. When I left the bench and turned my back to the lake, my mind was again clear and calm. I realized, just as I had earlier this day, that I couldn't run from my passions and worrying myself senseless over them was purely keezworky in itself, because my passions would remain. I discovered that all my running, questioning, and worrying was only making me miserable. Therefore, the only thing I could do was to accept my feelings.

'There is neye more I need to think about and neye reason to discuss my feelings.... Not because I fear someone's laughter, but because it would only cause them to worry over something they can't fix or change any more than I can,' I thought, firming my determination while climbing my tree-home to go to bed.

I slept better that night than I had in many nights.

Jon cheerfully woke me in the morning, "Come on, Met Lord, rise from there and greet the day," he shouted upon entering my bedchamber

Peering out from within my bundle of bed covers, I saw—and smelled—that he brought our morning meal to my tree-home. Informing me that he would wait for me in my mainroom, he left my bedchamber with our food, taking the stairs back down to the mainroom. It was the aroma of my meal, rather than Jon's sunny disposition, that pulled me from my bed to dress and join him downstairs. Together we turned my mainroom into a dining area and celebrated my sixteenth day of birth with teasing and laughter throughout the morning meal.

Full of boyish exuberance, Jon eagerly pulled me to my feet the moment I scraped the last jott-full of theron eggs into my mouth. "Now, because you're not to be anywhere near the preparations for this evening's celebration, you and I are going take a long walk in the direction of Malinieum City. We are to return only when we are certain to arrive in the clearing at nightfall. Met Lordship High King Sayleen Cantabo and your Father have requested that we go as far as time will allow, and see if we can

PART I TENZENAR

discover what progress the Tenzenar have made on their *road*," he added, his tone playfully important.

I smiled, eager to get away for at least one day from Te'air and my feelings for her. "Master," I asked, detaining him a moment, "what if the Tenzenar and their *road* are farther than a day's walk? Do we keep going, or do we set out again a few days from now to get that information?"

He shook his head. "Let's just be on our way and find out, hmm? I'm not a teepatin Niki. I'm not going to let you delay me with questions just long enough to allow you to get a peek at some of the preparations being made for your celebration." Taking my arm, he led me to the door, "Anyway, I doubt the Tenzenar are even a full day's walk from New Malin. It has been many fortauns since our first journey, and their machines are more than efficient for what they were manufactured to do. It's not unlikely that the Tenzenar and their *road* are now less than a day from New Malin."

I frowned with genuine concern.

"Though, in all truth," Jon added with a smile of delight, diverting my concern easily, "on this day, it matters not where the Tenzenar happen to be—you just need to be out of New Malin until nightfall. Now, let's go, Niki. We can always find something to do... even terons from Tenzenar."

I laughed. "But being around Tenzenar, while different and often most disconcerting, is much more fun. Come, Jon, we can't deny their ability to waste an Airian's time, now can we?" I then laughed harder, remembering some of the things Conden and Salitarin told us about during their foray to Malinieum City. "And let's not even mention the amount of their own time they waste on the worthless pursuit of acquiring things and machines—or how blatantly ignorant they are of their wasted time."

Jon laughed. "I thought you said you weren't going to mention it?"

I pulled on his arm, a teasing twinkle in my gaze. "Come on, let's have neye further delays. We need to get moving before we're caught in the preparations for my day of birth celebrations," I remarked chuckling, as I tried to lead him in the direction of the clearing. Laughing over this obvious maneuver, Jon grabbed my shoulder and turned me away from the clearing, forcing me to go around through the trees.

At the border of New Malin, the guards stopped us and explained that we both needed to raise our shields of invisibility. It was neye longer safe to travel through Dindieum any other way. The Tenzenar were very close indeed.

Leaving the outer guard post, we raised our shields and walked in silence. Our attitudes were neye longer as carefree as when we left my tree-home. The tension in the air was as real as the near silence of the creatures within the trees and the warm breeze which periodically touched our faces. With each step away from New Malin, I could not help but remember the fear and uncanny tension that had surrounded each of us on our previous journey to learn about the Tenzenar.

Eight terons south of New Malin's border we encountered the first sign of our invaders. Along the path, a few pearons into the forest on either side, a bright orange substance was garishly splashed on the trunks of the trees. The marked trees had an eerie frightful look, as though each were broken in defeat and were waiting in line for their turn to be executed. My stomach lurched, and needing a sense of security, I grasped blindly for Jon's cape needing that tangible proof of my Thaytor's presence.

"Jon, what do you think those orange marks mean?" I asked, pulling on his cape to stop him, hoping his reply wouldn't echo what I had already feared.

"They're the trees the Tenzenar plan to cut down and uproot to widen the path so they can lay their *road*." Placing his hand unerringly on my shoulder, he gave it a squeeze before letting go. "Keep your eyes alert for Tenzenar. They should be very close, if not right on top of us," he warned while we continued walking.

Like a mootan, taking him literally for a moment, I looked up into the trees. I wondered, if we were as close to the Tenzenar as Jon believed, why we hadn't heard the horrendous roar of the huge machines and the screams from the trees. About to ask him if he thought it was what the Tenzenar called a *weekend*, I heard the heavy footfall of numerous Tenzenar coming our way.

PART I TENZENAR

"Hey! You there! Get a move on!" The harsh shout came from directly ahead of us. *"Mark more of those trees. We're almost sitting on top of you. We can't halt the machines much longer. Your delays are costing us money!"*

I almost jumped out of my skin when a big, husky Tenzenar male blundered up the path in front of us. *"Get on up here you idiots! Stop worrying about the turn in the road. For [blank] sake, that's about a mile and half north of here. Now quit your stalling and get to work!"* he yelled at the Tenzenar following him.

Jon grabbed me and pulled me to the side of the path enas before several Tenzenar careened by. Each of them was grumbling something unpleasant about the man in front of them or the work they were ordered to do. After the Tenzenar were out of sight, Jon started to chuckle quietly.

"Rather sad and silly creatures, aren't they, Niki?" he whispered, aware I needed to see the tragic humor in these people, so—in spite of my fear—I would not find myself freezing up again at the wrong moment.

"Ta, Master, most especially the way they seem to enjoy their own misery," I replied. Silently, I just felt very puzzled. Why were these Tenzenar so... revolting... when the Tenzenar family in their dwelling had touched my heart with their affection for one another? Sighing, I moved on, not telling Jon about my confusion. While we were there among the *road* workers we wanted to learn, but we also wanted to have fun while learning. My day of birth was not the time for puzzling or disturbing thoughts and questions.

There came the hums and growls of the Tenzenar machines starting up. Above their tremendous roar were the shouts and orders given by various Tenzenar as the work began in force. Jon and I took to the woods quickly, giving the marked trees a wide berth as we continued to make our way south. Once past the danger, we were assaulted by the familiar acrid odor obliterating the sweetly clean air. Emerging from the cover of the trees, pearons behind the machines that forced and flattened the black substance on the ground, we watched them work, following along with them slowly returning north.

As their work progressed, I watched with morbid fascination how they built their *road*. We listened to the Tenzenar work. Their harsh voices that seemed to constantly vibrate with anger and irritation nearly overwhelmed me with heartbreaking grief. The longer I watched, the weaker I became, as if I were somehow taken fraw by their contagious sense of bleak despair and irritated anger. It wasn't long before I began to understand why my great-great-grand uncle past in Sontall at so young an age. Watching these people for one hundred aanas would drain the life out of anyone.

"Jon," I began, still watching the action in front of me, "what is the necessity in this?"

"I know not, Niki," his voice but a whisper. "I weep for all that is lost. I can hear the screams from the trees as they are pulled and torn from life. My heart aches for the life within the soil, as it is smothered by this... unnatural substance. A substance which smells of all it brings... horrible, acrid Sontall. Keyenoa, where are we to go? What are we to do now that You have brought us this Tenzenar destruction?" his voice was as hollow and void of life as the Tenzenar around us. His words were for Keyenoa not me.

Shivering over his description and the lack of vibrancy in his voice, I felt compelled to do something to break the spell of despair that had woven itself around the both of us. Tugging on his cape, I turned blindly in his direction. "Let's go home, Master. I've had my fill of Tenzenar for this day. Should it not be about dusk when we arrive in New Malin? I mean... I wouldn't want to be breaking in on any surprises I wasn't supposed to," I urged, with a hopeful turn in my voice, uncertain if he even heard me.

His cape trembled for a moment in my hand. "Ta, Niki, thee are right. Let us take ourselves from this morbid place... and quickly, before we find ourselves hopelessly trapped in their miasma of despair." He shuddered again.

Heading deep into the trees, bypassing the shouting men, their spewing machines and the uprooted trees, we returned to the path well ahead of the danger. Several pearons ahead we nearly stumbled into four Tenzenar men, gathered on the path deep in conversation.

PART I TENZENAR

"Let's just go around them, Jon," I encouraged, eager to be away from all Tenzenar.

"Listen to what they are saying, Niki," Jon urged very quietly.

"Well, Ron, where do we begin this turn in the road?" one asked another.

"Here, look on the map. You're to begin the curve here," the man replied as he unfolded a map. The other men moved in closer to get a look at what he was showing them. *"You're to make the curve gradually slant westward, like so, and here, turn it back to its northward course,"* he elaborated, continuing to point at the map.

"All right, Ron, I see what you want. But would you mind telling me why we need to go to all that trouble? Look, it seems clear that if we just stay on this northward course, we would save both time and money?" the first man demanded.

All eyes turned to *Ron*. *"When Dick and I surveyed the land north of here we discovered many cliffs and deep crevices in the land along this section, here,"* he replied, directing the men's attention to the map once again. *"Taking the road along this route, the land is much less rugged. Therefore, we actually save time and money, not to mention energy, by following this route."*

"Jon, that's not right," I whispered very softly aware that my Thaytor shifted at my side. I did not need to see the map, I understood the directions *Ron* was giving them. "The land isn't what they describe north of here at all. It is neye more difficult to traverse than what they've managed to travel and destroy already."

Taking my arm, he walked me past the men in the group, giving them a wide berth for safety's sake. Then, leading me off the path, he went some pearons into the wild undergrowth. There he turned to face me, lowering his shield of invisibility he indicated that I should do the same. With a deep sigh of relief, I relaxed my shield and sat on a vine encrusted log nearby.

Putting his boot-clad foot on the log next to me, Jon rested his forearm on his bent knee while leaning near, his expression alight with excitement. "It's not really so strange, Niki. You're just not giving the matter as much thought as you should. Think about it, if they were to continue on their straight northern course, wouldn't they end up building their *road* right through the heart of New Malin?" He dropped his foot to the forest floor and began pacing in eager excitement. "I'd wager that your father and Met Lordship High King Sayleen Cantabo, having learned where the Tenzenar were planning to put this *road* of theirs, combined their power and put the belief into the Tenzenar minds that New Malin was this impassable rugged landscape they have described.

"I left you for a moment and got a closer look at the Tenzenar map. They now plan to lay this *road* across the stream only a few pearons ahead of us and then continue northward following the stream from other side. Coincidentally, this keeps the Tenzenar at least a teron from New Malin's borders, and several terons from Cetar's borders. The *road* reaches its end at the lake, just in sight of inlet's mouth. So while it's still not the most comfortable solution, it is a much better one than the *road* going straight through our clearing."

I smiled, feeling rather teepin when Jon made it quite clear, that I had missed what Met Lordship and Father had done. "Master, did you actually go up and stand with the men to get a look at their map?" I asked wondering about his judgment, especially after his lecture to me about sneaking into the Tenzenar dwelling tuevtauns ago.

He smiled sheepishly, yet there was a tell-tale twinkle within his eyes. "Curiosity gets us all once in a while, Niki," he coughed. "Now come, there's a celebration awaiting you, Met Lord."

Raising our shields of invisibility, we returned to the path and followed it to New Malin.

Just as dusk was giving way to night, we reached the southern edge of the lower clearing, and I was astonished to find that it had been transformed into a wondrous array of color and light. Strung all around the clearing, bobbing and swaying in the trees, were softly lit tesha lamps of wondrous sizes and colors. People crowded almost into the middle of the clearing. It seemed everyone who had been invited to the celebration had come. Each guest held a minca tellite candle with their strong sturdy flames flickering in the gentle breeze. The effect of the lights from the candles and the bobbing tesha lamps of various colors and sizes caused me to think that all the stars in the universe had settled into the clearing for a rest.

Jon, while remaining at my side, urged me forward. As I walked past them, the guests knelt respectfully one by one, keeping their heads bowed until I had moved on. Then, two by two, they fell in behind us, quietly singing a song of welcome and joy. I was thus guided down the center of both clearings brimming with guests. Finally, I stood before a large table at the northern most end of the clearing.

There, Jon stepped back and took his place at my right shoulder. The people of Airies had quietly filled the clearing behind me, taking seats on the grass. The guests seated at the long table in front of me were the families of all Six Kings. Father was sitting near the middle of the table, next to two empty chairs, while the princes, princesses, Kings and ladies, filled the remainder of the seats. Offering my father a nervous smile, I knelt on one knee while Jon continued to remain standing at my right shoulder. Father rose from his chair and transported himself across the table. Looking at me and the people gathered at my back, his expression was filled with pride.

"Gentle people of Airies, I give you all welcome and wish you great joy this night," he had raised his voice using his given power to allow all to hear him as he looked across the crowd. "On this night, sixteen aanas ago, I received a precious omnestera from my Joined and Keyenoa. Because of that omnestera... that gift... I gladly stand before you now, eager to share some minca part of him with you this night.

"To each and everyone, I present my most precious... omnestera and great joy, my only son, prince—and I hope heir to a throne—Nikita Markain Malin."

Cheers rang out from all the guests.

Father waited for the guests to grow quiet and then continued, "Together with all the Kings, their ladies, daughters, and sons present, I ask that you now join in this celebration of his birth, sixteen aanas past. Nikita has but two more aanas before he is to enter manhood through Con Sona Eata and with Keyenoa's arecean, take up a Kingdom's crown.

"To begin this celebration, I wish to honor Met Son, Nikita Markain Malin, with a new crown. A crown that now carries sixteen points."

As Father held out his hand, Conden stepped forward from the crowd behind me and gave Father a gold crown. I blushed, embarrassed and ashamed. A great deal of trouble had been made to produce this crown, either with Father's power or through his instructions to a goldsmith who then had to forge it. However it was made, I did not feel I deserved such effort. In my rush to leave Malinieum City after we had told my father the news of the Tenzenar landing, I had accidentally left my crown somewhere in Jon's home. Therefore, much to my father's consternation and grief, it was one of the items that had to be counted as confiscated by the Tenzenar.

Bowing my head humbly, I listened to him speak. "With Keyen, hope, faith, and a long, prosperous life ahead, I present to thee, Met Son, thy new crown, signifying thine aanas of boyhood before Con Sona Eata and manhood. I ask now, before all present here, that Keyenoa's arecean fall upon thee, Met Nikca, granting all He desires thee to grasp. Best wishes from us all."

Jon easily spread the leakas so that Father could slip the crown over them. Once the new crown rested on my head, Jon released leakas so they locked on to the crown and held it in place on my head. Cheers of joy and congratulations rose from the guests while I was escorted to the center seat at the table. Jon quietly sat at my right, while Father resumed his place on my left. At my father's nod of consent, I spoke the traditional prayer of leki to begin the feast.

The succulent meal was shared with all the guests. Everything I requested had been included, from the roast creasion to the largest moreanne cake I had ever seen. Father had ordered free-flowing quantities of leeksha wine served to all throughout the meal and everyone drank as though the potent wine was ghea neye more than water. The dinner lasted a full oona, with a minca more drink being consumed than food, though both quantities were high. Spirits were soaring as the dinner came to a ceremonious close and Father raised his hands, quieting the merrymaking.

Rising from his chair a bit unsteadily, he began to speak, "At my son's request, there will now be a theron hunt. Any boy desiring to join this challenging competition is welcome to do so. For those older and less inclined for such competition, there will be singing and dancing... which shall continue all through this glorious night, ceasing only when the sun has risen on the morrow."

Cheers filled the air.

Father waited patiently for them to quiet. "There will be prizes given to the best theron caught this night, and also for the best dancers and singers."

Again cheers rose from the crowd. Father shouted, making certain he could be heard, "Let these joyous festivities begin!"

As the music began, the dancers and singers eagerly rivaled for position.

Jon quickly gathered the boys to organize my desired theron hunt. First he spilt our eager masses into well defined age groups, making sure that neye boy was forced to compete unfairly against another much older than he. Then, we were instructed to find one partner and remain with this partner throughout the competition. Sornan Dorna and I found each other instantly. We stuck together as if we were glued—in an effort to keep us both upright—while Jon recited the rules of the game.

"Now, I am sure that all of you know these rules as well as you know how to write your names... but I'll repeat them for the younger players... and those who think they may find some way to circumnavigate the regulations." He smiled tipsily over our groans of impatience. "There is to be neye killing of the birds. Each player must use his wits, agility and a cautious hand to catch his theron and return here with the bird alive.

"Male birds will bring the most calu. Female theron will instantly dock the bearers fifteen calu. There's a one oona time limit, so don't be too picky about the theron you manage to capture. Remember, one in the hand is worth more than the best still in the forest," he chuckled… rather drunkenly.

"Once you've caught your bird, return with your capture to the clearing immediately. I'll be here awaiting your return and help in the judging at the end of the time limit. If you've not caught a bird within the one oona limit, return to the clearing in any case. You may help in the unbiased judging of the birds caught." Jon's voice had become more authoritative with each sentence. I guessed he was trying very hard not to reveal just how inebriated he was. "Time begins now!" he shouted, causing every contestant to scatter into the woods in various directions.

With excitement dancing in our eyes, Sornan and I stumbled into the forest. Every time one of us fell—which was rather often—we would both convulse with uproarious laughter. We couldn't understand why we had such difficulty remaining on our feet. Or why it seemed to each of us that the other was constantly swaying to and fro as if to purposely trip the other up. This of course was what caused us both to fall down, as we seemed to get caught up swaying in rhythm opposite each other.

"You know, Niki," Sornan said, slurring my name as he pulled himself to his feet, "we've managed to get only a few pearons into the forest. I think we've had…" he started to giggle convulsively which caused him to topple to the forest floor, again, "A bit too much to drink."

I stood staring blankly at the vacant spot where he'd been standing, completely baffled as to where he'd gone. Then, following the sound of his hysterical laughter, I discovered him sprawled on the forest floor looking positively ridiculous. Unable to help myself, I started to laugh. This, of course, caused me to sway back and forth on my own very unsteady feet. Wondering how I could possibly still be upright, I began to laugh harder.

"Yup," I agreed with his assessment of our condition. Then, while looking around to try and determine where we were, I became very dizzy and suddenly fraw to my stomach.

"Niki," Sornan gazed up at me sadly, unable to get back to his feet, "how are we going to catch a theron like this?" He began to giggle, again, "To be honest, we're both rather pathetic—don't you think?" His eyes tried to follow me as I swayed.

Unable to assimilate more than one question at a time, I shrugged my shoulders in answer to his first query. This movement was enough to cause me to topple to the ground beside him.

Following another unwarranted attack of the giggles, I turned to Sornan, "About catching that theron. How 'bout we lay very still… right here… maybe one of the birds will walk right up to us and then we can grab it."

Sniggering with glee, Sornan agreed. "We are certainly incapable of wandering around the forest, let alone getting to our feet at the moment, Niki, so why not."

There we stayed, sprawled drunkenly in the leaf debris for about half an oona. Duirng the occasional times we remembered what we were supposed to be hunting, Sornan—a bit more sober than I—would imitate the mating call of a female theron, hoping it might raise our chances for success. To our mutual astonishment—and with much credit to Sornan's superb imitation call of a female theron—a rather proud male bird sauntered right up to us. I jabbed my forlaynan in the ribs excitedly and Sornan—thinking quickly—clumsily grabbed the bird. He hung on grimly as it squawked and fought for its freedom while I cheered him on with drunken giggles.

Proud of our bird and aware of the teepin of trying for anything better, we agreed to return to the clearing. Sornan quickly hopped up and left me struggling to rise from my sprawled position. Having finally managed to find my feet, taking a moment to decide exactly where the clearing was, I realized that Sornan was gone. After shrugging, I began walking. I thought it best to keep going—until I remembered that he had the bird.

Sometime later, I managed to sober up just enough to realize that I was wandering around the edge of LeFold Lake, shouting like a mootan for Sornan. Not quite sober enough to think rationally or see with any clarity in the darkness, I bumped into someone, accidentally knocking them to the ground while I somehow remained on my feet. Certain I had found my forlaynan, I stammered an apology—one that was more insult than apology—as I offered to help him to his feet. Bending over, I was engulfed by the sweet, alluring odor of solleeta flowers and honey.

'Te'air!' my mind shouted while I shook my head in denial, only to nearly loose my balance. "Toenda, I honestly didn't see you there," I offered a better apology—just in case the person happened to be someone other than Sornan. By then, even my sluggish mind was forced to admit this was a high possibility.

The hand that found mine was feminine. 'Te'air!' my brain shouted at me again.

I swallowed nervously as another hand took hold of my shoulder. My heart raced as it lept into my throat, forcing my breath to puff passed my lips in shallow gasps. Trying to steady the female as she swayed against me, my hand clasped her softly indented waist. Speech instantly became impossible.

"Oh, Met Lord Nikita, truly it was my fault. I got in thy way." Her voice sang and danced on my pounding heart, confirming what I had guessed all along.

'Te'air!' my mind shouted with triumph.

Releasing my hand, she grasped my vest, her fingers caressing my flesh between the laces, as she leaned into my body. "I'm afraid, Met Lord, that I've twisted my ankle. I'm unable to walk without your help." Her sweet breath touched my lips.

I longed to say something that was filled with confidence and alluring masculinity so I could sweep her off her feet to some unknown romantic destination. However, I could do neye more than stand there, panting like an eshiday out of water, unable to make one coherent sound. Te'air sighed and nestled her head against my chest, sending wafts of sweet solleeta flowers and honey to my nostrils.

"Met Lord, there's a warm and dry cave tucked behind the waterfall. If you'd carry me in your arms, we could go there so I could rest in its shelter tonight and leave in the morning when my ankle is again strong." She sighed prettily against my chest, and I swear her lips touched my flesh between the leather ties. "I'd be most honored, Met Lord, if you'd consent to keep me company until the morning when I could walk. I really am afraid of the dark and don't like to be alone." Again her breath and lips caressed my chest. "It frightens me so… to be alone."

Puffed with masculine pride and delirious with desire and drunkenness, I found myself standing taller and thrusting out my chest—certain my scrawny sixteen aana shoulders had broadened to more a masculine dimension. Leaning down, I gently touched my lips to her hair, hoping she wouldn't notice. "It is I, Met lady, who'd be honored for thee to consent to my company while thy ankle heals," I replied, trying to sweep her up into my arms wanting so desperately to gallantly carry her into the cave. Instead, in my drunkenness, I nearly dropped her when my center of gravity shifted from her extra weight. Stumbling frantically for the cave, I fought to keep my shifting balance from decaying any further while hoping that I would not dump her into the water and have me tumbling in after her. I did manage to soak us both when I ducked beneath the waterfall, but she quickly assured me that it was all right.

Setting her as carefully as I could on her feet, I lit the tellite candle she had told me was on a rock shelf by the opening. As the minca light took hold and grew, it illuminated the murky darkness of the cave. I turned to face her nervously, aware that my whole body was betraying my affection and longing for her. Her glorious, shimmering blue eyes searched me with adoration. Then, her soft expression widened to horror even as she took a step closer to me.

"Oh, Met Lord, you are all wet, and in your fine clothes! Your micon tunic will be ruined if it does not dry quickly," she gasped. "It must come off to dry properly, and also keep you from becoming fraw," she whispered, moving ever nearer. As her hands ran up my vest her fingers tangled themselves in the leather ties, as she pleaded in a breathless whisper, "Let me help you, Met Lord."

Unable to stand, I dropped to my knees on the hard, rough surface of the cave floor, as her mouth covered mine. Te'air tumbled down after me, giggling like a minca nikca at play….

Chapter VII

The Breaking of a Heart

"Keyenoa knew if He allowed our youth to keep their desires, suffering the pains of passion and the misguided ideas of lustful longings, that we as a people would again be at war with one another, and Leyette Castrinair would once more be the ruler of Airies."

—Valcree Metlan Sontall,
first High King of Airies

I woke the following morning certain I was now a man, invincible and powerful to all. There was neye else I would ever need, except my Te'air.

Ignoring the pounding protest in my head, I looked eagerly around the cave hoping to find her. Instead, I discovered my Thaytor. He was sitting near the cave opening with a grim expression marring his face. My clothes lay in a sodden mass beside him. Te'air was gone. Ignoring him and my headache, I gathered up my wet clothes. Jon neither moved nor spoke as I struggled to dress.

Uncertain what he knew of last night and Te'air, I decided silence would be my best defense and forlana. Watching my Thaytor beneath lowered lids as I dressed in my sodden micon tunic, Jon expressed neither curiosity nor anger. Instead his mood

PART I TENZENAR

seemed to reflect shock, hurt, and confusion. I was fraw at the thought that he knew far more than I hoped.

"Nikita, we need to talk," he said quietly.

I sat on the cave floor and waited for him to continue. My stomach was churning and my head was pounding from my hangover. I felt chilled to the bone from my soaking wet tunic and the tone in his voice.

"Sornan returned to the clearing last night with a prize winning theron in his grasp... but you were neye to be seen. When asked about your absence, he explained that he was certain you were right behind him, confessing that both of you were more than a minca drunk. He thought you had probably gotten rather confused as to the direction of the clearing—if you could even get to your feet." Jon paused, watching me closely.

I fidgeted under his scrutiny and the clamminess of my sodden tunic.

Shaking his head, he continued, "Your father was notified that you were missing... and most likely hadn't all of your senses. Mark, though, wasn't terribly concerned. He was confident that neye harm could come your way in just one night... and he easily convinced me of the same. If you hadn't found your way home by morning, I was told to go looking for you.

"Well, needless to say, morning came and you hadn't returned. Heading to the clearing, I quickly found the location where you and Sornan had caught the theron, and picked up the trail of your boot prints stumbling along the winding lake path...." He looked down and murmured to himself, "I saw the feminine foot prints trailing yours... but I just didn't think much about them. Who would have thought I should? There was neye reason for me to believe there could possibly be any connection between the two of you... until I found you both...." His coal black eyes met mine, his expression stunned. Jon knew.

"Master...." I barely heard my own voice as I forced myself to speak.

He looked at me, his expression haunted and questioning.

I was truly afraid. He, who was always with me, always my firm foothold, who seemed—most times—to know me better than I knew myself… was now so far from me I could hardly say I knew him. He also looked as though he could say the same about me. Suddenly, we were neye more than strangers. I wasn't sure what to say to pull us closer together, but I was desperate to find the words. Somehow I had to re-bridge the growing chasm between us.

"Jon, she was always there!" I blurted out. "She was always so close, driving me keezworky with wants I knew I shouldn't have. She never got close. She never noticed me… and that seemed to make me want her all the more. I couldn't get her out of my mind! And neye matter what I did or what decisions I would make concerning her. I always found myself noticing her while my wanting her grew. I was afraid to speak to you… or anyone else about my feelings. I knew what I felt wasn't normal, and I thought… well, I thought you'd… laugh at me… like you did that time with Conden.…

"Then… last night… she spoke to me! She twisted her ankle when I nearly ran her down. She told me about the cave. She asked me to carry her here and stay with her until her ankle healed. She was so frightened of being alone. Then, I got her all wet going under the falls. Instead of worrying about herself, she was concerned about ruining my tunic and my becoming fraw if it weren't removed to dry. Jon… she.… Jon, she… touched me.…"

I gulped in deep breaths of cool, damp air hoping to ease the sudden desire that filled me as I remembered what had happened. "Oh Master, never in all my life have I felt like this. I am filled with Keyen for her! She is innocent and pure, and all that I desire," the exuberant words of youthful affection flowed from my lips. My feelings were real—they were a Keyen—as deep and heartfelt, to me as any true Keyen I would find later.

He sighed and slowly stood. "Well, we'd best get back to our respective tree-homes and into some dry clothes. Sitting in these wet things and feeling them slowly dry on one's person is most uncomfortable." He lifted his cape and squeezed the water from its hem. "We'll talk more about what happened, Niki... but later, after we're both dry and comfortable."

He took my arm, aware that I did not want to discuss last night any further. "Just be glad it is only I who'll hear your story and not your father too. Hear me, Niki," he commanded, "when I sent the girl on her way, I told her to speak neye word of what took place between you two. She gave her promise. Right now your father doesn't need to deal with this... this...." He waved his arm around the cave instead of completing his statement, "And I'm determined to keep it from reaching his ears. At least until I learn exactly how serious it is. I'm trying to protect him as much as you... so stop fighting me!"

Following Jon out of the cave entrance, I heard him mumble to himself, "It shouldn't be too difficult to keep this... this... incident from him. His mind's been overly preoccupied with other matters in recent days. I only hope, when things settle down, I'll have this problem solved. Na'chore, Mark has enough on his mind... he doesn't need to be worrying about Niki as well!"

He stepped under the waterfall, soaking his clothes again and not even reacting to the sudden cold dousing. Irritated by his reaction to the matter of Te'air, I turned away determined to have ghea neye to do with him. I wasn't more than three steps up the pinnacle, when he called to me from below. Offering him a dramatic huff, I leaned my back against the rock, folded my arms, and glared at him.

"Where are you going, Niki?" he asked calmly.

"Home to get dry, like you," I replied churlishly, thinking he'd gone keezworky. "You were the one who suggested we change in the first place, you know."

He smiled stiffly, "Come down from there and follow me. While you may well be angry with me... heed me on this. Going that way will just increase the distance of your walk home. Suffer my presence a few onas longer, and I'll have you at your door."

Reaching his side, I made a face he wasn't suppose to see.

"I'd say in three onas, Niki, if you don't drop that smug arrogance off your face rather quickly, you're going to not only be deeply embarrassed, but will also have to admit what a kutated mootan teepatin you are being right now," he warned as he continued walking.

I glanced his way skeptically and reconsidered my position. "Actually, I've wondered where this path would end," I murmured.

He said ghea neye, only grinned.

Just about to demand what he found so amusing—having already forgotten his warning about my attitude—I recognized my tree-home and realized I was nearly beneath Kingstree. Suddenly, it dawned on me that I was standing in the middle of the most populated section of all of New Malin—and felt very kutated indeed.

"This, you must admit is a bit quicker than walking six terons the other way, only to end up near the same spot."

Fed up, finding neye humor in the matter—especially because the humor was at my expense—I glared nastily at him. Then, in a typical youthful huff, I departed for my home. I felt humiliated, condemned, and put upon all at the same time. All I wanted to do was to get out of my wet clothes and as far away from the man at my back as fast as I could. I didn't want to share my feelings concerning Te'air with anyone. And I certainly didn't want to put them under Jon's scrutiny. My Keyen for her was real in my heart. I feared he wouldn't take my feelings seriously and instead do all he could to undermine the sweetness that was Te'air.

"Niki," he called.

I kept walking.

"We **will** talk after you've changed!"

Ducking under the gungas tree that held my house, I climbed the stairs to my bedchamber and changed my clothes, before returning to my mainroom to sulk. I didn't want to hear what Jon had to say. I understood exactly what had happened between me and Te'air. I knew my own feelings. Jon had neye right—or need—to interfere in this matter.

"What exactly does he think we have to talk about, anyway? That's something I'd like to know!" I said, venting my anger and frustration on the empty room.

"Oh not much, Niki," Jon answered sarcastically as he walked in. "Except your telling me what exactly happened between you and Te'air. How long you've had feelings of this sort for the woman. And what your feelings are now that you've had a few onas to cool off."

I glared at him. Honestly, I was more scared and embarrassed over his questions than I was angry at him. I knew exactly what my answers would be and I also knew he wouldn't like them. Having scrutinized my feelings for Te'air for weeks, I had already been through everything Jon was going to put me through. I just didn't want to get all tied up in knots over something that was impossible, yet was apparently possible for me.

He turned to a chair beneath one of the open window-doors and looked up at me as he dropped into the chair wearily. His expression showed neye sign of his previous sarcasm; rather, it was filled pain and confusion.

"Niki, don't you understand… I need these answers from you. I'm confused…. I am bewildered. I can see within your expression that you recognize that I understand what you're feeling even less than you do. And whether you believe it or not, Niki, I don't think you understand your feelings half as much as you think you do."

Suddenly before my eyes he looked like a man old and weak, worn out long before his taun. Looking at him, and being as connected as we were, I too felt as though I were weakening and growing old. I hated the idea of being the cause of his quiet and personal torment.

I began to talk, mostly babble at first, afraid that if I stopped I would lose what I needed most, my Thaytor and Fortulaynan, Jontair Alcone. I told him again about how Te'air seemed to hover nearby, but never noticed that I was there. Then, I shared with him exactly what had happened the night before. I stumbled in embarrassment over the details that took place after she and I had entered the cave, yet I knew he needed to understand everything.

"Master, every time she gets near me my heart jumps into my throat, choking me. When she is near, if I don't feel like I'm going to fade into Sontall from embarrassment, I feel certain I'll simply sweat myself into oblivion!" I exclaimed, finally falling silent.

Jon looked grim, but neye longer crushed.

I relaxed, comforted by his expression, knowing I wouldn't lose him. "I was scared to tell anyone about how I felt. I knew my feelings were abnormal, and so I was ashamed," I confessed. "I did a lot of praying and a lot of thinking, and I decided that it was silly to worry so much about my feelings. What is the purpose in worrying about something that can't be changed, Master?"

With his attention focused on the floor between us, Jon smiled sadly. As time wore on and he remained silent, I began to fidget while I waited for him to speak. I even began to regret that he hadn't laughed at me. Anything would have been better than having to witness the pain I had caused him by not sharing my feelings and desires with him before he'd found me in the cave.

Five eternally long onas later he raised his eyes to mine, piercing my soul with his grief. "Tell me again exactly what happened last night. Start from the time you left the clearing with Sornan to hunt a theron, until you saw me in the cave this morning."

I didn't want to cause him more pain. All I wanted to do was to tell him that it was all a joke and assure him I was still the boy he knew yesterday. But I recognized that this situation was far too important to castrin that way. I'd grown up enough in the last oona to understand, painful or not, Jon needed to know the truth. So I shared my story again. And as I did, I felt an aclusceaun greater than at any time since the Tenzenar landed on Airies. When my story came to an end, I was emptied inside of all my immature reactions, defenses, and responses.

Working through his thoughts, Jon spoke quietly to himself, "By Alleanne, any man—or boy—would have to be blind not to notice Te'air's… er…"—he cleared his throat—"attractions. She certainly sets out to display those attractions in quite a provocative manner. I admit, at times, she has a way about her that could bring a high priest to think solely of his flesh… so why not a boy? Now, along with her well-accomplished abilities and the great talent in her trade—these being a rather large part of it, there is another factor that could tip a boy from the norm—Niki was very inebriated at the time she had chosen to use him for her purposes. While she may not have expected to consummate the relationship last night, she would not be one to turn down such an opportunity when he was drunk enough to be swayed by her wiles."

While I had listened to everything he said, I heard only that Jon had come to accept that my sexual desire wasn't abnormal. Not wanting to hear the rest of what he'd said, I managed to completely block out all of Jon's implications concerning Te'air's morals.

"Jon, when I Con Sona Eata, do you think I could Join with her?" I asked him eagerly and sincerely.

He went very still for a moment. Then, slowly met my hopeful gaze and sighed, "Niki, this is going to be the hardest thing I have ever had to tell to you. Te salma, for my sake and more importantly yours, you must listen carefully to everything I say and listen with focused intent, keeping your silence until I am finished—all right?"

I nodded eagerly, certain he was going to tell me about the difficulties Kings face when Joining with any woman not born of royalty. Already having an answer for such a minca detail, I was prepared to defeat his argument. And if I couldn't sway him to my perspective, I knew Joining wasn't all that imperative… I could always just partner with her.

Jon stood and began to pace. "You see Niki…." at my hopeful expression he stammered and grimaced, "Allills, Niki! You're really making this very difficult!"

I just looked at him in confusion.

He sighed and continued pacing, this time being careful not to look at me. "Te'air is a, uh… um… oh, allills, Niki! Te'air is a sosceshpa, just as her mother is and her mother's mother was… probably going all the way back to the Ryder times," he shouted.

Instantly my mind closed off as I silently argued ferociously to myself that his accusation couldn't possibly be true. However, keeping my promise, I said ghea neye.

Jon lifted his face toward Alleanne, "Keyenoa, tella saa, grant to me Thy strength," he muttered, closing his eyes. He waited several enas in faithful patience, then looked at me and continued, "That's a fact, Niki, and one I can easily prove, if I must... but, tella saa, allow me to finish what I have to say, first."

Clenching my jaw, I nodded once, determined not to believe another word. I didn't want to let him destroy my joy and my belief in my Keyen.

He sighed and pressed on, "Remember, how you told me that Te'air always seemed to be close by, but never noticed you? I promise you that she was well aware of your presence. Her pretense otherwise was simply a ploy to gauge and further stir your interest. Te'air had decided upon a plan to ensnare you the first moment she had access to you—long before you ever noticed her.

"Think about it, Niki, not only are you Mark's son, you are very likely to take the throne from your father when you Con Sona Eata. The fact that you are a... good-looking youth is an added bonus. She knew that if there was any way she could let it be known that she spent a whole night with you—even if you couldn't consummate the relationship—it would make her a most prominent sosceshpa indeed. Discovering that she could seduce you, Te'air knew she would make herself name and raise her prominence above all other sosceshpa in New Malin.

"Niki, the girl used every lastna of skill and feminine wile she had against you for her own gain." He looked at me, daring me to argue with his logic.

My desperate need for her to be what I had led myself to believe was stronger than any logic Jon could lay before me. I was hurt and terrified, deep in my heart, that Jon was right. Yet still needing her to be what I wanted her to be more than anything else at that moment, I refused everything he said. "Neye Jon! You're wrong! All wrong!" I shouted, springing from my chair. "Te'air told me she cared for me. She warned me how we could never have each other. She must feel Keyen for me, because she gave me promises last night! She gave me herself! She never followed me on purpose, it just happened! All of it just happened!" I turned and walked several paces away.

Even while I had been determined otherwise, some of Jon's message managed to get through. I had begun to question her motives in my mind. I so need to trust that she honestly offered me what she had because it was something I never had before—a gentle, tender Keyen from a woman. If, instead, I believed my Thaytor's words, I would then have to accept that what I wanted and needed so desperately was ghea neye more than a… castrin. To do that was more than I could bear. Unwilling and unable to allow my heart to be destroyed by the truth he spoke, I hardened my heart and myself against Jon.

"Niki, as Keyenoa is my witness, I swear to you that my words are the truth. I give you my toenda omprice sorice for having to tell you this," he said, moving to my side.

I trembled with rage and panic, unable to speak.

"Her footprints trailed yours along the winding path. Then, they turned into the forest heading northeast into the tree-homes. I found them again along the lake shore moving from the tree-homes going in the direction of the falls. That is where they met with thine. Can thee not see, Niki? Te'air knew where thee were headed and deliberately reached that place before thee. All had been planned—premeditated—and then acted upon down to the last detail. She used a sprained ankle to get you to pick her up and take her into the cave. There was ghea neye wrong with her ankle this morn' when she sauntered triumphantly from the cave following my set down. She told me rumor would spread, even if, as she promised, she didn't start it. She assured me she would not bother thee again, since she had gotten what she wanted."

"Get out of my house!" I exploded as I swung to face him. "I've neye need for a ghea castrin Thaytor, who is out to destroy my heart in anyway he can! I despise your litkini insinuations! Te'air has to feel Keyen for me! What happened last night, just happened! Do you hear me! It was not planned! Get out of my house now and keep clear of my life!" I shouted as I pushed and shoved him from my mainroom and partially down the outside steps.

He stumbled, but I just kept pushing. Hanging onto the rail and tree branches, he managed to turn and take the steps down. Aware he would continue on his way, I remained where I was, watching him go. Pausing near the bottom step, Jon looked up beseechingly. I simply lifted an eyebrow and turned away, going into my mainroom and closing the door behind me.

Pacing through my tree-home, I spent the time desperately convincing myself of Te'air's innocence and her Keyen. Finally managing to convince myself, I went in search of her. Deciding it would be better not to call attention to myself, I dressed in one of my oldest micon tunics and removed my crown before I departed.

Uncomfortable that word would get back to Jon and my father if I asked anyone where she was, I searched for Te'air alone. It was surprising just how difficult the girl was to find in the minca forest Kingdom of New Malin. A frustrating two oonas went by before I spotted her in the lower clearing. She was standing near the cooking area laughing and talking with several other women. Glancing up, she seemed to shine with welcome as she smiled at me ever so sweetly. Extending a hand, she urged me closer. Mesmerized by her beauty, my reservations were forgotten. I didn't care who saw or heard of our meeting.

"Met Lord, did you brave the anger of your Thaytor to come to me?"

Putting my arms around her, I kissed her clumsily, expressing all the emotions, needs, and fears swamping me. I forgot all about the women nearby.

"Mmm, Met Lord, you make my heart stir so," she sighed loudly.

"Te'air," I murmured with awe, breathing in her scent of solleeta flowers and honey. "I need you so!" All my desperation for her Keyen could be heard in my voice.

The women begin to giggle and whisper, reminding me of hungry dara. Uncomfortable, sensing their malice and cynicism, I tried to lead Te'air away. She held me still. Embracing my arm, she laid her head against my shoulder and lifted her eyes to my face. Drowning in her gaze, I ignored my discomfort and let her keep me near the others.

"Oh, Niki," she sighed, squeezing my arm. Her touch made me feel stronger than I had a right to feel. "You know my heart after the night we spent in the cave." She cuddled closer, pressing her breasts against my arm.

My head swam. Everything was forgotten except for her.

"I believe in my heart that what took place between us last night was Keyen. I swear to thee, that when I Con Sona Eata, I will take thee for my Joined. I'll fight all on Airies for thy Keyen."

As if from another place far away I heard the women giggling and making snide comments in crass and noisy whispers. Fogged by desire and need, when Te'air glanced in their direction and offered a nod of victory I hardly noticed it. The implications of her actions were completely beyond my believed reality I refused to comprehend it. All I saw was her beautiful face rather than the satisfaction of gain in her expression. I was just grateful the women had grown silent around us, and I could again forget their disturbing presence. Te'air maneuvered me deeper within their growing numbers.

"Niki, how long until thee Con Sona Eata?" she asked, tucking her head beneath my chin as her fingers played with the ties on my vest.

"Two aanas from now, when I'm eighteen, I will likely enter Con Sona Eata. You can wait that long, can't you?" I begged, focused on her lips as they parted with invitation.

My longing was interrupted by crass whispering and giggling. Again, I tried to guide Te'air away from the women, only to freeze as she lifted her eyes to mine and parted her lips, licking them with her minca pink tongue.

"Oh, Niki!" she sighed.

Leaning down thinking to kiss her, Te'air suddenly squeaked and placed her hands against my chest. With her attention darting fearfully around the clearing, she pushed me away when she noticed a Dornian guard lingering near by talking to another woman several pearons away.

"Tella saa, you must go now… before someone… finds us together," she urged as she pushed against my chest a second time.

Still dazed with desire, I pulled her closer. "I care not if we're discovered. I want never to leave thy side. Come with me now and I'll show thee my house and all that will be thine," I urged desperately.

She shook her head. In the light blue depths of her gaze there was a harsh determination that stunned me into releasing her. Stepping away, I gave her the freedom she had silently demanded.

"I cannot. Not now, Met Lord. I've made the midday meal for my family and must take it to them. I fear, even now, the meal will be cold. You have caused me to forget my promises and duties too long already," she said in a rush as she moved away from me, her gaze searching the lower clearing. Finding the guard lingering but obviously impatient, she quickly lifted a hand to my cheek and caressed it. "I'll come to thee at moonrise, Met Lord, and we'll have the whole night to share thy home and thy warmth… not to mention thy passion," she promised, before running gracefully away.

The women surrounding me moved in ever closer, blocking me from watching Te'air. They were laughing and cooing as they pressed against me. Their mouths were leering slashes of brightly painted color, while their eyes mocked me with hard lurid stares. Several hands groped and touched my flesh in bold and vulgar intent. Desperate to get away, I swung around, only to have more women step in and take the opportunity to do the same. My obvious fear and confusion made them laugh and titter all the more among themselves. They jeered at me, repeating Te'air's many words with mocking cruelty, laughing at my masculinity and telling me in low, beckoning voices how sensuous I was. My head whirled with hurt and confusion as I continued to try and escape their ever enclosing circle.

Jon's words about Te'air rang in my head. In my mind, I could see her lovely face floating and mingling with those who now surrounded and taunted me. Her ever-enchanting voice echoed in my thoughts, as Jon's harsh words and the women tormented me. Unable to take anymore, I shouted angrily, shoving through the groping women, unconcerned with how many I pushed to the ground in my need to get free. Running from the lower clearing and into the tree-homes, I was chased by the sound of their calloused laughter and the echoing reminder of Jon's words… "She's a sosceshpa, Niki." Once within the trees, I turned and followed the direction where Te'air indicated she was taking the meal to her family.

Desperate for Te'air to dismiss my fears, I searched frantically for her, even daring to inquire from others in New Malin if they had seen her. Neye could help. Many didn't know her and even those that did didn't seem to know where she lived. Sorely confused by what had happened and the reactions I received when I politely asked of her, I decided to go to the lake and sit quietly inside our cave and think in the dark and quiet there.

I moved through New Malin like a specter, alone, uncertain and yet still full of hope. On the minca sandy beach near the waterfall, discarded and half hidden behind the rock pinnacle, was the rusty pot she had carried from the lower clearing. I didn't stop to wonder why it was there, I just knew she was in the cave and simply ran to the waterfall and dashed into the gloom behind it.

Halting just beyond the water, I waited for my eyes to adjust to the darkness. Te'air's alluring voice mingled with the huskier tones of a man. Their breathing was heavy, but their voices light and full of laughter. Slowly, my eyes adjusted to he darkness. Both were so caught in their own passion, they were unaware of my presence—as I stared—unable to turn away. All my hope and innocence lay shattered at my feet as I watched her with another man. Te'air's name was torn from my throat in shock and utter betrayal. Both turned, each gazing at me with a different expression of frustration and surprise. During those painful moments every infinite detail had etched itself in my memory. Everything I wanted and everything I so desperately needed and believed I had finally found was destroyed. In that ena I found myself forced to grow up with far greater speed than my soul could handle.

"Go on with thee. I'll be done soon. Take tha self out an' be quick about it. Thee can have 'er when I be done." The guard's green eyes were glazed with desire, seeing ghea minca-neye. His Dornian slur was thick with his irritation and lust.

I couldn't move.

Te'air sat up. Unable to salvage what she might have gained, she smiled with cruel, cold-hearted malice. "Ta, my manly one," she laughed. "Go away. It seems this Dornian guard desires his privacy." She shrugged a shoulder and smiled teasingly, "Though, if you chose to stay, perhaps it could help you learn a few things, hmm?" Then she moved, catching the attention of the Dornian. Caressing his face, she continued to address me, "Like he said, you can have me when he's through… if you are so eager you can't wait for tonight. It makes neye difference to me."

Her words filled me with disgust. My mind and soul were so devastated from the pain she caused that I could not think to move.

"Juss get on with thee, an' leave us be. I've bartered away half me precious goods fer an oona with 'er. She's laid with royalty, an' I want ma worth of 'er… alone, do tha hear ma, Cessan?" the Dornian guard growled at me, but his attention remained on Te'air.

I broke. Sudden rage and bitter humiliation exploded inside me. Lunging wildly at the two, I hollered with incoherent anger and devastation. The Dornian guard, taken by surprise, shielded Te'air with his body, as he twisted around to face me. His suddenly sharp, powerful green eyes blazed to life with defensive power as he instinctively thrust his hand out in my direction. Shards of power swept down his arm, forming a ball around his hand as he made a fist. Then throwing his hand open, that ball of power flew at me, forcing its way in and throughout my defenseless body. Every nerve within me was on fire. My organs twisted and shivered in agony. I had neye defense and neye power to shield myself or retaliate, and neye power to hold off the crippling pain, which catapulted though my body. It was as though I were being burned and torn asunder from the inside out.

Screaming, I doubled over, desperately trying to protect myself in anyway I could. As blood and vomit choked off my cry for mercy, the Dornian guard dropped his hand to the cave floor, releasing me. The pain was gone, leaving me as if I'd been burned in an inferno. Curled and broken, in a growing pool of my own blood and vomit, I waited for Sontall, longing for the aclusceaun it offered. I wanted to never to feel such pain again—unsure which hurt was the worst, Te'air's betrayal, or the guards attack. Mercifully, I quickly lost consciousness.

Chapter VIII

Whateshan Eyette Sontall

"When thee releases the hand of Keyenoa, the enemy stands waiting to grasp it, filling the emptiness of thy soul with an ever growing bitterness, fouler in flavor than the flesh of a zewaller's heart."

—Valcree Metlan Sontall,
First High Kingof Airies

"Jon?"

I opened my eyes. I thought I'd spoken but discovered I was unable to open my mouth.

I was in bed. The shadows of the room moved and shifted with the flickering and muted candlelight. Looking around, I realized that I was in my tree-home. Jon stood near the end of my bed, facing a window with the shutter panels open staring blindly out into the darkness. The night had turned the window into a reflecting glass, revealing the haunted and shadowy distortion of my Thaytor's face to the room behind him.

My heart hammered wildly for a moment as I remembered the re-occurring horror I experienced during my unconscious dreams. In them all would be as it was now. Jon standing before the window, the room dimly lit, and the silence oppressive. I'd be so racked with pain, I'd have neye choice but to call out... and Jon would turn. But it wouldn't be my Thaytor who faced me. Instead, it would be a Leyette come to take my soul and be condemned.

I stared at the man near the window, fighting the remembered horror of those dreams. Determined to discover if my dream was going to turn out to be reality, I forced my lips to part... then hesitated, almost weary beyond bearing. I had to know, whatever the consequence. I had to know who stood by my window in the dim light of night... life or Sontall.

"Jon?"

What passed my lips was a mere grunt, sounding like the rustle of tinder-dry leaves as they scurried across the ground before being lifted to flight by a flurry of wind.

Uncertain if he had heard right, Jon hesitated before he turned. Then, my clambering heart grew calm and steady as I looked at my Thaytor's worried face. I tried to smile, but I was too weak to move even that minca part of my battered body. He rushed to my bedside, laying a warm and tender hand against my cheek. I felt his power flow through my bruised body, all too clearly reminding me of the attack and so filling me with fear.

"Shhh, Niki, speak not. Not yet," his voice was restoring, reminding me that his power would never hurt me. "I don't know, if thee would believe how greatly I leki Keyenoa for returning thee to us alive." He sighed with relief and gentle humor. "Ta, thee should sleep now. Thee will soon be back to the Niki we know and Keyen. Thee need but a bit of taun to heal." Unable to move or even voice my gratitude, I closed my eyes, allowing his voice to wash over me. Again, his hand caressed my face as sleep took hold through the touch of his power. "I will be away from thee but a minca taun. I must go to assure thy father, who be waiting in thy mainroom, that I've indeed seen thine eyes open and that thee are aware of thy surroundings before he becomes fraw from lack of sleep and concern," he murmured, his hand slipping from my cheek.

At his words, his power left me and I opened my eyes. My desire for sleep faded instantly when I heard I would be alone.

As he turned from the bed, I tried to call out, but the only sound I uttered was a pitiful moan. Ghea leki'anne, Jon turned with a puzzled frown on his face as he leaned near the bed.

"What is it, Niki?"

He smiled tenderly at my effort to speak.

"Take your time, master. Give your exhausted body a moment to adjust and the words will come," he explained with his usual intuitive wisdom.

I opened my mouth, tasting dried, stale blood. "You were…" I began only to falter. "I… I…. Te'…" my voice gave out in pain and exhaustion.

He nodded in encouragement but did not understand what I was trying to say.

To speak of Te'air hurt me too much. Gathering another slow and painful breath of air, I forced different words from my mouth, "Toenda omprice sorice. I need thee… very… much, Master."

He closed his eyes as a wave of emotion washed over his face. "Sorice leki omprice, Niki," he said with affection. Ruffling the hair on my forehead, he smiled. "Now let me go to your father, so—once I assure him that you're fine—he will go home and get some much-needed sleep."

As Jon left, I closed my eyes and waited, lying in limbo more asleep than awake. When my father reached my bedside, I was aware of his presence but had neye strength to open my eyes. Bonfinar quietly urged Father to leave, telling him we both needed our rest. When Jon added his insistence that I was fine and only exhausted, Father relented and obeyed Bonfinar's urging.

⌘⌘⌘⌘

The following dawn, Jon carried in our morning meal, filling my bedchambers with succulent odors. I smiled weakly as he set the tray on the table beside my bed and lifted me higher on my pillows. He apologized quietly when I couldn't help but groan in pain, and then tucked my coverlets around me. Murmuring something about our meal, he turned, careful not to jostle me further.

"How did you find me in the cave?" I asked quietly, my voice raspy and worn.

His hands stilled and he looked at me sharply. "Later. I'll tell you later. Right now, eating is what you must do."

He carefully set the tray on my lap. Closing my eyes, I inhaled deeply, imagining the taste of the theron eggs, gessa eshiday, honey bread, and the warm saflee, which I could smell. Staring at my tray, I frowned... discovering only a bowl of mild broth. Jon ate from the plate I had longed for. Suddenly, the odor of his food soured and my stomach revolted at the idea of eating at all. I was weak, emptied of everything clear down to my soul. Even Keyenoa's presence within me seemed distant and far away.

"Try to eat, Niki. It's been five long days, Fortulaynan," he said.

I stared at him in surprise, then looked at my bowl and reached for my jott with a trembling hand. Everything hurt when I moved. Still, I struggled to lift the heavy jott and drag it to my mouth. Sighing, I managed to slurp down what few drops remained in the bowl of the jott when I finally got the utensil to my mouth. After I managed two more tries, both being more successful than the last, Jon smiled and turned his attention back to his meal.

"If you keep eating that well, I should be able to answer all your questions... oh, maybe later today. And when you're feeling up to it, you can tell your father and me what happened... and who it was who had the audacity to attack an untried youth."

His words brought to my mind the clear memory of Te'air and the guard in the cave. In a matter of enas, I relived the whole humiliating and horrible incident. "Neye, Jon, I will never speak of what happened!" I declared in a venomous whisper, shame and hurt filling the emptiness in my soul.

"Trust in me, as you used to, Niki," he urged. "I'm not sure I can bear the pain of your rejection again." Jon's face was a mask of anguish as he looked at my nearly broken body. Leaving his food half eaten he turned to go.

"Master!" I called out when he reached the bedchamber door.

He turned, hopeful.

NIKITA'S STORY

Looking down at my bowl of broth, unable to meet his gaze, I whispered, "Ask Te'air, Jon. She knows."

I looked up and saw rage flaming in his black gaze. There was an expression of determination etched in the sudden lines on his face before he swung around and left my home. I closed my eyes, smiling with bitter anticipation, knowing Te'air would rue the day she crossed Jontair Alcone.

I slept deeply until his return at midday.

Waking, I took in his expression of both tenderness and smoldering rage as he looked into my sleep-drugged eyes. "She tried to weave a tale of castrin, believing you'd past in Sontall and so couldn't refute her story… but I eventually forced the truth from her."

I winced in pain her remembered betrayal.

Jon's anger swiftly left his expression as he witnessed my reaction. "I know, in your heart, you felt Keyen for her, Niki. Toenda omprice sorice, Met Fortulaynan, I wish with all my being that she could've been what you so wanted her to be."

I shook my head, silencing him quickly. That pain was too fresh to endure. "Don't apologize, Jon, not a bit of it was your doing. Tella saa, tell me what happened."

He studied me a moment shaken by my response. I felt him probe my thoughts with his power suspiciously. As he did so, I held my breath and concentrated on concealing what was within me, all the while meeting his gaze without fear. I didn't want him to discover the corrosion and emptiness in my soul because of her cruelty. I wanted his answers, and knew he wouldn't give them if he sensed my state of mind. Slowly, his power receded and I relaxed my defenses while awaiting his decision.

"All right, Niki," he sighed. Putting his hands on his thighs, he leaned back in his chair, his expression satisfied. Somehow I'd been able to teepin him. "The man who attacked you is named Mackien. He's one of Dorna's top guards." A frown appeared on his brow. "Tell me, is it true Niki? Did you come at them intending to attack… and the guard, not knowing who you were or your age, defended himself with his power?"

I closed my eyes in bitter shame and nodded, remembering my actions all to well.

"Okay," he said gently, easing my shame with his quiet acceptance. "Well, here's what I surmised from Te'air's story," he continued, "when Mackien realized what he had done—even believing you would soon to pass in Sontall—he was prepared to take you to the clearing and confess. Unfortunately, his honor was forestalled when Te'air told him your age and who you were. She begged him, using all her feminine charms, to leave you inside the cave where—upon your Sontall—you would vanish, leaving neye but the two of them aware of the truth. Mackien condemned himself even as he followed her advice; leaving you on the cave floor, he then fled to Dorna."

My Thaytor grew silent, anger dancing in his gaze.

"How did you find me? I remember trying not to be noticed when I went to the cave?"

Struggling to recover from the emotions sweeping through him, Jon moved to the window across from the bed and opened the shuttered window-doors to look at the gray-green haze of the leaves beyond. "A lady of the court by the name of Corina noticed you heading to the lake. When you failed to make an appearance in the clearing for both the mid and evening meals, and learning that I was greatly concerned over your absence, she approached me with her suspicions as to where you had gone.

"Knowing the significance of the cave, it was rather simple to find you." He turned and looked at me. "I leki Keyenoa Lady Corina noticed you, Niki. If she hadn't, Te'air's plan would've worked and you'd be gone. As it was, I found you nearly drowned in your own blood and... well, never mind... just onas before you would have reached Sontall. Because you couldn't defend yourself, the loss of blood and internal damage done to you made it... difficult... to keep you alive." Taking in a deep breath, Jon exhaled slowly, and then forced himself to smile, easing the severity of his words. "I swear, Niki, sometimes I wonder if Keyenoa's keeping you alive for some special reason. You've managed to live a very charmed life for your short sixteen aanas," he murmured with a teasing lilt to his voice, while shaking his head in disbelief.

Leaning back against the window frame, he frowned. "Niki, Te'air has been banished from New Malin. She understands it will mean her execution if she enters this Kingdom again."

"You told Father? Father knows and has done this?" I whispered, thinking that he too had learned of my great shame, it felt as if my whole world had crashed apart.

Jon shook his head. "As of now, your father's not been informed of her involvement. Her banishment was accomplished on my order alone." He sighed, shifting his weight on the window sill, "After I spoke with Te'air and before coming here, I went to your father intending to tell him everything. But before I was able to speak, he stopped me. He explained that he knew—even while you were unconsciousness—of your agitation and desperate desire that he never discover why such an attack had happened. He confessed to me that as he sat with you that first night, when you had begun to fade away, he promised you upon Keyenoa's name, that he would never seek to learn what had happened. He feared that if he didn't make such an oath to you and Keyenoa that you would have welcomed Sontall. It was upon his promise, Niki, you began to make a turn for the better. Mark made it clear he wanted to know ghea neye—so long as the reasons for the incident wouldn't be repeated and that your life wasn't threatened in such a manner again.

"I honored his request and his promise to you. I told him ghea neye of what happened, Niki." Jon held up his hand, forestalling my sigh of relief, "I did so in respect of his wishes—not yours," he continued, "and I told him plainly, if I didn't receive a few honest answers from you, I would be back in his chambers before this day was out."

A power-filled brilliance lit his eyes as he watched me closely. I returned his gaze, almost eager to face his questions. I was determined to keep my embarrassment from anyone else. Jon's knowledge was crushing enough.

"Niki, do you now feel Keyen… or have any desire for Te'air or any other woman you know?"

Holding his gaze, I replied with unflinching honesty, "I vow, Master, those feelings are quite gone." Not only were my feelings for Te'air obliterated, so was every other tender feeling in my soul. Her betrayal and the harsh loss of what I so desperately wanted had nearly destroyed me five short days past. To be able to survive, despite that desolation, I had encased my heart in stone.

Jon watched me a moment longer, then satisfied, he leaned back in his chair and sighed with relief, "Leki te ghea Alleanne!"

I was momentarily surprised that Jon hadn't realized the full scope of my honesty. However, grateful that he wouldn't tell Father and relieved I wouldn't have to do any further explaining of my emotional instability, I relaxed and listened to the end of his story.

"Mackien has been found, arrested, and jailed," Jon said. "He will await your Con Sona Eata when you shall then judge him yourself—as our laws decree. Due to those laws, Mackien is bound to silence, just as Te'air is on threat of her life. Therefore, neye will ever know what really happened."

"Do you think it's possible Father might change his mind and want to know?" I asked fearfully.

Jon shook his head. "I doubt he'll have much time to even contemplate such a thing. But time or not, Niki, he is a man of honor. Your father will keep his promise. His honor will overcome any curiosity he may have, believe me."

"Master, what's going on to keep Father so preoccupied?" I asked, remembering Jon had muttered something about Father's preoccupation when he had discovered me and Te'air in the cave.

He sighed, "Of course, you wouldn't know because everything happened on the same day," he murmured mostly to himself. "Niki, the Tenzenar *road* has made its curve to the west and crossed the river not even a teron south of New Malin. Their *road* has been laid all the way to LeFold Lake cutting a line between the borders of Malin and Cetar. It has been open and in use by *thacars* for several days." After making a short snort of derision, Jon looked at me and continued, "Listen to this, Niki. At the lake, these Tenzenar have made some sort of visitation site. They've put up what they call *picnic* tables and carefully scattered them about a portion of land between Malin and Cetar." He then gave another snort of disgust. "These *picnic* tables are for Tenzenar to put food on to share a pre-made meal. This enables them to '*experience the wilderness,*'" he chuckled quietly.

His voice changed subtlety when he noticed my need for sleep. He talked quietly of other changes around New Malin, waiting for my body to tell me what he already knew. Gently the hypnotizing power in his voice lulled me into sleep. Jon quietly left only after I was deeply asleep.

⌘⌘⌘⌘

I was confined to my bed for two fortauns. Often left to myself during that time, I spent many oonas carefully hardening myself and my heart against trust and affection. In those two fortauns I accomplished this goal. Neye was the wiser of this intent. Jon and Father visited often. They would bring meals and share news of New Malin and fascinating stories of the things the Tenzenar were doing at their '*recreation sight.*'

"How high do you consider the danger of discovery is to us and Cetar, with the Tenzenar so close?" I asked both men after we had finished our midday meal. I was thinking that the idea of many Tenzenar blundering around in New Malin might be the best thing to happen. It would certainly be something that would keep me entertained.

"It is less of a worry than before, Niki," Father assured me, "Met Lordship High King Sayleen Cantabo has used his power to confuse the Tenzenar minds. Every one of their senses and their machines tells them that the land surrounding the *recreation area* is dangerously impassable. As long as the Tenzenar see the land around them and trust in their machines and gadgets, they'll not dare cross the borders into either Kingdom."

Disappointed, I sighed. "When do you think I can get out and watch the Tenzenar… *picnic*?" I asked. By that time, my body was neye longer as bruised and lifeless as my soul.

"Soon, Niki, soon," Father assured me, after looking to Jon for confirmation.

As the days slowly passed, Father continued to visit. Each day I sensed that he had something he wanted to say but couldn't seem to get the words passed his lips—to his own growing frustration. Finally, three days before the end of my confinement Father came to my bedchamber, his expression strained—he was clearly ready and determined to talk.

"Niki, you know that I… well… that I will never seek to discover why this guard attacked you," he sighed. "I admit though, that I am mighty curious… it is an Airian trait, after all." Aware of my sudden panic, he sighed and shook his head swiftly, "Neye, son, whether I am curious or not, I am aware of your feelings… that's what I came to assure you. I give you my vow that I'll never pry into what transpired. I respect you, Niki, and your privacy. I honor your right to that privacy. If ever you find you feel differently or need to tell me, I will listen, eager to help in any way I can. Until then, Niki, I will speak neye more of the matter—this too I vow."

"Sorice leki omprice, Met Father," I murmured, running my fingers along the bed linen, "Thy understanding over this matter means more to me than I am able to express."

He patted my hand uncomfortably. "Neye, except Jon and I even know of the attack. Not even the woman, Corina, who told Jon of your whereabouts, knows of this assault. I also promise, son, that neye will ever hear of it unless you tell them—not even Met Lordship High King Sayleen Cantabo." To my surprise, he bent over the bed and placed a kiss on my forehead before swiftly leaving my room.

With every tender emotion I possessed near Sontall, I was unable to express how special his promise was to me. However, by Keyenoa's grace, the knowledge of his Keyen remained with me, locked away from the poison that had begun to grow and fill my soul.

During those last three days of confinement it was difficult to remain in bed. More than anything I wanted to escape all that was a reminder of what I had lost. I longed to turn my attention on the Tenzenar. I was itchy and eager to witness them *'picnicking.'*

Once I was released from my bed, I walked through each day in a haze of eager vindictiveness and volatile anger. When around my own people, I took great enjoyment in causing malicious mischief which would bring on the disapproval of others concerning my behavior and attitude. I purposely set out to alienate those closest to me and received perverse pleasure in hurting them as well as others. With each vindictive accomplishment, I was spurred on to find even more ways to drive anyone away teepin enough to get too close. I had even managed to shut Keyenoa out of my life—leaving me alive, though not living. It wasn't long before there were many in New Malin—including the guards that watched our boarders—who had become so disgusted with my behavior they silently wished me a short life and eternal anguish upon its end. Finally assuring myself I was free from all watchful and overprotective eyes, I began to make intrusive forays into the Tenzenar *recreation area*.

I would rise each morning, snatch food from the clearing and go directly to New Malin's border near the *road* and *recreation area*. At first I would climb the branches of a zumfouler tree watching my quarry from a safe distance, but I quickly grew uncomfortable and board. These two factors soon overcame any fear I had of discovery. I then began to move among the Tenzenar, and even got daring enough to steal food right from their *picnic* hampers, happily ending my morning jaunts in the clearing among my own people.

I began to stay at the *recreation area* for whole days, returning to New Malin only when I felt the need to cause my own people trouble and to remind them to be glad of my absences. Then, I expanded my times away from New Malin, spending fortauns living and sleeping among the Tenzenar in the *recreation area*, surviving by partaking of their unknowing hospitality.

I even dared to climb into a *thacar* and traveled with them back to their dwellings. The speed of the vehicle and how close I was forced to sit next to the Tenzenar as we traveled meant ghea

PART I TENZENAR

neye to me. All that mattered was how far they could take me and the speed in which they got me away from my own people. I derived such great pleasure from the challenge of stealing and maneuvering my way into the Tenzenar machines, I decided to intensify my daring adventures. I then began to create mischief and havoc among the Tenzenar, straining and pushing the limits of my invisibility through its frequent use. By holding my shield as long as I could, this seemed to gradually lengthen the time I was able to hold my invisibility.

I quickly learned that each *thacar* had to stop at the home Jon and I visited. These *thacar* seemed to need something called *fuel* to make them run, and if they didn't stop at *Bill* and *Ruth's* home, they would run out of this *fuel* before reaching the city. I discovered that *Bill* and *Ruth's* dwelling was also called a *farm* and the family called themselves the *Masters*. *Bill* and *Ruth* were the parents of *Lisa*, and *Michael*. Their kindness to all who visited was affirmed each time I stopped with the Tenzenar in their *thacar*. The *Masters'* were generous people, making a living from *farming*, selling *fuel*, and even offering rooms for the night. I often remained with the *Masters*, feeling a sense of aclusceaun living on the fringes of their lives.

At first I was concerned that *Lisa* would reveal my presence, but quickly ascertained that such a danger was minimal. *Lisa* never volunteered any information or knowledge of me, though it was apparent she knew when I was around. Sometimes she'd get caught staring at something neye could see, or was heard talking to *Sam*, their logone, about me. When asked, *Lisa* would answer with sincere honesty—but neye would believe her. It quickly became an accepted fact in her family that *Lisa* had acquired an *"imaginary friend"* and neye more was said about her 'odd' behavior. This conclusion was also indulgently explained in a quiet way to guests when they noticed *Lisa's* behavior.

Lisa was also clearly aware of my mental instability. She never once spoke directly to me, understanding that I needed to be left alone. I was grateful that she kept her distance. I had great affection for the nikca; but despite that affection, if *Lisa* had tried

171

to be a forlana, I would have ruthlessly hurt her… if only to purposely hurt myself.

I quickly learned that *Lisa* had incredible sensitivity and discernment, and it was this that aided her ability to see beyond my invisibility shield. It wasn't long before I discovered that there were other Tenzenar who seemed to have a similar sensitivity to *Lisa's*. Some would notice vague shadows or would giggle uncontrollably when I got too near. Traveling in their vehicles for oonas at a time, I learned that many Tenzenar would grow solemn and still. If I were careless and accidentally made contact with them, that person would shiver violently and make some inane comment. Occasionally, a Tenzenar would get hysterical either laughing uncontrollably or weeping in deep grief. This happened only in an enclosed space like their *thacars*. It was an arecean that neye other Tenzenar, nikca or adult, seemed to have the depth of sensitivity that enabled *Lisa* to see me so clearly.

I remained content to travel between the *recreation sight* and the *Masters'* home. I had neye desire to see the Tenzenar town or to visit Malinieum City. I might not have cared about living around the Tenzenar, but I wasn't fond of the idea of being inundated by them, their buildings, and various machines. Malinieum City was also too much of a reminder of everything I fought to leave behind. I wanted neye reminders of my people, their Keyen, or Keyenoa.

As the tuevtauns went by, I learned many minca things about the Tenzenar. I discovered their vehicles were called *cars* or a *car* if it was just one. I often overheard discussions about those Tenzenar which they called *scientists* and *archeologists*. These were the people gathering what information they could from the Airian cities they had discovered. There were also some *scientists* that recorded details of what the Tenzenar called "Airian *sightings*." These were encounters of unexplainable and unusual events or occurrences which took place. Far from a surprise, many of these described encounters were very similar to the pranks I continued to play on any worthwhile and unsuspecting Tenzenar. Having neye proof of these encounters save the word of the Tenzenar reporting an incident, many of these *scientists* discounted such reports. However, the Tenzenar population quickly began to realize, discounted or not, a great number of experiences were too similar in nature to completely ignore and Airian encounters quickly became a fad of folklore and legend.

It wasn't long before the rumor of sightings and missing food from pantries and defackas started a custom that spread throughout the Tenzenar population. Each night, succulent meals would be set outside the Tenzenar dwellings to appease these mischievous 'Airian' sprites. While neye adult actually believed in these sprites, it was a custom they created to entertain and excite their nikca. Unconcerned over their reasons for the custom, I was simply grateful to have food at my disposal. It kept me from having to raid anymore defackas or pantries in the dwellings popping up around the *Masters' farm*. I was careful in my habits of pilfering from these 'offerings,' being certain to utilize offerings at different dwellings in the area. I was aware that if I raided only from the *Masters'* home, Tenzenar suspicions might rise, causing many to question that *Lisa's* invisible forlana just might not be as imaginary as they first believed. I confess it was hard to turn down *Ruth's* offerings. I enjoyed her cooking so much that there were many nights when I bravely snuck into the house and shared a meal with them at their table with only *Lisa* aware of my presence.

As the tuevtauns passed, I came to understand why some Tenzenar lived life with joy, while others seemed to go through life simply existing. Those, like the *Masters*, who lived with joy, believed in Keyenoa—or *God* as they called Him—and had a strong belief in someone named *Jesus* who was also Keyenoa… or *God*. While this confused me very much, I couldn't deny there was a difference to those people who believed in Him. The Tenzenar who lived their lives without *God* and *Jesus*—neye matter how hard they tried to make themselves happy—never quite succeeded in finding that unshakable joy found in the Tenzenar like the *Masters*.

Because I'd chosen to ignore Keyenoa in my life, I gave up all interest in the subject once I learned He was the reason why there was a vast difference between many Tenzenar. Turning my attention to other matters, I continued with my self-destructive behavior.

My conduct, of course, didn't go unnoticed or ignored by my own people. There was a great deal of worry, along with many quiet discussions and conferences concerning my actions. Father understood that my misdeeds and Tenzenar focused activities were caused by what had taken place before my attack, but he never once confronted me or Jon when I was in New Malin. He recognized that his learning the details of what had happened would do ghea neye to stop my destructive course. He knew that instead of bringing me back to my old self, it would only spur me on to further angry and destructive actions. Because of Father's and Bonfinar's counsel, Jon also gave me my freedom while the conferences and quiet discussions continued in the hopes that someone would find a solution to bring me back home and back to myself. Therefore, free to do as I desired, I continued running from myself, Keyenoa, and the concern of those closest to me.

On the seventh tuevtaun following my sixteenth day of birth, all three men had reached their wit's end. Failing miserably with every idea they tried, Father called upon the wisdom of Met Lordship High King Sayleen Cantabo.

The night before the private meeting, the people of New Malin were gathered in the upper and lower clearings to celebrate and honor the High King's visit. I was ordered to remain in New Malin and told to join our people in their celebrations. Father hoped that by Met Lordship witnessing my behavior, the High King would have some answers as to what to do about me.

It was a joyously happy night filled with laughter, drinking, and dancing—a night very much like my day of birth celebration—filled with everything I'd come to despise, fear, and mistrust. Obeying Father's orders, I remained in New Malin deciding to unleash my own type of entertainment. Before Met Lordship had even made an appearance, I was well involved in my own efforts to celebrate. With the skill of a brutal and vocal surgeon, I managed to dim the happiness of many people. Success bubbled in my veins, spurring me onto more destruction. Craftily, I managed to start fights between innocent bystanders and ruined jokes by revealing the punch line before the story was half told. I deliberately made extremely poisonous and cruel remarks concerning appearances, the motives for gifts being given and complements being offered. I was so successful I left almost everyone I encountered either in tears or fighting mad. Every one of them was personally ready to leave the celebration before it even officially began.

Quickly learning of my behavior, Father caught up with me and ordered me to my tree-home with an angry reproach. But that night I danced on the edge between sanity and destruction. Ignoring my father's orders, I left the clearing and started across the bridge toward the Tenzenar recreation area. I was determined to find a *car* to the *Masters' farm*, and do what damage I could among the Tenzenar.

I had started across the bridge only to I freeze at its center. Three shrill, long whistles pierced the night. New Malin's borders had been breached by a Tenzenar. My heart pounded with dread and excitement. I for one was not about to run for cover and hide. I was going to seek out the intruding Tenzenar and discover how they had entered New Malin.

Chapter IX

Jeanitear

"My Keyen for thee will ever remain, even during those days when thee deny Me. Always and ever will I strive to lead thee home if thee should ever stray."

—Book of Keyenoa

Three whistles pierced the night for a second time, now nearer to the clearing. The guards, who were following the intruder, sounded their warnings each time another guard post had been breached. Conden, seeing me, lowered his shield of invisibility as he ran onto the bridge. His eyes were glazed with fear as he focused on me as I blocked his escape.

"Nikita, raise your shield! The Tenzenar comes in this direction!" he exclaimed.

I stared at him, completely confused by his fear. Again, the whistles were heard as other guard posts were breached, and they too began their exodus from the invader. The guards would precede the intruder until they reached their last defensive position—just beyond the bridge where I stood. There, the intruder would be surrounded and killed by an arrow shot from a Loreann bow. Conden, tired of waiting for me to move on my own, grabbed my shoulders and shoved me to one side as he ran across the bridge to take his position of last defense.

PART I TENZENAR

"Niki, come on!" he urged, pulling his Loreann bow off his shoulder, he notched an arrow into position as he took up his assigned station at the edge of the clearing. There he raised his shield and vanished from sight, bow and all.

The soft rustling of underbrush behind me indicated that other guards had also crossed the stream and took up their positions, drawing their arms in preparation. I raised my invisibility shield, but didn't run for my tree-home. Instead, I crossed the bridge heading away from New Malin, determined to see who this Tenzenar was who had found a way beyond the shield Met Lordship had placed around New Malin. A Tenzenar destined not to live long, if it continued on its course. I was filled with morbid curiosity. I wondered how Tenzenar passed in Sontall and if it would be Conden who would make the kill.

The quiet of the night was suddenly breached by a cacophony of noise. Breaking twigs, tearing briars, and the crushing of leaves beneath clumsy feet shattered the still of the night. These noises were swiftly followed with strangled cries of protest, pain, and mounting frustration. Smiling, I waited patiently for the clumsy Tenzenar to blunder through the underbrush, find the bridge, and cross it. There, a swift arrow or lackna thrust would meet it and end its life. I was determined I would not miss such a sight.

The Tenzenar crashed through the trees, landing on its hands and knees less than a pearon from the bridge. It mumbled something, voice cracked and trembling, so very near to tears that my heart raced in eager anticipation. Then, the Tenzenar pushed itself to its feet.

It brushed tangled hair from its face and looked around with fearful desperation. The ena it took for my sharp-sighted Airian gaze to take in the pitiful sight, there was a rush of stabbing, biting pain which pierced my heart and spread swiftly to my soul. With my breath, momentarily knocked from my lungs, I could do ghea neye but stare in wonder and awe at the woman before me.

She wore a light tan coat that reached her knees and covered a silky, misty-blue dress nearly the same length. Her legs trembled. Both knees were skinned and bleeding a dark red color. Both her knees and legs were coated in leaf debris and muck. She carried a minca, odd-looking metal container tightly in one hand. In her fear she swung it defensively back and forth in front of her. She stood so close to the bridge she barely missed grazing the rail with each pass. However, with the moon still hidden behind the clouds and the night so dark, her weak Tenzenar eyes couldn't see the bridge before her. Blinded, she had blundered into New Malin unaware. It was a ghea teepin mistake, and one I knew could prove fatal if she ever noticed the bridge and crossed it.

Her fear was palatable to my senses, tasting of salt, sweat, and ground decay. It vibrated around me, moving with the air she disturbed by her swinging container. Her breath, sweet in odor, puffed from her lips as she fought to still her mounting terror.

Empathy filled my broken heart along with tenderness and affection, instantly washing away the searing pain and darkness eroding my soul. I didn't want her killed. This plain, ghea teepin woman, with her fear, uncertainty, and determination to let ghea neye defeat her, had so moved me that I managed to forget my own anger and fear. Finally I was able to let go of my own determination that ghea neye would ever hurt or touch me again. Having my ability to feel Keyen restored, I couldn't sacrifice this woman to what would come if she discovered the bridge. However, I had neye idea what I could do to stop her. Praying for the first time in seven tuevtauns, I humbly pleaded that Keyenoa show me how to spare this woman while I watched and waited, taking in her strange beauty.

Her long, brown hair was in a tangle. Sharing the silky strands, was damp earth and grass, and bits of twigs and leaves, scattered and matted in it. I wondered if she'd ever manage to comb the mess out. There were tears in her enormous brown eyes, which had begun to trickle down her face, causing her eyes and cheeks to glisten and shimmer in the darkness. Her face was roughly scratched and bruised, smudged by dirt, dampened by tears and dew. She was beautiful to my eyes. In her expression was a longing and a need for someone to care for her… a need equal to my own in all ways. It was in that ena of recognition that I gave her my heart.

PART I TENZENAR

Those hauntingly sad eyes continued their blind search, hoping to see something or someone who could help her. I was relieved that her search would prove hopeless in the darkness. It kept her safe. It kept her alive.

Without warning, the fickle moon rose above the trees, pierced the cloudy sky with its silvery light. My heart leapt into my throat as I took in the details of her beauty. She was filled with Keyenoa's presence. He seemed to overflow from her like a fountain pouring out cool, healing spring water. Then, those forlorn Tenzenar eyes lit with joy as they fell on the sight of the bridge, filling me with dread.

"Oh! Thank You, God! A bridge! There has to be someone nearby living in this wild place," gratitude and relief filled her voice. It had neye melodic ring or sing-song cadence, but it was soft and gentle, reminding me of the rustle of crisp dry leaves when one scuffles their feet through them on a chilly day.

I stepped out of her way when she started to cross the bridge before coming to my senses. This Tenzenar had somehow awakened me from my emotional Sontall. I was more alive than I had been in seven long tuevtauns and I couldn't allow her life to be taken after giving me such a gift. Not knowing what else to do, I started to reach out, planning to grasp her arm and keep her from crossing.

Another whistle rent the air from just across the bridge. I recognized it as Conden's as he made his claim to make the kill if the woman crossed the bridge. Suddenly the Tenzenar halted, stumbling backward in her fear. Relieved, I let my hand fall to my side. Closing her eyes she sagged. I watched in awe as her dirty face softened and became serene. Then, with a sigh the woman opened those eyes again, revealing that she had replaced her fear—which had nearly paralyzed her—with both faith and trust. In her expression was a steely determination to go forward. Focusing her gaze blindly beyond the bridge, she tried to see the source of the whistle. To my horror, she straightened with a rather frightened but determined jerk of her shoulders and took a step toward the bridge a second time. I heard the slight rustle of Conden taking aim with his Loreann bow.

"Neye, tella saa, neye, don't go any further!" I shouted in Airian without thought.

She stopped and twisted around, swinging the metal container up and out with deliberate malice. I jumped back as it barely missed my head. Her breathing had again grown uneasy as she peered blindly and desperately in my direction. Slowly, the clouds enclosed the moon, dimming the silvery light around us. In that fading light, having found ghea neye, her knees buckled beneath her, and she slumped to the base of the stone bridge. Broken and in utter defeat, terror, and exhaustion she began to weep pathetically.

Moving beside her, I watched helplessly as I argued with myself, questioning my sanity and courage. Sighing, I lifted my eyes to Alleanne and prayed. "My alon was sealed long before my eyes beheld her, wasn't it?" I asked Him silently. "I can neye more leave her at the edge of this bridge, terrified and exhausted, than I can shut Thee from my soul and heart any longer."

Forcing myself to relax, I lowered my shield. Instantly my tunic picked up the minca light from my limited boyish power, radiating a soft, silvery glow around me. Conden cried out, and then silenced himself, uttering only an odd-choked syllable.

Over his protest, Jon's shouted in greif, "Neye! For Alleanne's sake don't! Te salma tella saa, Niki, don't!"

I hesitated, aware of my Thaytor's fear and grief. Hearing the strange voices, the woman curled tightly in on herself. If I left her here to finally muster the courage to once again cross that bridge and so meet her Sontall, Jon would be able to do ghea neye to help me return to life. If I allowed this woman to come to harm, I knew my soul would be utterly destroyed. My people and home had minca hold on my heart, whereas this woman fully held my heart in her hands. I simply could not stand by and see her hurt or frightened any longer. This Tenzenar, in all her strange, alluring beauty had somehow aroused emotions in me I thought long since obliterated and unattainable.

With my own hands trembling, I took her cold, trembling fingers into my warm grasp. At my gentle contact, she flinched and glanced up fearfully, ready to attack to save herself if necessary.

She was far too frightened to speak, but I knew I had to say something to ease her fear... or find myself maimed by her defense. I also had to talk to her in Tenzenar or I would be unable to halt her defensive attack.

Mustering my courage, I quickly cleared my throat, *"Please... do not be... frightened... anymore. I am quite real and very harmless."* I stumbled abominably over the pronunciation of her flat lifeless language.

She trusted me immediately. With a hesitant smile, she relaxed and withdrew her hands from mine to roughly scrub the tears from her face. Her hands, as filthy and scraped as her knees, only soiled her cheeks all the more. I couldn't help but smile at picture she made. Gathering her emotions and putting them in order, she glanced up at me as she struggled to get to her feet. When I rose with her, my silver neron lox tunic caught a minca shaft of moonlight and illuminated her delicate face in sharp clarity. I gasped in wonder all over again. Even streaked with mud, she was beautiful. She stared at me, puzzled by my reaction to her.

We stared at one another, both mesmerized by the strong current of emotion that danced between us. Unable to help myself, I caressed the tears and dirt smudges from her face. She blinked in surprise at my touch and lowered her eyes. Disconcerted by it, she shyly broke the contact between us by taking a step back.

I smiled and took her hand. While I was also stunned by the powerful feelings between us, I sensed her need for some kind of reassuring contact. Picking up the metal container she had dropped when I spoke to her, I turned her away from the bridge and New Malin.

Holding her hand, I guided her south, around the inlet, and then pointed in the direction she needed to go. *"If you walk straight through there, you will come to the road you lost and find someone to give you aid,"* I said softly, fighting the sudden urge to take her lips in a gentle kiss. Reluctantly, I returned the metal container and turned to go.

She grasped my arm. *"Please don't leave me here alone,"* her voice trembled as much as she did.

Cupping her face with my hands, I looked into her eyes, discovering the remains of old emotional scars, along with that loneliness and a need for Keyen that so echoed within my own gaze. Along with those emotions I was also aware of the blazing and healing evidence of Keyenoa's presence. Then, I saw in those flat, brown colored orbs, a sharp and real terror of being left alone in this place so strange to her. I instantly recognized it was a terror spawned from the memories of whatever had caused her to run blindly into New Malin. I caressed her cheek, wanting to remain, but knowing I should go, and forced my hands to my side.

She clasped at my hand desperately, *"I haven't got a car, and no one will likely come looking for me—at least until tomorrow. A man… he… left me here… and I am afraid he might decide to come looking for me. I can't… I don't… he can't find me."* Her voice caught on an uncontrollable sob. *"All the strange sounds… so much like voices… and the whistling when no one was there. Please, please don't leave me alone,"* she begged.

I released her hand and rubbed my thumb along her jaw, "How could anyone be so cruel as to abandon such a jeanitear omnistera as thee?" I asked, unaware I had spoken in my language.

"What…?"

Before I could answer, her gaze left my face and she looked me over. She took in the sight of my clothing, and finally realized that I was the one generating the soft light around us rather than the moon. She gasped, suddenly recognizing that I was not Tenzenar. Like a dree before the dassishon strikes, her fear became so great she froze.

Hating that I had frightened her even more, I simply started to talk. Speaking softly at first, as I would to a helop uncertain of my intentions, I was careful to use her language rather than my own. *"My name is* Nikita Markain Malin. *I am an* Airian, *the son and hopeful heir to the throne of the* Sixth King of Airies, *who is named* Markain Malin.*"* To my relief, her expression of terror slowly faded, becoming interested and bemused.

A theron suddenly startled from the trees close by. Crying out in alarm it burst from its resting place and flew over our heads in the direction of New Malin. She jumped, and stifling a cry, she moved closer to me for protection. I was awed by her sudden trust. Lifting my eyes I offered my leki to Keyenoa and watched as the bird as it disappeared beyond the trees. Then, I thought of New Malin and was aware it was time I return to those waiting for me there.

"Knowing what I am, do you still want me to stay with you?" I asked. *"I can take you to a place where I know you will be safe and very near the road. There you can wait for help and I can return to my people."*

"Please stay... um... your majesty," she stammered for a title unable to pronounce the one I told her that my father held.

At my smile, she curtsied rather saucily in an effort to cover for her embarrassment or possible mistake in my title. Leaving her head cocked to one side, she peeked up at me, revealing a pair of flat brown eyes that suddenly glittered with tenderness and mischief. I found myself even more ensnared by her strange beauty. A beauty that went far deeper than her skin.

Surrendering to her playfulness, I smiled while lowering myself in a sweeping bow. *"I shall stay most gladly, fair lady, and protect you while you sleep from all fearsome things of the night. Promise me but two favors and one gift, my beautiful treasure, and I will be your servant till dawn brings forth the sun."*

Remaining in my playful bow, I angled my head upward watching her while awaiting her answer. Her smile radiated a joyous pleasure. She dropped the metal container to the ground—completely forgotten—clasping her hands in nikca-like glee.

"Speak your favors and request your gift, your majesty, and I will hold you honor bound," she declared.

Straightening from my bow with consummate flourish, I kneeled before her and held out my hand. *"First, my beautiful treasure, you must promise never to wander anywhere in this forest without me at your side. Second, I would have your promise that you will never mention what has happened this night after you fled into this forest. And my treasure, the gift I dare to ask would be the simple utterance of your name."*

She lowered her head, pretending to lift a long, flowing gown off the ground and curtsied in regal formality. *"Kind lord, I solemnly and dutifully vow to keep both promises."* She looked up at me while in her curtsy, her expression solemn and earnest. *"I promise these things, fully aware of the importance of each, and gratefully aware that my lord is only making light of the situation to ease my fear."*

"And my requested gift?" I asked her, not sure how to respond to her astute observation.

She lowered her head in a slow and regal nod, *"My name is Jennifer Anne MacArthur."*

Surpised to learn she had three names, I urged her to stand from her cursty and face me, realizing that she had to be at leaset equal to my status as a prince. *"You must be a... queen!"* I stammered searching for a fitting title in *English*, *"a most important one at that.* Met Lady*, it is I who must kneel at your feet!"* I exclaimed.

"What? No, I'm not a queen... why would you think so?" she stammered in bemusement.

Embarrassed and feeling very ghea teepin, I looked away. *"Never mind,"* I mumbled, while picking up her metal container. *"Come, let me help you find a warm place to sleep."*

Confused, her eyes begged me for an answer as she took my offered hand. Far too embarrassed, I refused to explain as I led her nearer to the *recreation area*. Finding a dry and protected area under a large gungas tree about a pearon from the *road*, I lifted the low branches and indicated she enter and explore her sleeping area.

She eyed me skeptically, before hesitantly ducking under the branches. *"Oh! This is nice!"* she exclaimed after I followed her in. My tunic illuminated the minca area from the continual glow of my limited youthful power. *"Thank you... um... what do you... uh...? What is your title?"* she asked, while settling herself in the soft dry leaf debris.

I coughed, further embarrassed, *"*Niki. *Just call me,* Niki. *I do not like titles much. Most people use my name—at least until* *it is learned if I am to be a king or not. Do you like to be called Jennifer, or something different?"*

"*Jenny,*" she answered comfortably.

"*Jenny...*" I rolled the foreign sound of her name on my tongue, "*I like that name very much,*" I said, causing her to blush.

Again my heart was tugged. My affection and desire for her was growing, and I realized the difficulty suddenly before me. Forcing my thoughts to the matters of chivalry, I dug the toe of my boot into the soil and leaf debris at my feet and stammered, "*I will find a place a bit farther around the tree to rest, so you need not worry about... uhm... er... well—so you do not worry.*"

"Niki?"

I looked up.

"*Oh rats! I don't want to sound... well.... Oh, just spit it out Jenny,*" she demanded of herself, "*Please don't leave, even if it's just a few feet around the tree trunk.*" She looked away in shame. "*I'm afraid. I'm shaking like a leaf and I can't seem to stop.*" Then gathering her courage she looked at me and continued, "*I know it may sound crazy to you. I mean, I can't even say why... but I know I can trust you. And if you don't stay... the things I'll remember, and imagine...*" she faltered a moment, then blurted, "*Oh, Niki, what he did... what he tried... and then to leave me here... I'm afraid!*"

Lost to her enchantment, I couldn't refuse. With a sigh of defeat, I sat beside her. "*I will stay, fair maiden. Your request is my command,*" I spoke lightly, hoping my return to our playful banter would ease the terrible pain that seemed to suddenly surround her. "*Now, lay here and sleep. I promise to keep you warm and safe. Fold away your fears, little one, until you can bring them out and place them in the light of day.*"

She sighed and snuggled into my arms and the leaves beside me. As we drifted to sleep, my body slowly grew insubstantial and mist-like. I thought it was a dream—even when my body and my thoughts begin to merge with hers and we formed one being. Only as my heartbeat accelerated to meet the cadence that hers, did I drowsily question my dream, but could not seem to wake.

'This seems like something Jon described as Keyen Sapato. What a strange dream,' I thought to myself in my half awake and half asleep state. 'I can't merge with another until after Con Sona Eata. But it's a nice dream, nonetheless… and so real. I like being one with her, even if it is all in my imagination.' I sighed, falling deeper into sleep and merging further with her body and mind.

Jenny slept on unaware of what was happening.

Our thoughts swiftly joined, and we openly shared our many hopes, hurts, wants, and fears—all as if in a dream. Loneliness and a longing for Keyen was an emotion we both experienced. I began to know her soul as Keyenoa created it at the beginning of time, and I welcomed her to learn all she desired about me. Eagerly, she reached into the depth of my soul and with a simple nikca-like innocence and curiosity she absorbed all that I was, just as I did with her.

An oona later I awoke suddenly. Instantly, I separated from *Jenny*, only then realizing our sharing had not been the dream I had thought. *Jenny* didn't stir. Alerted by my instincts, I rose to my knees and cocked my head to one side listening for any unnatural sound, trying to hone in on the danger I knew was nearby. Something was ready to enter the forest. Raising my shield, I crawled out from beneath the branches, just as a harsh yellow light flashed through the trees in a searching arc. There was the sound of muffled and metallic chatter nearer the *road*, sending shivers along my arms. After a moment it became clear that this odd-sounding chatter wasn't moving but remained on the *road*. That harsh light flashed through the trees once again. Focusing on the light, a sound of snapping twigs reached my ears. Whoever had command of that light had entered the forest and was moving cautiously in my direction.

"Jennifer!?" a male Tenzenar voice shattered the quiet night with booming authority.

She stirred beneath the tree behind me.

Again the Tenzenar shouted her name. His voice resounded through the trees with firm authority.

PART I TENZENAR

She murmured something incoherent and crawled out from under the gungas tree, her eyes still blurred by sleep. The yellow light arced through the trees, this time closer.

"Jennifer Anne MacArthur!?" her name was shouted for a third time as the light arced past her, brushing over her coat for the barest of enas.

She quickly stepped toward the light. *"Here! I'm here! Over here!"*

She rushed past me. Unaware of my presence, she was intent only on finding the man who had called her name. With a cylindrical portable light source, the man easily moved toward the sound of her voice, emerging from the brush only a few furons away. *Jenny* rushed toward him, falling into his arms. The man comforted her a moment, before he stepped back and looked her over very carefully.

He wore a stiff, uncomfortable-looking dark blue coat with gold buttons glittering brightly down the front. The buttons, along with a gold medal star pinned to the coat over his breast reflected the light from the silver object he held in his hand. He wore a hat on his head with a black shiny brim and a minca metal shield attached to it with Tenzenar writing on it.

"Are you all right, Ms. MacArthur?" he asked. *"The station dispatcher received an anonymous report that you were lost up here. While the caller refused to give his name, we felt it prudent to investigate after checking at your home and then with your parents."* He frowned. *"Good thing we did. There have been far too many strange reports received around here. You've been a brave little lady being up here alone for the better part of a night. All the gold on Gareross would have to be offered for me to endure a night up here,"* he said, praising her in an effort to calm her.

"Thank you, Officer," she began said with relief, *"I've been wandering around, lost for hours. I got all turned around and couldn't find the road, and had no idea how to get back to it. Only an hour or two ago, I was lucky enough to stumble...."* She clamped her mouth shut, realizing she nearly broke her promise and told the man of my rescue. Covering for her near blunder, she

continued rapidly, *"Stumble under this tree and found a warm and dry place to sleep."*

The man leaned back on his heels, his eyebrows raised when she ended her story. *"Yes, I would say very lucky indeed. If you'd wandered more than half a mile east, you'd have encountered some real nasty cliffs, treacherous sand bogs, and shale rock that can crumble away with the slightest provocation."*

Jenny paled in shock.

"It's okay, Ms, MacArthur, don't give it another thought," he stammered, ashamed he'd frightened her. *"You're safe now, and obviously must have never gotten close to that area. Come, I'll get you to the Masters' farm. They're expecting you. Even now, Ruth Masters is likely warming up a good warm meal and making up a room for you to sleep in tonight. They're real fine folk and will take good care of you until your parents are able to leave Second Site in the morning and drive out to pick you up."*

I nearly choked with laughter at the man's gullibility to believe everything he saw, and his misinterpretation of *Jenny's* expression. She had instantly realized that she wandered much farther than a teron to the east. Instead of stumbling over a cliff, into sand bogs, or careened down a rock slide, she ran smack into me.

"Come along, Ms. MacArthur, you must be cold and tired. The road's up there, approximately fifty feet away," he said, as he pointed the cylindrical light in the direction he spoke, and placing his arm around her shoulder urged *Jenny* forward in a comforting manner. *"As I said, I'll be taking you down to the Masters' farm, so there's nothing more for you to worry about. Ruth Masters is a dear woman, full of warmth and understanding. Both she and Bill love to have company and are eager for yours."*

"Thank you, Officer," she murmured, her head falling against his shoulder in exhaustion.

I followed them back to the *road*. The man kept his arm around her as he carefully eased her across the uneven ground and guided her through the forest by the use of the portable light in his free hand. I looked around at the place I called home. In the

PART I TENZENAR

last few tuevtauns, I'd shut my eyes to the land I was now seeing, admitting that had refused to acknowledged it as my home. Returning my attention to the Tenzenar female tucked against the man's shoulder, I thought about what we had shared and had restored within each other.

"She pulls me, Met Keyenoa, and I know not what to do. How is it that You chose her—a Tenzenar—to so touch my heart that my will to live has been restored? However it was done, she did renew my desire to return to You. How then can I stay here and let her leave me behind? How can I let her go... without going with her? I'm afraid, Met Keyenoa, that if I allow her to leave, I'll fall once again into decay. I see this land, yet it neye longer is mine. Your people neye longer seem like my people. Forgive me, Father, if I wrong You and Your people, but I know I cannot remain without her and keep from ending my own life because of my grief. I need to go with her if I'm ever to fully live again," I said silently, still following *Jennifer* and the man.

They stopped at a black-and-white painted *car* parked on the *road*. In the forest I heard the muted trill of three, short whistles. The guards of New Malin, having followed her departure, signaled that all was safe for the people within Malin's protective boundaries. *Jenny* glanced over her shoulder. Her eyes, sad and full of longing, filled with tears. Then she sighed and turned back to the *car*. I quietly hoped she would be happy when she learned we hadn't actually parted.

I prepared myself as the man opened the back door of the *car*. When *Jenny* slid inside, she ghea leki'anne slid over to the far door. Then, just as the man put his hand on the door to shove it closed, I placed my hand on the inside of the *car* door and exerted just enough pressure to hold it open for the matter of enas I needed to get inside. He felt the door's hesitation for less than a moment before he pushed it closed with a smooth shove. I was relieved that *Jenny* had unknowingly left me plenty of room to make myself comfortable without having to brush against her.

The man quickly climbed into the front seat and started the motor of the *car*. *Jenny* laid her head wearily against the window beside her and gazed out at the silhouetted trees watching as they swayed in the night breeze. Her face was reflected in the glass of the *car* window, and I watched her as she continued to look out longingly at the forest while tears slid down her cheeks.

The *car* slowly picked up speed after it turned around at the north end of the *recreation area*. When we swept past the place where the vehicle had been parked moments before, *Jenny* slumped in her seat and sighed deeply. Turning from the window, she wiped her eyes and stared blindly up at the ceiling above her. My breath caught, I hoped she was despondent because she thought I'd been left behind.

"*Is anything wrong, miss?*" the man asked, glancing into his *rearview mirror*.

"No, not really, Officer." *Jenny* forced herself to sit upright. "*I feel empty... as though I'd gained something for just a moment.... Something so incredibly priceless and very special that I couldn't begin to count its true worth.... Only to lose it just as quickly as I'd gained it.*" She sighed, "*Oh, I can't seem to explain it right. It's rather like being given the most wondrous gift in the world, and with it so many things to learn and understand... then loose it before you can even look at it. It's gone so fast, you're not even sure it was actually there—let alone was ever really yours to begin with.*"

The man grunted and nodded. "*I think I understand, Ms. MacArthur. Whether you know it or not, you're talking about love. Are you perhaps thinking about the young man who called the station and told us where to find you?*" he asked gently, thinking he had the answer to her problems. "*Don't you worry about losing a thing. Do you hear me? He's not worth your trouble let alone your love. Believe me, I know! Anyone who would leave another person up here is not worth a plug nickel, in my book. Though, if you're determined he's the one, I wouldn't let him know or forgive him too quickly for leaving you up here.*" He looked in the rear view mirror and smiled with reassurance.

Jenny shook her head, looking down at her hands, unable to face him with the shame that suddenly filled her expression, "*No,*

Officer, you're right. He isn't worth even a plug nickel. He left me behind because he wouldn't take no for an answer and I had to fight him off. What I think of him now is not fit to be spoken, let alone thought," she said quietly, bravely lifting her grief-stricken face to meet the man's eyes through the rear view mirror.

The *officer* flushed red with embarrassment and made some comment about *prosecuting* him if she wanted to *press charges*. Blushing, *Jenny* whispered *"No"* while fighting sudden tears.

"Please let it go. I'd just like to forget him and hold onto the dreams I had as I slept under that tree in the forest. They were wonderful dreams, and more precious because they seem more real to me than my previous… date."

The man straightened in his seat and glanced back at her, his expression one of tenderness and respect. *"Ms. MacArthur, believe it or not, I understand better than you could imagine. I know you might find this hard to believe, but such dreams are not restricted just to the young. We adults are blessed by them as well. I'm sorry you had to face such ugliness before experiencing such joy only in a dream. I hope some day, your dream comes true."*

Both of them fell silent, concentrating on their own personal thoughts as the metallic chatter continued from a box beside him under the *dashboard*. With her head resting against the *car* window, *Jenny* soon fell asleep. I just watched her, hoping I had done the right thing in following her.

When we turned into the *Masters' driveway* and slowly came to a stop, I sat up and prepared myself. While the *officer* got out of the *car* and walked around to the back door, I shifted as quietly as I could on the seat. Ghea leki'anne, *Jenny* had fallen asleep against her door, so the man moved around to my door and opened it carefully.

"Ms. MacArthur, wake up, now. We've arrived at the Masters' farm," he said, blocking my exit as he leaned into the *car*.

Jenny woke suddenly and began to slide across the seat. Afraid she'd bump into me, I put my shoulder against the man's chest and shoved so I could squeeze past him. At my brief contact, he drew back and shuddered violently, grimacing in discomfort.

NIKITA'S STORY

Jenny hesitated, watching him with confused concern. The man shrugged and smiled in embarrassment, murmuring something about *"someone walking over his grave,"* before offering a hand to help her from the *car*.

She yawned. *"Thank you so much, Officer, you've been more than nice."*

As they headed toward the house, they talked about things such as *phone numbers* and *addresses*—none of which I understood—while *Ruth* darted off her front *porch* and rushed out to meet them. A faint light shone through the *living room* window, while all the other rooms remained dark, cloaking much of the house in the night's shadows. I smiled. It suddenly felt as if I was coming home, and *Ruth's* excited welcome was as much for me as *Jenny*.

Stopping halfway across the yard, *Ruth* waved frantically at *Jenny* and the *officer*. She'd put on a few unneeded lastnas since I'd last took a long look at her and made use of their unknowing hospitality. Nonetheless, she looked healthy, robust, and full of joy. I knew it was safe for *Jenny* to be left in the *Master's* care. *Ruth's* affectionate and giving nature would quickly surround her with genuine Keyen, comforting the fear that lingered in *Jenny's* expression.

The logone began barking somewhere inside the house and *Bill's* night-hushed voice commanded him to quiet down. I shuddered, trapped in the memories of several near encounters with the beast. Shaking them off, refusing to wonder over the wisdom of my actions, I followed *Jenny* to the house.

Ruth surrounded *Jenny* with her warm and welcoming arms. *"You poor child, you must be terribly cold and frightfully hungry,"* she murmured tenderly. Without pause, she turned to the man and gave him a warm smile. *"Thank you, Matt. You go on home to that pretty wife of yours. Bill and I'll take good care of her. You can count on that."*

He nodded, also smiling knowingly and returned to his car. Tipping his hat in their direction, he wished them, *"Good night."*

Ruth offered the man one last wave, before guiding *Jenny* inside. As usual, she spoke nonstop, inserting important information with things of minca or neye importance. She often repeated

PART I TENZENAR

herself and then laughed at herself when she realized what she had done. I smiled warmly, following them through the front door.

"I'm sure Matt told you already, but I'll tell you again. I'm Ruth Masters—but just call me Ruth. Bill and I—oh, he's my husband—are most glad to hear you'd been found. And we are even happier to have you with us for the night. Now, I've made some hot chicken soup—thinking you'd be chilled to the bone and hungry—and it's warming on the stove, ready when you are. Oh here, let me take that lunch box—you don't need to be lugging it all over anymore. I'll have Bill put it up in your room for you—he won't mind at all." She reached for the metal container in *Jenny's* hand.

Having gotten *Jenny* in the front door, *Ruth* swung her arm behind her in a maneuver born of great practice. Catching the open door, she gave it a good shove. The door flew toward my face. I tried to turn sideways and slip through before it hit me... but didn't quite make it. The door balked suddenly, a mere furon before meshing with the frame.

"That's strange," she said frowning over her shoulder.

The cessation of movement was so sudden the door had rebounded in the opposite direction, vibrating in confusion over which direction to go.

"It's never done that before." She turned back and pushed it closed. *"Oh well... there it goes,"* she added with a shrug before continuing down the hall, the door quickly forgotten.

I leaned against the wall. Lifting my tender, throbbing fingers, I pressed them against my lips, kissing and sucking at them frantically. Irrationally, I believed this action might somehow take away the bounding pain rushing through them with every beat of my heart. Halfway down the hall, *Jenny* had turned and looked at the front door, a quizzical expression wrinkling her brow. All pain from my bruised and bleeding joints was instantly forgotten while my heart hammered with hope. Then, shaking her head, *Jenny* turned back to *Ruth*, dismissing her speculations and dashing my hopes. My fingers began to throb with even greater pain to further my misery.

Forcing myself to follow—condemning myself for being a glutton for punishment—I stopped at the threshold to the defacka. *Ruth*,

Bill, and *Jenny* were in the room… with *Sam*. In all my forays to this house, I had always been ever vigilant concerning the logone's whereabouts. I had never dared entered the *Master's* home when *Sam* was inside. The moment I reached the doorway to their defacka that beastly logone caught my scent and raised his hackles, growling fiercely.

Ruth had yet to stop talking, *"Here we go now,"* showing *Jenny* to a chair at the table before easing her into it, *"have a seat and I'll get you a nice hot bowl of soup."* Not missing a beat in the conversation, she looked at *Bill* then the massive tip-tilted eared logone standing behind *Bill's* legs. *"Oh, Bill, do put that dog out! I swear, I don't know what gets into him. He usually likes people we bring into the house. Don't you worry, Jenny, it isn't you. That darn dog is getting senile. More often than not, these days Bill and I catch him growling when there is nothing around to growl at, at all."*

Ruth went to the stove. *"I'll just get you a bowl here and fill it with some warm soup.… Thank you, Bill, you're such a dear,"* this was said after he put *Sam* out the back door.

I agreed with her sentiments, and silently leki'an *Bill* myself, yet chose to remain in the hall, not daring to enter the defacka. I had learned that to do such a thing, one needed to be wide awake and feeling quite agile. Pilfering in a populated defacka was very much like dancing with lacknas, bits extended.

"Here, Bill, would you mind taking this up to Jenny's room for me?" Handing over *Jenny's* lunch box, *Ruth* promptly forgot it. *"There's your bowl of soup, eat up, child. My own children are asleep, so when we go up to your room, do try and be quiet. Those kids of mine seem to have ears tuned especially for excitement, and if we wake them, no one will get to sleep until they ferret out every bit of news they can concerning your adventure this night. Now, you just slurp that soup right down, it'll do you wonders."*

Bill winked at *Jenny* as he left the defacka. I nimbly stepped aside, letting him go by.

After *Jenny* lifted a *spoonful* of soup into her mouth, *Ruth* suddenly pulled herself upright, gathered a deep breath of air, and slowly exhaled, forcing herself to relax. *"Oh my, just listen to me carry on—you'd think I hadn't had another female to talk to in ages! I'm sorry, child, I'm not always this talkative—Bill say's I'm often worse,"* she laughed at herself and her pun. *"But honestly, sweetie, it's just that when Matt got word to us about what you've been through, and how you'd been stranded up at the lake... well we were shocked and terribly worried about you."*

Jenny smiled shyly, having just placed her forth *spoonful* of soup in her mouth. Swallowing quickly, she murmured in genuine consternation, *"You don't even know me, why would you worry about me, Mrs. Masters?"*

"Oh, now, call me Ruth, all right? And about our worry... you're one of Christ's children aren't you? Aren't we all? And shouldn't we then care for and about each other because we're family?" Ruth's genuine, tender smile melted *Jenny's* reserve.

Much of her fear and exhaustion became suddenly etched on her face. *"I guess... I never quite thought about it that way. Thank you, and may God bless you and yours," Jenny* whispered, putting a hand over *Ruth's* tentatively *"I confess, there were quite a few times I was worried about myself,"* she added wearily.

"Oh, shame on me!" Ruth exclaimed, lifting *Jenny's* bowl from the table before she'd managed another spoonful. With tender firmness that only a parent can master, she eased *Jenny* to her feet. *"Here I've been, yammering away, telling you how concerned we were and I didn't give one thought to your need for sleep. I'll tell you Jenny, that's just like me... I don't like it much, but I talk too much... and I can't seem to stop. Now, let's get you to bed before I head off on another tangent of senseless yammering."*

"Don't say that! You've been so kind, and have really made me feel at home. The soup was just what I needed... it really was delicious. You and Bill have already gone to so much trouble... I can't thank you enoug...." Jenny protested while *Ruth* guided her to the stairway.

"Now, now, no need for thanks. I love to.... Ewww!" Ruth cried out, shivering from head to toe after walking into me.

Our impact and mutual surprise was so great she knocked me to the floor. Then *Ruth* fell backward herself in her hurry to get away from the strange sensation our contact had caused. Stunned, I remained on the floor.

"*Oh Ruth, are you all right?!*"

Jenny walked around in front of her, then bracing herself to offer *Ruth* some leverage so she could stand, *Jenny* stepped right on my sore fingers, grinding my knuckles into the floor with her heel. I closed my eyes, biting my lip so I'd not make a sound as spots of white light flashed behind my eye and waves of pain rushed up my arm from my sore, mangled hand.

"*Oh yes, I'm fine, just fine. It's been a terribly strange and tiring night for the both of us, my dear… and we'll just leave it at that. Come on, let's not waste any more time in getting you to bed before we both fall asleep right here in the hall. Bill and I'll be sure to pray that tomorrow turns out to be a much better day for everyone concerned.*"

Jenny shifted her weight and moved her foot, while I slunk to a corner, well out of danger. Closing my eyes, I prayed that Keyenoa would heed *Ruth's* words for all concerned.

As they climbed the stairs murmuring quietly together, I followed a few steps behind. The stairway creaked and groaned in an oddly welcoming way, while *Jenny's* fingers squeaked periodically against the highly polished banister railing. Despite my hand, I again felt as though I had indeed come home.

Ruth stopped at one of the rooms on the right side of the upstairs hall, and opened the door.

"*Oh, Ruth, what a lovely room!*" *Jenny* exclaimed.

I maneuvered behind the women to see inside. In the room's center, with braided rugs all around, was one of the biggest beds I'd ever seen. Four massive wooden legs held it a learon off the floor, and with a thick down coverlet piled on an even thicker and cushier palate, it took a minca set of steps placed beside the bed to get up onto it. On either side of the bed sat wooden tables, with Tenzenar 'wax-less' lamps on each. *Ruth* pressed a button on the wall and the lamps instantly filled the room with a bright light. There was a fire enclosed in its own pit against the wall near the foot of the bed, crackling and popping noisily, warming the whole room. The walls were blue, a color very much like the Airian sky in summer, and all along them were hung many strange but lovely pictures of an unfamiliar land, similar to the ones I had seen in the *Masters'* mainroom.

Jenny stopped at the edge of the bed, running her hand gently over the thick, hand-sewn coverlet, and *Ruth* smiled with tender pride. *"Yes,"* she sighed warmly, *"I must confess this is my favorite room too. Bill and I wanted at least one room to remind us of our home planet. This room was copied from an ancient photo past down through Bill's family—they once lived in a place called Missouri in the old United States, oh in about the 1940s."*

I cautiously moved across the room and backed against the wall near the fire pit, certain to be out of the way.

Jenny looked away from the bed cover toward *Ruth*, appreciation gleaming in her eyes. *"I don't know how to thank you for all you've done. You and your husband have been most kind and generous to me—and you don't even know me. Honestly, I haven't the faintest idea how I can ever repay you. Part of me wishes you were my mom, and I'd never have to leave here again."*

"Now, now, child, you'll make me want to cry," Ruth stammered, while pulling down many layers of the bed coverlets. *"There's a bathroom down the hall, leave the light on when you're done, and then climb right in this bed and get some rest. It is close to two in the morning and long past both our bedtimes."* She walked to a big piece of furniture and pulled open a drawer. *"Here's a nightgown, so you'll be warm and comfy. It really was sweet of Bill to light that fire. It sure makes it nice and cozy in here. God's blessings to you, sweetie, and good night,"* Ruth murmured as she left the room, closing the door quietly behind her. *Jenny* picked up the *nightgown*, looked at her dirty hands and legs, and left the room heading to the *bathroom* to wash. I sighed and lowered my invisibility shield. Sitting on the floor beside the fire pit, I rested my head on my knees and listened for *Jenny's* return, raising my shield just as she opened the door.

Chapter X

Disclosures and Discoveries

"Truth is the light which leads My nikca to walk with Me."

—Book of Keyenoa

Jenny flopped on the bed and sighed contentedly. Then, looking around the room, she took in every detail of its warm beauty at her leisure. I watched with affection as she wiggled her toes while looking about the room. Then, glancing over the edge of the bed, she began swinging her feet while picking up one of the feather stuffed pillows beside her and burying her face in its soft folds.

I remained by the fire, feeling very much like a mootan. She neye longer seemed as lonely as me, let alone in need of my strength or comfort. Her world was back to normal, while mine remained in disarray. Flopping back against the mattress, *Jenny* laughed quietly as she pressed the pillow over her face. I wondered if I should have followed her after all—neye matter how much I still needed and wanted her. Watching her nikca-like joy, I could not abandon all my hope. I could neye more leave her now than I could cease to breathe and remain alive.

"Keyenoa, what am I to do? I can't simply appear and say, *'Surprise! Here I am!'* She might scream and alert the whole household to my presence. Or she could simply demand I leave before I could explain why I followed her," I asked Keyenoa while watching her, wishing I had the courage to speak. My aching knuckles, still throbbing in rhythm with my heart, bled on the floor as I watched her and considered going home, where—if all were normal within myself—I should have belonged.

Jenny rolled over and slid her feet to the floor. She was suddenly pensive and unhappy. Walking around the room, she picked up a knickknack and examined it before putting it back and moving on to something else. Her expression was distant as if she pondered a very weighty matter, and the items she looked at were just a distraction while she thought. Stopping barely three furons in front of me, forcing me to back against the wall, she sighed.

"Nikita?" she asked softly, hopefully.

Her breath brushed my cheek before she moved to the window. Leaning heavily against the sill, she gazed out at the darkness. Restless, she then turned and faced the room. My heart hammered in my chest. I was too afraid to respond. I both feared and longed for her to want me as I did her.

"Oh boy, do I feel silly right now... and I know in a few minutes I may feel even sillier—especially if you aren't in the room—and you really did happen to be another of my dreams." Her voice, dry and plain, filled me with hope. *"My heart tells me you can't be a dream, what with the policeman shivering like that for no reason... and the way Ruth Masters couldn't shut the front door... and in the hall when she shivered like the policeman after running into something... when there was nothing to be seen in her way.*

"Oh, you must be here... or at least another being like you." She paused, shivering uncontrollably. Fear flooded her expression as she searched the room. *"No! No, no, no, you aren't a ghost. You can't be a ghost of one of those beings who lived here before we came to this planet,"* she murmured, before regaining control of herself and continuing her thoughts. *"No, I know you can't be a ghost... I remember your touch—and I remember touching you. Other things happened though, while I slept, I...."* She closed her eyes and shivered. *"But that was just a dream."*

NIKITA'S STORY

Opening her eyes she scanned the room again, her expression now desperate as well as hopeful. *"Please,"* she implored, *"if you're here, show yourself. Talk to me again. Tell me who and what you are at least one more time."* Then, she pleaded, mostly to herself, *"Please, oh please, be here."*

I forced myself to concentrate and dropped my shield. Slowly, as I became visible, she gasped with surprise. Looking at her, I smiled boyishly and blushed. Our eyes met and held.

How this woman could enthrall me I didn't know. I just knew I never wanted to leave her side. *"I call myself an* Airian,*"* I began. *"I do not understand what 'ghost' is, but there was fear in your voice when you said the word, so I do not think I am one. I do not think I am something to fear, and I have no desire to frighten you, or anyone else."*

She leaned against the window sill, uncertain, *"Are you living or dead? A ghost is something that's not alive."* The odd diversity of this female who could be both brave and afraid at the same time fascinated me.

"Oh, I am quite alive. To prove it—here look—I have been bleeding on the floor," I teased, pointing at my blood on the floor.

Jenny found neye humor in my statement at all. Concerned, she moved to my side. *"Are you all right?"* she asked, looking me over, searching for an injury. Finding ghea neye obvious, she looked at me with innocent expectation, destroying all the male bravado I'd been trying to display. I saw only her face and funny flat brown eyes, as I set my bleeding hand into hers. She inspected my wounds, tenderly caressing my torn fingers.

"Niki, your blood is white!" she exclaimed glancing from my hand, to the floor and back into my eyes.

I smiled tenderly. *"I should hope so, it has been that color since the day I was born, except of course, when it is low on oxygen. Then, it is red. Is it possible you have forgotten so soon that I am an* Airian?*"* I teased.

Blushing in embarrassment, she looked down. *"My blood is red when exposed to the air and blue when not."* She moved a

PART I TENZENAR

few steps away, and I heard her mumble very quietly, *"Boy, Jesus, when You answer a prayer, You really answer a prayer."*

"Who is... Jesus?" I asked, hoping she could explain my confusion where He was concerned.

She swung around in surprise and seeing my expression, she smiled. *"He is God's only Son, given to man so we may have companionship with* Keyenoa, *and eternal life."*

Frowning she shook her head sharply. *"What am I saying... what is* Keyenoa? *I must be more tired than I thought."*

"It is all right." I touched her shoulder, turning her to face me. *"What you said made complete sense... to me. It seems you got more from me than I realized."*

Her eyes went to mine revealing her puzzlement. Uncomfortable with what I had to explain, I turned away. *"We—my people—call God:* Keyenoa. *We call Him this because, translated to your language* Keyen *means... love, and He is the origin of all love, therefore He is* Keyenoa.*"*

A frown formed along her brow as more questions filled her mind after my answer.

"I guess I should explain how you came to know the word in the first place," I admitted shamefully, not sure how she would react to my explanation.

Sighing, I moved to the window she had occupied moments earlier and leaned against the sill. *"Jenny, somehow—and I am not certain how—we joined as we slept side by side under the* gungas *tree. This joining is known to my people as a very special and very personal way to share one's self with another.* Jon *explained that this sharing is called* Keyen Sapato. *It means* Keyenoa's *given love allowing us to truly become one... umm... being, united within one another. This is what happened to you and I. And this is why you knew my people's word for God."* I looked at her. *"I did not do this sharing with you consciously, but that does not lessen the depth of what took place—especially when it happened without your consent or knowledge... and if you are angry, well, I cannot blame you. I am not sorry we shared in this way, but I am most sorry that it seems as if I took advantage of you in some way by this sharing. I say again in my defense that I did not even know I had this ability."*

Her smile seemed to brighten the room. *"I'm not angry Niki, I am awed. What a precious and wonderful gift you've given me. Hearing your explanation answers so much. I understand now why I have all these words, questions and names floating around in my head. Would you explain them?"* She climbed on the bed, rolling on her stomach so she could look at me. *"Who are... Jontair Alcone, and... Te'air... and what does whateshan eyette Sontall mean? Those are the names and words that seem the... loudest."*

A flood of raw pain washed through me. Turning, I looked out the window. I couldn't face her and let her see the pain she'd unknowingly cause, even if I felt I owed her some response.

"Ta, I too have many names and questions I hope thee will explain to me, Met Jeanitear Omnestera. But the moon has long since dimmed her soft light so all on Airies may sleep before the sun lifts his fiery head, bringing on a new day. Allow me but to remain with thee, and...."

She hadn't understood a thing I said. In my exhaustion and pain I'd slipped into Airian—even using the name I had given to her in my heart. Blinking and rubbing at my eyes, I turned to face her, *"I am sorry, Jenny. I am tired. What I said was that I too have many questions, but it is late and we both need to get some sleep,"* I explained. *"I think I had better tell you why I am here, before we do sleep. When I saw you in* Dindieum, *you healed something in me that I had very nearly destroyed. And in healing me, you saved my life before I utterly destroyed that too. I want to remain with you—if you will let me—and I will gladly answer any questions you have about me and my people. Will you let me remain... or should I go?"* Fearing her rejection, I looked at my boots, and got caught up remembering my interrogation in the Chamber of the Kings when I had wondered why my boots had been wet.

Without warning I was enveloped in her embrace. *"Oh, Niki, you may stay with me forever and ever!"* she answered with undeniable sincerity.

Smiling, I leaned back drawing her head from my shoulder and looked into her eyes. Cupping my hands around her face, I held her as a strong current of emotion surged from my soul. She put her arms around my waist, and I became aware of the woman beneath the light, linen gown. As desire slammed into my belly, I set her from me gently, and moved to the fire pit, needing more distance between us, while I sought Keyenoa's strength and wisdom.

Jenny was definitely not Te'air—a sosceshpa. Watching her through my lowered lashes, I was well aware of her purity and confusion. Determined to protect and honor that innocence, I saw neye recourse to my dilemma but to begin making my bed on the floor, a few learons from the warm fire. As I grabbed coverlets from the end of the bed and began to work, I could not help but notice the hurt in her expression. Swiftly, I began to pray about my ability to honor her purity without damaging the woman, asking Keyenoa again to fill me with His strength.

"*Niki, what...? Did I do something wrong?*"

I sighed, determined to keep us both from embarrassment. *"No, Jenny, you did nothing wrong. I am simply preparing a place for me to sleep. Go ahead and get in bed. The Masters family rises very early in the morning."*

She was more astute than I'd given her credit for. *"Thank you for your gallantry, kind lord, but let us both be sensible concerning this matter,"* she began in the same playful manner we'd used in Dindieum. *"If you're going to stay with me and..."*—she held up a finger as I began to answer, silencing me instantly—*"keep your presence unknown to others—not to mention saving wear and tear on your fingers—you, my gallant lord, will have to share the bed with me. Though,"* she blurted, raising her finger higher, *"because you're a fine and upstanding young gentleman of royal birth, I'd expect your behavior to be one of virtue and decorum. You may sleep with your clothes on beneath the bedspread, and I'll be buttoned up tight in my nightgown under the bedspread and the covers."*

Shaking my head, I moved to the bed, dragging the extra coverlets I'd taken from the end of the bed back with me. Though she called me gallant, I wasn't gallant enough to turn down her offer of comfort... and the chance to be near her. *"I shall strive to protect you even from myself, fair maid,"* I murmured, then swiftly changed the subject, *"Now, most virtuous maiden, tell me how you knew what happened to my hand?"*

She looked away. *"I remember stepping on something when I rushed to Ruth after she'd fallen. As soon as I saw your hand, I realized what I did.* Niki, *I'm really sorry, does it hurt terribly much?"*

"Ta," I said quietly as she reached for my hand, knowing she wouldn't understand my answer. Then chuckling, I pulled her close and held her. *"It does not hurt much, Jenny. The front door was the first to cause them harm... so please do not feel you are to blame."*

She nestled her head beneath my chin as her arms surrounded my waist. With a deep and contented sigh, she relaxed. I closed my eyes and reveled in my own contentment having her in my arms. Suddenly, she pulled back, looking at me with surprise, *"You went through all that just for me? Why?"*

"Because I finally found...." I began only to realize the depth of my Keyen for her. Getting up, I walked around the bed and tossed the spare coverlet in a heap on the far side. *"My reasons involve a long and painful explanation, too long for what is left of this night,"* I murmured while straightening out the heap. *"Jenny, I swear I will tell you as soon as I can... perhaps even later this morning, but right now... I cannot."*

She smiled then sighed. *"Well, I can't admit to being blessed with patience, but I'll try and wait,* Niki. *Anyway, I'm tired too, so I'll agree to everything waiting till the morning."*

She pulled down the lighter coverlets on her side, then went to the door and pushed a switch that blanketed the room in darkness. My sharp eyes adjusted quickly to the firelight and watched as she grabbed up the linen nightgown, lifting it to her thighs, before throwing the coverlets over her.

Saying ghea neye, I sat on the edge of the bed and pulled off my boots, then removed my Loreann bow and quiver from my shoulders. After placing these items by the fire pit doors, I returned to my side of the bed, smiling as she tucked the coverlets tightly beneath her chin. Leaving on my tunic britches, I took off my vest, and crawled onto the bed. While *Jenny* moved only her head to look at me, I laid down and tossed the heavier coverlet over the both of us, being very careful not to intrude on her side. Murmuring something about sleeping well, I forced my eyes shut.

She lay just as stiffly as I a few furons away. Unable to relax, I began thinking of all I'd done this long night. When I remembered I'd missed the feast in New Malin and hadn't eaten since the morning meal, I admitted I was hungry—really hungry—for the first time in a very long while.

"*Jenny, I am hungry,*" I whispered as my stomach growled loudly in confirmation. There was a muffled a giggle from her side of the bed before she sat up and looked at me. I smiled. *"I will be right back."*

"Where do you think you're going?" she whispered in surprise.

"Well, if I can get down the stairs and out the front door without too much noise, I will find, a treasure trove of food on the porch. It is put there for Airians*, and I am an* Airian, *so... I am going to eat it."*

She stared at me skeptically.

"Jenny, I have been eating this way for months. The only difference is that I am in the house and need to go out to get it."

"All right, I should have something left in my box to drink," she said, still skeptical.

Climbing out of bed, I hoped I could make it outside quietly. Raising my shield of invisibility, I started to the door only to pull up short after I'd opened it.

"Jennie where's the... *where is the dog?"* I asked, realizing I had not spoken in her language.

"He's in the backyard, Niki. *I thought you were inside when Bill put him out. Good luck, and do try and be quiet!"*

"Thanks," I muttered with minca gratitude, remembering that I had been there when *Bill* put *Sam* out and embarrassed I had forgotten.

NIKITA'S STORY

I wasn't feeling enthusiastic about wandering through a dark house simply to eat, but my stomach was complaining loudly, and I knew I'd not be able to sleep until I did eat. However, the quieter I tried to be, the more noise I seemed to make. The stairs creaked and squeaked on every step. Then, misjudging a step, I stubbed my bare toe and nearly fell down the last few in my effort to recover. This caused the rail to also groan in protest as I hung onto it for dear life. After that, the front door rattled and clanked as I unbolted it and forced it open. While snatching the food off the shelf, plates, and dishes clattered together musically. They continued to do so while I carried them inside, fumbled with the lock on the door and returned up the stairs to our room. It was a relief not to find *Ruth* or *Bill* waiting for me out side *Jenny's* room.

"I am back," I announced inanely, closing the *bedroom* door.

"Niki, why didn't you eat it out on the porch?" she asked, refraining from commenting on the noise I'd made.

I ignored her and the light button on the wall, preferring the firelight. Without a word I dropped my invisibility shield and moved to the bed, placing the stolen booty on the coverlets between us.

"I'll get that soda for you," she murmured, going for her metal box.

"Soda?" I whispered skeptically.

"Never mind, Niki, *it's good, I promise,"* came her giggled response, realizing she had neye way to explain what a *"soda"* was. Handing me a cold bottle filled with some sort of fizzy liquid, she giggled again at my hesitancy to take it. *"It tastes good,* Niki. *Really it does."*

Without further comment or delay, I ate my meal of *cold chicken, chocolate cake,* and *soda.* While I had eaten all these things before—except the *soda*—it was the first time I had an opportunity to learn their names, as *Jenny* ate the food with me.

When the meal was consumed, she set the dishes on the floor beneath the bed—so she wouldn't step on them in the morning—and lay down to sleep. Neither of us was as nervous with each other as we'd been before my impromptu raid on the food outside. As soon as I was beneath my *bedspread* and she beneath the coverlets, with both our heads nestled comfortably on the feather stuffed pillows, we fell asleep.

⌘⌘⌘⌘

Later that morning, we woke to the most wondrous odors reaching us from the defacka. *Jenny* and I peered at each other through a pile of tangled bed covers and smiled eagerly.

"Food!" she exclaimed, her eyes lighting up with mischievous delight.

I nodded, promptly climbing off the bed. I may have eaten a few oonas earlier, but it had been just enough to take the edge off of my first true hunger in tuevtauns. With the bright light of day streaming through the windows I began pulling on my boots near the fire pit. *Jenny's* gasp caused me to slowly pivot and face my awed roommate.

"You look like a human male, but you don't exactly look like one. Niki *you... glow... not your clothes but you.... You're beautiful!"* she exclaimed, her voice filled with genuine delight.

All I could do was stand there, one boot on, the other in my hands, feeling stunned and embarrassed.

Her eyes twinkled with mischief as she stared, absorbing every inch of me. *"You, my lord, are definitely, infinitely, better! Oh, what a pair of shoulders!"* she gushed, teasing me unrepentantly.

With as much false dignity as I could muster, I thrust my foot in the other boot, picked up my vest from the floor, put it on and laced the front closed. I had kept my eyes on her as I worked, forcing my expression to be one of affronted indignation. The longer I stared, the more lost to her charm I became. Slowly my gaze softened and I smiled at her with affection and embarrassment. *Jenny*, still surrounded within the soft warmth of the covers suddenly began to giggle, her eyes sparkling, her expression glowing in adoring joy.

"I love you, Nikita Markain Malin,*"* she whispered while her Keyen spilled from her heart as if it were water flowing from a fountain.

I gaped at her, feeling overwhelmed with my own Keyen. I'd so wanted to hear those words from her, yet I never believed she would really say them. *Jenny* sprang from the bed, and flung her arms around my neck. Tucking her head between her arms, she rested it against my chest.

"Keyen, Niki," she sighed.

Lifting her head with my hands, I gazed into her eyes, and then leaned down and kissed her trembling mouth. My heart swelled as if it were breaking as I allowed myself to accept her Keyen and offered my own through that trembling kiss.

"Keyen Renli, Jeanitear Omnestera," I murmured in Airian against her warm lips, knowing neye other way to express the depths of my feelings for her. *"I love you. I do, and I have since the* ena *I first saw you all smeared with dirt and tangled in leaves,"* I explained, when our kiss had ended. She smiled and wiped the dampness from my eyes, even as a minca tear rolled down her cheek.

"Jenny?" Ruth called through the door, causing us to jump apart. She spoke again and knocked.

Instinctively, I went invisible stepping away from *Jenny*. She stared at the door, unable to move or answer. Grasping my hand, she squeezed it tightly and shivered in reaction to my invisibility shield but refused to let go. Neither of us noticed that the hand I held was also invisible.

"Jenny, honey, are you awake?" Ruth called again, turning the door handle.

I noticed my Loreann bow and quiver lying on the floor in front of the fire pit in plain sight. *Jenny* shivered again when I released her hand and frantically dove for the weapons. Slinging the items over my shoulder, I sighed, relieved to find everything had vanished.

"Oh, you are awake, child," Ruth murmured as she opened the door.

Jenny stood in the center of the room with eyes as large as saucers.

"Oh! Sweetie… I didn't mean to frighten you. I'm so sorry for intruding. I came to tell you that Matt was able to contact

your parents about an hour ago, and confirmed that they're on there way here from Second Site. They should be here in just a few short hours. While you're waiting for them, I have breakfast ready downstairs whenever you are."

Jenny managed to murmur something about a nightmare, as she fingered the linen nightgown she wore, looking at her clothes now cleaned and folded in *Ruth's* hands.

"*Oh, I'm sorry, honey!*" Ruth exclaimed sincerely, handing *Jenny* her clothes. "*After what you went through last night, it's no wonder you're having nightmares. I know it won't be easy but, try and think no more about it. Oh, I found your clothes in the bathroom and gave them a good wash. Just come down for breakfast whenever you're ready. Putting something in your stomach should make you feel much better and help your nightmares fade away.*"

Without another word she left, quietly closing the door behind her. I waited until I heard her go downstairs before lowering my shield. *Jenny* looked at me warily, to try and reassure her, I smiled. Shaking her head, she sighed. Then, setting the cleaned clothes on a chair, she began making the bed in nervous distraction.

"*I'm worried about you,* Niki,*"* she confessed patting the pillows in place. "*How are you going to stay out of their way, not to mention mine, and still get something to eat? Oh,* Niki, *how are you going to survive without discovery while you stay with me?*"

Having fended for myself among Tenzenar for many tuevtauns, I had neye such fears. Going to her, I cupped her chin in my hands and promised, "*I can find ways, Jenny, as I have many times before. There is no need to worry. This house and its occupants are quite familiar to me and I know the dangers before me. My only real problem is a little girl by the name of Lisa. She can see me as clearly as I see you even with my shield of invisibility raised, but everyone believes I am her imaginary friend, nothing more.*"

"*Lisa?*"

"Ta, *Lisa.*

"*As you have begun to discover, Ruth and Bill Masters are kind, gentle people who own a small farm, sell fuel for those pass-*

ing through and take in an occasional boarder as they work on building a church fellowship. Bill's a pastor as well as a farmer. They have two children, a boy who is around nine aanas *and a girl, who is about four. Now, the boy is no threat to me, but as I told you, Lisa can see me even when I am invisible... however, as I said before, they think I am her imaginary friend. It seems you* Tenzenar *do not take your children seriously."*

Jenny shook her head in disbelief as she retrieved her clothes and went down the hall to the *bathroom*. After changing, she went down stairs to the defacka. I followed, after stopping in the *bathroom* myself. *Jenny* remained concerned and uncertain of my reassurances, yet chose not to argue.

As usual, food covered the defacka table, leaving just enough room for plates. The exotic smells seemed to invade my senses, greedily saturating the air and torturing me with every breath I drew. The *Masters'* seating arrangement had changed to accommodate *Jenny*. The nikca sat at the head and foot of the table, while *Bill* and *Ruth* faced one another across its width. There was an extra chair between *Ruth* and *Michael*. This arrangement put *Lisa's* back to me, while her brother faced the entrance. I waited at the door while *Jenny* entered and everyone turned to look her way.

Instantly, *Lisa's* focus skittered from *Jenny* to me, and after a moment of further scrutiny, she smiled at me in ghea forlaynan welcome for the first time. *Lisa* had clearly recognized the change in me. I put my finger against my lips, silently imploring her to say ghea neye. Understanding, she nodded eagerly, covering her mouth to stifle an errant giggle. With a nikca's innocence, she struggled to keep her eyes on *Jenny*, yet couldn't help but smile in my direction as her focus kept sliding my way.

Ruth stood and urged *Jenny* to sit. *"Help yourself, child, and don't be shy, as you can see there's plenty here."* Then taking the spare plate, *Ruth* began filling it before *Jenny* could, *"You remember my Bill from last night. This is Michael, my firstborn... and this is my daughter, Lisa."* She nodded in the direction of her nikca too busy adding food to the plate to point them out.

I watched with ravenous envy when *Jenny* began to eat, obviously enjoying every bite. With *Lisa* aware of my presence, hunger overrode any further need for me to be cautious. With the ease of practice, I moved between *Michael* and *Jenny* and knelt on the floor, returning *Lisa's* smile. Whispering to *Jenny*, I let her know where I was and waited impatiently for an opportunity to steal some food. *Lisa* watched my every move, smiling impishly, but remained silent concerning my presence.

"Dad, Dad." *Michael* poked and prodded at *Bill* while whispering excitedly under his breath, far too shy to speak to *Jenny* himself. *"Tell her what happened last night. You know, about the food, Dad. Come on, tell her about the food!"* he urged. In his growing excitement, aware his father was hesitant for some reason that he couldn't understand, he blurted out his news. *"An* Airian *came and ate our food! See, we leave it out every night, hoping one would like Mom's cooking as much as Dad does, and last night one did!"* he exclaimed, excitedly, *"They've come before, but it's been a long time. Lisa and I thought they were mad at us or something, but one came last night, that's for sure!"*

"Now *Michael*," *Bill* started to intervene, *"I told you it could have been anyone, maybe even Je...."*

"Oh, no, Dad, it was an Airian *for sure!"* *Michael* insisted. *"You remember the piece of fur you found that night when Sam went crazy? You said that could be an* Airian's *remember? And the food's been taken before. So how can you say that an* Airian *didn't eat the food last night?"* *Michael* insisted, trying to sway his father to his side of the debate.

Jenny, guessing what *Bill* had tried to say, eagerly jumped into the conversation in an effort to redirect it. *"Mr. Masters, do you have this piece of fur handy?"*

He hesitated a moment ready to press the issue at hand, then changed his mind. *"Why... uh, yes I do... I'll go get it. Ruth was telling me your parents study the old ruins and claims of encounters. I guess this piece of fur would be something they'd have an interest in."* He left the room, with *Michael* tagging along.

Hearing what *Bill* had said about *Jenny's* parents, I suddenly began to question my sanity and my 'chore. How could I have given my heart and Keyen to someone whose parents were deeply involved in Airian study and discovery? Shaking my head, I put aside this fact. Knowing there was ghea neye I could do to change what was, I saw minca sense in worrying about it any further.

Lisa left her place at the table holding some sort of food combination smashed between two pieces of bread looking as though she might drop it at any moment.

"Jenny...." *Ruth* interrupted herself, *"Lisa! What are you doing?"* It was obvious *Ruth* had intended to ask *Jenny* about the missing food before she noticed her daughter starting around the table.

"Jenny looks very hungry, momma. So I made her a sandwich to take with her when she goes home." I was reminded of *Ruth* in that moment.

Lisa came to a sudden stop between me and *Jenny*, and before *Ruth* could say anything more she started to hand the concoction to *Jenny* only to drop it before *Jenny* had a chance to reach for it. This caused the delectable-looking *'sandwich'* to drop right into my waiting hands.

"Oh! Well, never mind. I'll go make you another." *Lisa* didn't sound quite as sorry as she should.

Knowing exactly what had happened, *Jenny* struggled not to laugh out loud. *"Thank you very much, Lisa, but there's no need. What I have here will certainly fill me up."*

Ruth chuckled mildly over *Lisa's* attempt to be hospitable. Unconcerned, she instructed her daughter to do her best to clean up the mess, murmuring something about *Sam* getting whatever was left behind. As *Ruth* focused sharply on *Jenny*, *Lisa* began to pretend to clean the mess.

"Jenny, honey, Bill and I want to clear up something about the 'Airian' *visit last night,"* she said with patient determination. *"We believe in allowing our children to have an imagination, but we don't want to perpetuate any... lies, well intentioned or not."* At this point in her conversation *Bill* and *Michael* had returned

PART I TENZENAR

so *Ruth* paused to smile at them. *Bill* understanding the message relayed in her smile, went to stand behind her in a supportive manner. All the while both continued smiling gently at *Jenny*. "*Honey,*" she continued, *"we heard... someone walking down the stairs last night, out the front door, then back up them a few minutes later."* She waited hoping *Jenny* would confess without further pressure.

I ate, hardly listening, certain *Jenny* would simply apologize and that would be that.

"Jenny, did you go down and take that food with the innocent idea of giving my children a thrill this morning?" Bill asked. *"Please, understand we're not angry. It was a sweet thing to do. We just want our children to realize the truth in this instance. You see, Lisa believes she sees* Airians*... and when we heard you go outside last night, well, we just don't want to encourage her falsely."*

Jenny cleared her throat, and there was a long moment of silence, as she bowed her head. I continued eating. Watching her lips move silently I knew she was praying. Still, confident that she would take the blame, I didn't bother to take note of her expression, or consider the fact that Keyenoa would clearly instruct her to tell the truth.

Lifting her head, she met *Bill's* gaze, *"I didn't take the food last night.* Niki *did—though I did eat some of it—and it was quite good."*

I froze, nearly choking on the last bite of my egg *sandwich*, while the blood in my head suddenly pooled in my stomach, causing it to flip-flop in revolt. *Michael* looked at *Jenny* as if she had offered him a treasure beyond belief, while *Lisa* clapped her hands gleefully. *Ruth* and *Bill* were stunned. They stared at *Jenny* in horror. *Jenny* turned looking blindly in my direction.

"Please, Niki... *I couldn't lie. They asked me outright, and I just can't lie to them. For me, will you show yourself?"* she begged.

I didn't move. I barely managed to swallow.

"Ms. MacArthur, *there is no one there. Please, this is enough!" Bill's* horror changed into deep concern over *Jenny's* mental state even as he grew angry.

Stepping from behind *Ruth*, he went to stand close to *Jenny* struggling with his outrage and worry. I moved near *Lisa*, knowing she'd not accidentally step on me in all the excitement. While I wanted to do something to stop what was quickly getting out of hand, the fear of revealing my presence to any Tenzenar other than *Jenny* was simply too great. I hoped *Jenny* would somehow find a way out of her situation without me.

Lisa glanced up at me, then handed me a cloth she'd taken from the table. *"You got egg all on your face,"* she said loud enough for anyone to hear her if they'd only been paying attention.

I wiped at my mouth frantically.

"Ms. MacArthur, you are either the most outrageous liar I've ever had the displeasure of opening my home to or you need to be put away!" Bill shouted harshly, his outrage winning out over his concern.

Suddenly there were large tears pooling in *Jenny's* eyes which quickly escaped and streaked down her cheeks only so more could take their place. Having her yelled at and forced to watch her cry was more than I could tolerate. Without thinking, I thrust the cloth in *Lisa's* hand and stepped from her side.

"That is enough!" I exclaimed.

Determined to protect her from further pain, I forced myself to lower my shield and appear. *Bill*, *Ruth*, *Michael*, and even *Jenny* froze in surprise, each turning to stare in my direction. *Ruth* gave a half-hearted cry of distress and fainted clean away—ghea leki'anee, she was still in her chair. However, once in her faint, she did slide out of the chair in a tangled heap under the table. As I watched her, the realization of what I'd done flooded my mind. The room began to spin and everything wavered before my eyes, sliding in and out of focus, even as the room gradually seemed to get darker and darker. As I fell forward, I saw Jon's face forming clearly in the darkness. Calling out to him, I was engulfed by an instant moment of excruciating pain, causing a bright flash of light to explode behind my eyes.… Then ghea neye, everything went serenely and wonderfully blank.

⌘⌘⌘⌘

PART I TENZENAR

"Jon!"

I opened my eyes upon hearing my own voice. Expecting to find my Thaytor leaning over my bed with concern glimmering in his coal-black eyes, I discovered I was laying on the long puffy piece of furniture—for which I was certain I had at one time learned the Tenzenar word to describe it. Scrambling through my muddled thoughts, I finally remembered that the furniture's proper name was, *couch*. I'd yet to realize that I was visible, lying on this *couch* in front of the whole *Masters'* family. *Jenny* was kneeling on the floor by my side, holding my hand. Smiling at her, I asked her through my expression, to explain why I was on a *couch* in my tree-home and would she tell me where Jon had gone.

Then, thinking she would probably never understand all that I wanted, I decided to ask her outright. *"What...?"* I began.

Ruth and *Bill* suddenly leaned into my line of sight, halting my question before it really got started. My head ached terribly. *Ruth* carefully lifted a blood stained cloth from my forehead. *Lisa* and *Michael* shifted uneasily at the end of the couch, leaning forward so they could see the damage. *Michael* looked a bit frightened, uncertain what to make of me, while *Lisa* just watched with grave concern.

I looked back at *Jenny*, desperate to know why my head ached so and whose blood was on the cloth that was taken from my forehead.

She smiled and squeezed my hand. *"You had the misfortune to faint too close to the kitchen table, so when you fell, you hit your head on its edge."*

"Are you all right?" *Bill* asked.

"His blood is white, Bill! Look at the cloth, it's white!" *Ruth* whispered, staring at the cloth in her hand.

Bill commandeered the cloth from *Ruth* and set it in a bowl of water above my head. He rinsed it and then returned it to the wound on my forehead.

I gingerly touched the cloth, my attention flitting between *Bill* and *Ruth*. Aware of my confusion, *Bill* asked again if I thought I was all right.

"*Ta, I think so,*" I murmured. My reply suddenly brought everything flooding back. And realizing I was visible, I remembered my own people and the implications my presence could mean if the *Masters* chose to be indiscrete.

"I guess I must have fainted, before I hit my head," I said inanely. Then pleased with the sound of my own voice—it being the only thing familiar to me at the moment—I began to babble just hear myself talk a minca longer, "*I fainted, because... well... to be honest... I am not comfortable appearing before* Tenzenar. *I mean I hadn't even intended to lower my* shield, *but Jenny began to cry so... well... I discovered I don't like her to cry—even for an* ena. *Then when I realized I did appear... I guess I fainted.*"

Remembering I wasn't the only one who fainted, I sat up intending to look at *Ruth* only to lie back down as my head spun ghea-kezky and my stomach flip-flopped.

"*You fainted too, did you not, Mrs. Masters?*" I asked softly, closing my eyes, unable to focus for the moment. "*Are you* benna*?*"

"*Oh, I'm... umm...*" she stammered self-consciously. "*Jenny what is* benna, *and* Tenzenar, shield *and* enas*?*" she asked in confusion. Then her eyes opened in dawning realization. "*Oh my heavens—strange words and white blood—he really has to be an* Airian*!*" she exclaimed, turning immediately to *Bill* for support.

I smiled, understanding exactly how she felt since I was feeling very much the same way. Finding a commonality in the situation helped me to gain a bit more control and find comfort in the situation. Slowly, so as not to jostle my tender head or frighten *Ruth*, I sat up and clasped her hand in mine.

"*I am sorry to have frightened you. And I apologize that my knowledge of your language is not complete.* Tenzenar *is a word my people use to describe your people.* Ena *is a short increment of time. I do not know what you call yourselves, and understand no equivalent of time to describe it in your language,*" I explained.

She squeezed my hand with affection and understanding. "*Bill's always telling me I talk too much... and now, when I have so many things to ask, so much to say, I can't seem to find the words to say anything.*"

PART I TENZENAR

"Please, Bill, Ruth," I began, shifting uncomfortably. I had to face the consequences of my appearing before them and deal with the situation as best I could, praying I would be able to forestall any danger to my people. *"I need to explain. I appeared because Jenny needed me. Yet in doing so, I have done my own people a great disservice and possible harm, depending on what you plan to do with this knowledge.*

"I have a responsibility to my people. One, I must admit, until now I have ignored for far too long. What destruction my behavior has caused in the past, I can only leave in Keyenoa's *hands... but what I have done today, is far worse than anything I have done previously. I humbly beg each one of you to never tell anyone of my appearance here. My life and my people's lives depend on your silence. If your people gain knowledge of our existence, there would be an overwhelming flood of* Tenzenar *searching for a glimpse of us, striving to find out where we live and trampling our lands and our homes—unknowingly destroying our peace and our way of life, thus ultimately destroying us.*

"I hope you understand why I have asked this of you. I have been here visiting often, and I know you are honest and trustworthy people of great honor and understanding. Therefore, I know if you promise to tell no one of my existence, you will keep it.

"My name is, Lord Nikita Markain Malin, *I am the firstborn son to* Lord Markain Malin, *the* Sixth King of Airies.*"* I forced myself to my feet. The damp cloth fell from my forehead to my hand, and hanging on to it, I bowed slightly. *"I humbly and sincerely ask your forgiveness for my illicit appropriation of your food and hospitality. I apologize for the times your family has been frightened or disturbed by the things I have done. I hope by my explanations already made and those to come, that any of your concerns are comforted and any lingering misunderstanding between us be henceforth cleared up."*

Completing my formal apology, which I had carefully translated from my language to theirs, I slowly sat back on the *couch*. *Ruth* took the cloth from my hand and began to rinse it clean.

"*Your apology—though unnecessary—is accepted. Feel free to pilfer in our home at any time,*" Bill said, chuckling over his pun, as he extended his hand.

I took it gladly, noticing the flash of silver fur in his other hand.

"*That piece of fur you hold, Bill, is the result of one of my first visits here,*" I confessed, staring at the item in question.

He held up the mangled piece of fur before looking at me and noticing that it matched my clothing.

"*Your* logone, *Sam, expressing his displeasure over my trespassing into his fenced area, tore it from my boot while I was leaping back over said fence in a rather frantic effort to get away. The white stains are blood, caused when he bit through the boot into my flesh.*

"*Please, I beg that you show it to no one. I have come to learn—through my limited experiences with your kind—that you are a very determined race of beings. If you share that bit of fur with anyone, it will raise too many questions... questions which would cause your people to begin a search for mine. If my people are discovered... well, I say again, this will result in our destruction.*"

Bill crushed the piece of fur in his fist and squeezed it tightly. "*I honestly don't understand why you believe that your discovery would ultimately destroy your people,* Niki. *I'm a simple man, who has a hard time seeing and accepting the evils of his own people. But because you believe this would happen, to refuse your wishes would only bring shame to this family. I also don't want to possibly be the instrument that confirms your beliefs about my race or be the cause of you thinking less of us as a people than you already do. I give you my word,* Niki, *we will keep our silence about your existence and everything we learn from you—in what I hope will be a lasting friendship,*" he said earnestly, then chuckled. "*To be honest, most people would think we were crazy if we did say anything, anyway,*" he added with another chuckle, lightening the mood in the room.

"*Amen,*" Ruth affirmed.

Both nikca began to giggle, though neither understood what they were laughing about. I motioned for *Lisa* to come to me. She eagerly scrambled into my lap as I looked at *Bill* and *Ruth*.

"You have always known she is unique, just as all children are. However, now that my existence is a fact, are you beginning to realize that Lisa is even more unique than either of you have comprehended. If you haven't realized it by now, I have always been Lisa's 'imaginary' friend."

Their expressions widened with dawning understanding.

"I cannot fully explain or understand why, but she has been able to see me and my people even when we cannot see one another. But understanding it or not, Lisa is able to see us. This makes her very special in the eyes of the Airian *people. Nothing in this life is so certain that you should discount it, and* tella saa *do not ever question her gift again.* Keyenoa's *ways are not our ways, and His gifts should never be taken lightly."*

Looking at *Lisa*, I still spoke to her parents, *"I want to give your family a gift, in thanks of your kindness to Jenny and me. Because of Lisa's abilities, I ask that you allow her to be the one to hold this gift for her family."*

I took a lock of my hair firmly between my fingers and pulling on the strands, I exerted pressure until it broke free. Lifting it to the air, a gold substance poured from the broken hair shafts coating the ends and then hardening. Taking a leakna from my left spannel, I poked a hole through the metallic coating. Then I removed a thin gold chain from my neck, slipped it through the hole, and placed it around *Lisa's* neck.

"It is important that this never come off, and you must never show it to anyone. It is a special gift and while I entrust it to you, it is up to your parents to decide if they want to use it. Do you understand?" I asked.

Lisa nodded solemnly. Her very young face reflected both understanding and awe over what was taking place. While terribly young, her understanding was far greater than her age. Smiling, she hopped off my lap and went to *Bill* and *Ruth*, showing them the necklace.

NIKITA'S STORY

"If there comes a time when your family needs my help, or the help of my people, this lock of hair will enable you to reach me. All you have to do is take the chain, hold my hair in the palms of your hands, and think of me... concentrating as hard as you can. I will be aware of your need and will find some way to come to you, no matter where I am. Just use this gift only if it is important. Because, once used, the lock of hair will instantly decompose and can be used no more."

Bill, *Ruth*, and *Michael* nodded in numb understanding. *Lisa*, having neye trouble accepting what I said, solemnly tucked the chain beneath her clothes hiding it from sight.

"Please, would you mind telling me how...?" *Ruth* began, breaking off when a shrill, vibrating ring from the direction of the defacka interrupted her.

Sighing with frustration, *Ruth* looked at *Bill* and shrugged her shoulders. Leaving the room, she went in the direction of the noise. A moment later, the ringing stopped, only to be replaced by the muffled sound of her voice as she responded to questions I couldn't hear.

Noticing my confusion, *Jenny* smiled. *"It's a phone,* Niki.*"*

This did minca to clarify matters, but before I could ask for more information, *Ruth* returned. *"That was your parents, Jenny. They wanted me to assure you they'll be here within the next hour."*

This news seemed to stun us all. I regretted the thought of leaving the *Masters'* home as much as they seemed to regret having us go. *Jenny* shifted restlessly, as she looked at me with worry marring her expression.

"Do you want to come with me... or stay..." she faltered, unable to finish.

Bill and *Ruth* were forgotten along with their nikca. I saw only *Jenny*. *"I want to come with you,"* I declared passionately. *"If you but understood how true my words were, that there is nothing to hold me to my home—and everything to hold me to you—you would never have asked such a question of me. I love you. I need you. I want to remain with you,"* I declared.

"*Michael, Lisa, it's time to go on out and play,*" *Bill's* statement clearly wouldn't tolerate any argument. The nikca quickly left the house without a sound.

Ruth was the only one who dared question *Bill*, but he shook his head the moment she opened her mouth to ask, instantly silencing her.

"*How the necklace works can be answered later, if we have time,*" he said as he looked at me and *Jenny*, his expression gravely serious. "*These two people have a dilemma facing them.* Niki, *you have spoken of* Keyenoa, *and. ... Well, I strongly sense that you're speaking of God. Am I right in this?*"

I nodded, confused with his line of questioning.

"*Jenny, what are your feelings about God?*" Bill asked solemnly.

Despite being perplexed herself, *Jenny* smiled as an incredible presence of aclusceaun washed over her face. "*I'm born again, Mr. Masters. Jesus Christ is my Lord and Savior.*"

Bill sighed. His expression grew even more concerned. "*Then you both had best sit down and listen to what I have to say.* Niki, *I don't know what your people believe, but I do know what every believer like Jenny has been taught... virginal purity before marriage. What you two face—if you go with Jenny,* Niki, *can put her in jeopardy.* Niki, *with your feelings for her, can you swear you'd not at some time want to be physically intimate with her?*" He held up his hand before I could answer. "*No, there is no need to answer, son. I can see by your expression that you know you can't. And Jenny, can you promise to honor God with your body, no matter how much you love* Niki?"

Jenny blushed and looked away.

"*How, may I ask, do you propose to solve this problem? And, Jenny, if you think you can just ignore this part of your Christian walk, search your heart. I think you will find that you would regret very much failing God in this matter,*" he said, then fell silent, giving us time to think.

"*Mr. Masters, will you marry us?*" *Jenny* asked quietly.

Poor *Bill* looked stunned. I grasped *Jenny's* hand and held my breath, hoping. *Ruth* sat on the arm of *Bill's* chair, watching him with the same hope as *Jenny* and I. He closed his eyes in obvious prayer, then some moments later, sighed and nodded. With a gasp of delight, *Ruth* ran to a drawer and pulled out some official looking documents. Then, in her usual rush she quizzed us on our full names, *Jenny* having to spell mine because I didn't understand their writing. Then we were urged to sign the documents. I again ran into trouble but *Bill* said I should sign by my own script. *Ruth* then signed the document as did *Bill*.

"I'll just keep this marriage certificate safe, here. There's no need for you to take it with you. If you ever need it, just call us... or if you are here, just look behind my mantle clock and it'll be there," *Ruth* promised, tucking the document behind the clock.

Bill then instructed that we face him and he guided us through our *marriage* vows before Keyenoa. It was a solemn and moving ceremony, reminding me very much of the partnering ceremony many of my people take part in. At the completion of the ceremony, he declared us man and *wife*, yet I sensed he was troubled. *Jenny*, after kissing me shyly, pulled me aside where she and I had a whispered conference that caused us both to blush several times before we reached an agreement.

"*Bill*," I cleared my throat nervously. *Jenny* squeezed my hand in encouragement, "*we want you to know... we want to assure you.... Jenny and I are aware you are concerned that we may not be... ready for the seriousness of the commitment we just made. I'm not going to try and convince you we are. Honestly, nobody knows if they are ready until they try. What we want to tell you... and Ruth... is... is...*" I sighed, then forced the words out, "*We pledge not to... to... consummate this union, until* Keyen... God reveals to us that our affection and devotion to each other is as lasting as we believe it to be. We understand that we need time for our love to mature, and we just wanted you to know that we both honor Ke... I mean, God, enough to take that time and our vows seriously."

Ruth rushed over to us enveloping both of us in a hug, speaking her arecean and ghea leki to Keyenoa. *Bill* quickly joined the embrace. His gratitude, while less exuberant, revealed his joy and relief over our promise.

"*Now, please tell me... how does that necklace work?*" *Ruth* blurted, wiping tears from her very curious eyes.

At that moment, the nikca rushed through the front door, exclaiming excitedly that *Jenny's* parents had arrived. We heard the slam of *car* doors and the crunch of feet on the stone walkway. Instinctively, I went invisible and *Ruth's* expression crumpled in disappointment. Unable to let her down, after all they had done for both me and *Jenny*; I lowered my shield and took her hand.

"Within me rests a very strong power that I am not able to draw upon until a time that God chooses. The lock of hair, like every other part of me, holds some of that power. The gold substance that formed on the broken ends is actually a form of that power leaching out. I cannot explain it fully, but it is this power that will bring me to you... if you have the need."

Squeezing *Ruth's* hand, I kissed her cheek, before raising my invisibility shield. For a moment she looked confused by my sudden invisibility. Smiling, I leaned near, careful not to get too close.

"Ghea Keyenoa benna arecean. *Thank you,*" I whispered, quickly stepping aside so I'd not be accidentally stepped on. The *doorbell* chimed, and *Ruth* rushed to the door as she and *Bill* looked worriedly at one another. They had clearly begun to realize the danger I was eagerly walking into.

With their usual heartwarming affection she and *Bill* greeted *Jenny's* parents and welcomed them into their home. Their open welcome helped the *MacArthur's* feel more at home as refreshments were offered and served. Uncomfortable with so many Tenzenar in the *Masters'* front room, I sat on the stairs out of sight waiting for the impromptu gathering to be over.

Chapter XI

Among the Tenzenar

"If a youth is trained in the ways of Keyenoa, when he leaves his Thaytor's side, Keyenoa's laws go with him."
—Thaytoric Book of Wisdom

Following the refreshments, everyone gathered at the front door, making a fuss over *Jenny*. She finally managed to retrieve her *lunch* container and get out to the *car*. Recognizing the opportunity for what it was, I followed her. Like mischievous nikca, giggling uncontrollably, we climbed into the back seat. *Ruth*, still engaging the *MacArthur's* in conversation, walked out with them while *Bill* and the nikca trailed behind.

"Jonathan and I had to rush away to Second Town on the day of Jenny's date. We were trying to work out a problem there. Honestly, we'd no idea anything had happened at home until we received the call from your sheriff over the emergency radio late last night. I thought that boy such a nice young man too. But I'm sure you can imagine, Ruth, just how frightened we were, until your Sheriff Matt told us that Jenny would be staying with you. What wonderful people you are to take in a young collage student who had some sort of spat with her date. I just knew my Jenny would be perfectly safe until we could solve our problem and get

PART I TENZENAR

away from the site to pick her up," Mrs. MacArthur explained in an off-handed manner.

"I assure you she's been a pleasure to have and no trouble at all. I hope you will allow her to come back and visit soon. We'd love to have her stay as long as she wants," Ruth assured *Jenny's* mother.

Mr. *MacArthur* shook *Bill's* hand, murmuring his gratitude distractedly before he followed his *wife* to the *car*.

I had watched her parents from the stairs, curious to see which qualities *Jenny* had inherited and from what parent. Mrs. *MacArthur* was a beautiful woman of about forty-five aanas and *Jenny* clearly resembled her physically. Evidently age wouldn't damage *Jenny's* beauty in any way. *Jonathan* seemed more like his daughter in spirit, radiating the same serine rationality and an innate honesty. Yet *Jenny's* beauty and spirit was purer than either of her parents, and I wondered how these two had ever nurtured such qualities in *Jenny* when they were both dulled and tainted by lifelessness. Where had she learned about Keyenoa? Who taught her that He alone was life and hope and the reason for joy?

Jonathan started the car and maneuvered onto the *road*. I sat stiffly in the back, keeping myself as far from *Jenny's* side as possible and tried not to breathe too loudly. Because of their occupations, her parents were a great danger to me. I was afraid even a minca noise would result in my discovery. Morosely, I began to wonder how I would survive living in a home with two Airian research *scientists*.

When her mother began firing questions at *Jenny* concerning what had happened the night before, *Jenny* began to explain how the night transpired. I wondered—with a great deal of trepidation—if she would be as open with her parents as she had been with the *Masters*. *Jenny* artfully avoided all mention of me or my people's existence in her explanations. She even glossed over the reasons she had been left at the park by her *date*, never mentioning to them what had caused the *officer* to say something about *prosecution*. While relieved she had kept her secret of me, I also wondered about it. I understood that confiding in her parents wouldn't be easy because they were both clearly wrapped up in their own interests. However, while my father was much the same way, having to rule Malin, I still often confided in him, despite his distracted and somewhat stiff manner.

Frustrated that I couldn't talk with *Jenny* and aware of the strain on my invisibility shield, I stared out the window watching the Tenzenar homes grow in number and flash by with increasing frequency. The *car* ride to the *MacArthur* home took a minca over an oona. *Mrs. MacArthur*, having listened to *Jenny's* story with an air of distracted impatience, began discussing *Second Town* with *Jonathan*. She did not console or enquire about *Jenny's* feelings concerning her experience. It almost seemed to me that she listened with the sole intention to assure herself that the blame for the evening's debacle lay fully on *Jenny's* shoulders and not on theirs because of their absence.

Mr. MacArthur looked in the rearview *mirror* of the car and cleared his throat. He murmured something gentle to his daughter, before eagerly responding to *Evelynn's* questions.

Listening to their conversation, my assessment of their personalities and priorities became startlingly clear. *Mrs. MacArthur*, while involving herself with Tenzenar and their Airian sightings, managed to keep her heart and compassion unmoved by anything but the data and the work. She was a rather empty and shallow woman who, while obviously concerned with appearances and how she was perceived by others, was careful to make certain her interests were the first to be met.

Jonathan MacArthur was exclusively work focused. He was happily distracted by his work so he wouldn't have to deal with the day to day irritations of life. *Jonathan* was completely indifferent and unconcerned with the opinions of others or how he was perceived. The only thing that could draw his attention and hold it was the physical science of some unknown life form and how they once lived. Eagerly caught up in his own chosen world, he studied that very confining world continually, filing away every lestna of information for further, in-depth examination. This happily separated him from involvement in his own world and offered him an easy justification as to why he should distance himself from the lives of those around him.

Jonathan stopped the *car* in front of a shockingly familiar structure—an exact duplicate of the private living quarters of Loreann—my old home. I followed the outline of the long, sloping structure molded into the hillside with great affection and unconsciously began comparing its craftsmanship to that part of Loreann I knew so well. Every vent and lattice surrounding the windows, eves and door frames looked as if they'd been taken from my home and placed here. Somehow the builders had even managed to duplicate the pattern of fine, feathery moss which hung over certain places along the eves. My heart ached. Overwhelmed with fraw-tieyee, I gasped with longing and anguish.

"What did you say, Jenny? I'm sorry, honey, I wasn't listening," Jonathan murmured, stepping out of the *car*. Mrs. MacArthur was at the front door fiddling with a bunch of minca objects jingling on a ring and ghea leki'anee hadn't heard a thing.

Jenny glanced my way in wide eyed disbelief before she looked at her father. *"I didn't say anything important, Dad. It's just so good to be home… and to have last night over with, that's all,"* she explained quickly.

He nodded, his question forgotten before she had even answered him. Going to the back of the *car* he retrieved the *luggage* and *data* collected from *Second Town*. *Jenny* and I wasted neye time. We scrambled out of the *car* and entered the house only moments behind *Mrs. MacArthur*. *Evelynne* called from the defacka explaining that "*lunch*" would be ready in "*half hour*."

I paused at the base of the three shallow steps which *Jenny* had climbed, leading to one section of the sleeping quarters. Looking around, I found the familiar house filled with harsh and unfamiliar objects. I was home, but I was not. I found myself wondering if this was a judgment from Keyenoa or an arecean in disguise. Taking the stairs, I hurried after *Jenny*, following her into the first room on the left. With *Jonathan* coming in the front door and *Evelynne* rushing from the defacka to take half of the things he'd brought into the house, I tried not to let my boots clatter on the wooden stairs as I moved swiftly out of their way.

My body had begun to shake from the strain of keeping my invisibility shield raised for so long. Reaching her room, I pushed the door closed quickly. Leaning heavily against the door, I relaxed, dropping my shield and looked at *Jenny.*

"Niki, what in the world possessed you to gasp like that? Hey, are you all right?" she asked, noticing my tremors.

"Ta, I am fine," I assured her, still leaning against the door. *"It is just the reaction of staying invisible for so long. I honestly did not mean to say anything in the car. It is your house! It is a replica of the king's private living quarters in the castle* Loreann. *It's my old home. What possessed your parents to copy it?"*

She smiled while considering my question. *"I always did think Dad liked to live like royalty,"* she giggled to herself. Then focused on me, noticing the sadness in my expression she added, *"Oh,* Niki, *I'm so sorry, I didn't know it was replicated from your home. I would've warned you if I had, I swear,"* she said. *"I knew it was* Airian *in design, that's all. You see, my parents are fascinated with everything concerning your people… your culture, your way of life, and especially the architecture of your buildings."*

"Arch-i-tex-ture?" I interrupted, horribly mangling the pronunciation.

She laughed lightly over my atrocious pronunciation. *"The artistic style of your buildings,"* she said, diplomatically refraining from commenting on how I said the word. *"Mom and Dad thought there was most likely a good reason for the houses in* Malinieum *to be built the way they are, so they copied it. They also believe that living in a reproduction of an* Airian *home might help them better understand your people.*

"Dad chose to copy from… Loreann. *Because, other than liking its layout, he decided that of all the homes in the city,* Loreann *was the truest example of your people's unique architecture."* Her eyes twinkled with mischief as she added, *"He would have loved to build all of* Loreann, *but he didn't have enough land allotted to him to do so."*

I smiled and began rocking on the heels of my boots with an impish gleam in my eyes. *"There is a reason why the homes in* Malinieum City *are built the way they are."* I said, deliberately saying neye more.

She watched me, trying desperately not to laugh, as she waited. *Jenny* knew I wouldn't be able to remain quiet for long—especially when I was so obviously proud of the answer. Defeated, I laughed outright and bowed before her in courtly surrender, causing *Jenny* to laugh as well.

"When Airians *walk through* Malinieum City, *it... well, it kind of... sings. In some way, I don't fully understand, the currents of energy created by our power work through the vents and lattices around the buildings and create notes. They flow around the house joining with notes made from the power of others and, thus, become blended together to create a kind of music. The long sloping ways in which the homes are built help the currents of power to move along and meld without obstruction."*

I smiled wistfully, remembering the many times I'd walked through Malinieum City just to hear it sing. *"Think of it, Jenny, all the houses built to make music! It was a sound so wonderful... so beautiful..."* I murmured dreamily, unaware I hadn't completed my thought, having lost myself in remembering the day I had asked Conden about the music in an effort to stall him from leading me before my father for punishment.

"I like the way you make it sound, Niki, *but...* Malinieum City *doesn't sing anymore,"* Jenny whispered with regret as she copied the way I spoke my city's name.

My heart fell. Malinieum City would never sing again. *"Because,* Keyen, *there are no longer any* Airians *living there to make it sing."*

Sighing, she lowered her eyes sharing my regret. *"I wish there was some way I could hear it sing,* Niki,*"* she said wistfully, aware there was minca hope that her wish would ever be granted.

Sharing our feelings of loss over Malinieum City's music and the life it once held, I was flooded with feelings of affection and desire. While wondering about my adoration for this strange

Tenzenar female, I remembered my promise to *Bill*. Clearing my throat, I struggled to refocus my thoughts, and only then realized that she had said the name of my city before I had, though it had been said incorrectly.

"How did you know to even say Malinieum *for the city's name? And how is it your people seem to know so much about us?"* I asked.

"You weren't listening to what my parents were talking about on the way home, were you? They were discussing some of their discoveries and suppositions. I grant you that most of it has been educated guess work, from studying the buildings and other items left in them... oh, and through some of the writings on the walls throughout Malinieum City."

"But did your father not say something about having trouble deciphering our written word? Jenny, I am most confused. If he is unable to decipher our words, how does he know Malinieum *is part of the city's name, and that we call ourselves* Airians?"

She smiled with understanding as she flopped on her bed. Rolling onto her stomach, she propped her chin on her elbows. Placing her feet at the head of the bed, she tucked them beneath the pillows. *"We don't know as much about your people as you seem to think we do,* Niki. *Dad's an archeologist, and so is one of the first to learn about your way of life. He knows a lot of disjointed facts concerning how you lived because he has studied your buildings and the stuff you left behind. But all he's learned from your writings is that you call yourselves* Airians, *that the planet is named* Airies, *and that the city he knows only as* Malinieum *possibly housed a king."*

"He knows no more?" I asked in surprise, relieved to realize I had inflated the Tenzenar's knowledge of Airians because of my own guilt, after finally acknowledging my past behavior and the damage I might have done through it.

"No, Dad has learned nothing more, Niki. *I think you know that there is now a growing subculture that believes your people are still alive. This subculture uses the many strange incidents being reported in the forest and around the outskirts of our city as*

proof of their suppositions. However, these incidents are difficult to prove. So overall, these believers aren't taken very seriously by the majority of the scientific community. Dad is interested only in facts, and therefore doesn't concern himself with those stories at all. My mother... well, it's now her job to document these incidents. So she conveys an interest in such beliefs in order to engender a trust with those who make such claims so they will be more forthcoming. Then, she makes and keeps a file of such incidences, crosschecking all the occurrences in order to compile a list of those stories with similar descriptions and locations.

"*Dad's so absorbed in trying to translate your writing that this occupies much of his time and all of his thought. Now that he's recently been able to travel to Second Town his frustration is compounded. He's not been able to translate its name—let alone any other words than the two I mentioned. Dad's also aware of another* Airian *town on this continent, but as yet has had no time to travel there. The archeology team is strained just exploring* Malinieum City *and Second Town. Therefore, he's in no hurry to make an expedition to the third town.*"

At her mention of "*Second Town,*" I straightened up off the doorway, putting aside all thought concerning her mother's new job. "*Jenny, do you know the direction of Second Town?*" I asked in a whisper.

Pointing offhandedly, she waved in the general direction she guessed the city to be. "*Somewhere off to the west, that way. I'm not exactly sure where. I've never been myself.*"

"Markainieum City."

I spoke the name more to myself, confirming what Jon, Scaun, Conden, Salitarin, and I had shared with Father and the High King... the Tenzenar were indeed closer to Oreon, New Malin, and the other Kingdoms than was comfortable. We hadn't known which city had been discovered, but we knew it wouldn't be long before both of Malin's cities were found and explored. New Cetar's boarders were under a minca more threat with Markainieum City's discovery, while New Tarton was safe for only a short while longer. I could only hope that Markainieum City would keep the Tenzenar too busy to explore the forest beyond it. Silently, I leki'an Keyenoa for their decision to explore Markainieum City before Lizingham, aware that Markainieum City was located much farther south and west of our new Kingdoms. Sighing, I pointed to the northeast. *"The other city, the one your father has yet to explore is called* Lizingham. *It is nearly due east of* Markainieum City *resting on the opposite coast of* Malin. *I fear that your father will not wait too long before sending a team out there, no matter how much it thins his workers,"* I murmured with bitter frustration. Having learned firsthand about the tenacity of Tenzenar, I began to wonder if my people were really as safe as they thought hiding within Dindieum and being shielded by Met Lordship's power. Aware that I could do ghea neye to halt the Tenzenar encroachment, I placed my fears into Keyenoa's hands. In a quick and silent prayer, I asked Him to bring someone forward who would find a solution to the extinction facing my people.

Aware of *Jenny's* interest and concern, I explained to her about my people and how we used to live on Airies. *"Before your people came here, each island continent on* Airies *was ruled by a king whose right to reign was made evident by his* Keyenoa-*given power. With the exception of the castle* Oreon *on top of* Mount Oron—*my father's realm spanned this continent.* Malinieum City, Lizingham, *and* Markainieum City *were the three major cities in his realm."*

She closed her eyes, mentally visualizing each island continent on Airies. I continued my explanation about our Seven Kings and the ruling system of Airies. Halfway through my explanation, I began to laugh at myself. I sounded very much like Rugan, when he droned on about the first High King, and our illustrious history.

Jenny listened avidly—being a much better student than I ever was—and as she listened she began to realize just how important my father was in the power structure of Airies. *"Where are all the kings and their people now? Are they still on their separate continents?"*

"No, we all now live around Oreon, *the* High King's *castle I told you about, which is actually the top of* Mount Oron *in the center of* Dindieum—*the large forest you were lost in."*

PART I TENZENAR

I then told her about my people, the power Keyenoa gave us and the powers He gives to each King. She was fascinated about the women's very different abilities and the arecean Keyenoa had bestowed upon them during the Taun of Change and Eta Medee-an Aclusceaun. I was frustrated that could tell her ghea minca-eye about Con Sona Eata. I admitted my own frustration concerning my ignorance of Con Sona Eata and confessed I was just as curious to learn the mysteries that surrounded my passage into manhood as she was. Then, I spent more time explaining our reasons for fleeing from their invasion and how the High King had moved us all to Oreon. *Jenny* was stunned to discover that our abhorrence of killing was so great that we instead chose to secret ourselves away rather than defending our land from invasion.

Just as I finished my explanations, *Jenny* was called to *lunch*. I agreed to wait in her room rather than foraging for myself around the table. She was dreadfully uncomfortable with the idea of my spending too much time around her parents. I was very tired from holding my invisibility so long, and so was more than happy to wait in her room. Promising to return with something for me to eat, she left quickly, not wanting anyone to come looking for her. I wondered how she'd leave the table carrying another meal after just finishing one, yet when she returned she had enough food to satisfy even my hunger. When I asked how she did it, she shrugged it off, saying her parents didn't even notice.

"Niki," she said quietly.

I looked up. Instead of continuing, she gazed at me with a troubled expression. Sensing she needed time to choose her words, I returned my attention to my meal.

"Niki..." she repeated, only to shake her head frantically when I looked at her again, *"No! Don't look at me. It'll be easier if you don't look at me,"* she blurted. I looked at the food, but was neye longer hungry. I was suddenly suspicious that I wouldn't like the conversation to come. *"Last night I mentioned two people named...* Jontair Alcone *and...* Te'air.*"* She stopped the instant she saw my expression. Then, taking a deep breath she forced herself to continue, almost tripping over the words to get them said, *"I knew last night when I mentioned them that I'd caused you great emotional pain... just like I'm doing now. But I know in my heart that we must talk about them. Are they the reason why you don't want to go home? I need to understand what made you decide to leave your people and why you feel you can't go back to them. I have sat here and listened to you speak of your people with such great love and pride,* Niki. *I can't explain to you why it's so important that I understand what happened between you and your people, but I know it is... because God is convicting me it is."*

Setting my nearly empty plate on a desk cluttered with several strange mechanical devices, I looked at her. I couldn't hide the pain I was experiencing, neye how much I wanted to. I also knew she was right. This was something she needed to know. We had pledged our lives to the other. Beginning that bond while still withholding parts of ourselves would destroy our union before it began to grow.

"Te'air was a woman to whom I foolishly gave my heart—and even a part of my soul. She took these gifts and used them to further her own acclaim. She told me, using great and passionate declarations, of her deep... love for me... and I was too stupid to see that she only had a desire for how I could increase her status. You see, to her, gaining a prince's attention—one who is a promising heir to a throne—and... the extra unexpected bonus of being the first woman to ever... ever..." I faltered to a stop overcome by shame and the growing frustration that I couldn't think of the words I needed to explain what I was trying to say.

Almost whispering, I struggled to go on, *"I was nothing more than a name she could drop to gain her more importance... to.... Ah, Jenny, she was a...* Te'air *was... well, a...* sosceshpa. *To her I was a... sort of... well, using my name... helped to bring her a higher... clientele... and give her more profit in trade for her services. I was warned, but I was simply too much a* teepatin *to believe these things were really her motives, let alone what she truly was. So instead of believing the warning, I chose to believe everything she said, only to find her in the act of being... intimate with another man."*

PART I TENZENAR

"Who is Jontair Alcone?*"* she asked quietly.

"My Thaytor.*"* I swallowed a pain that nearly choked me. It was neye longer Te'air's name and actions that caused me such anguish; it was my thoughts of Jon. Why had I allowed so much to be destroyed between he and I for a woman who cared ghea neye for anyone but herself?

Puzzled by the Airian word, *Jenny* waited for me to explain.

I went to the window. Tucking my hands behind the frilly curtains, I leaned heavily on the frame and looked through the glass. *"I do not know your word for him. I really do not think you have a word to describe what he is and does.* Thaytors *are men, who at their* Con Sona Eata *are given a power from* Keyenoa *to match the given power of a specific youth expected to be a king upon that youth's* Con Sona Eata*. When a* Thaytor *and the youth are matched to one another, the* Thaytor *begins to instruct and guide this youth throughout the* Thaytor's *life, aiding that youth on how to be and become a good king. I am not sure how anyone knew that* Jon *and I were matched by* Keyenoa's *hand, but, we were.*

"Just as it is with every male before Con Sona Eata—*I have* minca *power to speak of, with the exception of invisibility. So as* Jon *waits for my* Con Sona Eata*, he teaches me what it means to be a good prince and heir to a throne. If I had remained with my people, and if, upon my* Con Sona Eata, Keyenoa *gives me the power to be a king. Then,* Jon *would have continued to guide my decisions with his wisdom, always having enough power of his own to keep me from doing harm with mine.*

"But more than that, Jenny, Jon *was a part of me and I was a part of him*—*oh, I think somehow we still remain part of each other. Because even though I have abandoned him, I cannot truly escape him. I am aware of him, even now, here inside me."* I pressed a hand to the center of my chest, where it ached. *"I am not sure it is even possible for one of us to live if the other passes in* Sontall*. I think this is true with all* Thaytors *and their charges, not just* Jon *and I."*

Jenny moved to the edge of the bed very near me. Drawn to her, I turned from the window and knelt before her. There was such depth of emotion and confusion in her eyes as she spoke, *"Why are you here with me, when your* Thaytor *could help you so much more than I?"*

"He tried, Jenny, but I only became more uncontrollable. He was the one who tried to warn me what Te'air *was, but I refused to listen. Then, like a* teepatin *I ordered him from my life. After I learned the truth, I felt like such a...* kutated mootan teepatin, *I was too embarrassed, hurt, and angry to face him. Every time I saw* Jon, *I was reminded of my shame with* Te'air *and the painful way I had learned the truth about what she was. Jenny, I so wanted what was between me and this woman to be* Keyen, *that when what I believed and wanted was ripped from me as it was, I sort of went a bit* keezworky. *After that, it just got increasingly impossible to be around* Jon *or actually any* Airian. *So I set out to destroy the bond I had between my people and* Jon *and I.*

"The day I discovered the truth about Te'air, *I closed a part of myself off—as a sort of protection against further pain.* Jon *tried to bring me back to my normal self, but even he did not understand what was happening to me.* Neye *among my people could understand. When I saw you, crying and frightened, lost in* Dindieum... *somehow, Jenny,* Keyenoa *allowed you to open my heart and soul, which I had shut to everything and everyone else.*

"*Seeing you,* Keyenoa *revealed to me what true* Keyen *should be and could be... and needing your* Keyen *as much as I wanted to give you mine, I took the chance* Keyenoa *offered.*

"*Jenny, I followed you because I fell in love with you. Believe me when I say, that you are all I want and need right now."*

A spark of desire and need flared between us and I took her in my arms, fighting my passion as I remembered my promise to Keyenoa and *Bill*. Sighing, I prayed for strength as I tenderly kissed her forehead. Then, unable to help it I lowered my mouth to hers. Taking in the sweetness of her lips for a long and gentle moment, I then rested my chin on the top of her silken brown hair, content to simply cherish her in my arms.

PART I TENZENAR

She nestled against my chest. *"Ummm,"* she sighed. *"I know you must be frustrated by all my questions,* Niki, *but when we shared minds, I took in so much and understood so little. Would you mind if I keep asking you things? I don't want to go crazy trying to figure them out by myself."* she murmured softly.

I chuckled, drew her from my arms and stood up. I was relieved she didn't question or fight my sudden separation from her. *"I do not mind. I too have a thousand questions I want to ask you."*

Tilting her head, she met my gaze with a mischievous smile. *"What did you mean when you said I must be a queen?"* she asked before I could voice one of my questions.

I blushed, just as she knew I would. *"I was not thinking. I forgot that, unlike* Airians, *names to* Tenzenar...."

"Humans," she corrected automatically.

"What?" Thrown from my train of thought, I missed what she said.

"We call ourselves humans, Niki.*"*

"Oh," I murmured, rolling the word around in my head before trying to use it. *"Anyway, I forgot that to you... hue-mains..."* I fumbled terribly over the pronunciation. *"That a name is only... a name, and that they have no other meanings.* Airians *name their children with great consideration, because to them each name holds a deep meaning. The number of names given to a child indicates their station among the* Airian *people, or the amount of power the child is believed to carry.*

"So when I heard your name, I assumed, because we carry the same number of names, you were royal born like myself."

She smiled with understanding and moved nearer. Embracing me, she gazed pleadingly into my eyes, saying ghea neye, simply absorbing my expressions with hungered joy. I felt as if I had been knocked kezky or walked smack into a wall unaware it was there.

*"*Niki, *will you teach me your language?"* she asked eagerly. *"I want to learn all I can about you and your people. I'll teach you everything I can about humans... anything you wish to know.*

I know you're going to need such knowledge, since you're going to stay with me here."

I'd given up on keeping my distance. Her touch was like sweet perfume. Each time she moved close, it became harder for me to step away. So kneeling again, I relaxed into her embrace even while praying that Keyenoa would give me the needed restraint. I searched for some question to ask her, hoping this might distract us both. Then, I remembered one of the things she'd said that had puzzled me last night.

"I will teach anything you want to know, but would you tell me first what you meant last night about... well when you said to that man... Matt... I think that was his name—that, your... date... wouldn't take no for an answer and you had to fight him off. What did you say no to, and why did you have to fight him off? Was that what made you so frightened that you ran blindly into the forest?"

Her eyes had grown large and round while her mouth fell open in remembered fear and embarrassment. Slowly a flush of bright pink crept across her face. *"What?"* her voice squeaked out in surprise.

Confused, and strangely ashamed over what I asked, I leaned back from her embrace. Not understanding that she had spoken in shock and not desiring clarification, I began to explain, *"You told the... um... officer... that the man you were with at the park would not take no for an answer...."*

"I know!" she snapped as she struggled for composure.

I knelt there watching her helplessly, not understanding why my question had disturbed her. I wanted to retract everything I'd said, but it was too late. Witnessing my confused and repentant expression, she sighed and smiled hesitantly.

"I'm not mad at you for asking, it's just that this isn't going to be easy for me to explain, Niki,*"* she said. *"It means, he wanted me to do what.... At least I think what* Te'air *and you...."* she stammered to a halt and looked at me.

Suddenly, having a benna idea where she was going with her explanation, I realized we would both have a difficult time continuing our conversation without embarrassment. Cupping her chin in my hand, lifting her face to mine, I smiled into her eyes letting her see my understanding and Keyen.

"Let my mind touch yours, as we did last night. Then, it will be possible for me to learn what it is you find difficult to tell me. Also, you will be able to learn what happened to me. With our minds joined, we will be able to both understand these things and save ourselves the embarrassment of finding words to describe something very personal."

She smiled in relief and eager acceptance. Her hand shook with emotion as she placed it against my cheek. Keeping my eyes locked with hers, I sought Keyenoa's arecean, careful to keep my body from touching hers. Though I longed to share all of myself, I understood that to Keyenoa this would be the same as taking her physically and therefore an offense against our promise to wait.

Laying my forehead against hers, our minds slowly drifted together. As I opened my thoughts, I took her back to when I had first struggled with my feelings for Te'air and allowed her to relive the last eight tuevtauns of my life. I kept ghea neye from her. *Jenny* relived everyone of my memories as if every experience had happened to her. She came to know the faces of all who were important to me as each person passed through that time in my life, from Father to Sornan and Jon, to Te'air, Conden, and Mackien. I halted the memories at the point in time when she stumbled into my life. As she shared my emotions and thoughts, I was aware of her tears of Keyen, her understanding... and her acceptance of everything she received.

Blindly, I caressed the tears from her cheeks, turning my thoughts so I could give her my language. Greedily, *Jenny* absorbed all I offered. However, because of my lack of power, it quickly became apparent that it would take several of these 'joinings' before she would be as proficient in my language as I was with hers.

Then, it was her turn to share her memories with me. I assumed, because she was Tenzenar, that I'd be shielded somewhat by the feelings and experiences of her memories... but this was not so. She gave unreservedly and honestly, searing me to my soul with what happened to her the night before....

Instantly, I was sitting in the front seat of a sporty and expensive looking car. Paul was sitting next to me. We had just pulled into a picnic area to talk—so why was I suddenly feeling frightened of him? He hadn't even moved from the driver's seat and the stick shift was strategically placed between us. However, he didn't need to come here for us to talk. Is that why I'm so frightened? I felt foolish to have kept silent and let him drive us here. Somehow, somewhere, I gave him all the control.

"Take me home, Paul," I demanded, trying so hard not to show how afraid I was.

He didn't listen, just smiled and told me to relax. He moved, managing to climb over the stick shift all too easily. His hands are suddenly rough and cruel. I know I didn't want this! He is hurting me with his hands and mouth. He was getting more aroused each time I tried to fight him off. I would scratch him and try and kick him, but all he did was laugh! Then, his hands force their way up my dress! "Dear God, help me!" I have to do something!

Yes! I need to use my lunch box! I have it. It's right at my fingers. Just reach a bit further... I... got it! I tell myself to take a breath, pretend... pretend to relax... then smash him over the head with it. I have to hit him hard, I have to stop him! I have to get free before he.... Before he....

WHAM!

"Is he stunned, God? Yes! Yes, he's stunned!"

PART I TENZENAR

WHAM! I hit him again for good measure and to be certain he doesn't recover too quickly.

I have to run! I have to run! I see the trees. I must run into the trees. He groans and stirs. "Okay, God, I didn't kill him, that's a good thing, I guess." I scramble out of the car, fall on the pavement as he grabs for my coat. I kick at him and catch his arm with my foot and his face with my lunch box. He groans and releases me. I have to run to the trees! Run as fast as I can to those trees!

It is so dark... and even darker under the canopy of the forest. I am sure to be safe there. My heart is pounding in my ears so loudly that I'm terrified Paul can hear it. "Did I hear him call out to me? Is he coming after me? God, please help me to run faster, get deeper into the trees." The forest scares me... but Paul is coming. I'm in the trees... but Paul is coming! He'll find me here. I need to go deeper into the forest. Keep running. I have to keep running.

Brambles pull at my clothes. Trees scratch at my face. "Ouch!" I fall, but I can't stay here, I'm still not safe yet. I see nothing and hear only my heart. Vines tangle around my legs. "Oomph!" I've fallen again, but scramble up only to get a few yards further only to fall once more. Exhausted, I lay still, crouching in the tangled ground cover and debris, prepared to run if I hear him coming.

"Dear God, help me! Tell me, can Paul hear my breathing and heartbeat too? Will it lead him to me?"

There's a rustle in the brush behind me. Run! Run! Run! Water! I stumble into swampy, smelly water! Run! Just run through it! He's heard the splash and will soon be on me! I look desperately for the moon, needing it to help me see. I force myself to ignore the pain and the stinging cuts as I crouch down in the tangling bushes on the other side of the water and listen. "God, is he following? I have to know if he's following.

"God, I'm praying. Can you hear me praying? Help me. Oh, please help me. Tell me, is it safe? Can I catch my breath here? I'm tired, God... and I'm scared! Okay, I'll keep moving. Yes, there is no need to run now... You're right, God, I don't hear him."

I stumble into swampy water again! I'm so cold! I have to keep moving, assuring myself that I can worry about the pain and the cold later. "My hands hurt, God.... Wait! Was that a car? Yes, that's his car! He's gone! He's gone! Thank You, God. Thank You! He's gone. I'm safe.... I can go back to the road, now. He won't get me. I can go back to the road now."

I begin walking in the direction I was sure would take me to the road. But in my fear and confusion I had unknowingly turned in the wrong direction....

"*Jenny! Jenny, are you all right?*" her father shouted while banging on the door. Instantly, our connection was broken.

Jonathan banged on the door again, while twisting the resistant door knob.

I vanished and backed to the wall, feeling my Loreann bow bite into my flesh.

Jenny unlocked and opened the door a crack, looking out at her father. *"I'm fine, Dad,"* she mumbled, clearly looking as though she'd just awakened from a sound sleep. *"I'm sorry I worried you. I honestly didn't hear you. I think I must have fallen asleep... or something,"* she stammered, reading his concern as clearly as I did. *"Did you need me for anything?"* she asked, realizing he had to be there for a reason.

"Uh... er.... Oh, yes, I.... I mean... I'm sorry I woke, you, honey... but Paula called. She heard what happened last night and wants you to phone her as soon as possible."

Jenny frowned in confusion, looking at the odd machinery cluttering her desk. *"I wonder why she didn't call my number."*

Jonathan MacArthur watched her, as if he were examining a strange artifact. *"She tried twice and got no answer, so she called our private line. That's when your mother sent me up here to check on you. I tried the door but... it was locked."*

She blushed, *"I guess... I must have been sleeping pretty soundly, Dad. I didn't mean to frighten you. I locked the door because I didn't want you or Mom to wander in and... wake me up by accident,"* she faltered, aware she was babbling.

"That's okay, sweetness," he murmured. Having ascertained she was fine, he allowed his mind wander from his daughter, completely unaware that she was making minca sense and not acting at all like her usual self. *"Go ahead and rest—I'm sure you need it after last night. Give Paula a call later, when you're ready. I'll have your mother let you know when it's time for dinner."*

Jenny offered her father a patient smile and a kiss on his cheek. *"Thanks, Dad,"* she murmured and patted his cheek when he blushed over her show of affection.

Quietly closing the door, *Jenny* made sure to relock it. Reappearing, I stumbled into the chair near the window, feeling utterly exhausted. I'd used so much energy merging our minds and then shielding myself from detection that I felt completely drained. As I slumped in the chair, *Jenny* rushed to my side.

"Niki, are you all right?" Falling to her knees, she threw her arms around my waist and laid her head in my lap. *"I really do love you so,"* she sighed contentedly. *"Sometimes, I find it hard to understand why I feel so deeply about you in such a short time, but I do! I really and truly do love you!"* she murmured happily.

I caressed the silkiness of her hair, touched by her affection. *"How can we not love one another? We have shared our deepest thoughts and most intimate feelings, discovering how much we are alike. You complement me, just as I complement you, so that together, we make a fuller and better whole. You and I also know that* Keyenoa *makes no mistakes. Nothing is ever just a coincidence where He is concerned. He brought us together because He wants us together."*

Pulling her gently into my arms, I kissed her. Her response revealed the same need that filled me. Leaning on Keyenoa, I gently released her, all the while aware of her reluctance to end our kiss. Gazing at her pouting expression, I shook my head slowly, hoping my indulgent smile silently chided her. She, at that moment, clearly didn't want to consider the consequences, so I had to point them out to her before my desires took over for the both of us. Shifting, I grinned wickedly at her, allowing her to witness, through my expression, the passion I felt. A passion I had been holding in check and keeping her from witnessing. *Jenny* drew back warily, while still wanting to test her ability to arouse me.

"Jennie," my voice was rough with passion as I finally spoke the Airian name I had given her upon seeing her that first time in the forest. *"May I suggest that you do what you need to do to get in touch with this Paula person, before you tease me into something I know deep in my heart you and I are not yet ready for?"* I wiggled my eyebrows suggestively, causing her to laugh, even as she wisely moved away.

Going to the machine-cluttered desk, she put her hand on a silver-colored, metal box that had tiny buttons on its front. Facing a round reflecting glass on the top of the box, she surveyed the buttons. Curious, I moved to look over her shoulder.

"It's called a phone," she explained. *"Like the one in the Masters' house, you heard ringing. People use it when they want to talk to someone without having to go to that person's home, which could be many miles away. The only difference with Masters' phone is that theirs won't allow you to see the person you're talking to—whereas, with my phone you can."*

PART I TENZENAR

"*Miles?*" I asked, remembering her telling me that the ringing noise at the *Masters'* house was the *phone*, and how her explanation had at the time explained ghea neye just as it did now.

Jenny smiled, realizing that I was too embarrassed to admit I'd yet to understand anything about *phones*. "Terons *are close enough to the same distance, I suppose. Here, let me try and explain it better. I simply punch a few of these numbered buttons, and that sends a code though these wires. When the machine matching that code is found, it rings to alert the person on the other end—that's what you heard at the Masters. Now, we will hear the ringing here as well, but at a different tone, so we know the machine is working.*

"Once someone at the other house presses this button, I will then be able to speak into this part here, and they'll also be able to hear and see me... just as I'm able to hear and see them—if they also have a view phone—which Paula does."

"You mean to say you can see and speak to people as far away as the Masters' house with this machine... and not have to go there in a car?" I peered at the device doubtfully.

Her eyes twinkled with suppressed humor at my expression, *"Yes,* Niki, *that's exactly what I mean. So if you don't want to be seen by Paula, I'd suggest you move away from this mirror device, here,"* she warned, pointing at the circular disk at the top of the machine.

I wasted neye time moving out of the way. By sitting at the head of her bed, I was both away from the view phone but still able to watch what she was doing. Giggling over my hurried retreat, she pressed the buttons in a sort of pattern. There was a short pause before I could hear a burring noise, sounding something like muffled ringing. This continued for a short time before it stopped with a loud click, to be followed by a voice booming from the box, causing me to jump, and *Jenny* to giggle again.

"Hey! Yo Jenns! Spill it, what happened last night?"

Though nearly squirming with curiosity, I didn't dare lean over to see if there was a face in the reflecting glass. I understood all too well that if I were able to see *Paula*, she'd be able to see me... and I didn't care for that idea at all! So I forced myself to be content with listening.

Jenny reached out for my hand and held it out of view of the screen as she told *Paula* nearly the same story she had shared with her parents. The only thing she included was a simplified reason for leaving *Paul's* car... hinting at, yet still evading the complete truth. She never mentioned or alluded to me or what she found in the woods. While grateful she kept silent about me and my people, I was confused why she had confided in the *Masters* when she dared not confide in anyone else who seemed closer to her and knew her longer.

Paula's voice broke into my revere, *"Well, I'll see you at classes tomorrow, Jenns. Take care of yourself and don't let your parents get you down. Bye."* There was another loud click and *Jenny* turned to face me.

"So what do you think?" she asked eagerly, while getting up to sit next to me on the bed.

"What is classes?" I asked, suspicious of the word and not sure what to say about the *view phone*.

"I go to college and take classes where I learn a profession. I guess you could say we have classes instead of Thaytors,*"* she offered, thoughtfully.

"Tell me about it," I encouraged, curious to discover if *college* and *classes* were anything like my dreaded learning house experiences before I met Jon.

"Well..." She flopped back against the bed. *"Let me give you a little background before I tell you about college and the classes I am taking now. First, we humans start school when we're about three years old. The first few years we learn how to learn and behave in class, how to read, write, and work with numbers. Then, from the ages of seven to sixteen we're taught the finer points of reading, writing, social behavior and arithmetic, working on improving these basic skills. When we turn sixteen, we then choose to either go on to higher education, or learn a specific job or trade. This is called college or vocational school, depending on your choice. And as I told you, I'm now attending college and*

PART I TENZENAR

in my fourth year, taking double courses to finish early. I should graduate in a few months."

I understood this explanation better than I did the *phone*. Pleased to hear that *school*—at least until *college*—was very much like learning house, I wondered if *Jenny* had any unbearable teaching masters, as I had in Rugan.

Flopping back on the bed, I looked at her lying beside me and smiled. *"I learned very much like you in my younger* aanas,*"* I said. *"But instead of school, I went to what we call* learning house, *where the* Airian *basics were drilled into my head until I was fourteen* aanas *old. While in the* House *I learned how to read, write, count, and work with numbers. I also studied our* Airian *history and some of your history. When I was fourteen, I became bored and dissatisfied with the* House, *so I began to find other things to do away from the* House. *That is when* Father *sent for* Jon.*"*

Thinking about my recent behavior toward Jon and how I missed him, I changed the direction of conversation, *"There were about fifteen children in the* learning house *when I attended in* Malinieum City. *Now, after our move into* Dindieum, *the class size is smaller... maybe ten. If I had not shown signs of boredom, or had no promise in becoming a king, I would have been left in the* House *until* Con Sona Eata. *Then, I would have vied for an apprenticeship of some sort. But we do not have anything like college or voc... cat... shonal school."*

Jenny smiled, biting her lip to keep from giggling over my pronunciation. She then sighed wistfully, *"I wish our schools were small like that, but they're not. At the college I'm going to now we've around two hundred different classrooms, with about three thousand people to fill them. From the hours of seven in the morning till four or five in the afternoon it's a mad house. Everyone's fighting to get where they want to be. And night school is only permitted for those who already have a trade but want to move up or change their profession."*

"Alleanne, *that many Tenzenar altogether... and for how long?!"* I shuddered in horror, imagining myself surrounded by so many Tenzenar for what sounded like a great length of time.

"Yup, needless to say, it's rather impersonal," she sighed, looking up at the ceiling.

"How long will you be gone? I do not understand your time," I asked again and received a giggle for my honesty. I didn't like the idea of these *classes,* realizing they would take her from me for what sounded like oonas everyday.

"Like I said, I attend classes on a double schedule, so I am gone for around three oonas, *or eight hours—as I would describe it,"* she explained. *"I leave here just over an* oona *after sunrise and come home about an* oona *and a half after midday. I attend classes for five days, and then have two days off. I'm also allowed semester breaks and vacations… but you don't need to know about them, since none will come up before I graduate."*

"You learn fast!" I muttered, amazed at her ability to translate her time into mine. I rolled over to face her. *"You do understand that I cannot go with you to your college? All those… humans… would have me* keezworky *in no time. With so many people about, the possibility of my being discovered would increase at least… two thousand ninety-eight times."*

She frowned. *"We have a problem, don't we?"* It was said more as a statement than a question.

"Jenny, come down for supper!" her mother's call forestalled my answer.

Having to postpone our present discussion, we both smiled at each other and shrugged. Needing a chance to get out of her room, I convinced her that I could go with her down to dinner. She agreed only after I promised to take food from her plate only.

Before I vanished, I stopped her at her door, *"Can you do me a favor?"*

"Of course I will, anything, Niki.*"*

"Can you try and learn how your father deciphered the few words he knows of my language?" I asked while raising my shield.

"Sure, but why?" she asked under her breath, shivering when my shield brushed against her as we left her room.

"Airian curiosity,*"* I whispered quietly, removing my hand from her back, so she wouldn't shiver.

PART I TENZENAR

Mrs. MacArthur passed the dishes around the table after everyone sat down. I found myself a comfortable place on the floor by *Jenny's* left elbow. As each item reached her, she innocently loaded her plate with extra portions. There were five big servings of this, two servings of that, a gargantuan glass of milk and three hot rolls crammed, piled or placed somewhere on or near her plate.

Her father froze in the middle of scooping up some sort of white frothy-looking mixture, his eyes focused on her heaping plate. Lifting his gaze from her plate, he stared at his daughter, dumfounded over her behavior. I bit my lip in a desperate effort not to laugh outright at the scene unfolding before my eyes.

Mrs. MacArthur, noticing the strange expression on her husband's face, looked toward *Jenny*. She became so focused on her daughter's plate that the piece of meat she had begun to lift from the serving plate dropped to the floor. Not one to miss an opportunity, I managed to catch it an ena before it touched the floor. Neye noticed a thing. Hoping it would help hold in my laughter, I stuffed the meat in my mouth while continuing to take in the scene unfolding around the table.

Jenny looked at her mother in wide-eyed innocence. *"What's the matter, Mom?"* she asked with the perfect amount of bewilderment, astounding me with her acting ability.

"Jennifer Anne MacArthur, don't you give me that look as if to ask, 'What's the matter with you!' Explain the meaning of all that food on your plate?" Evelynne demanded.

Jenny glanced at her plate, then looked at her mother and shrugged. *"I'm just hungry today—it must be from all that excitement yesterday,"* she explained as if none of this was unusual.

Then, bowing her head she leki'an Keyenoa for her meal before muttering under her breath, "Niki Malin, *you better help me eat all this… or I swear I'll find some way to have you stuffed and mounted over the fireplace."*

"I could never be as stuffed full as you if you eat all that— even if you did mount me on the fireplace," I whispered, choking down the piece of meat and my laughter. *"Do not worry, I will eat*

it happily," I added, knowing it would be a while before *Jenny* would see the humor in the situation like I did.

She sighed and closed her eyes in exasperation. *"May my Lord Jesus Christ forgive me for all this lieing?"*

Just as it was meant to, her statement sobered me. I nodded and bowed my head, pleading her case as well. I hoped Keyenoa realized the necessity for her behavior, and so asked for His forgiveness for both the necessity of her ghea castrinair and for my being the cause.

Aware that her patience had been strained to its limit, I said ghea neye about her having avoided the whole situation by taking second servings when her plate was empty rather than piling it so high to start with. Swiftly snatching one of her rolls, I began to eat quietly, listening to her parents lecture her over the ills of overeating and missing meals that would cause one to overeat in the first place.

"Will you do me a favor? Drop that extra eating utensil in your lap when you can," I murmured to her quietly during her parent's diatribe.

Never acknowledging that she heard me, *Jenny* maneuvered her elbow in front of the pronged instrument. Then with consummate skill, she slowly slid her elbow to the edge of the table, pushing the utensil until it dropped unnoticed into her lap, where I easily retrieved it.

As I ate, I discovered that the utensil was also as invisible as the food on it, and began to consider the far reaching possibilities that my invisibility shield might provide. I wondered, since I was clearly able to envelop certain things behind my shield, if it were possible to cover *Jenny* with my shield as well?

"Jonathan, you've been working all afternoon on your latest theory to decipher the stone writings. Is there any indication you're on the right track?" Evelynne's question drew me from my musings.

He sighed and leaned back in his chair. *"No,"* he admitted with frustration. *"My phonetical theory seems plausible, at least to me. But the computer-based linguistic simulation I put together* won't correlate with the few words and associated meanings I already understand. I confess I'm just about ready to throw in the towel and take myself and my team out to Third Sight to see what we can learn there."

"Dad," Jenny spoke up after retrieving her empty glass of milk from her lap, shivering as we accidentally touched. *"How'd you ever decipher the words* Airian *and* Malinieum, *let alone understand their pronunciation as well as their meaning?"*

I smiled proudly. Even *Evelynne* leaned forward to hear his answer. It seemed neye had never thought to ask *Jonathan* about this before.

"That was the strangest thing," he began reflectively. Clearing his throat, he wiped his mouth with a cloth before pushing his plate toward the center of the table. *"I haven't told anyone this,"* he confessed, looking in *Evelynn's* direction with guilty expression. *"I was afraid my colleagues would think I'd lost my wits.... But now, who's to say for sure? The words I learned have checked out perfectly in every context where they appear, and I've now found several different areas in which I could compare them.*

"Let's see, it happened about two months after we landed. The shops weren't even...."

"Yes, Dad, but what happened?" Jenny interrupted.

It seemed *Jonathan* was used to this type of redirection, because he smiled guiltily, and took a moment to regroup his thoughts while muttering an apology of some sort.

"Well," he started again, tipping his head back and closing his eyes, while taking himself back in memory to the day he'd learned the Airian words. *"I was standing under the stone arch in front of the city staring—with great frustration, I might add—at the symbols engraved there. I was certain those symbols represented either the name of the city or a greeting of some sort, but for the life of me I'd no idea which... or how to decipher the writing. Days before, I scanned hundreds of similar symbols into the computer and attempted to map some symbol matches, both with the sample I'd taken from the city and with other known languages. There was absolutely no correlation with any other symbol sets from other*

planets, but I did come up with a number of identical symbols that appeared frequently throughout the city. The most frustrating issue was that the computer algorithms were unable to even classify the language as pictographic, phonetic, or alphabetic in nature. I also ran into a dead end with the grammar analysis routines. I couldn't even tell which symbols represent names, nouns, or verbs. No matter which way I attacked the problem, nothing seemed to work. I tell you, I was feeling about the way I do now. I wanted to just give up, throw in the towel and walk away. I think I'd even muttered something to that effect, when from somewhere behind me, I heard a voice whisper, 'Malinieum.' Startled, I swung around to see who'd spoken, but there was no one... not a single solitary soul around." Jonathan chuckled uncomfortably. He was fully aware his story was beginning to sound rather far-fetched.

"Well, I just shook my head. I thought I'd been working too hard and decided it might be wise to walk into the city and find my assistant, Joe. I assured myself that being around another human being for a while would make things seem—well, less strange. Joe was standing by the dry fountain in the center of the city, near the large building... the one we copied part of when building this home. You know the fountain I mean, don't you, Evelynne?" He waited for her response.

She nodded quickly, a frustrated frown pinching her eyebrows, as she waited for him to continue his story. He smiled happily over his wife's response and leaned back in his chair, relaxing into his tale.

"When Joe saw me, he called excitedly, exclaiming he'd found a great number of symbols carved on the sides and base of the fountain. They also seemed to resemble those on the arch in front of the city, and one word, he swore was the same. I rushed over to see what he was talking about, and began examining the symbols.

"In my excitement, I forgot about my desire for company and sent Joe off to get my portable computer and hand scanner. I wanted to get an accurate copy of the symbols, so I could compare them and increase my data base.

PART I TENZENAR

"As soon as he'd left the courtyard, the voice spoke again. 'Malinieum,' it urged. I dared not turn around, not wanting the helpful voice to go away. There was insistence in the voice, this time, urging me to heed it. Then, it suddenly felt as though a thousand ants were crawling over my arm and hand as something forced my fingers onto the symbols that matched those on the arch.

"'Malinieum City,' the king's city," the voice urged, before my hand was lifted and placed over the first group of symbols around the fountain.

"'Airians, the people of this planet,' the voice said before moving my hand once again to the next group of symbols that lay between the words Airians, and Malinieum. Then I heard him say very quietly and rather reverently, 'Santall,' born, or given life,' it whispered at me.

"To my frustration, Joe returned at that moment. My hand was quickly released and the tingling feeling vanished. I never heard the voice again. I said nothing to Joe of what I'd experienced. Well, to be honest... I was afraid to say anything. I just told him I thought I found a way to decipher some of the words, hoping he wouldn't ask me how or why I couldn't decipher more. Well, Joe didn't question a thing and together we added the three words into the computer, for further analysis in the lab.

"The voice had taught me a three or four word phrase, Airians Santall Malinieum City, meaning 'The people born in the king's city.' From that, it stands to reason the following symbols are most probably a list of names... but unfortunately, it seems for now, there's no way to prove it. I simply can't decipher anymore."

He sat forward, resting his elbows on the table as he looked at *Jenny* and *Evelynne*. "All my research so far has brought me to the hypotheses that the Airians have at least two different types of script for writing. The styles of symbols that I've been discussing are the only type we know anything about. The problem is, this style seems to be used infrequently, and mostly in genealogies or official records... and even this supposition can't fully be proven. Between our limited access to this type of script and our limited knowledge of it, not to mention the other style—whose meaning we *have yet to consider even researching—we will probably be kept very much in the dark for a long time to come—unless I am offered some sort of 'Rosetta Stone,' or that mysterious voice returns. And even if it did return, I would have to admit that it is far from scientific to count on a voice that I have been the only one to hear,"* Jonathan *added as he smiled sheepishly, his attention drifting to* Jenny.

"There is another archway, like the one here, at the main entrance of Second Town and its name is clearly engraved on it in the same style of script as the arch over Malinieum. *The first symbol looks similar to the first symbol in the word* Malinieum, *and the last is also identical, so I'm assuming the ending must mean city.*

"Here, let me show you, Jenny... Evelynne's already had a look at this."

Mr. MacArthur left the table eagerly. He went to a cluttered table sitting against the wall, and pulled out a piece of parchment and a strange-looking writing implement. Returning to the dining table, he jotted down the Airian symbols he'd memorized from the archway, then wrote the symbols spelling Markainieum beneath that leaving a large space between them. Then, he wrote Ma___ieum in his language. Below that he wrote the symbols for Malinieum, before writing Malinieum in his language beneath it. Standing by *Jenny's* left elbow, I leaned over her shoulder to look at what he was doing:

♋ ♍ ♏ ♌
Ma -ieum

♋ ☼ ♏ ♌
Malinieum

He had a good hand when it came to writing Airian words. I thought I could even take a few pointers from him. *Jenny,* as if reading the name with me, spoke out loud, "Markainieum... Malinieum."

PART I TENZENAR

"What did you say, Jenny?" her father exclaimed excitedly. Stepping behind her, he nearly kicked me as he leaned over the table to look at his daughter's face and the words he'd written.

Eyes wide in horror, she stared at the floor beside her, thinking I was still there. Sighing, she met her father's excited gaze as he awaited her response.

"Jenny, did you say, 'Markainieum'*?"* he asked, oblivious of her distress.

She looked at the paper, *"Yes... but I don't know why I said it... I didn't mean to say it out loud,"* she mumbled to me rather than to her father. Then, all too aware of her father's excitement, her expression softened in defeat. *"Could it fit, Dad? I mean, do you think my guess could be right?"* she asked, unwilling to disappoint him, all too aware that she had the answer he desired.

"Well, honey, I don't know, but after my experience at the fountain I'm willing to rerun the computer and encode Markainieum *as a symbol fact, adding it to the other known words,"* he replied eagerly. *"From the looks of this, syllabic-phonetics may well be the key to this type of their writing!"* he added as he rushed from the room, paper in hand, and into the conference room on the opposite side of the fire pit wall.

Evelynne followed after him quickly, *Jenny* forgotten by both parents.

She sat miserably in her chair, staring at the table. *"I'm sorry, Niki,"* she whispered. *"It just slipped out... and then, seeing how much it meant to him, I couldn't let him down... even though he forgot me the moment...."* she didn't complete her thought.

Understanding, I spoke softly. I needed to say the words, yet was afraid she had yet to learn enough to understand my Airian, "Keyen Renli, Jeanitear Omnestera. Seek your aclusceaun from Keyenoa who dwells within you, and know you did the right thing. Hold fast to the truth that you already possess the Keyen you so desire from the only true and real Father there is. He will never disappoint you and He has placed you first in His heart."

"I love you and God too, thank you, Niki. *Aren't you at all angry with me?"* she asked, not fully understanding everything I said.

"No, Jenny, I am not angry. To be honest, I wanted you to tell him. Hearing his story, it seems someone else on Airies *has also taught him a little of our language. I cannot see how anymore would hurt,"* I answered her.

She turned, following the sound of my voice to the far corner of the room. Forcing a smile to her face, she called to her parents, never taking her eyes from where she knew I was. *"Mom, Dad, I'm going out for a walk. Paula told me she'd be at Deer Tread Park. Don't plan on me being back for a few hours."*

There was neye reply from the conference room, yet it was clear *Jenny* hadn't expected one. I sighed with regret over her parents, understanding her feelings all too well. What she had with her parents and what she longed for would never be the same. I found myself thinking of my own parent while following her to the front door. Father at least cared, even if at times I thought him distant and difficult to approach. Sighing again, I decided to put all parents from my mind for a taun to come. Choosing to heed my own advice, I decided to rely on Keyenoa for His Keyen and direction, and stop condemning my parent for those times I felt he'd somehow let me down.

Chapter XII

A Clearer Understanding

"Where you go, I will be with you—even if you travel to the end of your lands. For I cherish you and will not allow you to fall from My hand again, nor allow you to separate yourself from the laws I have placed within your heart."
—Book of Keyenoa

Following *Jenny*, I watched closely as I purposely brushed against her, letting her know I was outside. My shield shimmered with a silver light where it enveloped parts of her in invisibility. The touch of my shield was what caused her to shudder uncontrollably.

"Eeee-u!" she exclaimed, closing the front door behind her. *"That's the most... eeee-u... feeling I've ever experienced."* She shivered from head to toe once again. *"When you did that to the policeman and Ruth, they must've thought someone was dancing on their graves or the dead had just walked through them."*

Reaching the paved walkway in front of her home, I frowned over her strange and morbid phrases as well as all the varied names she gave to the man who found her at the lake. *"Jenny, you called that man... Matt, policeman, sheriff, officer... and while on the phone to Paula, you referred to him as cop—what is his* name? And those morbid phrases—do people really dance on top of the dead? Jenny, your language confuses me more every time you speak,"* I grumbled, deciding it'd be kutated to ask about the Sontall walking though others, certain I would never understand that.

Jenny giggled at me and began to explain the complexities of what she called the *English language* as we walked along a paved walkway. *"I'm sorry,* Niki. *No, people don't really dance on the dead or on graves—at least not anymore. Those are just colorful phrases, used to get a feeling across to someone else. We humans also have different words that mean the same thing, and the same-sounding words that mean totally different things. The only way to differentiate between their meanings is through the context in which they're used."* She wasn't helping me to understand at all. *"Words like sheriff and officer are titles that refer to the same man. The titles are used to show respect, as well as revealing his profession. There are other words like policeman, detective, and even cop, which also refer to the job he does... and in some cases can be used as titles also."*

Completely confused, I made a face at her, knowing she couldn't see me. Not wanting to continue on this subject, aware that she would soon realize my complete confusion, I looked around at the Tenzenar homes. The land known to me as Golden Meadow was so changed, that I had neye idea where I was. I wasn't even certain if we were walking north, south, east, or west. Sighing, totally frustrated, I looked for the moon. Knowing it rose in the east, I hoped it would reveal my direction... but the moon had yet to rise.

Looking at *Jenny* I quickly got distracted by her strange beauty, marveling over my attraction to her. She managed to move my heart and stir my desire without even meaning to. Tempted to touch her, I forced my hand into a fist and kept it at my side, knowing my touch would only cause part of her to disappear and her to shiver *"as if dancing on the dead."* Silently, while still watching her, I humbly sorice leki Keyenoa that He had brought us together.

"So are you taking me someplace special?" I asked, only because I wanted to hear her voice.

PART I TENZENAR

She shrugged. *"No, I just needed to get out of the house. We need to talk about my going to school and figure out some place safe for you to stay while I'm gone. I thought that by taking a walk, there wouldn't be as many interruptions or distractions."* Jenny paused and looked blindly in my direction. *"Niki, I'm not an idiot, I know it must be hard to be cooped up in a house that looks like your old home, yet, stuffed full of things and beings alien to you."* Shrugging, she sighed, *"I think we both needed to get out of that house."*

Touched by her intuitive understanding, I quickly graced her cheek with my lips. She shivered as my shield enveloped half of her face. Then, aware of my kiss, she giggled shyly in embarrassment. Smiling over her reaction, I suddenly thought of a place I wanted to go. I knew I would feel comfortable there.

"Could we go to Malinieum City?*"* I asked eagerly.

"Not tonight... it's a bit too far to walk." She tilted her head to one side, revealing a twinkle of mischievousness glittering in her gaze as she peeked in my direction as if she could see me. *"Anyway, my prince, I thought you were supposed to be learning something about my culture. If you take me to* Malinieum City, *I'll be much too curious to even think of teaching you about humans. Therefore, to make sure that doesn't happen, I know of a nice park..."* She fell silent as we past an older couple strolling along hand in hand, *"Where we can go. It's not crowded at this time of night, so it'll be safe for you to appear. And there we can talk without being discovered,"* she finished.

"Ah, my fair maid, I am but your humble and loving servant. I shall follow you with adoration and eagerness wherever you lead," I said, playing along with her, feeling a spirit of joy begin to fill me the farther I got from her home.

"What are those?" I asked a few moments later, pointing to a long pole stuck in the ground with a light at the top that illuminated an area around us as if we were standing in a patch of daylight.

"What are what, Niki?*"* she asked in confusion.

Starting to answer, only to discover that not only had I neye name for the object, I had neye words to describe it either. Grasping her arm, I pointed with it to the direction of the pole. She shivered uncontrollably over my contact, while her arm and part of her shoulder disappeared completely.

"That! Jenny, what is that?" I asked in frustration, releasing her arm, sorry for the discomfort I'd caused.

She smiled. There was a bright twinkle of humor that gleamed in her eyes as she looked blindly in my direction. *"They're called light poles, or street lights,* Niki. *We use them to see better at night."*

I murmured some sort of acknowledgment, embarrassed by my question, realizing she hadn't told me anything I hadn't already figured out for myself. We walked together in compatible silence for a while.

"Niki," she began, quietly breaking the silence between us, *"Do you know why we came here—to this planet, I mean?"*

"Ta. *The second time* Jon *and I visited the Masters' home, I went into their house—invisible of course. Ruth and Bill talked about being able to free themselves from the sterility of progress, saying something about letting their children grow up as they used to on some place I heard them call Earth."* I found myself remembering all the ideas I had about Tenzenar back then and compared it to all the things I had learned since.

Turning off the paved walkway we stepped onto a dirt path surrounded by trees and grass. *Jenny* led me into a wooded glen and sat beside me on a stone bench. The minca glen was lit only by the edges of light coming from delicate and fancy looking light poles which lined the dirt path several pearons away. Sighing contentedly, she gazed at the stars overhead. Completely sheltered by the trees and a fair distance from the dirt path, I felt it was unlikely anyone would think to wander in so I relaxed and lowered my shield.

Taking her hands in mine I squeezed them tenderly. *"There is something which has confused me since I first saw the Masters in their kitc-hen."* I frowned at mangling the pronunciation, but

PART I TENZENAR

continued, *"I think I have the answer to this, but hear me out and let me know if I'm right... will you?"*

She nodded, her brow creasing like her father's as she concentrated.

"My people call your people Tenzenar *because we believed you to be without life as we know it—selfish, self-focused, and self-serving. When I watched the landing of the* lunata, *I saw many people who portrayed the lifeless, black monsters we believed you to be. Then, in the Masters'* defacka, *when I looked at their faces, saw their eyes and heard their voices, I knew that they were different. They had life inside them... and in you, Jenny. I can see this life in you as well. Yet I do not see it in your parents, nor in the faces of the older couple we passed back there on the road. I have been greatly confused why some of you are truly alive, while others live in what we call* whateshan eyette sontall... *existing without ever truly living, simply surviving till death. Is this difference which I have described because you and the Masters have* Keyenoa *and the others have not? And if this is so... why do these others not have Him, while you and the Masters do?"*

Her expression seemed suddenly lit as if by a flame, *Jenny* smiled with tender understanding. *"Yes,* Niki, *it's because of* Keyenoa *that some—like me and the Masters—are different. Bill, Ruth, myself and I believe even Lisa—though I'm not certain of Michael—and many other humans have received what we call eternal life, because the Holy Spirit lives in us. This light you see, and the differences you describe, are caused by our belief in the Son of God—*Keyenoa *as you call Him. Through our belief in the Son of God, Jesus Christ, we are given eternal life and the Holy Spirit. It is our walk with Him and His Spirit that brings us great joy, as we live our life for Him, rather than simply existing in our world. The reason not all people have The Son of God living in them is because not all accept or choose to believe in Jesus. God allows us to choose freely, and many simply have not yet chosen Him, or have made the choice against Him."*

The idea of choosing was foreign to me. Airians were born with Keyenoa's presence living in us. I was surprised that anyone could choose not to have it be this way. I pondered my limited knowledge of *Jesus Christ* from the sharing of *Jenny's* thoughts, but I still had a hard time understanding how He could be man, Keyenoa, and Spirit. So I was not surprised to find I didn't understand why the Tenzenar chose Him or didn't choose Him. Closing my eyes, I turned to Keyenoa, and through prayer I asked for His guidance and understanding.

His answer, though not terribly clarifying, came immediately. Opening my eyes, I smiled and caressed *Jenny's* face. "Who am I to fully understand the ways of Keyenoa? He deals differently with all His people. To you *humans*, *Jenny*, Keyenoa gave His Son, and through Him comes eternal life and camaraderie with Keyenoa. Airians were given those things on the day Keyenoa gave the first High King his powers," I spoke in Airian.

Jenny's smile revealed that she had understood enough of my language to comprehend the essence of what I had said. Kneeling in front of her, I gazed at her face. *"This is why you told the Masters' of me, but not your parents or your friend Paula! The Masters' believe, but your parents and Paula do not."*

She nodded and kissed my forehead. *"I find it incredible and humbling that God, in His unfathomable desire for communion with each of His creations—and there are more than just human and Airian—that He makes one way and only one way for each separate creation."*

We sat silently, our gazes locked, awed by what we had learned. As I lay myself before Keyenoa with ghea sorice leki omprice, slowly my Keyen for *Jenny* grew and blossomed, while Keyenoa gave me a glimpse of His desire for all of Airies. Even as He gave me this glimpse, Keyenoa cautioned that I hold it in trust and wait on Him for the rest of His direction.

Turning from her gaze, my attention drifted over the bench we occupied. Instantly, I recognized that it had been built by the stone masons of Malinieum City. Reading some of the words carved on it, I realized it had been placed very close to Dreamers Lake just outside the main gate of Malinieum City. The path we were on when entering her *park*, would lead straight to Malinieum City's gate about one hundred pearons beyond the bench. Perplexed, I wondered why *Jenny* would claim that Malinieum City was too far away, when we were actually very close to the main gate. Absently stroking the stone-etched words, I struggled with my confusion and the sense of betrayal I felt because *Jenny* hadn't told me the truth. Before I spoke and accused her of ghea castrin, I sought Keyenoa's direction. First, Keyenoa reminded me how I also needed to learn that truth was truth—neye matter the circumstances—and until I lived this lesson I shouldn't find fault in her. Keyenoa also made it clear that this was not the time to confront *Jenny* over her 'misleading' words—she hadn't ghea castrin to hurt me. Instead, *Jenny* had an honorable reason for her castrin just as I did when I asked *Bill* and *Ruth Masters* to castrin for me. So Keyenoa urged me to trust her and let the matter go. Keyenoa then promised that He would see to it that she and I would both learn the lesson of truth… in His taun, not mine. Accepting His wisdom and chastisement, I still could not quite quell my uneasy feelings when I began to wonder why she didn't want me to go to Malinieum City. Even as I said ghea neye to her about where we were, I did know she would never castrin to hurt me. *Jenny* had to have a very benna reason for not taking me to Malinieum City.

With a sigh, I returned to the subject we'd been discussing before our talk about Keyenoa. *"So, Jenny, did I understand Ruth correctly concerning your peoples reasons for coming to* Airies*?"*

"Yes. However, our just wanting these things from Airies *didn't make them so. There was more that had to take place before we were allowed to fulfill our dreams and be able to inhabit this planet,"* she answered with a tentative smile. *"Airies first drew the Alliance's interest approximately four years ago. And the Interplanetary Explorers were sent here to gather information about* Airies. *First, they took a life reading from their ship, never sending anyone down to this planet—as you must know. While on the ship orbiting* Airies, *they learned that your atmosphere was quite similar to Earth's, that there was wildlife and plenty of eatable vegetation. It was also concluded that there were no intelligent life forms inhabiting your planet at this time.* Airies *was*

then determined to have everything our select group of people had petitioned the Alliance for many years earlier.

"I swear, Niki, *no one would have dared settle on* Airies *if the IE discovered there were intelligent humanoid or animoid life forms on* Airies *already,"* she finished, clasping my hands in hers, urging me to believe her.

"Hu-mane-oide and anne-moyed?" I repeated, confused by the words, but understanding what she was trying to tell me.

She giggled. My pronunciation was horrid. *"Humanoid is how your people would be classified... if we had known of your existence. They are terms used for any life form that's similar to humans—or the way I like to put it is—any beings created in God's image. Then there's another classification known as animoid, and that describes beings of high intelligence but look more animal than human,"* she explained, while still smiling over my mispronunciation. Shaking her head she continued, *"I simply don't understand why your life readings have never registered on the original I.E. ship's sensors or the sensors now on the planet. All that has ever registered were your towns, scattered dwellings and a few farm plots—all of which seemed to indicate they had long been deserted."*

"That, I can explain, Jenny," I said. *"A long time ago before your people mastered interstellar travel,* Airies *got her first* High King. *When Keyenoa gave him his power he gave all the people the ability to raise shields of invisibility. He also set a protective cover of power over all the people of* Airies, *and this shield has been maintained by each new reigning* High King *from that* taun *on. It was* aanas *upon* aanas *later that another* High King *was given power to span the universe. He watched your people as they began their explorations into space and learned of your peoples' nature. Killing to humans is... well... something your people consider possible. It is a thing human's might ponder before doing, but killing is to the human mind a thing that is not only possible it is oftentimes acceptable. Humans kill to protect, to force another to their way of thinking, to gain land, and even for simple pleasure. To Airians, it is abhorrent. It is a thing that can only be con-*

sidered if neye *other solution presents itself for the safety of our whole population. We would rather flee danger than kill. And if faced with killing for our survival... the act of killing often sends the killer into such decline they too end up in* Sontall.*"*

"But our people have changed, Niki. *We no longer choose to destroy life, nor try to impose our way of life on others. Oh, I really can't explain it, not well enough for you to believe me. While you stay with me, promise that you'll watch us as a people and as individuals, and then decide for yourself if we're now what we once were."*

I climbed up and sat on the back of the bench, letting my booted feet rest beside *Jenny*. *"I have heard Father say that sometimes seeing is more convincing than the word of a most trusted* forlaynan... *but only on rare occasions should one put his trusted* forlaynan *to such a test.*

"By being with you, I am given a chance to learn many things my people don't understand. I would be a ghea mootan teepatin *if I didn't take it. However, I remain with you, not for the purpose of learning, but because... I love you."* I looked at her. *"Now, that brings us back to the problem we left your home to solve. What is to be done with this sometimes invisible* Airian*, who has followed you home like a stray beastie, while you are off each day attending collage classes?"*

A gust of wind crept through the trees and caught her hair, lifting it from her face as she stood. Walking across the minca expanse of grass in our enclosed clearing, she stopped near the edge of the trees. Taking in a deep breath, she drew her arms around herself and then let them drop back to her side as she sighed. She faced me with an expression of resignation on her plain, yet endearing face.

"Well, Niki, *when I think about you staying at the house without me, there is one thing that makes me quite nervous. My mother works from the house."* She watched me closely, hoping I would recognize the ramifications of what she was saying, but I saw neye problem. "Nikita Malin, s*he records and analyzes all alleged* Airian *sightings, encounters, or other strange, unexplainable hap-*

*penings on this planet. From what I've heard of the calls and her reactions to them—comparing them to what I now know about your people—*Niki, *she's one sharp lady, and very good at her job! My mother also has this rather scary and very accurate intuition, that neither I nor Dad can figure—it drives us both crazy, much to her enjoyment. Considering her intuition and her occupation, I'm afraid she'll discover you in no time—especially, if you are in close contact with her for long periods of time with no one around to distract her."*

Jenny sighed with frustration, both over having neye better solution, and my continued cavalier expression. *"I also believe it when you say it'd be suicide for you to go to classes with me. You're right, there are just too many humans and humanoids hurrying and scurrying all over campus for you to watch out for them all. There also might be other's gifted with Lisa's uncanny ability to see you. Going to school with me would be more of a risk than the risks you face at home—but only a very small, infinitesimal, microscopic bit more of a risk—"*

She held up her hand as I opened my mouth to make a suggestion. *"Now before you suggest it…"* she cut me off. *"There's no way that it's safe for you to wander through First Settlement without me.* Niki, *it'd be just as suicidal for you to wander the city streets as it is for you to come with me to college. It'd actually be worse without me being with you, because you still understand very little about us and our culture. I'm sure you haven't the faintest idea of our traffic and pedestrian rules, or even that we have them. I shudder at the thought of you crossing a busy, bustling street on a red light."*

I'd been prepared to argue with her until her last statement. I had absolutely neye idea what a *red light* was or the rules she spoke of, let alone what a *pedestrian* or *traffic* was.

"What if I stay in Malinieum City*?"* I offered helpfully.

"No!" she nearly shrieked. *"How would you get there, without having to deal with the streets? Then, there are people wandering around* Malinieum *all the time, and since you can make the city sing, they'd be on you like bees in search of nectar.*

PART I TENZENAR

"No.... The only solution is the one I'm not very happy with, but like it or not, I think it's better than our alternatives—and I really did consider them all," she finished unhappily.

"I will not go back to my people without you!" I interrupted defiantly, accepting her logic about Malinieum City, though I knew she hadn't told me everything.

Jenny looked horrified by my statement. *"No,* Niki,*"* she corrected, *"The solution isn't either that drastic or that final. You simply have to stay in my room—with the door closed—until I come home. Since it's my responsibility to take care my own room, Mom doesn't go in there. That means you will be safe from discovery—so long as you remain in my room. Then, as soon as I get home, I'll get you out of the house so you won't go stir-crazy. With me taking you around First Settlement, I'll be able teach you everything you want to know about my way of life, and I hope as I teach you about us, you will also teach me about your people and laws. If you can stand this for a couple of weeks or so, you should be able to wander out alone after that."*

I opened my mouth to comment, and again she held up her hand. *"If you have to leave my room—for any reason—please, be sure my mother isn't anywhere around. The best times to forage for food, or go to the bathroom, would be when she leaves the house and checks her post office box or goes shopping. Because she has no idea you exist, it seems Dad and I are enough to distract her when were in the house. Therefore, I don't see why you can't come down and eat dinner with the family, so you're not always cooped up in my room. Oh, and don't worry, I'll do my best to come up with some believable reason for eating so much at dinner,"* she added proudly, finally offering me an opportunity to respond.

Climbing off the bench, I took her in my arms, chuckling quietly over her long and unnecessary speech. Another couple could be heard heading in our direction, so I raised my shield of invisibility. As the shield slid around me, I looked down at her and confirmed that she too was fully hidden behind my shield. The tell-tale line of hazy silver light, indicating the edge of my shield, extended a furon behind her, moving as we moved.

"I will do what you suggest, Jenny," I murmured, my lips nearly touching hers, *"because, like you, I have no better solution. But about my...."*

"Niki, I can still see you!" she whispered sharply as she twisted in my arms, aware of the impending intrusion. *"Be careful, for heavens sake, people are starting to walk through here!"*

I hung on to her, keeping her from slipping beyond my shield. *"Shh,"* I chided, *"they will hear you and think you are an* Airian *come to haunt them. I am invisible, my* Keyen*, I assure you. While you are in my arms like this, you are as invisible as I am, keep squirming and your backside will be showing."*

She stilled instantly but looked at me skeptically, even as she drew her arms around my waist and relaxed against me. I caressed her cheek, fighting the passion she'd stirred in me, until she lifted her face to mine. Sighing in defeat, I lowered my head and claimed her lips in a tender kiss. The intruding couple, having heard *Jenny's* exclamation of alarm, had chosen another secluded spot, leaving us blissfully alone.

Reluctantly, I stepped back from our embrace, watching as my shield past through her body, causing her to shiver. Closing my eyes, I relaxed and lowered my shield, becoming visible.

"About having to come up with an excuse for eating so much, Jenny..." I began hesitantly. Feeling guilty for not mentioning this before the meal, and afraid she'd see the tell-tale twinkle of humor in my gaze, I looked at my boots. *"You see,* Keyen*... well... I thought you understood before we went down to the table... but obviously you did not."*

"Understood what?" she asked with such sincere concern.

I looked at her, scrunching my face in trepidation, knowing she was gong to hate my answer. *"There was no need to pile your plate with so much food all at once. If you serve yourself what you normally eat, I will help myself to your plate, and all you need to do is go for seconds if one of us is still hungry. That way your parents might not notice that you are suddenly eating enough to feed two, and not gaining a* lastna *for your effort."*

PART I TENZENAR

Swiftly clasping a hand over her own mouth, her eyes growing as round as saucers, a flush of embarrassment spread across her face. *"Nikita Markain Malin, that was a shameless and shameful thing, neglecting to tell me something so important,"* she chided even as her eyes twinkled in humor and her lips twitched with the desire to laugh.

I pulled her back into my arms, laughing. *"I love you… so much,"* I whispered. Closing my eyes, I struggled with the force of emotion I felt for her. *"Let us go home, Jenny, before your parents begin to worry over your long absence. I have so many more questions to ask before we go to sleep tonight, and if I ask them now, I fear we will be here for the remainder of the night."*

Discovering that my shield expanded to accommodate her so long as she remained close to my side I covered us both in invisibility, as we left the park arm in arm. After letting Jenny know that we couldn't be seen, we carefully avoided the few humanoids strolling along the walkways. Our return to her home was made in companionable silence.

At the front steps, I looked around the darkened street. Certain neye was nearby, I stepped from her side, apologizing as she shivered when my shield slipped away from her. She opened the front door with a minca, flat metal object which she fitted into a slot in the door, then stepped aside to allow me to enter first. I decided—mundane or not—it'd be better to murmur something about being in the house, rather than touch her and have her relive the sensation of my shield passing through her body anymore this night.

She went to the back of the house to inform her parents of her return and tell them benna callray and I went to her room. Closing the bedchamber door quietly, I lowered my shield weary and drained from the almost constant use of my limited power. Removing my Loreann bow and quiver, I tucked them beneath the bed, completely out of sight. *Jenny* entered a few moments later, shutting out the light, to prepare for bed. I sat on the bed to remove my boots, listening to her rustling in clothing drawers.

Suddenly, out of nowhere, *Jenny* rushed at me, while grabbing one of the pillows from the head of the bed. Before I had a chance to protect myself, I was soundly pummeled about the head and shoulders by a giggling female. Having neye recourse, I of course defended myself as any gentleman would in such a situation—I cheated. Tickling her unmercifully, the pillow was quickly dropped in her effort to protect herself, leaving me with a quivering, giggling mass of *'humanoid'* at my mercy. To my relief, my fingers revealed that she had on very prim and proper nightwear of light weight cloth britches and a soft, high buttoned cloth shirt. Exhausted by our romping and both of us fearful of being overheard, I encouraged her to settle into my arms. *Jenny* sighed and happily snuggled against me.

"You said you had more questions to ask," she reminded me sleepily.

I nodded brushing the top of her head with my cheek, *"I understand the reasons for your coming to* Airies. *And from what I have witnessed, I would say you people live very much like they did when our* High King *discovered your existence."*

"Umm, yes, probably, why?" she asked as she kissed my cheek and slid beneath all the coverlets, yawning.

I slid off the bed, unlaced my vest, and dropped it to the floor, before tucking myself between the heavy top coverlets, and the lighter ones underneath.

Making myself comfortable, I continued, *"Well, I understood it was during that time that your people were slowly destroying your world through poisoning the air, water, and land—with little concern or awareness of what you were doing. If that were so—and your silence confirms it must have been—then have not your people condemned* Airies *to the same destruction, by living this way here?"*

"No, Niki. *No! We're not doing that, I promise you!"* She sat up and looked at me in the darkness. *"We really have learned from our mistakes. We may live a similar lifestyle, but because of our increased knowledge and technological skills, we've discovered different ways of manufacturing those things without causing the*

poisoning called pollution. The electricity, cars, and other things, are designed to look similar, but were made in consideration for the protection of Airies. *The pollution done in that era was the one thing we wanted to have stay in that time. Every humanoid who had petitioned to live here came with a desire to live and work with the land, giving back what we take. All the materials that couldn't be made from resources here that we could replenish were made on another planet and brought here. I don't know all the technical mishmash, but I know there will never be any pollution of* Airies," she finished passionately.

"*I want to trust you, but somewhere inside me, I am uneasy. I know you are honest and firmly believe all you have said, but, Jenny, I have seen many humanoids that are not honest or scrupulous. Therefore, I am not able to fully accept that* Airies *will not and has not already begun to suffer the fate of your Earth. I have already seen much damage done to my world from your roads and houses,*" I replied quietly, touching her cheek in reassurance.

"*You can learn as you stay with me,* Niki, *that while things look the same as in that time, nothing is being poisoned by pollution,*" she answered softly.

"*One more question. Then, I promise, we will sleep,*" I said as I pulled her, covers and all, into my arms.

"*Confess,* Niki, *you're just trying to keep me awake hoping I'll be too tired to go to classes tomorrow?*" she teased.

"*No.... But... now that you have mentioned it....*" I let my sentence falter with a chuckle. "*No, that was not my intention. Though I admit to enjoying the sound of your voice, it is so different from mine, dry and raspy, and somewhat smoky... well, it fascinates me,* Keyen,*"* I murmured, kissing her hair as she giggled at me.

"Tell me about the Intern-plaine-a-tary Ex-plour-ars," I struggled to get the words past my uncooperative tongue.

She laughed, turning her face against my chest to stifle the outburst. "*I like hearing your voice too, especially when you try and pronounce new words,*" her response was muffled against my chest as she laughed all the harder.

I swatted her backside, causing her to yelp. Lifting her head, she managed to get control of her laughter, *"Okay, okay, no more laughing at you, I promise. The Interplanetary Explorers are simply a branch of our government."*

"Gov... ern... ment?" I interrupted.

"All right, let me try and explain," she sighed wearily, recognizing the enormity of what I'd asked. *"Government is a term used to describe the way people are ruled. Here, let me give you an example you will understand, your kings are what we would call your Government. In our case, we have a group of leaders, chosen from each of the different planets in the Alliance, who decide our universal laws and ways of keeping interstellar peace in the Alliance. These leaders are called the Interplanetary Board, and they work as a part of the Interplanetary Alliance, which is contrived of those people living on the aforementioned planets."*

She sighed knowing she wasn't doing the best job explaining. *"I'm sorry, it's confusing,* Niki, *but I can't explain it very well when I'm tired,"* she said and forcing herself to continue. *"It's something like your ruling system, but instead of kings ruling each continent, we have leaders, who in their own way rule each of the different planets. When these leaders get together they form a board, where they make decisions concerning the planets and the space between them together. Do you understand this much?"*

"Ta, *I think so. The people who live on the planets, who have chosen to align themselves in this type of unification, call themselves the Interplanetary Alliance. Then, these people choose one person to represent them from each planet, and when they get together they are called The Interplanetary Alliance Board."*

Her silky hair brushed my cheek as she nodded. *"Uh-huh. Now, each planet in the Alliance keeps its own type of government and set of laws, and takes care of itself. Then there's a section of the Alliance called the Interplanetary Police, who enforce the laws of that planet and of space. They patrol the area of space around the individual planets, keeping the peace and taking custody of any lawbreaker who breaks the IA laws or the planets laws that is not a resident of that planet.*

"Another section of the Alliance is called the Interplanetary Defense. They keep other forms of government from invading Alliance space.

"Then there is the Interplanetary Explorers. They travel around the universe exploring new planets and searching for different life forms. When they find a new planet with intelligent life existing there, they first study those beings from a distance. If they discover the life forms are aware of other intelligent life existing beyond their world, they try to make contact with the new beings. Knowledge is then shared, along with offers to join the Alliance. If these beings are found to be ignorant of life on other planets, the Explorers send word to the Interplanetary Defense alerting them of a new planet in need of protection. Thus, the Alliance gives these people protection from any other alien invasion and allows them to live the way they always have, without their ever learning of the Alliance's protection.

"Do you understand all that?" she asked, tilting her head to look at me and again tickling my cheek with her hair.

The coverlets were bundled around her head as if she wore a hood, so that her nose was the only thing my sharp eyes could discern in the darkness. Smiling over the comically, adorable picture she made, I considered her question.

"Ta, *I understand. In the case of* Airies, *if they knew of our existence, we would have been studied. Since we do know of other planets and life forms living on them, we would have been contacted by the Explorers sooner or later. When they learned that we did not wish to have contact with other beings, we would have been left to ourselves. But if we had decided that our two cultures could in some way be mutually beneficial for each other, we would then have been invited into the Alliance. No matter which way we chose to deal with the Alliance, we would have been left to rule* Airies *as we have been ruling her since the day* Keyenoa *gave us our first* High King."

"*Yes!*" she exclaimed in a whisper, kissing me in reward for my understanding. Yawning widely, she rolled away from me and straightened the wayward covers before re-tucking them around her shoulders. *"Now, you should have quite a lot to think about, while I'm in school tomorrow,"* she murmured, already beginning to drift off to sleep, *"Good night, my love, sleep well."*

"Keyen, Met Jeanitear. May the night treat you well in your rest and Keyenoa watch over your heart, till morn's bright day shines once again upon your pretty face," I murmured tiredly in Airian, slurring the words of an old salutation I had heard when very fraw at five aanas and was being cared for by a Cressa Orate.

"What?" she asked, waking at the sound of my voice.

I rolled over and kissed her. *"I love you,"* I said in explanation. *"Good night, Jenny,"* I murmured, reluctantly rolling over to sleep.

"That was an awfully long way of saying I love you and good night," she murmured, then said, *"good night"* again, before burying herself deeper in the coverlets and instantly falling fast asleep.

I sighed and closed my eyes, ghea sorice leki omprice Keyenoa once more for this woman He had given me. I asked Him to help me honor her with my affection and consideration as He would want. She had been given to me through His hand as I had been given to her, and so I trusted that He would find a way to not only bring *Jenny* and me closer together, but also keep us from ever being torn apart.

Chapter XIII

Promises to Keyenoa

"If you make a pledge to partner before your Lord Keyenoa, speak it with your heart and know, once spoken, you shall be bound by it until your Sontall, and areceta every day of your life by the holding of it."

—Book of Keyenoa

I woke the next morning an oona before *Jenny*. Lying beside her, I watched with adoring fascination as she slept. Again, I was moved by her strange and alluring beauty. Her face, with skin as soft and smooth as the petals of a keya flower, carried an expression of innocence and a minca measure of the joy that Keyenoa placed in all the Airian people. It was a joy I'd known all my life. I smiled as I remembered what she had told me about Keyenoa's Son and that she'd come to accept Him only recently. Keyenoa had told me this was why she was just now awakening to the joy I had always known, and why there remained a touch of sadness in her face.

If any of my people were to touch her mind before seeing her face, I was certain she could be mistaken for Airian. I also knew that at this moment, she—even being totally alien—had more of the heart and mind of an Airian than I. Having for so long pulled away from Keyenoa and my own people, I was only now struggling to reclaim what I'd lost.

Leaning near her, I touched her soft cheek, turning her face to mine. *"Jenny,"* I whispered pressing my lips to hers, *"come on,* Met heart, *wake up before someone decides you have slept long enough and comes to wake you."*

She woke instantly, her with eyes lit in joy when she found my face. Stretching slowly, she let her outstretched arms encircle my neck. Needing neye further encouragement I kissed her again, allowing the kiss to deepen.

"Mmmm, good morning, Niki,*"* she purred, then sighed and forced herself out of bed.

Looking at a mechanical object beside her *view phone*, she sighed in exasperation while suddenly scurrying around the room. With haste and efficiency she changed her clothing and organized what she needed to take with her. Intent on her tasks, she'd forgotten I was there, and I chose not remind her, finding the view quite pleasant and enlightening.

After dressing, laying her books and papers to one side, she sat in front of the *viewphone* and pulled out a case from one of the desk drawers and opened it. She set out several minca containers, then one at a time dipped into them, placing color and gook all over her face and eyes. Fearful of the alarming change she'd do to herself—considering all those different colors she was applying—I sat up and gaped at her. Finished, *Jenny* turned and smiled at me, and to my amazement, all those strange colors had blended in harmony, subtly enhancing her beauty, rather than destroying it as I had feared.

Gathering up her stuff, she paused at the bedchamber door on her way out. *"I'm going to get you some toast and coffee for breakfast,* Niki. *Then, whether I want to or not, I'll have to rush for the campus bus."* She blew me a quick kiss, and rushed out.

A few onas later, she returned with a plate holding several pieces of warmed bread smothered in something called *butter*, and a heavy mug filled with a dark black liquid. The liquid's aroma hung in the air, tickling my nostrils with a scent I had come to associate with mornings at the *Masters'* home. Kissing me on the cheek, she offered me a sad wave, and headed off for whatever a… *bus* was.

Understanding the danger of remaining in only my tunic breeches, I quickly dressed, even placing my Loreann bow and quiver on my shoulders, cumbersome as they were. I wanted to take every precaution, just in case *Evelynne MacArthur* happened to enter the room during the day without *Jenny's* knowledge. Then, I sat at her desk and ate my morning meal.

The first oona was passed by my pacing, sitting in the chair by the desk and looking at the symbols on the strange buttons attached to the *view phone*, or bouncing like a minca boy on the bed. I was forced to stop the bouncing when the springs began to squeak—even though that was the most enjoyable thing I had done all morning. While the second oona wore on, I began to wish *Jenny* had one of those idiotic machines in her room. The *Masters'* had one in their home which I heard *Lisa* call a *television set*. I thought at least if I turned the abominable thing on, I would've had something to capture a portion of my attention until her return. Heaving a sigh of frustration, I flopped backward on the bed and admitted I'd soon go keezworky if I didn't find something to occupy my attention.

Going to the window I had opened earlier, I looked out at the *road* and walkway with great longing. Breathing in the cool air, finding it more sustaining than the meal I had consumed, I considered escaping to the outside world for just a minca taun. *Cars* sped along the *road*, and it looked as if every Tenzenar in the town had chosen to go out, filling the walkway with their presence as they scurried along. Shuddering at the unaccustomed sight and the thought of being among them as they rushed here and there, I wondered if there was any aclusceaun in these creatures' lives and abandoned the idea and the window. I also began to wonder how well I would handle the stress and depression Tenzenar seemed to cause while I lived among them. When I had been among them before, lost in whateshan eyette Sontall, I had not cared what the Tenzenar did to my already damaged soul. Now that I had *Jenny* and a purpose in my life again, I cared about my ability to withstand the emotional turmoil the Tenzenar caused, and deep in my heart I knew I had benna reason to worry.

Pacing the room like a caged animal, a burring noise broke the silence in the house. It came from outside *Jenny's* room somewhere up the next landing and along the hall. Immediately my desperate mind and over active curiosity became caught. I could hear *Evelynne* walking up the three short steps and passing by *Jenny's* room before taking the next two steps, on her way to intercept the ringing. I moved cautiously to the door and eased it open. Eager to discover what was going on, I didn't stop to consider *Jenny's* warnings about her mother and the ghea teepin of my actions.

Poking my head out the door, I saw *Evelynne* sitting at the end of the hall to my left, seated on a stool with her back to me. She was speaking into a *view phone*, which sat at the end of the upper hallway, near her and *Jonathan's* bedchamber. From where I stood, only a minca corner of the carved table and the machine was visible. Ghea leki'anee *Evelynne* blocked the reflection *mirror*. I didn't trust the thing… despite the fact that I was invisible.

Invisible?! I ducked back into the room so quickly I even got dizzy. My heart thumped ghea kezky as I swiftly raised my shield relieved as I sensed it surround me. Scaring myself as I had, I decided it was wiser to remain in *Jenny's* room—bored or not—and moved back to the bed… forgetting to close the door.

With the door open, bits and pieces of *Evelynne's* conversation caught my attention and drew me back to the door. Assuring myself that my shield was raised, I stepped into the hallway, hoping I could hear the conversation better. The ena I stood in the center of the long hallway, on that short, two-step landing just below hers, *Evelynne* swung around, her eyes searching with terrifying intensity. I froze, hardly daring to breathe.

The expression on her face and the unfocused search of her gaze gave proof that she couldn't see me, but that knowledge wasn't comforting. *Jenny* had been right about her mother, and I called myself all sorts of names for not listening to her. *Evelynne* most definitely possessed an uncanny and accurate discernment,

PART I TENZENAR

and so was a great danger to me... and my people. Because I was determined to remain with *Jenny*, I realized that I would be laying my life and those of my people on the blade of a very sharp lackna. One slip—and I admitted I might have made that slip already—and I would destroy everything.

The voice from the *view phone* called to *Mrs. MacArthur*. Distracted, she shrugged her shoulders as if questioning her own sanity, before returning to the caller and continuing her conversation. I dove back in *Jenny's* room, and finding the corner near the window—as far from the open door as possible—I crouched there, trembling like a frightened dree, unable to go to the door and close it.

Not even five onas later, *Evelynne* ended her conversation. Then taking the short steps down the landing, she paused at *Jenny's* room. Cocking her head to one side, she focused on *Jenny's* bedchamber door before stepping into the doorway. I focused on her feet, not daring to look at her, and held my breath as I remained pressed into the corner under the window. I began praying while utilizing every lestna of power I possessed to deepen my shield and keep from being discovered. My bow, quiver and arrows dug into my back, but I continued to force myself against the wall and brave looking up at her. *Evelynne* remained just as still while she scanned the room, focusing both her sight and senses into every minca space she could see, before centering her attention upon the corner where I was.

Taking a few steps forward, she reached out her arm. The clock in the mainroom began to chime causing her to startle. *Evelynne* suddenly blinked catching sight of herself in *Jenny's* dressing glass and shook her head. *"I must be loosing my mind!"* she murmured, dropping her arm while laughing at herself in the glass. *"I'm starting to be as jumpy and hypersensitive as some of my callers."* She sighed, still looking at her image in the glass, *"Well, listening to some of those stories... green people popping out of the shrubbery, unexplainable feelings of always being watched, voices and things that go bump in the night. It's a wonder I haven't gone a bit batty sooner."* She left *Jenny's* room with her laughter floating behind her.

In my desperation, I had managed to not only lock up every muscle in my body, but my ability to lower my shield as well. I had gone numb from the pain of the arrows digging in my back and my muscles cramping in protest, even as my whole body began to tremble in reaction and exhaustion. I was stuck as I was until *Jenny* returned home. The oonas now seemed to pass at the pace of a gobbiyon.

⌘ ⌘ ⌘ ⌘

The front door opened, and I heard *Jenny* call to her mother, before slamming the door closed behind her. Eagerly, she dashed up the first short flight of steps and down the landing to her room. Kicking the bedchamber door shut with the back of her foot—probably the same way she had closed the front door—she tossed her books on the bed with careless regard, simply eager to get rid of their weight. Eyes alight in eagerness, she searched the room. Slowly, her expression changed to puzzlement, then to concern as I did not appear.

Her sweet face blanched a pale white, as she looked back at the door, comprehending that since she had shut it that morning and shut it again just now upon entering, that it had to have been opened sometime following her departure that morning. Spinning around, she frantically began to look for some sign of my presence.

"Niki?"

Closing my eyes, I struggled to remember at least one *English* word that would help her to understand my dilemma and allow her to find me. She was the only hope I had of helping me unlock my unnatural state, before my energies were exhausted and I simply passed in Sontall.

"Here, under your window," I whispered in Airian when I realized that *English* didn't matter. My words were so faint I thought she wouldn't hear me, let alone understand what I said.

"Te salma, help me. Keyenoa, help me," I whispered, turning my pleas to the One who could hear… even if I never uttered a sound.

Sticking her arms out in front of her, *Jenny* felt her way over to where I sat, groping blindly for my arms. While aware of her touch, I was beyond helping her as she forced me to my feet. All I could do was repeat my prayer to Keyenoa despite the fact that I knew He had answered me. Running her fingers up my arms to my shoulders and neck, she cupped her palms along either side of my cheeks. Tilting my face, she kissed my muttering lips, silencing me with her tenderness.

"What's wrong? I can't see you, or understand much of what you're saying. Please, try to tell me what you need me to do!" she said.

"Help me get me out of this house," I replied hoarsely.

Grasping me under my arms, she supported my weight with strength born of desperation. I moaned as my legs tingled in painful protest while they began to awaken. Leaning heavily on her shoulders, we left her bed chamber. Locked in my invisibility and my strength nearly gone, my shield had shrunk tightly around me. I was unable to cover *Jenny* behind my shield as well. Assuring me that her mother was in the laundry room at the far back of the house and wouldn't see us, she helped me out the front door.

Remembering the many people on the *road* and not wanting to draw any attention, I forced myself to move under my own power as soon as we were out the door. *Jenny* called to her mother, informing her she was going out for a few *hours* before following me. She accurately grabbed for my arm—unconcerned with any possible witnesses on the street—and pulled me around to the side of the house.

"What happened to you, Niki?*"* she asked again, after we were well out of sight of prying eyes and curious ears.

Leaning heavily against the stone wall of the house, I struggled to catch my breath. *"Not here, it's too close,"* I panted, more afraid of *Evelynne* than my Sontall. *"I want to go to the park where we went last night. There, we can talk safely."* I knew that just getting my muscles to moving and the blood flowing through my limbs would help me to relax and allow me to lower my shield when we were safe.

The walkways and streets were crowded, yet it hardly mattered to me. Careful to walk only on the grass in front of the Tenzenar homes, I was able to stay clear of the masses so I wouldn't be stepped on or bumped into. It took all my concentration to keep my feet moving to a place where I could begin the battle to regain my visibility.

We quickly left the pathway going to the same secluded spot we had occupied the night before. The park was more crowded in the daylight, intensifying the chance of someone stumbling into our private glade, so taking *Jenny's* hand I led her to a large gungas tree nearby. Bending low, I urged her to crawl under the branches and followed behind her.

Collapsing on my stomach, my arms and legs now feeling like stone weights, I continued to pray. Every muscle screamed in protest as I forced myself to relax, while assuring myself that I was safe. *Jenny* sat next to me, listening to my moans of pain, unable see me or help. My body protested as it was slowly eased from its contracted state, bringing tears to my eyes. Finally, my muscles loosened and my shield fell.

"Are you all right?" Jenny asked with tears in her eyes.

I lay where I was, unable to answer. My arms were flung above my head and my legs extended, while my cheek pressed against the loamy leaf detritus. I waited a blissful moment, simply breathing deeply and enjoying the aclusceaun, before answering. Opening my eyes, I looked at her, far too comfortable to move any other part of my weary body.

"Ta, *I am fine... now,"* I assured her. Pulling my arms toward my face, I tucked them under my head and then explained, *"Jenny, I grew bored and restless and that made me* ghea teepin *and careless. I was so ready to jump at any diversion to come along that when it did, I did not think about how dangerous it might be. You see, the view phone rang and your mother came up the stairs to answer it."* I closed my eyes. Her fingers brushed gently against my cheek, encouraging me to look at her. Her expression of understanding mingled with tender reproach made me close them again and nod. *"You might as well know,* Keyen, *my people are cursed with a deep seated curiosity. Having such a fascinating disturbance come at my weakest moment... well, I was lost to all common sense. I opened the door of your room and looked out. Finding your mother sitting at the view phone, I had to step out to hear the conversation better... after all it was about* Airians, *you know."*

She tried to frown at me, but her smile of understanding kept defeating the frown.

"I know—now—I should have listened to your warning last night. There is no need to ever remind me of that again, I assure you, Keyen. I know your mother is dangerous. Because as soon as I stepped into the hallway, after making certain I was invisible, your mother knew someone was there. The caller not happy with being ignored, was what saved me from discovery. I was able to dash back into your room when the caller insisted your mother turn her attention back to the view phone.

"Shocked into the reality of my danger where your mother is concerned, I found that corner near your window and huddled in it like a frightened dree. *However, the moment her phone interview was over your mother went looking for me. The* ena *she walked into your room, I used every* lestna *of my limited power, strength, and energy to hold my shield at its maximum ability. I then added prayer to the rest of my efforts and that finally worked. By* Keyenoa's *grace, and His protective hand, your mother finally attributed her feelings to an over active imagination,"* I sighed, closing my eyes and humbly ghea sorice leki omprice Keyenoa for His protection.

"Why couldn't you appear when I came home?" she asked.

I rolled over lifted my head cupping my chin in my hands. I had finally begun to feel stronger and more like I should. *"Remember my telling you of* Con Sona Eata, *and how I have not gotten my gift of power and so cannot hold my invisibility for a long time?" Jenny* nodded, and I continued. *"Well, to shield myself from your mother's sensitivity, I over extended my abilities and... I ended up locked in my invisibility, rather like a whole body muscle cramp. If you had not gotten me up and away from your mother, I would never have been able to drop my shield. Getting me up and moving and out of that house, saved my life. I would have died in another few* oonas *if you hadn't come along."*

"Oh, Niki, *what are we going to do?"* she was clearly both defeated and frightened, ready to give up her idea of having me stay in the house when she was off at school.

My irrational fear of *Evelynne MacArthur* had begun to decrease as I continued to recover. I wasn't teepin enough to forget the danger she presented, but now that I was aware of the challenge she presented, I began to ponder the resources and talents that I had not utilized in my first encounter simply because I had not expected her to be so intuitive. Rolling on my side, I caressed *Jenny's* cheek with the back of my fingers and smiled confidently.

"Your mother is not such a big problem. I can go back, Jenny. I understand the danger now and know how far to push things. Remember, Keyen, *I know that house—maybe even better than she—and I also have a few tricks I have learned when dealing with* Tenzenar. *Truly,* Keyen, *I can play* dodge the Tenzenar *with the best of them. It will be a challenge, and I promise I will not be* teepin *enough to engage with her in that game—she is far too dangerous for that. However, I can and will protect myself and my people from discovery. I have not been caught for the last eight* tuevtauns, *and I was never as careful as I will be with your mother. Now that I know what to expect, I am better prepared, I promise you."*

Jenny spent several onas arguing with me, but my mind was set. I'd begun to think of the time with *Evelynne* as an adventurous challenge, one that would keep me from boredom. Airian's are notably curios and stubborn. They are a people determined to meet every challenge put before them head on and never give in until futility is a proven fact. *Jenny*, faced with these aspects of my Airian nature, relented only because she hadn't anything better to offer—Tenzenar, I learned, are just as stubborn and curious as Airians, and only a minca more pragmatic.

When I was rested enough that I could again raise my shield, we returned to her house and her room, locking the door behind us. As she did her homework, I observed her with affection, curi-

PART I TENZENAR

osity and growing frustration. Because I was unable to decipher the strange symbols scrawled in her books and she wrote on her papers, I understood ghea neye of what she was doing. This caused me to fidget at times in boredom and for *Jenny* to chastise me for distracting her. Discovering that I could irritate her and so garner some attention that way, I began to fidget and distract her on purpose. *Jenny* caught on quickly and simply laughed at me before resorting to hitting me with one of her pillows.

When she finally managed to finish her work, we laid down on the bed, cuddled together and talked about her *college* and the many forlaynan she had there. She told me about *Carrie Lynne*, and *Karen*, two women she had met shortly after arriving on Airies. Their ghea forlaynan was formed by their common bond of faith. She joined the two girls every *Sunday* for services at the *campus* chapel. *Jenny* then talked about her *"best friend in the entire universe," Paula.* The two girls had grown up together because *Paula's* father was also an *archeologist* and traveled with the *MacArthur's* from planet to planet. *Paula's* parents had recently separated due to job conflicts and subsequent personal problems, which had given *Paula* a choice to live with either parent. She had chosen to live with her father and travel to Airies so she could stay near *Jenny*.

"She lives in the dorm at college and her father pays the extra tuition to board her there, since he's uncomfortable dealing with all the 'female baggage and emotions' as he put it. Paula's dad is much more comfortable letting Paula's mom deal with that stuff, and since she isn't here right now, he'll pay extra so he doesn't have to deal with it alone. Paula says I'm her only true family, right now." Jenny sighed and smiled rather sadly. *"I've talked with her about how I found my joy and my 'true' family, but she doesn't want to hear anything about 'all that religious stuff'... as she puts it. Paula's pretty smart, though. I've faith she'll someday recognize that it's not religion but living that I'm talking about, and so come to accept Him. Then... well, I won't miss her so much. I mean it seems that lately we have so little in common..."*

"Hearing what she is like, I do not think Keyenoa *will allow her to slip from His hand,"* I said. *"From all the mischief she has* managed to get you into, you friendship reminds me a bit of me and *Jon when we lived in* Malinieum City. *Paula is more like me and you more like* Jon. *My* Master *tried so hard to keep me from trouble, yet I always managed to find a way to entangle him into that trouble right along with me."*

Jenny laughed, *"Then* Niki, *you have my condolences, both for dealing with a friend like that and not having him around anymore."*

To pass the time until *Jenny* was called for *dinner*, we compared some of the things Jon and I had done to things she and *Paula* had done. There were many times we couldn't help but laugh because our stories sounded all too similar.

I followed *Jenny* to the family table, fighting my fear and nerves all the way. To my relief, *Evelynne* showed neye indication that she had any awareness of my presence. She also never mentioned her experience to anyone concerning sensing my presence earlier in the afternoon. *Jenny* refrained from piling her plate high with food and so never drew her parents attention to how much food actually made it onto her plate. The only time anything was mentioned about *Jenny's* eating habits came at the beginning of the meal when *Evelynne* pointedly asked *Jenny* if she had taken their advice and eaten that day. When *Jenny* replied that she had, the subject was forgotten and the remainder of the meal passed in relative harmony, as both parents focused the conversation on their own interests.

At the end of the meal, *Evelynne* expressed some surprise that there wasn't a single leftover to put away. But having neye idea who had overeaten, she was at a loss as to whom she should counsel. While she and *Jonathan* cleared the empty dishes from the table, *Evelynne*, having decided that he must have been the one who had consumed far more than he should, decided to lecture the poor man concerning his overeating. From the defacka, *Jenny* and I could hear her telling him that such over indulgence could lead to a possible heart attack and stroke.

"Mom, Dad, I'm going for a walk, I'll be back in about an hour," Jenny shouted, quickly heading toward the front door,

PART I TENZENAR

while we could hear *Jonathan* staunchly defending himself and his reasonable eating habits.

Once outside, I tried to steer *Jenny* toward Malinieum City, but she managed to turn us off the paved walkway just before we reached the gates, leading me into another park. Following Keyenoa's instructions of last night, I let the incident pass and followed her eagerly to a secluded spot where I could drop my shield. Together we crawled under the branches of a large gungas tree a few paces off the dirt path. There, I became visible and leaned against the tree trunk. Letting her sit in between my legs, I enfolded her in my arms so I could hold her and listen to her talk.

"Niki, *why haven't you asked me what I'm studying in college?"* she asked with a teasing smile as she tipped her head back and looked up at my face.

Looking into her warm, brown eyes, I blushed. *"I didn't know you studied specific things, I thought you just took classes."*

She chuckled lightly while shifting out of my arms so she could lay her head in my lap, allowing us to look at one another as she spoke. *"I'm studying alien research. Being with Mom and Dad and moving all over the galaxy has encouraged my fascination about different beings and their various cultures. However, unlike my parents, I like studying about present beings and their cultures not ones long gone. Also, I've always wanted to join an Explorer ship and travel through the galaxy studying and learning about newly discovered life forms and their cultures. The problem is that there are so many young people just like me—all of us having the same dream—that many of us never make it into the Explorers. There are simply more people than there are positions. But when I learned about this sad fact while I was talking with a recruiter, I also learned that I chose a highly difficult field to study that not many students qualify to get into. That fact along with the amount of work I have put into my studies and keeping my grades in the top one percent of my graduating class, the recruiter said, the chances were high I would be one of the dedicated and lucky few who made it into the Explorers."*

I bit my lip and tried to hide a growing smile, aware she hadn't considered what it would mean to us if she did make it on an *Explorer* ship. "Keyen, *I am not so sure you will be one of those few to make it into the Explorers.*"

She sat up, her eyes flashing with indignant anger. *"Why would you say such a horrible thing like that? I've only a few more months till I graduate, and unless I really foul up on my finals, I'll remain in the top one percent of my graduating class. When the Explorers see a record like that, they'd be hard put not to find a place for me before my graduation gown grows cold. My recruiter tells me Research Specialists are in more demand than ever before... except for Captains, and that takes decades after getting into the Explorers to accomplish,"* she argued heatedly.

I smiled, further infuriating her, though that wasn't my intention. *"Jenny, listen to what you are telling me. Do you mean you would leave me behind if you were offered a position on an Explorer Ship?* Keyen, *I cannot leave* Airies... *even if you, who are my whole heart, did leave."*

She looked as if I had hit her.

Cupping her cheek in my hand, I gently kissed her lips. "Keyen, *I will never keep you from going, if that remains your desire now that you know I cannot go with you. I would hold you fast in my heart, and await your return, bonded to you through our promise before Ruth and Bill Masters and our* Keyen,*"* I explained gently, pulling her onto my lap and tucking her head against my shoulder.

Instantly, she threw her arms around me and buried her face against that shoulder. Sobbing almost uncontrollably, she swore she'd never leave me. I held her close and sadly listened to the shattering of her dream all because of her need for my Keyen. I was ashamed of my words, knowing I had used them in order to carefully maneuver her into choosing to stay on Airies and remain with me. Lifting her head from my shoulder, I looked at her tender minca face with regret. How utterly kutated I had been not to understand the depth of her dream until I had taken it from her.

PART I TENZENAR

And why, why hadn't she realized that fulfilling her dream would have separated us?

"Oh, Keyen, what have we done to ourselves?" I said in Airian, overwhelmed with a feeling of hopelessness and shame. Suddenly, I found myself forced to look at our relationship from a different and very impossible angle.

Aware of her struggle to translate my words, I switched to *English*. The words were frustratingly empty in the translation, keeping me from saying what I wanted with the pure expression of emotion my language possessed so naturally. *"I have suddenly realized that because of our love we have trapped ourselves into something which—in many ways—leaves us both barren and unfulfilled. You know Jenny that I love you as deeply and strongly as you love me. Therefore, neither of us will leave the other—we are bound together for our whole lives by what we share and feel. It is not the words we spoke in front of Bill and Ruth that binds us, but the One far greater. However, because I am* Airian *and you are human we cannot go and claim our marriage to your people with boldness, or seek out mine and ask that we be* Joined *for life before* Keyenoa. *Though my* Keyenoa *and your God are one and the same, our people are not, nor do I believe your people will ever come to know of mine. Therefore, Jenny, we are trapped in our love, united by* Keyenoa *but unable to claim it to either of our peoples, unable to be openly one.*

"How can I consummate our union knowing this, and how can I not... knowing you alone were chosen for me by Keyenoa's *own hand? I can but swear by my faith in* Keyenoa *that I will never leave you or pledge myself unto another, even if it means never consummating our union. The only way I shall part from your side will be if you ask it of me... and even then, there will be no other for me but you."*

Her expression radiated with joy, accord, and sorrow that matched my own. She cupped my face in her hands, her touch and expression revealing her understanding as we shared our pain. *"My feelings for you are as strong and as everlasting as yours. I've been foolish and selfishly blind in my love for you. And I am ashamed I didn't respect what you've been struggling to honor and do*, Niki. *I realize that, now. And I thank you for not taking advantage of my passion and naiveté... when I've almost demanded you take what I wanted to give.*

"But don't you see, Niki? *You said it, though I'm not really sure you heard what you said. Our love for each other was given to us by God and is therefore sanctioned by Him. He wanted us to meet. He wanted us to love each other. I know now that God has some purpose in mind for our love that neither of us can begin to understand right now. So why must we keep our union celibate just because we can't proclaim it before our people? While our union is unorthodox because all we have is each other and God—oh, and the Masters. We have nonetheless made the promises of marriage before God through Bill, who has the authority to marry us and did perform a binding marriage ceremony... this makes our union real in the sight of all my people. Now, here we are* Niki *making these promises again before each other as well as God, and both of us willing to make them everyday for the remainder of our lives despite the difficulties it places upon us. Why can we not just trust in God and consummate that which God has already blessed, giving ourselves into His hands in faith to direct our future—wholly and completely promising to follow God's direction?"*

Closing my eyes I prayed, seeking Keyenoa's wisdom and sanction for all *Jenny* had said. Then crying out jubilantly, not concerned with who would hear me, I voiced my praises to Keyenoa for showing *Jenny* what I too had seen but hadn't the faith to believe. Because of my separation from Him, it remained difficult for me to trust in Keyenoa for such answers, or trust in my ear to hear them. I continually expected Him to throw hurt and disappointment my way rather than tender understanding and wisdom.

"Jenny, can we go to Malinieum City? *If we go to the sanctuary there and offer Him our promise to be faithful in His will for our lives, we can ask for His blessing over what we now face together with and for Him?"*

"No, Niki, *you're not thinking. We can't go to* Malinieum City. *You're forgetting, you make the city sing. There are always*

PART I TENZENAR

at least four men assigned to guard the city from vandals during the day, and even more men are added at night. We could look for an open church here... but I don't think God cares if we come to Him in a church or in a football stadium or under a gungas *tree, so long as our hearts are pure and sincere,"* she explained.

I didn't even take the time to ask her what a *football stadium* was. I was so filled with joy that all I wanted to do was kneel before Keyenoa and share in our prayer to Him together. So kneeling where we were, we lowered our heads solemnly and quietly. I prayed in Airian, as *Jenny* prayed in *English*. To my surprise—though it had not been planned—we prayed in such unison, even our words were the same despite the different languages spoken. Soberly, holding each other's hands, we told Keyenoa of our problem and ghea leki Him for the ghea arecean of His Keyen which we felt for each other. Humbly, withour eyes raised beseechingly toward Alleanne, we asked Him that He guide us in His will and that we honor Him with our obedience and Keyen. Then with tears in our eyes, we closed our prayer and bowed our heads in silence. As *Jenny* and I looked at each other we could see the same overwhelming aclusceaun and warmth in each other. Then slowly, as if a hand other than ours guided us, we were drawn together, our lips meeting in a kiss. Both of us knew we had taken a daring step forward, committing ourselves to something far larger than she or I could comprehend at that moment while we recommitted ourselves to each other and gave ourselves over to Keyenoa's plans.

Walking home, I held *Jenny* close in my arms, cloaking her behind my shield. In her bed that night, we joined in Keyen Sapato, sharing both bodies and minds as we became one, just as we had on the night beneath the trees of Dindieum. Knowing our joining was sanctified by Keyenoa, I gave all of myself to her, having neye guilt or fear. Through this union of sharing, I was also careful to make sure that *Jenny* could speak and understand my language as well as any Airian. We opened ourselves to each other, sharing many full and rich experiences and emotions from our souls, aware that Keyenoa joined with us in our sharing.

An oona before dawn, with unspoken agreement, we parted our minds and separated our bodies and then joined as man and woman. Each of us existing separately, feeling separate feelings, we shared and expressed our passion and our love for each other in that way which is common to both Airian and *human*. Through that physical union we confirmed that while we were different creations, we were still both made by Keyenoa's hand and in His image.

Jenny and I were one. We had each other—a wondrous gift from Keyenoa—and in faith, we gave ourselves to Him, promising to follow His guidance as we worked together to meet our future.

Glossary

Aaleyen: Last name. Nicholina Aleria Aaleyen Malin. Nikita's mother.
Aana: Year.
    Aanas: Plural.
    Aanaling: One year old.
Achool: Chosen.
Aclusceaun: Peace.
    Aclusceaun (medeerla): Peace be to thee/peace is what I offer.
    Aclusceaun (medee-an): Be at peace.
Acron: Name. The Guard Master of the 907th Regiment.
Airian: Race of beings.
    Airians: Plural.
Airianite: Colonists to Airies.
    Airianites: Plural.
Airies: Planet.
Alcone: Last name. Jontair Alcone, Thaytor to Nikita.
Alda (leone): I understand/know so I won't argue.
Aleria: Name. Nicholina Aleria Aaleyen. Nikita's mother.
Aliakan (heater): Device to keep a room warm.
Alleanne: Heaven.
Allearan: Safe place.
Allica'te: Name. Cressa Orate.
Allills: Awful pain.
Alltryon: Species of lox.
Alon: Destiny.

Alon: Name. King Alon Tarton.
Amfrack: Frog-like creature.
    Amfracks: Plural.
Animoid: Part human and part animal.
Antron: Bird, similar to an eagle but larger than a condor.
Aray: Morning.
Arece: Bless.
    (Ghea) **Arece:** Blesses
    Arecean: Blessing.
    Areceta: Blessed.
Arlue: We, together.
Aron: Distance approximate to an acre.
    Arons: Plural.
Atcheeda: Barbaric.
Autet: Augmented with.
Bachalyon: Drink given at Con Sona Eata.
Batearda: Grief, sorrow.
Beblina: Name. Known as the most beautiful Airian woman of her erra.
    Beb: Nickname.
Belapheus: Name. Personal Guard to Nikita Malin.
Benna: Good.
    Benna'nay: Goodness.
Billon: Vegetable like a potato.
    Billons: Plural.
Bonfinar: Name. Personal Guard to Nikita Malin.
Bruic: Name. Little boy.
    Bru: Nickname.
Callon: Container for toting water.
    Callons: Plural.
Callray: Night.
Calu: Points measured in a spar.
Calufant: Referee.
Cantabo: Last name. High King Sayleen Cantabo.
Cassa~eede: Thaytor command word.

Castrin: Deception. Lie. Falsehood.
    Ghea Castrin: lied, deceived.
Castrinair: A deceiver; or to deceive someone.
Leyette Castrinair: The Angel of Darkness and Deception (Satan).
Ceranon: Name. King Ceranon Letark.
Cessan: Title of respect for man.
Cetar: Fifth Kingdom of Airies.
Cetarieum: King's City on Cetar.
Chalday: To fish.
    Chaldayan: Fisherman.
Cholin: Play.
    Cholina: Playing.
    Cholinta: Plaything.
'Chore: Luck, chance, or fate.
Colen (en donahae): Devotion and trust forever.
Con (Sona Eata): Come of Age.
    Conay Sona Eata: Came of Age.
Con de reyna: Help one so ashamed/Can you forgive me?
Conden: Name. A guard to Markain Malin.
Contie: Name. Oreon Guard who bars Niki's way in to see his Thaytor.
Corina: Name. Jontair Alcone's woman.
    Corie: Nickname.
Coule: Space.
Creasion: Meat-like, lamb in flavor.
Cressa: Title of respect for woman.
Dachstan: Hit the dirt, dive for cover.
Dachta: Thaytor command word.
Dachtan: Stop, cease immediately.
Dadan: Daddy.
Dara: Hunting/carrion feeders which roam in packs.
Dasho: Red bulbous root – crunchy, sweet, single stalk.
    Dashos: Plural.
Dassishon: Snake.
De: Connecting word.
Defacka: Kitchen.

Degos: Name. Ruemassan male.
Dentie: Tree species.
   Denyadda: Little mammals easily frightened. looked.
Derrian: Mountain range.
Dindieum: Forest on the continent of Malin.
Doege: Change.
Donolyn (keyen): Love for a parent.
Dorna: Second Kingdom of Airies.
Dornian Slur: Accent on the Continent of Dorna.
Dorieum: King's City on Dorna.
Dree: Rodent like a rabbit.
Eata: Age.
   Eatas: Plural.
Effica: Drink given during Con Sona Eata.
Ellinan: Thaytor's command word.
Ena: Second.
   Enas: Plural.
Enna (trucan fortulaynan): Share the same feelings of heart.
Eshiday: Fish.
Eyea: If not for.
Eyette: The same as, compared to, similar to.
Fae: Small community or town.
   Faes: Plural.
Feleena: Name. King's partnered woman.
Flet: Feathers on the end of an arrow.
Forlana: Companion, friend.
Forlaynan: Very close friend.
   (ghea) **Forlaynan**: friendship
Fortaun: Week.
   Fortauns: Plural.
Fortu: Thaytor's command word.
Fortulaynan: Feeling of heart, bonded by heart.
Frawman: Person ill or diseased. **Fraw**: Ill or diseased.
   Fraw-nall: Illness or disease.
Furon: Two inches.
   Furons: Plural.

PART I TENZENAR

Gareross: Planet.
Garzan: Creature that lives in high mountains, has a heavy pelt and thick fur.
Gangee: Strategy game like chess.
Gaphela: Wheat.
Geehowl: Pig.
Ge-inall: Towel.
Gessa (eshiday): Type of fish.
Ghea: Connecting word signifying tense change.
Gleets: Peas grown like peanuts.
Gnurlin: Maggots
Gobbiyon: Snail.
Gontlin: Drink used in Con Sona Eata.
Granlier: Semiprecious stone. Color between ruby and garnet.
Gungas: Species of tree.
Helop: Horse.
    Helop: Plural.
Illishya: Diamonds.
Jaquietan: Name. Little boy.
    Jaquie: Nickname.
Jareen: Free.
Jatiell: Carries, brings, returns.
Jauna: Giving over to slavery/surrender.
Jeanitear: Beautiful. Also, Airian name for Jennifer MacArthur.
    Jennie: Nickname.
    Jen'nan: Beauty.
Jelisya: Planet.
Jophty: Plant, tastes like chocolate.
Joining: State of being partnered for life through the power of Keyenoa so that no other partnering can occur or death will befall both partners.
Jontair: Name. Jontair Alcone Niki's Thaytor.
    Jon: Nickname.
Jorinar: Throwing weapon like a spear or javelin.
Jott: Fork and spoon combination.
    Jotts: Plural.

Keedton (poe): Damning, damnable.
Keena (lay alda soona leone): Your feelings I understand and are known to me.
Keesa'nye: There you have it.
Keesh (de la torda): Bond between us.
Keya: Fruit like an apple.
    Keyeas: Plural.
Keyen: Love.
Keyen toolay: Extended family.
Keyeniya: God given patience.
Keyenoa: God.
Keyenoay: Sunday, or God's day.
Keyloss: Plant, juice is used as a combustible; ignites when wet.
Keyna: Like.
Keysa~narann: Telekinesis.
Keysla: Life.
Kezky: A bit off the norm, slightly nuts.
Keznakhile: Irrational, temporary insanity.
Keezworky: Crazy.
Kileiha: Dedication to God.
Konturn de le ata: Feeling opposite emotions at the same time.
Kreatar: Name. Kreatar Sornan Dorna. Friend of Nikita Malin and next Sixth King of Airies.
Kutated: Really stupid.
Lackna: Sword with bits.
    Lacknas: Plural.
Lareina: Thaytor command word.
Lastna: Pound.
    Lastnas: Plural.
Leagonenn: Ryder war factions.
Le~arren: Weaving.
    Le~ar: Weavers.
Leakas: Gold clips attached to the head at birth to hold the crown in place.
Leakna: Knife with bits.
Learna: September.

Learon: Approximately two feet.
    Learons: Plural.
Leastna: measurement of weight, i.e. gram
Ledo: Animal like a deer.
Leeksha: Wine.
LeFold Lake: Lake up by Oreon.
Leki: Thanks
    Leki'an: Thanked
    Leki'anee: Thankful
    (ghea) **Leki**: Thanking
    (ghea) **Leki'anee**: Thankfully
Lendor: Name. Oreon Guard who barred Niki's way to his Thaytor. Nikita's Story.
Lestna: Ounce.
    Lestnas: Plural.
Letark: Third Kingdom of Airies.
Letarkieum: City of the King in the Third Kingdom.
Leyette: Angel.
Litkini: Disgusting.
Lizingham: City on Malin.
Locar: First Kingdom of Airies.
Locarieum: King's City on Locar.
Loga: June.
Logone: Wild dog or wolf.
Lonay: Saturday.
Loomby: Large rodent, often a pet.
Loreann: Bow, and the castle in Malinieum.
Lortna: Ton.
    Lortnas: Plural.
Lox: Fox-like creature with thick pelts.
Lumballer: Poisonous mammal.
    Lumballers: Plural.
Lunatas: Sky-house or spaceship.
Mackien: Name. Used his power against Nikita and was imprisoned for the offense.
Malin: Sixth Kingdom of Airies.

Malinieum: King's City on Malin.
Mantobar: Mountain lion, panther.
Markain: Name. Markain Malin Sixth King of Airies.
Markainieum: City on Malin.
Medde-an: Everyone included/we all be.
Merrinin: Name. Personal Guard of Nikita Malin.
    Merri: Nickname.
Met: Title of respect.
Me'talm: A-men.
Metlan: Name. Valcree Metlan Sontall.
Micon: Tunic and vest combination.
Milisha: Flowers.
Minca: Small, little, tiny.
    (ghea) **Minca**: Smaller, littler, tinier.
    (ghea) **Minca-eyee**: Infinitesimally small.
    (ghea) **Minca-neye**: So small as to almost not be counted or noticed.
Minca-coule: Fearful of small places.
Minsle~ar: Little weaver, spider.
Mirrimar: Mountains.
Mootan: Idiot/mentally handicaped
    Mootan'eye: Idiotic, addlepated.
Moreanne: Type of cake.
Motulayna (Keyen): Deep unshakable adoration.
Na'chore: Bad luck.
    Nathaneyellan: Name. Son of Nikita Markain Malin.
    Nathan: Nickname.
Neesa: In spite of, but for.
Nema (leaf): Plant used for healing.
Nematoe: Blowfly.
    Nematoes: Plural.
Neron (lox): Type of lox.
Neye: No.
    Ghea neye: Nothing.
    Ghea neyean: Nowhere.
Nicholina: Name. Nicholina Aaylen Aleria Malin.

Nikca: Child.
    Ghea nikca: Childish.
Nikita: Name. Nikita Markain Malin.
    Niki: Nickname.
Omnestera: Treasure. Name. Jeanitear Omnestera.
Omprice: Earnestly, with conviction and respect.
Ona: Minute.
    Onas: Plural.
Oolanay: Three gold chains to denote Joining.
Oona: Hour.
    Oonas: Plural.
Operbus: Mammal like a skunk; tastes bitter.
Orate: Servants.
Oreon: Castle of High King.
Oron: Mountain where the High King's castle sits.
Pacean: accepted and obeyed
Palana: Group of people.
    Palana'ta: Ourselves.
Palona: Name. Palona Cetar Fifth King of Airies.
Partnered: A promised union between man and woman.
    Partnering: The ceremony of this union.
Pe'atron: Name. Oreon Guard. Older brother of Terensann.
Pearon: Yards.
    Pearons: Plural.
Pentar: Name. Kreatar Sornan Donra's Thaytor.
Peterla: Liqueur made from fermented flower petals.
Pieckta: Pecan's taste like pecans.
Plesnockeal: Psychological.
Poe: Damn.
    Poed: Damned.
    Poe-keedton: Damning, damnable.
Quintie: Like beef cattle; hides are saved also.
Raborre: Plant that extracts tannic acid.
Ralla: Safe, okay.
'Ram-Dam': Ghost Steed.
Rearlonn: Welcome.

Reinta: Thaytor's command word.
Renlets: Like pearls.
Renli (Keyen Renli): Love between man and woman.
Reyena: Ashamed
Richon: Name. Richon Locar First King of Airies.
Rugan: Name. Learning House Instructor.
Rulakeeyon (seeyan): This is what I, we, seek.
    Rulakeeyon seeya: You have what we seek, we have found what we seek.
Rulieha (norice): See us through.
Rupas: A vegetable, corn in flavor.
Ryde: Sit on helop-back.
    Ryden: Past tense.
    Ryders: Plural.
Ryder: Person who lives from the back of a helop.
Saflee: Hot drink like tea.
Saleet: Unchangeable.
Salitarin: Name. Guard of Markain Malin.
Salma: Urge you.
Santall: Birth.
Sapato: Physical and emotional joining to become one being.
Saybar: Stringy fibrous plant.
Sayleen: Name. High King Sayleen Cantabo.
Scaun: Name. High King's guard.
Scripp: Larva or not full-grown, but not an infant.
Scureel: Night insect.
Seeya: Have found.
Seh: This.
Sey: He/she.
Seya: Us
Seya'te: Us all.
Sha: The place where one belongs.
Shaliyle: Messenger.
Shashon: Dance.
    Shashonu: Dances.
Shenon: Hell.

Silvan: Name. Oreon Guard who guards the private chambers of the High King.
Sinca: Mountain range.
Solleeta: Flower with intoxicating odor.
Sontall: Death.
Soona: Completely understood/understand.
Sorice: Very much, felt deeply, earnestly.
Sorice Leki Omprice: Thank you very much.
Soreleann: Departure.
Sornan: Name. Middle name of Kreatar Sornan Dorna.
Sosceshpa: Unclaimed woman, prostitute.
Spannel: Protective metal armband. Can be used as a weapon.
Spar: One-on-one challenge or a mock battle.
Speal: Ornate wrist-guard. Can be used as a weapon.
    Speals: Plural.
Ta: Yes.
Ta met taul: Known to me.
Tafta: Nightwear.
Tal: It is, it be.
Tamould: Offering oneself to another unconditionally.
Taniger: Ants or termites.
Tartiniuem: King's City on Tarton. Nikita's Story.
Tarton: Fourth Kingdom of Airies.
Taun: Unknown amount of time.
Te: I.
Te'air: Name. Sosceshpa.
Teepatin: Foolish person.
    (Ghea) **teepin**: Foolish.
    (Ghea) **Teepin-eye**: foolishness
    Teepin: Fool.
Tellalay: Drink at Con Sona Eata.
Tella saa: Please.
Tellite: Candle with wick soaked in keyloss juice.
Tenzenar: Frightful enemy.
Terensann: Name. Little boy.
    Teri: Nickname.

Teron: Approximately one and a half miles.
> **Terons**: Plural.

Terrak: Name. Guard Master of all Regiments.
Tesha (lamp): Made of large colorful flowers.
Tezzar: Species of tree.
Thaytor: Teacher, mentor, friend, conscience.
> **Thaytors**: Plural.

Theron: Bird.
> **Therons**: Plural.

Thormar: Name. Guard Master of Castle Torquille.
Tieyee: A feeling of home or belonging.
Toenda: Apology.
Toguss: Name. Master Woodcarver.
Toern: Great power.
Tolbad: Mountain range.
Tomenan: Title of respect for a group, i.e. gentleman.
Toolamay: Worms.
Toolay: feeling from the heart and soul. Felt or shared soul deep.
Tor: Thaytor command word.
Torquille: Castle on Dorna.
Truson: Deer-like animal with high shoulder blades and a looped tail.
Tuevtaun: Month.
> **Tuevtauns**: Months.

Valcree Metlan Sontall (Leyette): Angel of Death.
Valcree Metlan Sontall: Name. First High King of Aries.
> **Cree**: Nickname.

Waterman: Boatman.
Whateshan (eyette sontall): Living like death.
X~za'te: Insulting word, highly offensive.
Zeppa: Flower. Yellow color used for dye.
Zewaller: Dragon-like creature.
Zilphas: vegetable that tastes like carrots.
Zumfouler: Species of tree.

PART I TENZENAR

Phrases to Translate

Achool Saleet Alon: Pre-chosen, unchangeable destiny.
Aclusceaun Medeerla: Peace is what I offer.
Alda leone colen en donahae: I understand and will not argue.
Allills, Allills de caw litkini frawman: Awful pain, awful pain, here come disgusting illness.
Benna neye: No good.
Benna rearlonn: Good welcome.
Benna soreleann: Heartfelt goodbye.
Ghea de arlue toolay Fortulaynan: Mutually together deep heart-bonded friend of the opposite sex, i.e. fiancé.
Colen en donahae: My devotion and trust forever.
Con de reyena: Help one so ashamed, i.e. forgive me.
Te ghea con de reyena: I am so ashamed.
Ena trucan Fortulaynan: We share the same feelings of souls, my heart-bonded friend.
Eata Medee-an Aclusceaun: Age of All-inclusive Peace.
Frawman toolay tieyee: A person ill/diseased in the heart for the feeling of home or belonging, i.e. homesickness.
Ghea minca-neye: Almost less than nothing.
Ghea mootan-eye: I am such an idiot/How absolutely idotic, mentally deficient of me.
Ghea neye: no one/nothing.
Ghea omprice'ta: Thankfully.
Ghea rulakeeyon seeyan: This is what we seek/ have we come to the right place?
Jen'nan dee thy omnestera: Beauty be thy treasure.
Keena lay alda soona leone: Your feelings I understand, I know them too.
Keesh de la torda dee benna: The bond between us is good.
Minca ghea mootan: a little not right in the head.
Seah taun: This time.
Sorice leki omprice: Thank you very much.

Ta rulakeeyon seeya: Yes, this is what you seek/you have come to the right place.
Te salma: I urge you.
Te soona pacean: I understand completely.
Tella saa: please.

About the Author

Gayle Hansen lives in Phoenix, Arizona, with her family and two precocious golden retrievers. When not writing or caring for her family, she enjoys reading and online gaming. Her experiences include multiple moves throughout the United States, which exposed her to many different landscapes and people. These experiences have all helped to develop her unique view of the world, bits and pieces of which can be found throughout her writing.

Gayle was always interested and fascinated with learning about God, questioning her pastors and ministers incessantly. Becoming saved at the age of fourteen, her interest grew and the questions continued in each church attended in her many moves throughout the United States. These questions and answers are also revealed throughout her characters interactions and their faith-based choices.

CPSIA information can be obtained
at www.ICGtesting.com
Printed in the USA
LVHW090510091219
639877LV00001B/23/P